A
Terrible
Beauty

Also by Katie Hanrahan

The Leaven Of The Pharisees

A
Terrible
Beauty

A NOVEL

KATIE HANRAHAN

Newcastlewest Books

Newcastle Books

First Edition: April 2011

The characters and events in this book are fictitious.
Any similarity to real persons, living or dead, is coincidental
And not intended by the author.

Too long a sacrifice
Can make a stone of the heart.
O when may it suffice?...

...Now and in time to be,
Wherever green is worn.
Are changed, changed utterly;
A terrible beauty is born.

-----William Butler Yeats
Easter, 1916

One

Disheveled, unwashed convicts lined the walls, eyes hazy with sleep. The cook's mates threaded their wheelbarrows through the confusion in the dark corridor, in a great hurry to deliver the morning ration, but why the haste? Mary Claire asked where they were being taken, but no one had so much as a second to spare in giving an answer. She tipped the mug to her lips and swallowed half of the gruel before handing the rest to Bridie. They weren't fed enough to keep body and soul together, so she'd mind the souls while Bridie tended the bodies and they'd parcel out the rations to their liking. The very idea of acting with a touch of independence, infringing the jail's regulations, led to a giggle that Mary Claire couldn't hold inside.

Sure it would be trouble this time. Just as she tucked her crust of bread into Bridie's bodice, an officer standing near them was splashed with gruel. It was the laugh that made him glare at her, a dark frown that as much as accused her of mocking his anger at the smear on his trousers, which was not the case at all. He kept looking at her, even after she'd wiped the smile from her face, like he was searching for someone he had never met but expected to recognize.

Mary Claire put her shoulders back, to stand without fear while the officer examined the group of women who shone in proud contrast to the rest of the female prisoners. With their hair neatly braided, black and red and yellow and brown, they could have been a group of proper young ladies at a country house party, just roused from sleep by their mischievous host. Except for Mary Claire, they were none of them ladies at all, but the infamous Dublin Doxies. The officer scanned their faces and Mary Claire stared right back. The company of whores had been good enough for the Lord God himself, and she'd not flinch at the company of fallen women, not even if he thought she was one of them. What did his British opinion matter, to a woman whose only crime was being Irish?

"Chains," a deep voice echoed off the cold stones, the cry arising from the men's section and moving forward.

The armorers pounded shackles onto the wrists of the last two women, and the officer startled, as if he had been shaken awake by a bad dream. "Is this necessary?" he said to an older man who must have been in charge. "They are weak and defenseless females, sir. You would chain these peaceful, passive creatures?"

"Where are they taking us?" someone else asked, but if there was a reply it was drowned out by the clatter of metal against stone. The officer stepped back, to avoid the long length of chain that was being threaded through the rings on the ankle shackles.

"Damn your orders," the officer murmured under his breath, speaking to the back of his superior. The armorer went about his business until he had two rows of ten women strung together like fish on a line, not caring if the women were peaceful or blood-thirsty harridans.

Lt. Plowman's ears were deaf to the high-pitched caterwauling and the whispered threats and vulgarities. In three months time, and the clock was running, he had to turn a determined enemy into a loyal friend, and accomplish the task in utter secrecy. They had given him the job because he was the one best suited to it, with a list of turncoats to his credit, but the

Fenians were not easily broken. Ready to embark, he had no idea how he was going to carry out his order, to take a political prisoner and bend her to his will, to plant his spy in the middle of the Fenians in Western Australia. He had no idea who he was even looking for in the writhing masses, not when he expected to find a child and the twenty prisoners were women grown old before their time.

"Where are we going?" one of the female prisoners asked.

The distinctive sound of feet scuffling on damp-slicked stones, mixed with the clatter of leg irons, lifted up from the men's section. The jangle meant it was time to stop fretting about the days ahead, to stop admiring the four beautiful women who must have been the infamous Dublin Doxies he had heard so much about. Plowman cleared his mind of all lascivious thoughts, to better collect memories as a witness to the end of an era. Milling before him was a human cargo, the scum of Queen Victoria's realm, about to walk into history.

"Where?" The anguished whisper passed through the two columns as the women were propelled into the middle of the corridor by shoves from the guards.

"You're bound for Australia," a guard said. It was an abbreviation for their true fate, a slow death at hard labor, a fate that made hanging a comparative act of mercy.

The convict gang stirred in alarm, the women commencing an ear-splitting chorus of sobs and howls that echoed and re-echoed from wall to floor to ceiling in a swirl of terrified grief. Only the Dublin Doxies maintained their composure, heads high and mouths pulled tight into tense nonchalance. Plowman's eyes met those of the raven-haired girl, clear eyes that flashed fire. She stared at him, glaring with a deeply burning hatred. It was the murderous glower of a soldier in battle, an attitude that he had never seen in a woman. Transfixed, he could not look away.

From the far reaches of the dimly lit space, a voice rose up and echoed through the cavernous depths of the prison. "Eireann go Bragh," an Irishman proclaimed, an act of daring that was answered with the dull thump of hard fist ramming a soft gut. A few others picked up the call, the phrase repeated by some of the political prisoners, the civilian and military Fenians who were now aware that they were sailing to their death.

Her lips moved, pale and dry, the words not spoken but spat out, slapped into Plowman's face. "Eireann go Bragh," the pile of dirty rags echoed the chorus of rebellion, daring him to silence her with his fist.

"Eireann's going to Australia, miss," Simon replied, amused by the outburst.

In a way, there was something sweetly charming in the girl's naiveté. Her strong political leanings were quite rare in a female, and a fair colleen at that, but it was her spirited impudence that brought the smile to his face. The Dublin Doxies were members of the highest echelon of the profession, women who could command the most exorbitant fees for flirtation, conversation and sex. He would give the little black-haired sprite about a month before she stopped being so outspoken, with her Irish ardor cooled in the hold of a prison ship. By then, she would trade her favors for a biscuit or a handful of raisins, her arrogance tempered by hunger and her pride cast aside by want. She might glare at him now, but before long, when her belly grumbled with hunger, she would have nothing but smiles and kisses for Lt. Plowman.

The warder barked out a command, "Stand. Ready. March," rousing Simon out of his lust-filled reverie. At once, the Marines and prison guards swung into action, prodding twenty women and two hundred fifty-eight men with rifle butts, bayonets, boots and strong arms until the columns began to move towards the door. The cries of the convicts nearly drowned out the harsh rasp of metal chains clanking and scraping on stone as all the feet began to shift in unison. Plowman reached out to give the lead group a push, only to find the Irish girl's backbone pressing into his palm. An image flashed into his mind, a recollection from his childhood during the Great Hunger, of taut skin stretched over sharp bones. The taste of bile was on his tongue, as it had been then.

They marched along the quay that led to a waiting steamship, bundles of ragged convicts and their guards in brilliant scarlet, all together in a driving rain. Among the crowd that watched the parade pass by were family members who came to say farewell to a loved one, to steal a last kiss or a final embrace that was roughly torn apart by a jailer. Lt. Plowman watched it play out, until he noticed that no one wept over the women. They were alone in the world, to make their way until they were caught and convicted. No one would miss them.

Through the mist and clouds it was impossible to see the tall-masted vessel that would be their prison for the next three months. The women noticed the small paddlewheel steamer, and they balked when they were propelled towards the gangplank, screaming that they would die of exposure on the open deck. As a group, they were convinced that the threat of transportation was merely a ruse, to cover up a far more brutal manner of execution followed by wholesale burial at sea to hide the evidence.

"Buck up, Bridie," Simon heard the Irish lass whisper to her mate. It was a soldier's daring bravado shared with a wavering colleague, spoken by a young woman who did not yet comprehend what she was facing. It was easy to be brave in the face of ignorance, to buck up against the unimaginable.

At the end of the procession were a group of men who knew all too well what their future held, men who once were proud soldiers in Her Majesty's Irish regiments. Every one of them had been found guilty of desertion and treason, willing participants in the Fenian movement who had taken up arms against the Crown. Plowman had run across them in the ranks, Irish men and boys who learned soldiering in the British Army so that they could turn that talent against England. Staring a brutal death in the face, they were soldiers still, marching with precision and pride as they made their way down Portland Hill.

Before the last passenger was put aboard the lighter, those already on deck were green with seasickness. The boat rocked violently in the chop of the harbor, the planks growing slick with the downpour that swabbed the deck. Shivering in her prison-issued gray wool dress, Mary Claire watched the gangplank, searching for a savior, for rescue, or a familiar face. Friends had sprung her brothers from a locked police van, spoiling the hangman's day. Surely they would do as much for her, to save her from seven years of torment in a God-forsaken wilderness.

"He's taken a fancy to you, that one." Bridie nudged Mary Claire. "Don't let pride get in your way."

"That's what put me here," Mary Claire said.

"Ah, now, 'tis good advice I'm giving you," Bridie said.

"You just stay close by, lamb, and we'll guide you through so that you come out hale and hearty at the other end," Moira Perkins said. "Free and independent, now that's a grand life for a woman."

"Quiet there, quiet," the guard ordered. He was a very young man, clearly puffing up with an overblown sense of importance.

"It's not our silence you'll be asking for tonight, love," Cornelia teased the fresh-faced Marine. Groaning in make-believe arousal, she attacked. "Oh, my angel, oh, yes, you are such a powerful man."

Uproarious laughter followed as the former residents of a rather tony bordello mocked the embarrassed blush of a virginal boy. Once wounded, the young victim was quickly torn to shreds by a torrent of verbal abuse. In self-defense and inexperience, he lashed out in turn, going after the one woman whose jaw was clenched in angry defiance.

"Here's one who knows how to keep her mouth shut," he sneered, jabbing at Mary Claire's middle with his bayonet. "Fine company you're keeping, Your Ladyship."

"Once a girl's put a knife in one soldier, it's nothing to cut another," Bridie lied.

"And that skinny neck won't need more than a penknife, not like the other gent who played too rough," Cornelia added.

"Shut up or I'll run you through," the man barked, but his voice cracked on a high note as he lost his courage.

"Run me through with your little pistol?" Cornelia cooed, reaching for his groin with her manacled hands. Chained to Hettie, and then to another eighteen women, the result was four female tentacles groping while the other convicts were forced into close proximity by the limited length of the chains.

"Oh, what a lovely big rifle you've got for me," Hettie tormented him. "Run me through, love, run me through."

Lt. Plowman generally ignored the low notes of prisoners' murmurings, knowing that women could not possibly keep silent any more than they could keep from weeping at the slightest provocation. When a throng began to mill around one of his men, he moved at once to quell a potential riot. Guarding women could be far easier, yet far more dangerous, than monitoring the male convicts, with the hazards falling on a green young Marine who had yet to learn the art of bantering with whores. Once women of that class detected a weakness, the word could be spread to the men's quarters, and the seeds of mutiny were planted as easily as that.

Shouting with authority, Simon waded into the churning mass with his revolver drawn, only to be met with sarcastic comments and shrieking guffaws as the women asked for men, rather than little boys, to look after them. Arkwright's cheeks burned red as another round of raucous feminine laughter filled his ears.

"Silence, the lot of you," Plowman shouted. In reply, he was bombarded with an onslaught of coquettish, sidelong glances and coy smiles as the fallen women played their games. Calling for order, he roughly shoved the women into regimented lines, to set the rules with a bit of force and signal an end to their fun.

The women sauntered into poses that implied submission to the authorities, two lines of ten side by side. Much to his surprise, Plowman found that he was watching the Irish girl, the set of her chin proudly obstinate as she ignored every scarlet coat that stood around the deck of the paddlewheel steamer, rain pouring down her face.

"This is where Eireann go Bragh has brought you," he whispered in the Irish girl's ear. "They steal your rations and you'll grow wise or be dead before this voyage ends."

"Who are you accusing of being a thief?" the plumper one hissed.

"He calls us thieves," the madam mumbled.

"Silence," Plowman screamed, so close to the woman's ear that she cringed.

Arkwright was sent to the middle of the column, where the civilian political prisoners would present less of a challenge, and Mr. Scofield came up to replace the boy. An older man who had seen much of the world, the pensioner guard looked no nonsense, and he was accorded a little respect.

The lieutenant walked away, but Moira took note of the backward glance that lingered on Mary Claire's rump. "Better to be one man's pet than a slave to all," she said. "You'll get more out of him if you play the game. The power to control your fate lies between your legs, and if you'll use what God gave you, you'll not go hungry."

"I'll starve to death before I'll sell myself to any man," Mary Claire said.

"Pride, Mary Claire," Bridie admonished. "Temper your pride and live."

A roll of the boat's hull nearly bowled them all over, and the misery of seasickness did more to silence the women than any orders from their jailers. Once the steamer began to move, the pitching grew worse, and the cries of the prisoners rose up through the storm. Under the driving rain, the menacing outline of the transport ship loomed out of the dark mists, and three women screamed at the sight of the black hulled *Hellebore*, the ship that was nicknamed "Hell's Door" by the men who sailed her. Looking at the masts, Mary Claire thought of Jesus on the cross. Christ had died for her sins, or so she was told as a child, and she feared that the time had come for her to die for her sins as well.

Almost before the boat had tied up alongside the *Hellebore*, the women were jostled and prodded up the steps of the gangplank, their pace slowed by nausea and the weight of the chains draped on their bodies. Outstretched arms heaved them up to the deck, using brute force to speed things along. The black-haired woman's limbs were trembling so violently that she could scarcely make one foot go in front of the other, and Mr. Scofield gave her a hearty shove by way of assistance. Plowman caught her as she tumbled against him.

"Watch your step, ladies," he sang out pleasantly, as agreeable as a guest at a picnic. He shared his smile with the Irish girl who had fallen into his arms, momentarily picturing her black hair twined in his fingers. She cut him, as ruthless in her disregard as any society matron, and Simon had the peculiar sensation of being utterly and completely invisible, nonexistent even as he stood at her side. Helping her to retain her balance, he whispered in her ear, "Steady as she goes, Miss Eireann go Bragh."

It was nearly impossible to stand at all as the prison ship heaved, up and down and side to side. Bodies undulated, keeping time to the shackles that scraped out a rhythm at their feet. Bridie squeezed Mary Claire's hand. "God help me, Mary Claire," Bridie moaned. "Holy Mary, Mother of God."

"Come on, Bridie, we'll have a prayer and take your mind off things. Heavenly Father," Mary Claire said, "send your Son to strike down the vile beasts that are all around us."

"All men are beasts," Varena growled. "Best learn that now, Mary Claire, before they eat you alive. Men are animals, filthy and disgusting animals."

Changing the topic swiftly, Moira repeated her mantra about free passage to Australia, crowing about the opportunity that Perth presented. Ignoring the madam's artificial cheer, and feeling a man's eyes on her, Mary Claire looked up and saw the Marine officer cast his gaze to his toes. So let him think she was a criminal; she was powerless to refute him. She possessed one thing the English could not bend or break, and that was an iron will. Whatever vile name they might paste on her, she would never give up the cause of freedom.

The gentleman's eyelashes flicked briefly as he peeked at his captives. Mary Claire wanted to laugh at his ridiculous posture, studying the seams in the deck as if his heart was empty of dirty thoughts and he was merely doing his duty in case the ladies should sprout wings likes Lir's children and fly away. When she caught his eye, she gave him a chilling glare, to let him know that she was above Her Majesty's petty humiliations. As far as she was concerned, the lieutenant was the pauper and she was the princess, not about to be humbled by such degradation. With one flash of her hazel eyes, she set him in his place.

Manhandled roughly into their ranks, the female prisoners stood on the deck with the rain still falling, no longer a downpour but a steady drizzle that added more misery to an existence that could not become more miserable. Weak and exhausted, Mary Claire wobbled when the armorers came through the row and knocked off the manacles. She was too feeble to lift her arms, to look at the abrasions that bled onto the sleeves of her coarse dress and the worn black wool of her stockings.

"Prisoners, attention," one of the warders shouted. He called out two numbers, and the women were jostled into place at the door of the iron cage that covered the forward hatchway. Two by two, a double line was formed that quickly grew ragged as those at the back shifted to see what was in front, while the warder barked out orders to straighten the line, over and over, before he would continue.

The amount of light on the prison deck was kept at a minimum, and the hold of the *Hellebore* looked like a deep and black pit, the very mouth of hell. The women at the head of the column were the first into the dark abyss, and their wailing erupted anew and spread through the group. Not one female was willing to enter the fearsome pit, and it took strong hands grabbing and pushing to send the first pair down the steps. Faltering in the darkness, side by side, they strained to see where they were in the very dim light of a single lantern.

"Prisoner 2564," a guard yelled, and Varena was thrust forward and sideways along a corridor, disappearing into the shadows. From the blackness came the sound of feet stumbling on unfamiliar footing, followed quickly by an order to "Get in your bunk and stay there until you are told to get out."

Standing at the foot of the stairs on the prison deck, Mary Claire was grabbed by a guard and sent down the corridor to an open door. Just in front of her, she could see Bridie being shoved towards a rack of cots that lined the walls where tall shadows danced like devils in the glow of a single lantern. It was quickly her turn, and Mary Claire was given the same rough treatment, heaved into the cot below Bridie as the guards stacked them, two layers of brutalized humanity. Shocked into paralysis, she lay on the coarse wooden planks and listened to the groans of the men who were just now experiencing what the women had already been through. All voices were extinguished by the fear that gripped the dark corner of the hold, where twenty human beings stared at dark shadows. In silence they remained as the hatches were shut; without a murmur they listened to the thunderous sound of the anchor chains rattling in the hawseholes directly below them. In silence they remained as the *Hellebore* groaned and began to move, starting on a fourteen thousand mile journey that tore the convicts away from home, family and friends, most likely forever. All at once, a howl rose up from the prison deck as two hundred seventy-eight terrified people lost all hope.

Two

Out in the Channel, the storm raged with greater violence, forcing everyone on board to stay below or risk being swept overboard. Gripping the edges of her bunk, Mary Claire curled up on the uncomfortable boards, her wet clothes clinging to her skin and stealing away the warmth of her body. The thin, ratty blanket that had been issued in Portland was as saturated as her dress, worthless for holding in heat. With her knees hugged to her chest, she shivered with cold and waited for a meal, her stomach rolling with every wave that struck the ship's hull.

Mary Claire knew hunger from her first days in prison, where she was incarcerated after a very hasty trial. Put on bread and water at the behest of her accuser because she was not sufficiently remorseful, she had learned that starvation could make a woman weak and submissive. It took all her courage to refuse to apologize and buckle under, but she then learned that a woman's pain could be used to her advantage. Half the county was in an uproar after her arrest, but when wild rumors of her ravishment began to fly, her case received more attention than she had ever thought possible. They sent her to Mountjoy Female Gaol to get her out of Limerick, and hunger became her ally.

"Buck up manly, *mo mhile gra*," her sweetheart had said when he went off to fight with the Fenians. Thinking of Padraig, it was well near impossible to buck up. Seven years in Australia seemed worse than a quick death from a bullet, for such had been his fate when the Fenian uprising in the hills of County Waterford had been ruthlessly crushed. Memories of Padraig had soothed her in Limerick and Mountjoy and Newgate, but the comfort began to fade when she was sent to Portland Gaol in England. Now she envied her beloved dairy farmer, because he was resting in peace while she faced what she could not bear to face.

"Mary Claire, do you have aught to spare?" Bridie spoke through the slats of her cot.

"I gave you my last crust of bread," Mary Claire said. "If I had even a crumb, Bridie, I'd give it up gladly."

"Do you think they plan to starve us to death?" Cornelia asked, her words coming in chopped syllables as her teeth chattered.

"And haven't they been doing it all along?" Varena grumbled. "Hypocritical bunch of bastards. Slow starvation to prolong the agony."

Waves broke over the forward deck and trickled through the ship's seams, leaving a layer of cold water on the surface of the prison deck. Every woman in the hold had soaked her feet in the puddle when she crouched in the dark to use the slop bucket, which had tipped over so often that no one bothered to set it upright any more. The odor was so foul that it defied description, and the air was made even more stifling by the need to batten down the hatches against the storm.

"Come lie with me, Mary Claire, and I'll tell you some things you should know before the door is opened again," Moira said.

She wrapped Mary Claire in a maternal embrace, warm and soothing, but there was nothing that could mask the chill of the harlot's rules of engagement. Mary Claire would have been sick again if her stomach were not empty.

"There, there, little lamb," Moira said, offering consolation. "Such is the world outside of the convent that sheltered you, and convent girls have the worst of it if they're not prepared. Someone will bribe the guard, or the captain will allow the door to be unlocked, but the men will come, Mary Claire, and soon, I promise you that. At least you won't be surprised or taken advantage of. Keep your wits about you, get what you can out of it, do you hear me? You have more sense in your head than any girl who has ever worked for me, and if you've listened to half of what I've said, you'll be running the finest house in all of Australia before too long. The men who govern that country will be crawling to you on hands and knees over sharp stones, begging to kiss your soft white arse."

"That little boy is itching to kiss anything in a skirt," Varena quipped in her heavy Belfast brogue, sending her bunkmates into a round of guffaws.

"He'd be an easy one, Mary Claire," Bridie said. "He'd be done before he got his English prick out of his royal trousers."

Mrs. Perkins held Mary Claire a little longer as the young woman's shoulders quaked with silent sobs. Swirling around them was the laughter and bawdy humor of condemned prisoners who were putting on a brave face. Unlike Mary Claire, the girls from a Dublin bordello had seen the world, the world that men ruled, and they knew how cruel and disgusting that place could be. Unlike Mary Claire, they had experience to help them along, while the girl who once spent her days studying the New Testament at St. Brendan's School for Girls had only prayer to rely on. Moira had stopped believing in God long ago, and she urged Mary Claire to see sense, or die.

Without light, without windows, without a sun or moon overhead, the women could not begin to guess if it was dawn, midnight, or quarter past noon. They were all exhausted when the shouting started, with red-rimmed eyes that betrayed the discomfort of rough wooden slats, cold and wet clothes, and suffocating, rank air. A pensioner-guard walked into the cramped corner of the hold, his lantern held aloft as he barked out an order that he must have issued every morning of his life.

"Show a leg," he shouted as he strolled past the racks, peering into each cot to determine if the prisoners had made it through their first night.

He was speaking to a crew of women who had never sailed before, and his command elicited nothing more than raised heads, as twenty pairs of eyes stared back at him in confusion.

"Is it time for work already, Mrs. Perkins?" Hettie said, as if she was asking the gray-haired guard if he was there on business.

Ignoring the invitation, the old tar canted his lantern toward a set of bunks, the ones that were empty. "Where are Prisoners 2566 and 2657?"

"Gone for a walk, love, with their sweethearts," an inmate sneered.

"That's enough out of you," another man threatened, and a scarlet-clad Marine stepped into the light. He addressed his question to the person who seemed best qualified to answer. "Sent them out whoring already, did you?"

"Are you looking for a little company, then?" Moira replied. "Those aren't my best, those two, you won't miss them."

"Prisoners, fall in," the officer said, disgust in his voice.

Mary Claire climbed down right behind Mrs. Perkins, having shared the narrow cot rather than sleep only inches from the layer of raw sewage that sloshed through their quarters. Bridie had joined Hettie, not so much to get away from the vapors as to avoid feeling so dismally alone. Teetering with every wave that hit the ship's hull, the women stood in the

26

muck and listened to the Marine officer repeat, with no patience, that each prisoner was assigned a berth and was to stay in that berth until told to leave that berth.

Holding hands, Mary Claire and Bridie stood with their heads held high, expressing their scorn without moving their lips. Even when the officer hovered just inches from her face, with drops of spittle splattering on her cheek, Mary Claire stared straight ahead, fearless and bold. Only Bridie could tell that her friend was trembling.

"Although I might be convinced to excuse a minor infraction of the rules," the corporal suggested very quietly, looking first at Mary Claire and then at Bridie. "Should I let it go, then, with an apology for old Ned Brightfelt?"

An order to quick march made Mary Claire jump and she began to move, only to feel Bridie let go of her hand. Quietly, seductively, Bridie offered to show Mr. Brightfelt just how sorry she was. When Mary Claire turned back, to see what the girl was up to, he touched her cheek with the bayonet attached to his gun and ordered her to keep her eyes front and keep her feet marching.

They had only gone a few steps from their beds when the cry came, "Prisoners, halt," and the column stopped. Unseen before, shrouded in darkness, was a plank laid across some barrels, with short stacks of boards lining either side. At the end of the makeshift table, nearest the cell door, was a haphazard array of wooden bowls and mugs, a large pot, and precisely one hundred sixty ounces of square, stale and molded ship's biscuits.

"Too rough for a fire," the galley mate almost apologized to Mary Claire as he ladled out a nasty smelling liquid into her cup. Pushed down the line by the pensioner-guard, she was next handed a bowl that held her day's supply of bread. The issuance of a ration was thus completed, and she was abruptly shoved towards the stack of lumber that served as seating.

"What is it?" Hettie asked Varena, who had already put the mug to her lips with desperate thirst.

"The finest chocolate we shall ever drink," Varena remarked with an edge to her voice. It was cocoa powder and stale water, served at room temperature, to wash down hardtack that had gone bad and been rejected by the Royal Navy.

Only a few feet away, Mary Claire could make out the silhouette of Corporal Brightfelt, his sinewy movements in the lower bunk clearly visible under the light of the lantern he had placed on the upper berth. Cutting through the chatter of all the other women, Mary Claire could hear Bridie's ecstasy with a clarity that was unworldly, mingled with an occasional deep groan from the corporal. Padraig had told her to buck up, but Padraig had it easy. Padraig had it easy because he was dead and Mary Claire wished that it were her head that had caught the bullet in Kilclooney Wood.

The Surgeon-Superintendent of the *Hellebore*, the insipid Dr. Charles Smith, made his grand entrance into the dark hold as the utensils were being collected. "Rules and regulations of the *Hellebore*," he roared in the tiny room. "You will conduct yourselves in a respectful and becoming manner to all the officers on board."

From that beginning he rattled on, enumerating countless infractions such as swearing, fighting, selling clothes or shouting, all of which would be punished severely. He made a very definite point of telling the ladies that they were, on no occasion, to hold a conversation with a guard or any member of the ship's company, a comment that brought a smirk, a snicker and a snort from the jailers who stood near the cell door.

"By my order, a table has been set up so that you may take your meals in a manner befitting your sex," he droned. "You are not required to procure your daily ration allowance out of deference to your weaker capacities. I anticipate that your display of appreciation for my kindness will be demonstrated throughout this cruise by your good behavior and quiet comportment, as I observe among you now."

Thus warned, the ladies stared back at him with empty eyes, far more interested in some arrangements for bathing, although that issue was never mentioned. Neither did the doctor explain how they were to wash their clothes or clean their quarters. No one dared to speak, and Dr. Smith nodded, satisfied that his message was delivered. He walked out the door, and the ladies stared blankly, blinking their eyes as if they had seen a ghost. The cell door was locked, and everything fell back into the numbing sameness of the day before.

There was no hope of exercise that day, not when they could feel the waves battering the hull with such force that the ship was on the verge of keeling over. Without books or light to read by, too depressed to talk and very much afraid that the ship would be broken to splinters in the rough sea, the lost souls grew even quieter as the minutes ticked away.

Precisely at noon, they were given a dinner of stinking, cold salt beef and one pint of a vile concoction called pea soup, with sour, diluted wine substituted for breakfast's unpalatable chocolate brew. The respite from monotony was brief, as the afternoon reprised a morning that was spent in waiting for time to go by. Boldly, Mary Claire left her bunk and climbed up to join Bridie, who was trying ever so hard to cry silently. "It's something to put in your stomach," she whispered as she slipped the biscuits into Bridie's hand. "Don't look, just eat. John Bull tried to make soda cake and sure 'tis a mess he's baked."

With animal greed, Bridie devoured the food, but it did little to appease the ferocious hunger that kept the girl awake at night. "That lad with the cook pot gave me four extra at dinner, sent from himself. It wasn't work, Mary Claire, not at all; it's not work. He popped in, did his business real quick, and he'll be good to us now."

"No, Bridie, I'll not give aught for one crumb of English bread," Mary Claire vowed. "I'd rather die."

After a couple of hours, and out of nowhere, the sound of the bolt in the lock sent Mary Claire scrambling back to her assigned spot, scared out of her wits that she would be the next one to pay off Mr. Brightfelt. Young Arkwright called out for Prisoner 2657, his voice ridiculously loud in the small space. Frozen into rigidity, Mary Claire could not move a muscle from the instant that she heard her number announced. Even when told to answer 'present' and then come when called, she was paralyzed with fear. It was the wrong way to respond, smacking of rebellion and insolence. Powerful hands grabbed her arms and legs and tossed her into the cesspool that sloshed on the deck.

Continuing his lesson, Arkwright ordered her to her feet, his point enunciated by a kick to Mary Claire's back. Unable to rise, the girl began to crawl, and she would have marched smartly on her hands and knees if two Royal Marines had not lifted her up by her arms. She was dragged out into the corridor so quickly that she never had a chance to move her legs, her feet stumbling clumsily behind her.

"So it's you, I should have guessed," the lieutenant chuckled. "Mr. Brightfelt was present at breakfast this morning and again at dinner this afternoon by my order. I was most displeased by his report, miss, and I have brought you out here so that you may speak freely. Every prisoner is issued a ration three times per day, and the penalty for stealing food is a severe one, and one which will be meted out without mercy."

Her lowered head and stooped shoulders began to rise, as majestically as a mountain range rising up on the horizon. Mary Claire had protected Bridie from the time they were shackled together in Newgate and then sent off to Portland, and she was not about to abandon her colleague in misery now. All men were animals, Varena was deadly accurate in her observation, and the men who wore the uniform of the Royal Marines were the most reprehensible of all. Her hazel eyes bored into Brightfelt's skull as she spoke the truth.

"He gave it to her," she glowered. "'Twas not stolen, sir, 'twas given in payment for a service."

Mr. Brightfelt gulped nervously, swallowing the bitter hatred that poured from her mouth. He tightened his grip on her upper arm as a stern warning to watch her words.

"Are you accusing one of my men, is that it?" the lieutenant pressed on. "Mr. Brightfelt took your ration and gave it to another prisoner?"

"No, sir, not my ration."

With a gentle hand on her arm, he took Mary Claire aside, escorting her to a dark corner where the water casks sloshed noisily. He lifted her up by her waist, "Light as a feather," he sighed, and he set her down on a barrel. Fighting back tears, Mary Claire folded her hands primly in her lap, as she had done at St. Brendan's chapel, and she lowered her eyes in prayer.

"We are here to protect you, miss, not to cause harm. Speak plainly, now, you have nothing to fear from me. Was your ration stolen by Mr. Brightfelt?"

"No, sir," Mary Claire said.

"Then one of your fellow prisoners took it?"

"No, sir."

"This is quite a puzzle, miss. What is your name?"

Silence was her reply, a refusal to answer any questions that required more than a yes or a no. She could feel his eyes on her, studying every twinge of muscle as if he was taking note of the frightened tremble of her upper lip. Just minutes ago, he had observed the opposite reaction, when she threw a fearless, and very menacing, scowl at the corporal. She had courage, she was intelligent, and she would be difficult to control. She would not make it easy for her captors.

"Forgotten it already? Pity. Or do you suspect that I am attempting to trick you into an infraction of the rules? You may answer my question by telling me your number, since that is the proper manner to interact with me. What is your number?"

The way that her jaw clenched indicated defiance, a flat-out refusal to cooperate. The tremble was gone, and Mary Claire dug in her heels. If he thought that he was in charge, that he could command her, he was mistaken.

"Forgotten that as well, my recalcitrant Irish firebrand? And it is stamped on your dress, or perhaps you are yet another illiterate Irish peasant who cannot read," he said. "Mr. Arkwright, the prisoner will be on her knees in the female mess until she can recall her number or her Christian name."

Leaving a weary sigh behind, Plowman walked out of the hold with Brightfelt, not looking back but confident that the unrepentant criminal was beginning to appreciate prison discipline. Within a span of twenty seconds he had forgotten all about her, too engrossed in his mission to worry about something as inconsequential as a hissing cat.

Over breakfast, he had listened to Dr. Smith wax prolific on the ungovernable sex drive of sailors while rationalizing the need to allow the women to service the men. The ship's surgeon had debated with himself, because not one officer would disagree, not when the conclusion would be of great benefit to a young man with healthy appetites. With the constant threat of a Fenian insurrection on the prison deck, Simon's men needed female companionship to ease their burden, and he would have found a way around the prison's rules if Smith had argued against a floating bordello. In the end, all Simon had to do was mention the dangers of mutiny, with sailors taking over the *Hellebore* to have access to the females, and Dr. Smith decreed that the women could ply their trade if they wished.

"They're the prettiest lot I've ever seen, sir," Brightfelt confided to his superior officer.

"Sorry? Oh, yes, yes, they are certainly a comely crew that we've shipped." Pausing at the foot of the ladder, Plowman issued a gentle rebuke. "You know the captain's policy, Mr. Brightfelt, don't abuse the privilege. You have sufficient free time to use as you wish."

"Aye, aye, sir. My apologies, sir."

"They are a clever group, sir, dangerously clever, and if you stop thinking with your brain they will be running this ship before you know it. Keep things in perspective, Mr. Brightfelt, remember that they are prison inmates who want to be out of prison."

"Pretty eyes, that skinny one," the corporal continued.

"Yes, indeed," Plowman concurred. "The loveliest hazel eyes I have ever seen. And I can't say that I've ever seen so many attractive women all together at one time. A veritable garden party."

Back in his small cabin in the stern, Plowman unbuttoned his coat and flopped wearily into his bunk. The storm that the *Hellebore* sailed through had kept him from sleeping, throwing him out of his cot at least four times during the night, and the waves had not begun to ease. Despite the discomfort, Plowman preferred heading out under rough water, but only because the passengers were all too seasick to stir up trouble. It gave the lieutenant a few days to set the tone, to let the inmates know that any infraction of the rules would be met with harsh punishment, but good discipline and behavior would be rewarded. Acquiescence could mean more time on deck, something that the prisoners would soon learn to cherish.

For everyone, the diet during the storm was cold food, and Simon absent-mindedly rubbed his empty stomach. He was looking forward to a hot meal, and he knew that his captives were thinking along those same lines. He also knew that grown men would not find enough in their bowls to fill their bellies, only enough to barely sustain life in a weakened, emaciated body. Before the *Hellebore* made port in Fremantle, more than one prisoner would be tied to the triangle and flogged for stealing. Before long, the strong would prey on the weak, and the ship's company and officers would find their every sexual fantasy gratified in exchange for a rock hard biscuit or a tin of potted meat.

The prison deck was quiet on the second day out, with the ship making little progress through a heaving chop. Shortly after dinner, Lt. Plowman was called to the captain's quarters, to discuss the official business that put a Royal Marine on a prison transport. He found the captain was seated at his desk, with his naval charts pushed aside and several newspapers spread open under his nose. The man was rubbing his eyes in a way that suggested trouble was waiting for them when they left the English Channel. Opening the conversation, Morse cursed the Irish, apologized to his wife for the vulgarity, and then cursed both Irish men, and Irish women, to the devil.

With a folded tabloid in his hand, Morse waved Plowman forward. Once he was close enough, the lieutenant could see that the sheets on the desk were old copies of American newsprint. On top of the stack were *The Boston Pilot* and *The New York Herald*; the latter was opened to a page that featured an engraved picture of a very attractive young lady at the edge of womanhood, a sweet maiden. Next to that, and it was obvious that the artist had taken great liberties with his very blurry etched rendering, was a copy of an official prison photograph. Reading upside down, Simon could determine that the Irish Republican Brotherhood had smuggled the original out of Newgate Gaol, but he doubted that the original bore much resemblance to the etching. The contrast between the pictures was stark, nauseating, and clearly overblown.

"We are transporting sixty Irish traitors, Mr. Plowman," Morse spoke as he paced his cabin. "Intelligence reports reaching London from our agents in New York have indicated that a plot is brewing. The O'Dwyer brothers have stirred up the immigrants halfway across America, with their lies freely broadcast within range of our ambassador. I wish to warn you that we may very well come under attack by agents or an army of Irish Brotherhood members, who have apparently been making plans to seize this transport and kidnap their fellows."

"My men are ready, sir," Plowman said.

"In addition to the aforementioned traitors, sir, it is possible that I have been blessed with the presence of a martyr on my ship as well." Morse exhaled his annoyance. "This is not from official sources, mind you, only rumor. I do not know if this Irish girl is aboard or not. Mrs. Morse followed the case with great interest."

"The trial was a mockery, my dear, you must grant me that," Mrs. Morse opined.

"As described in the American press." Morse tapped on the stack of papers. "Yes, well, if the courts had admitted to the perversions that were hidden under clerical robes, this never would have happened. Thanks to the local court, we have this claptrap to serve as an example of our fine legal system. And then the county gaol dumped the problem in Dublin's lap, and Dublin moved her around in their shell game, and who is at the bottom of their barrel of shit?"

Clearing his throat, the lieutenant reminded Mr. Morse that his wife was within earshot. A harrumphing "beg pardon" was grunted, but Morse did not alter his tone or his vulgar verbiage as he continued his diatribe.

"How those damned O'Dwyer boys made it out of Dublin, I will never know, but the day that they escaped justice at the end of a rope has become the Crown's worst nightmare," the captain fumed. "Leave it to an Irishman to string together a few choice words and turn one girl into a cause for justice and Irish rebellion. If I could once get my hands on the master who steamed out of Dublin harbor with them on board, I would wring his goddamned neck."

"The episode will be forgotten soon enough, I expect, sir," Plowman said. "If she is being transported as you suspect, Western Australia is a quiet place that retains the news that the convicts would like to relay."

"If she is, indeed, occupying a berth below deck, it would be in everyone's best interest that she reach Fremantle intact," Morse said. "One whole, pure and innocent female convict, and if God is kind to me she will be pure and innocent at this moment. Let there be no new cause for public outcry from these Irish agitators in America."

"Aye, aye, sir, I understand," the lieutenant nodded. "Have you determined exactly which prisoner she might be?"

"I never bother with records of prisoners; I leave that to Dr. Smith, and he is not to be made aware of this individual. He'd find a reason to hang her just to strike a blow for England. In passing, I did ask about the criminal records of the females, and apparently there are at least seven thieves among them. She is one of those seven, that is as much as I can narrow down her identity at this time," the captain said. "Keep your eyes open, Mr. Plowman. If she is here, one of those loudmouthed revolutionaries will undoubtedly give her away."

"Perhaps your luck will hold, sir, and Lord Derby chose incarceration over transportation as a display of clemency," Plowman said.

Morse mumbled his accord and waved Plowman away. "Perhaps Lord Derby came to his senses and realized that a switch applied to her ass would teach her a lesson. A switch and a husband is all any girl needs to set her straight."

The lieutenant bowed slightly to Mrs. Morse, ready to take his leave, but she held up her hand as if she wanted to make some important pronouncement. "If you would be so kind, Lieutenant," she said. "Your opinion about these reports."

She picked up *The Boston Pilot*, the sheet folded neatly to display the vitriolic prose that detailed the so-called trial of a seventeen-year-old orphan, accused of stealing meat when everyone in Rathkeale knew that she only snatched a soup bone from a dog. The author of the article implied that Reverend Wilkerson pressed charges because the young lady's brothers had escaped from a police van on the way to their hanging at Newgate Gaol, and he wished to punish her by proxy.

"His argument has a scent of legitimacy," Simon said, tactful and diplomatic. "To wait nearly a year to press charges, and to arrest the girl within hours of her brothers' escape. Yet these Fenians are a very real threat to our military, so that I could hardly quibble with one man's desire to make an example. A simple lesson is always the most clear."

"It is my opinion that the girl was persecuted for personal animosity, not Fenianism," Mrs. Morse continued. "No witnesses corroborated Reverend Wilkerson's testimony. He was the only one to claim that she stole a roast out of his oven."

"The word of a minister, Mrs. Morse," Plowman said.

"The very minister who made a sport of deflowering young virgins," the captain grunted. "The court was not listening to some twaddle, Mrs. Morse, they were listening to Whitehall. Support the Irish Brotherhood and suffer, those are the words that sent her down."

"Indeed," Simon agreed. "And the Fenians in America have certainly let us know what they think of our message."

Quickly scanning the entire article, Simon picked up on a few key points that Edward O'Dwyer, former prisoner of the Crown and still a wanted man, wished to make about life under British rule. Thanks to the man's heart-rending prose, readers all over the United States had learned that Thomas O'Dwyer was brought to penury when he refused to surrender his only daughter to a vile, and very Protestant, pervert. Wilkerson denounced Fenianism from his pulpit and squeezed O'Dwyer until the man was bankrupted, evicted, and left homeless on the back lanes around Rathkeale town where he sickened and died.

There was nothing particularly startling about the saga, not when Simon had heard of countless families that had suffered the same fate at the hands of a landlord. What made this family different was Michael O'Dwyer's experience with the 88th New York during the American Civil War. He had come home and trained his brothers, with a mind to do battle against the Queen. The O'Dwyer boys would never have taken the oath and gone off with the Fenians if they had not been provoked so forcefully. They would not be in America now, denouncing England and agitating for Irish freedom, raising funds from the descendants of the famine emigrants and stirring up trouble on this final transport to Australia.

"The situation could have been better handled," Plowman said in conclusion, and he bowed out of the captain's cabin. He had not gone more than three steps when Mr. Brightfelt came running up to him. There was trouble in the forward hold, something that worried the relatively experienced corporal.

Before reaching the women's quarters, Plowman could determine that there was trouble indeed, and not some catfight between whores. Not less than twelve women were chanting "Mercy" at the top of their lungs, pounding their mugs on the table to enunciate their point. Mr. Arkwright's scarlet coat was a bright beacon that illuminated the source of the entire conflict, and Plowman was at once infuriated and awestruck.

"Please, miss, please," the young Marine begged, on the verge of sobbing with frustration. "Please just say two, that's all, just the first number, just say two."

The prisoner had been on her knees for six hours, her body racked with pain as she weakly swayed, fighting to stay upright if she died in the process. Mealtime had proceeded as scheduled, and the women were up in arms over the cruel treatment that had begun after dinner and continued past supper. It was now time to get into bed, but the ladies had thus far refused to turn in their utensils, refused to leave the mess area, and they refused to be quiet in the face of threats of corporal punishment. Plowman was well aware that the riot had to be put down at once, because three Royal Marines would be no match for nineteen women armed only with outrage and the will to tear the guards to pieces.

"My apologies, miss, but you did tell me your name in Portland." Plowman deflated the tension. "Once a lady tells you her name, Mr. Arkwright, never ask her to repeat it two days later. There is no greater insult to the fairer sex, and no better way to demolish a budding courtship."

Plowman slipped a hand under her thin arm and lifted her to her feet as she cried out in pain. "Your name is Eireann go Bragh, I believe. Now say it."

"Ireland forever," she rasped defiantly, and two strong men dragged her to a seat at the table where a rancid smelling pint of gruel was sloshing in a dirty mug.

"There will be silence, or there will be no further need for this mess hall," Plowman bellowed fiercely.

Gradually, the clanking stopped and the shouts were reduced to curses and grumbling. Looking briefly at Prisoner 2657, Plowman was touched by her companions' solicitude. The plump redhead was tenderly cradling the girl's head, while the older member of the tribe carefully held the cheap wine to the convict's lips. He had not expected the denizens of a bordello to care for one another in the least, but this was genuine affection.

"When the weather breaks," Plowman continued, "you will be permitted to exercise on deck for a minimum of one hour each day. This time may be lengthened, or it may be eliminated, as you wish. There will be order. There will be discipline. There will be recreation. Or, there will be confinement in the hold, as you wish."

Surveying the twenty pairs of eyes that glowered at him, the lieutenant was satisfied that his message was clear. Checking on the condition of the hardheaded prisoner, Plowman watched her friend take a sip of barley gruel before helping her to eat, and they went back and forth until the modest ration was consumed. It was the oddest thing he had ever witnessed, and he caught himself staring, vacant and dreamy. Mumbling an order to carry on, he left the cell, his eyes beginning to sting as the fetid odor burned into his nose.

"A good soldier is brave," Mary Claire murmured as Cornelia and Bridie eased her into the cot.

"A good soldier knows when to retreat, and when to fight to the last drop of blood," Hettie said. "Now, take another bite or I'll shove this shit down your throat."

"For the babe." Mary Claire refused the biscuit crumbs as she blindly reached towards Bridie's middle.

"There's ways to get better than this," Mrs. Perkins noted. "John Bull won't starve the wee one to death, but we all work together, girl. There's only one way to do it."

With something in their bellies, the ladies felt a resurgence of seasickness, and the rancid smells of partially digested barley gruel and sour wine were soon added to the outhouse vapors that filled the room. Two days at sea had passed by, with another one hundred to go; the malaise that night sucked the last few drops of hope right out of their hearts.

Three

Only when the metal hatches were finally opened did they inhale the sweet, salty air of the outside world. After three days in a stuffy pen, the smell had become so bad that the guards who lived aft of the female quarters had begun to complain. There was hot food at last, although tepid was closer to the actual temperature of the unsweetened, bitter chocolate that was doled out, to wash down the dry, disgusting biscuit.

Breakfast was no sooner finished than a tramping of feet proclaimed the arrival of Mr. Hiram Hightower, an old constable from Lancashire who had accepted the position of Assistant Warder as a means to relocate to Australia with his wife, to be closer to their son and his sheep station. His assistants drifted at his side, ferrying buckets, brushes, lime and sulfur candles.

Scrub brushes were handed out, and each pair of women was issued a bucket of water before being jostled to various parts of the cell. Barely able to put pressure on her knees, Mary Claire leaned on one hip as she worked across from Bridie, head to head as they set about their chore. Before long, the sweet notes of feminine chatter began to mingle with a snippet of song as Mary Claire set a pace with an Irish tune that made the work flow more smoothly.

That task completed, Mr. Hightower barked, "Prisoners, fall in," and a guard set about sprinkling the planks with lime while a companion placed burning sulfur candles throughout the cell. As they were ordered, the ladies sorted themselves in line in the storage area of the room, to listen to Mr. Hightower explain his rules. They were exceedingly simple while utterly arbitrary; any infraction would be punished but there were too many regulations to enumerate them all. With a warning glare at the Irish girl who was already labeled as trouble, the man did mention that convicts would answer when spoken to, but other than that, it was anyone's guess what might bring on Mr. Hightower's retribution.

They were taught how to properly fold their blankets, a task to be completed promptly upon rising every morning. They learned how to remove the slats of their beds for a daily brushing, and then Hightower pointed to Phoebe Evarts and Sarah Thorpe and told them that they were the cleaners. For the rest of the trip, they would sweep out the female quarters every day, and whether it was a fair arrangement or not made no difference.

"Prisoners, quick march," the jailer proclaimed in the early afternoon of the following day, and the two regimented lines were forced up the steps and out of the hold. With their eyes accustomed to the darkness, the cloudy skies seemed so brilliant that the women all put their hands to their faces to shade the intense light.

Blinking and squinting, the cluster at the mouth of the hatchway looked around, surprised to discover that the edge of the deck was lined with guards and jailers, their rifles pointed, bayonets fixed and fingers on triggers. The weak and seasick group presented little threat, but a show of force was understood. The men stared down their sights and the women stared back, blank and vacuous, confused by this peculiar universe that was sailing southwest around the northern coast of Spain. For one brief moment, it seemed as if everyone and everything stopped, an entire ship frozen over and captured in amber.

Bridie put an arm around Mary Claire's waist to help her walk around the circuit. "May I have the next dance?" a sailor yelled down from the mainmast yardarm, making an obscene gesture along with the offer.

"There's no strings left in your old bow," she called back, giving the old tar a look of disdain. "You can fiddle with yourself."

"Look, another ship," Varena waved her friends towards the rail. "Something's up."

While the women milled closer to the port bulwarks, peaking between guards and hardly walking at all, the tall masts on the horizon grew taller as the vessel approached. They also detected an increased tension in the Marine guards, who suddenly became excessively alert. "Look up there, at the captain," Hettie whispered. "He's having kittens over it."

Trying to get a better spot from which to view the oncoming barque, one convict gave another a bump of the hip, which was returned with a shove. In a matter of seconds, they were trading punches and clawed scratches, with hair pulling added to the weaponry. Mrs. Perkins rounded up her troop and guided them to the middle of the forward deck, out of range of the shrieking fight that boiled over and singed the two pickpockets.

"Why don't they stop it?" Mary Claire asked Moira, but before she received an answer she called over to one of the red-coated pensioner guards. "Why don't you stop it?"

"No prisoner to make conversation, miss," the man said, but he answered anyway. "And no sane man would wade into that riptide."

Not one jailer lowered his rifle or took an eye off the prisoners, and the battle continued. A gunshot suddenly cracked through the screeching, with a sound so loud that all the women screamed in panic. Mr. Brightfelt's shot in the air gave him the response that he sought, for the combatants stopped fighting long enough to permit the guards to pull them apart without risking the fists, feet, teeth and nails of enraged, irrational females.

"Who instigated this fight?" the corporal demanded of the four Amazonian warriors who stood in front of him, held tightly in place by two burly guards.

It was a hasty and somewhat stupid question, one that Brightfelt swiftly regretted as a chorus of "She did" begin to bounce around the deck. Along with a waggling of fingers pointing, he would have to conclude that everyone had started the fight, and he was looking the fool when he meant to sound commanding. For the sake of appearances, he had to choose one, and he managed to pick out the woman who was the least bloodied. The unlucky convict was told to report to the punishment cell, while her three cohorts were brought to the mainmast to receive five blows to their rumps from the bosun's length of knotted hemp. It was a child's punishment, not unlike a nautical caning, but since women were regarded as children they were given the same penalty.

"Injustice," Mary Claire screeched. "The cruelty of the Crown is never ending."

"And she's next," Brightfelt pointed at Mary Claire while one of the fighters yelped in pain.

On the quarterdeck, Morse was swearing at the Stars and Stripes that waved at him from the other ship. With a spyglass pressed to his eye, he uttered a string of epithets while issuing orders to prepare for battle. His cargo of prison refuse was temporarily forgotten as he contemplated the wisdom of firing on the American flag in international waters. The possibility of sparking some sort of diplomatic debacle was weighed against the possibility that Irish-Americans were going to destroy Morse's career by taking his ship. There was no easy solution, short of dumping the Fenians overboard and letting the sharks have them. He looked out over the deck, lined with nervous guards, fingers twitching on the triggers of Enfield rifles, the tension rising as Yankee sails, and then Yankee rigging came into clear view.

"Do not come any closer, or you shall be fired upon," Morse threatened through his hailing trumpet.

There was a short pause before the ship's master responded. "I am in international waters, sir. And I believe that we settled our differences in 1812. When we whipped your royal ass."

The quarterdeck of the *Hellebore* did not flinch at the insult, which only ratcheted up the agitation that filled every officer present. Captains were in the habit of stopping at sea to pay social calls, to have a gam and pass along weather conditions, but everyone steered clear of the transport vessels and their cargo of criminals. A ship on a rescue mission, a Fenian ship, would not be so concerned, and Plowman kept his eyes glued to the weather-beaten Yankee with the full and bushy beard.

"State your business." Morse played for time, hoping to discover the other captain's true motives before the *Hellebore* was lost to Irish piracy.

"Sternwood Millhouse, sir, requesting permission to come aboard, to obtain your assistance," he replied, wearing good manners that failed to cloak his distaste of the Union Jack.

"We are a prison ship, sir, and have no assistance to offer," Morse retorted.

"If you have no assistance, sir, do you have a chronometer to spare?"

"Do you think it is a ruse, Mr. Plowman?" Morse pondered for a moment. "We'll keep our distance. One boatload of Irishmen can't do much damage, and if the merchantman is truly at risk, far be it from me to deny aid to a sailor."

A small boat tied up alongside the *Hellebore* and Captain Millhouse was cordially greeted on the quarterdeck. Plowman was satisfied that nothing was afoot, not after he looked down into the small boat and saw a few colored sailors, obviously unarmed and simply curious about the strangely painted craft that gave off an odor worse than a pigpen. The merchant master's explanation for the disruption was perfectly logical, with his claim that his chronometer had been destroyed during the storm that nearly wrecked his ship. Exhaling with weary relief, Plowman took advantage of the pleasant scenery on deck to find a few moments of peace from the press of his duties.

The plump little redhead was inspecting him, looking him over in the way that all young ladies discreetly examined the male sex. With a sly smile, she shared her assessment with her black-haired companion, jabbering away in the peculiar guttural tones of the Irish language. Two sparkling hazel eyes slipped quickly over his face and shoulders, followed by a lark's song of giggles as the two shared their confidences. To let the pair know that he was aware of their admiration he sent them a half-smile and a very slight nod, frustrated that he understood only a very few words of a language that was spoken in Ireland's most isolated areas. He would have to prevent them from conversing in Irish, and he made a mental note to alert the guards and Marines. There could be no greater danger than inmates freely plotting in a foreign tongue, even women who appeared harmless.

Hearing the language brought back pleasant memories of his childhood, of the maids who chattered in the hallways and sang strangely beautiful songs as they worked. Distracted, he found himself admiring the prisoner's captivating eyes when Brightfelt and a pensioner guard suddenly entered the scene, grabbed the woman by her arms and dragged her to the mainmast. Her screams broke the idyllic mood, forcing Plowman to look around and discover that a storm had erupted on the quarterdeck. Captain Morse was waving a newspaper at his guest, berating the merchant master about the girl from Rathkeale while inviting him to leave at once.

"Ireland forever," the girl proclaimed loudly, drawing Plowman's startled attention. Turning back to Mr. Millhouse, now standing at the gangway with a box under his arm, the Marine watched as the stern Yankee pointed to the Irish lass, every muscle moving in slow and deliberate motion.

"The name of O'Dwyer is on the lips of every man who loves Ireland. Know that you are not friendless or forgotten, Mary Claire O'Dwyer," Millhouse's deep voice resonated along the deck and seemed to echo off the water.

A bullet could not fly faster than Plowman at that moment as he sprang into action. Pushing the old guard aside and grabbing Mary Claire's arm, he picked her up and dashed to the forward hold with Brightfelt rendering rapid assistance. Mary Claire was hustled down to the prison deck so quickly she seemed to disappear in a puff of smoke.

"Prisoner, you are the most insolent brat I have ever encountered." Plowman stood in the women's mess, an anger that had been stoked by nerves permitted to rage out of control. "A cell may not reform you, but a good caning is more suitable punishment for such an infantile display of poor manners."

There was no sorrowful remorse, only a puerile smirk that meant she had scored a point against her captors. With exaggerated movements,

Mary Claire bent over at the waist and ran her hands across her bottom, smoothing her skirt and presenting her rump for beating. Ever so slightly, she jiggled her hips, as if she were laughing merrily and mocking him, taunting him into greater fury.

Her pose meant something altogether different to the lieutenant, who took her shoulder and lifted her upright, his cheeks flushed red in an embarrassment that increased when he suspected that she knew what he was thinking. Wearing a victor's laurels on her brow, she straightened her spine and held her head high. She was not forgotten, with friends in America, and her cruel smirk drove him over the edge. His hand rose of its own volition, his fingers tightened, palm flattened as his hand became a weapon that came within inches of striking her mouth. At the last second, he stopped short of striking her, but she ducked and stumbled to the deck, hitting her bruised knees and gasping with pain.

"Why do you seek to add more punishment, when clearly you are paying a high price for your crime?" Plowman said, forcing his every muscle into composure.   Going down on one knee, he crouched next to the stooped figure, his mouth so close to her ear that her hair brushed his lips. "When was the last time you bathed, 2657, can you recall when last you were immersed in hot water, with a cake of soap that smells of roses? And when was the last time that you dusted your fair skin with lavender scented powder? When was the last time that you brushed your hair and pinned it up on your head to display this long, graceful neck?"

As she folded her hands in prayer, Mary Claire glanced at her fingers, the nails so encrusted with dirt they were almost black.

"You smell worse than a cesspool, you are filthy. Your clothes are filthy. As for your figure, I cannot begin to tell you how appalling you have become. That can change, 2657, if you want this journey to be more tolerable you have the power to change all that."

Reaching into his coat pocket, Simon took out a piece of paper-wrapped candy and a neatly folded flannel. "Did you receive peppermint drops when you were little, when you did as you were told? If you will behave, 2657, and follow orders like a good little soldier, I can give you this, and there are more to be had. Would you like a piece of soap and a bit of fresh water to match this flannel? Yes, I see that you would like that very much, to scrub the dirt of Newgate and Portland off your skin."

"All these things I will give thee, if thou wilt fall down and worship me," Mary Claire hissed, glaring at Simon and enunciating her syllables with murder. "Begone, Satan."

"Never in my life have I witnessed such absolute, all-consuming, childish stubbornness. If there is any creature on God's earth that is more stupid than an Irish woman, I should like to see it," Plowman fumed, rising to his feet and kicking at an empty bucket.

"Look in a mirror," she retorted, her flinty gaze as cold as death. Brightfelt gave her the back of his hand on her temple, sending her sprawling sideways.

Roughly, Mary Claire was lifted to her feet and brought back to her bunk. "It's no punishment for such a saint as you to be on her knees for the next three months," Plowman said. "Perhaps confinement to your cot will help you see reason. I will send your regrets to Father McCabe tomorrow morning, and convey your lack of remorse at being unable to attend his religious service or participate in any Catholic sacraments."

The bolt jangled in the lock of the cell door. As they turned to go, the two Marines heard her voice, clear and beautiful, as Mary Claire sang, "Magnificat anima mea, Dominum." It was the Canticle of Mary, warbled in an act of adamant rebellion.

"I'm sorry, sir, but if I had known," Brightfelt said as they tramped up the steps out of the forward hold. "Bobby Arkwright paid out six apples and ten biscuits for the redhead last night. They drive a hard bargain, sir, but they give a fellow the full value. Best I've ever had, sir, treated like a king, to be honest. I suppose she's pretty angry over your offer, considering how much the others get and all."

"Thank you, Mr. Brightfelt," Plowman said. "Not a very well planned maneuver on my part."

"The madam, sir, she's the one to see if you're looking for a bit of quality snatch. That one there is going for a high price, we found out, because she's not been ridden yet." Brightfelt snorted with derision. "Or so the madam says. Bobby heard that and his tongue started to wag, drooling the boy was, believing that old whore's tall tales."

"She'd give a man a fine ride for his biscuits, first go or fiftieth," Plowman said. "Hard to pin a reasonable price on that kind of merchandise."

Morse met with his officers that evening, opening with a pleasant dinner before sinking into a battle plan in the event of attack. Instead of an armed escort, the *Hellebore* was given Lt. Wargrave and a few old naval guns. No British warships could be spared to safeguard the prison ship, and Morse was convinced that cost was the issue. Feeding and clothing prisoners was done as cheaply as possible, rather than waste a shilling on a pack of despicable wretches. As it was, the custom of transporting criminals to Australia had come under fire for the past ten years, and the government very much wanted this final delivery to be smooth and well executed. The government did not want to pay too much for the task.

At the end of the evening, Captain Morse took Simon aside for a private security briefing, held in hushed tones to prevent Mrs. Morse from listening in and contributing her opinions. She was a modern and progressive sort, one who subscribed to the newest philosophy regarding proper treatment of criminals. Her husband was not in agreement.

"There can be no doubt, Mr. Plowman, as much as I have prayed that the O'Dwyer girl was not on this ship, but our passenger 2657 and this miscreant are one and the same." Morse indicated the fuzzy etching of Mary Claire that was printed in an old edition of *The Irish World*, the so-called gift from Mr. Millhouse.

"Not with the confirmation that we received today, no sir," Plowman agreed. He scanned the essay briefly, picking up a few key words. Michael O'Dwyer had composed it, citing his own experiences with the Union Army at Appomattox as he called on Irishmen everywhere to take up arms. There was a rehash of his sister's misery, yet another mention of her persecution on behalf of the Irish Republican Brotherhood, but Plowman already knew all that. His thoughts elsewhere, he sighed and rubbed his eyes, recalling so vividly the day that he was told that he was just the man for the job. It had all sounded so simple at the time.

"Now I can tell you why I was assigned to the *Hellebore*," Simon began. "In strictest confidence, you understand, Mr. Morse. While it is true that I am under orders to closely monitor the military Fenians, I was also given a covert operation of which no one but you shall be made aware. I must confess that today's incident was actually very good news for me."

"You have been granted some remarkable liberties to act on your own initiative," Morse said, reading over the secret dispatch with great interest. "But as I am aware of your record with the Irish problem, Mr. Plowman, I agree with your superiors. You are made for this type of intrigue."

The mission was not going to be easy, especially since Mary Claire was under the protection of a highly successful madam. Their clique was tight, both physically and emotionally, whether they were strolling the deck or sharing food. The madam looked out for Mary Claire, but there was a rather sinister reason for the bond, one that Simon had discovered recently. On the prison ship, food was scarce and more valuable than gold, and Mary Claire was worth a small fortune.

Thanks to the redhead's insistence, "I'm so fond of a man who's never lain with a woman before, Bobby," and Brightfelt's impatience, the O'Dwyer girl was still on the market for a price that escalated rapidly between Friday night and Saturday morning. On a lark, Brightfelt asked again on Saturday afternoon, and had reported to Plowman that the virgin could be had for two dozen apples, a pound of sugar and two of tea, three bottles of wine, and probably more if any man were foolish enough to follow through on the deal. Plucking a cherry being a once in a lifetime encounter, no one seemed to be able to offer enough.

That Mrs. Perkins was a smart businesswoman was apparent, but Plowman had to consider the possibility that there was more to her salesmanship than a week's rations. With her skill, she could build up the excitement until she found a man hungry enough to pay whatever was asked. Men could be stupid when there was a woman involved, and Plowman was not so certain that the top price might not be the keys to the locks and few rifles. The Fenians were everywhere and nowhere, a dangerous group that had infiltrated the armed forces and come very close to overthrowing British rule in Ireland. They could be anywhere, invisible until they struck, and who could say if there was a Fenian ship nearby, waiting for just such a moment.

Prisoner 2657 was pacing the planks between the racks while Father McCabe said Mass on the forward deck above her. She strained to hear the priest's words, responding when she thought she heard a prayer, the Kyrie and later the Agnus Dei. At the stern, Dr. Smith was warbling a

Protestant hymn, with his Anglican congregation apparently matching his volume in an attempt to drown out the Catholic liturgy. Back and forth, only a few steps she walked and turned, walked and turned, asking God if it was a sin to be more ashamed of being a stinking, unwashed woman than in sorrowing over a Mass missed because of a great weakness.

"Mea culpa, mea culpa, mea maxima culpa," she beat her breast in an act of contrition, seeking His forgiveness for her sins, for her unremitting pride.

The door was opened and the lieutenant strolled in, his face a gentle mask of concern. With great effort, he struggled to hold his expression, but he was unquestionably surprised by her appearance. Her eyes had been held open by force of will and pure fear, not shutting since Friday night, and she cast her dark-ringed, bloodshot eyes on his jaw, observing the muscles tighten and relax. Taking a step back as he came closer, she stumbled over her feet, her legs too weary to move with grace.

"I have heard you are for sale," he said.

Clutching her prison dress close to her neck, Mary Claire flew into a panic that was elevated beyond reason. She began to scream as if she was under attack, falling to the floor where she could curl up into a tight and inaccessible ball.

"Silence," he ordered. Taking a firm grasp of her shoulders, he knelt on the deck and yelled in her face, shaking her like a disobedient and willful child. "You will be assigned to the laundry detail on Monday if you will behave. Will you behave, 2657?"

She stopped screaming and scurried backwards on her bottom, pushing up against the bulkhead in search of an escape. "No, no, I won't do it," she rasped in terror.

"If you work in the laundry you will have access to water. You could at least wash your face and hands after the clothes are taken out of the tubs. But you must be a good girl, and do as you are told."

Silently, she cringed against the wall, staring at him with the horrified visage of a cornered doe. The lieutenant had the upper hand, a power that could be used to break down the resistance of a woman who was barely out of childhood.

"You can no longer stomp your little foot and pout, and then expect to have your way," he began. He was soft and tender now, an abrupt change from the stern, raging officer who had spoken only seconds ago. "Do you regret your outburst of Saturday afternoon?"

"No," she answered.

"Did you hear the men? Their voices carried out of the hatchways, I was certain that you heard them shouting about the Yankee ship and grew more obstinate because of it."

Learning of such great success, Mary Claire straightened up, glad of a victory and better able to stomach what she feared was about to come next. The men on the prison deck had been so loud that it seemed as if the whole world must have heard them. Without a doubt, the Yankee master had been treated to a rousing chorus, and from him the word would spread to her brothers in America. In two or three weeks, Ed and Mike would know that she was well, and she was still full of fighting spirit

"Among the prisoners are nine men who are Fenians, deserters from Her Majesty's armed forces. Some of the finest soldiers, I might add, brave men who bear the scars of battle from conflicts in the Punjab. None of that matters, 2657, because they are deserters, and a deserter is a traitor, anathema to every loyal soldier. They spoke out for you when they were ordered to be quiet, but their punishment was not confinement to their quarters. Do you feel sorry for yourself, eh, do you?"

A touch of disgust curled her lip, and she slapped his face with the contempt that shot from her eyes. For a brief instant she had begun to bow, but she had not broken, although his penetrating gaze must have detected the slight wavering of her will. The Marine continued to heap on the sort of punishment that hurt her deeply, pummeling her sense of piety and goodness to others. Already he had found her weak spot, something that she was too tired to fully disguise.

"Their punishment, 2657, was to be beaten with fists and rifle butts. Because of you, Eireann go Bragh, all because of you, there are men writhing in pain, noses smashed, guts bruised. Now I ask you if you regret your outburst, but your self-pity is so all-consuming that you do not seem to care, and you continue to disobey."

Shame and remorse swamped Mary Claire, enough sorrow to bring the tears to her eyes. She realized the consequences of her actions and she ached with compassion for those who had to pay the price that was not exacted of her because of her sex. A sob rose in her throat and she held her fist in her mouth to stifle a moan that threatened to give away her weak position. The officer slid down to join her on the deck, resting his back against the bulkhead while curling his arm around her shoulders, offering consolation with tender words and soft whispers.

"Not twenty feet away from you, less than twenty feet, are evil men who are being sent away because they are murderers and rapists. Your guards do not wish to see any crime committed upon your lovely person, but if you stir up trouble and make things difficult for them," he said, leaving the threat to dangle in mid-air. He whispered in her ear, his cheek so close that she could smell sandalwood soap and bay rum. "Those same criminals will serve fourteen years, or even more, at hard labor. Do you know what that means?"

"No, sir," she gulped.

"It is unlikely that they will live long enough to complete their sentence and return to England. Quarrying stone, cutting roads, in a heat so brutal I cannot begin to describe it. The sun is so bright that men go blind, the work so grueling that they are half-dead at the end of every miserable day. And I have not even mentioned the snakes and the fevers."

"What of the Fenians, sir?" she asked.

"A lifetime of penal servitude at hard labor," he said softly, letting her figure out the rest. "You see what they face, and if you would be a true friend to them, you would not do things that result in further punishment. Can I be your friend, 2657, will you listen to my advice?"

Aware that she had very nearly fallen into his trap, she pulled away and popped to her feet. "No man in regimental scarlet is a friend to Ireland," she said.

Slowly and methodically, the lieutenant rose to his full five feet ten inches and began to unbutton his coat. Fire flashed from his eyes, a heat that Mary Claire detected on her face as she began to back up, step by slow step, until she was trapped against the end of the bunk. In a fury, the officer tore off the jacket and threw it, with force, at Mary Claire's arms.

"Learn to look beneath the surface, girl, and find your true friends. Your plump colleague, is that a friend beneath her fleshy form? She takes your ration, and do not try to deny it because my men have seen you give half of every meal to her. She grows fat while you are transformed into a walking skeleton. And that is a friend?"

An insult to Bridie was more than Mary Claire could tolerate. With a sneer on her lips, she took the coat in her dirty fingers and threw it on the deck. "You're a right idiot."

"We'll soon see who the 'eejit' is," he hissed, aping her Irish brogue. "There is a price on your maidenhead, my dear, put there by a woman who has made her living by using innocent young girls in ways that are more depraved than you could ever imagine. You think you are a grown woman, well, just wait. One man can do a great deal of damage in thirty minutes time, and if you were wise you would pay close attention to my words."

He had intentionally managed to jab at the one thing that Mary Claire feared more than starvation. Out in the normal world, men were restrained by respect, but she had discovered months ago that prison inmates were not treated with respect. Knowing that, she could not fully understand what the lieutenant was trying to suggest. Either he was sincere in his warning or he was attempting to separate her from the only people she trusted.

"I am capable of choosing my friends, sir," she proclaimed, daring him to try anything that a gentleman would never do.

"Then choose wisely, 2657, choose well and live. If you do not, you are finished." Changing his manner, the lieutenant grew more personable. "Surely, a pretty girl like you has a sweetheart who longs for your return. Do you not wish to join him again? How I envy the boy who has captured your heart, for he is the luckiest man on earth."

"As I envy him, sir," she said. "I envy his freedom. Free for all eternity from the persecution of your evil queen, with his blood staining the floor of Kilclooney Wood and his soul in paradise, where no English heretic may wander."

Her frenzied ramblings had an unexpected result, bringing on a complete change in the lieutenant's mien. Fatigued and dazed from lack of sleep, she kept babbling on, claiming that she had lost her darling and had no reason to carry on, not when he had given his life for Irish freedom. "Better to die for Ireland," she concluded, not sure where the words were coming from or even if she was making any sense.

"I am so very sorry, Mary Claire, so very sorry," he said. "But there are men all over the world who would long for a chance to win your heart. Listen to me, as a friend, without my scarlet coat and the trappings of the Crown. You have a long life before you, and I will see to it that you live for as long as you are aboard this ship. Don't make yourself a martyr, don't waste the life that God has given you."

"Idiot," she spat back, glaring daggers at him.

She had gone a step too far, triggering his temper after he had been relatively kind to her. He was seething with anger as he grabbed her shoulders and gave her a hard push that sent her sprawling into the lower bunk. Fearing the worst, she clung tightly to her skirts as if she could hold them in place through the strongest assault. The smirk on his face was cruel as he towered over her, his hand moving towards the fly of his trousers.

"Be prepared then, 2657, be ready for the worst. It is coming, girl, and those whom you think are your friends will show their true colors. You'll be a whore when you land at Fremantle, and you'll die a whore in Fremantle. May God have mercy on your soul."

With that, he turned on his heel and strode towards the door, picking up his coat in a graceful swoop without breaking stride. Shattering under the strain, she burst into wretched sobs, a pitiable and violent wailing that betrayed her. At the door of the cell, he paused and called out to her. "If you are intent on destroying yourself, Mary Claire O'Dwyer, there is nothing that I can do to stop you. Do you think anyone will care if you kill yourself? Will you make Ireland free? Or will you burn in hell for all eternity?"

Four

With nothing to do all day, and no exercise period to look forward to when bad weather set in, the prisoners grew restless and they took out their frustrations on each other. There was endless bickering that often lapsed into violence, scratching and clawing with fury that found no respite. Every infraction meant five strokes of the bosun's cane, but still the female mess was a scene of frequent squabbles followed by swift retribution, regular discipline, and dire warnings.

After a full seven days at sea, Captain Morse decided that he had put enough distance between the *Hellebore* and civilization to preclude any attempt at Fenian piracy. The prisoners were roused from their cells and assembled on deck, with the females granted the best spot, out of deference to their femininity, to view the spectacle that was about to unfold.

Under close guard, a brutal looking gorilla of a man was paraded to the mainmast and tied to the metal rings that were attached to a gaff on the mast. Bolted to the deck was another ring that was used to bind his legs. Following a reading of his crime, which appeared to be brawling, a powerful bosun's mate wound up and swung the cat. Bridie fainted on the spot while the other women screamed in horror.

For those who had sailed in the Royal Navy or spent time in prison, flogging was not something out of the ordinary. Not that a man enjoyed watching it, but many of them were somewhat accustomed to the sight. Mary Claire closed her eyes at the sickening exhibition and she prayed. She prayed for the prisoner and she prayed for all the men who had to live through more than she would ever know. She entreated God to give her strength as her will wavered, and she was deep in contemplation when Mr. Hightower pushed a scrub brush into her stomach to rouse her. An Irish scrubwoman to wash away English blood, Mary Claire was ordered to swab the deck until it was spotless.

Working at the gore that was splattered on the teak planks, she could see the shadow of the noose dancing on the deck, the rope that was ever present on the main yard to provide a constant reminder of the speedy execution that could be delivered to those who did not behave. She thought of death, of the view from the end of the noose, and she wondered if it was so bad after all. Suicide was a sin, but God could not fault her if she were executed.

The evening star was rising in the eastern sky when the female prisoners were given an extra exercise period. For the first time, they were on deck at the same time as the men, though they were carefully segregated by armed guards and several feet of empty space. The ladies were grateful for an opportunity to inhale some clean air before retiring, and they appreciated the timbre of male voices that drifted forward, carrying the sounds of poetry and prose that had been written on scraps of memory and delivered by rote. Between the women and the armed guards, a group of sailors were taking their ease.

One man had a fiddle and another a tin whistle, and they struck up a song to pass the time. The women joined in, to tell a sorrowful ballad of famine and hardship. A calm descended on the forward deck as the high voices of the ladies told of the Irish girl who left home during the Great Hunger, only to die at sea. It was a protest song, to be sure, one that subtly blasted the brutality of the English government during the famine years.

A pall of hopeless misery hung on the deck, as impenetrable as fog. When the fiddler struck up a rollicking tune to lighten the mood, Varena accepted the challenge. Taking to the stage in the center of the circle of women, she lustily warned the gentlemen of the dangers of pretty young damsels who were pickpockets, inveigling a man to transportation to Van Diemen's Land. Bridie jumped to her feet, giggling merrily, and took Mary Claire's hand. They waltzed without a care in the world, twirling away from what awaited them in the future.

A tap on the shoulder, an irresistible smile, and a courtly bow brought Mary Claire into the lieutenant's arms while the ship's purser, with a wicked grin, put his hand on Bridie's waist and danced away with the jolly redhead. The officer and the convict could have been a courting couple at the crossroads dance, smiling with delight and unaware of the world around them. Music had the power to take the dancers far away, to a place where Mary Claire saw the face of the most handsome man she had ever met, eyes glowing with love, someone so appealing that she wanted him to kiss her and let his silky whiskers tickle her lips.

As *The Black Velvet Band* ended, someone called out a request for *Star of the County Down*. A naval officer began to walk towards Mary Claire, thinking he could claim a dance, but Lt. Plowman swiftly put an arm across her back and led her away, bringing her to the starboard rail for a quiet chat.

"Can I be your friend, Mary Claire?" he asked the sky as he leaned against the bulwarks, his eyes savoring the gentle light of sunset.

His words reminded her of all the cruelty and the mean punishments inflicted, and she was pulled back to the reality of a prison ship. "No," she said, straight to the point.

"You choose to learn the whore's trade, apparently," he pressed.

"I choose not to starve, John Bull, and if it's a fallen woman I must be, 'tis your queen who is the Royal Madam to all her subjugated slaves, an Anglican betrayer of decency, Queen of the harlots sitting on her throne of sin."

"Bold talk for a maiden," he chuckled.

"As bold as the stupidity that falls from your lips," she countered. "You've put many a girl in a family way, I'd guess, with your fine ways, but it's an idiot who claims a girl fleshy when she carries a child."

She made a move to storm off, but the lieutenant had a solid grip on her arm. "*The Maid Who Sold Her Barley*," he begged, and the fiddler sawed away while his toe tapped to the quick rhythm. With an iron hold, Plowman dragged Mary Claire through the reel, singing the words with a lewd air, practically bellowing in her face. "If twenty guineas would gain the heart of the maid I love so dearly, all for to tarry with me one night and go home in the morning early."

He was laughing at her, at the fire that blazed in her eyes, at the look that promised brutal and bloody murder. "Better an Irish whore than an English queen," she hissed.

"Better to die of the French pox than go back to Ireland after you've served your time? Ireland must be a wretched place indeed." She tried to pull away but he held her wrist, his grin now threatening. "And when a man buys you, you cannot run off if you do not fancy him."

He did not so much release her grip as he flung her hand away. Bridie left the dance and ran after her friend, who had fled to the port bulwarks.

"I can't go on Bridie, this life is no life at all," Mary Claire sobbed.

"'Tis the only life we have, don't let them take it. Such a great sin, to kill yourself; you know that. You'd go straight to hell and never see your sweetheart again."

"I'm in hell now," the girl wailed, despondent to the depths of her soul.

"Buck up," Bridie soothed, hugging Mary Claire and rocking her, two lost lambs huddled together seeking shelter from the storm.

The naval lieutenant was oblivious to the desolate mood of the black-haired girl whose hand he grabbed, unaware of the tears on her cheeks as he put an arm around her waist and started to dance. Smiling broadly with the charm of a seducer, he took a few steps before he noticed that his partner was sobbing.

"Oh, forgive me, did I step on your toes?" Mr. Wargrave babbled nervously. "I'm truly sorry, 2657, I become so clumsy when a pretty girl is next to me."

"No, you did not step on my toes," she screeched. At the top of her lungs, she tore the air in two. "God bless Ireland, and every man who sheds his blood for freedom."

The bewildered officer held the weeping convict at arm's length while the guards hastily cleared the deck, using the toes of their boots to prod the seething mass of political prisoners into the hold. Mary Claire was forcibly pulled away from Lt. Wargrave, a sudden movement that sent her sprawling. It was so clear to her at that instant, what she had to do, and she scrambled to her feet as hands clutched at her, trying to grab her legs.

Plowman caught her just as she reached the rail, one foot on a coil of rope as she struggled to climb over the side. He wrestled her to the deck, all the while shouting orders to his men as the convicts were returned to their dark, stuffy quarters. Despite his threats to clap her in irons so heavy that she would not be able to lift a toe, she continued to kick and flail while the guards hauled her forward to the punishment cell at the bow.

While the *Hellebore*'s prow sliced through the Atlantic, the spray that broke overhead splashed Mary Claire. Pulling off her shoes and stockings, balling up the black wool, she began to scrub her face with every wave that soaked her. Next she worked on her hands, focusing on scouring off the dirt that had shamed her. In imitation of wash day, she rubbed the stockings, putting them back on dripping wet. She let the salt water saturate her under drawers and she rubbed at her petticoats, concentrating on her task so that she would not think about where she was or how frightened she was.

After a while, the slap of the waves on her body made her weary, like a boxer being pummeled until she fell to the ground. Mary Claire was exhausted by the effort of surviving, exhausted by a lack of sleep and exhausted by hunger. Before long, she lay down on the planks and closed her eyes, to be battered all night and not feel it anymore.

She thought that she heard Mr. Scofield, but when she opened her eyes it was dark, and she was shivering uncontrollably. Her arms and legs were too heavy and too cold to move, and as she forced her aching knees to bend, she heard the rattle of metal chains rubbing on wood. Lt. Plowman had followed through on his promise.

"I'll be good, I'll be good," she whispered, her face pressed to the cold, wet planks. "I hate you, Paddy, for leaving me. You and my brothers, I hate you all. I hate you all."

She did not notice that she had begun to scream, over and over again, that she hated them all. "There's a nut that won't be cracked," came a man's voice, but she could not see who was laughing at her, mocking her, not when she had no energy left to raise her head.

"Do you still wish to earn your keep on your back?" Mr. Plowman asked.

Mary Claire dragged her face across the deck to turn her head, to look him in the eye. "I'll do what I must to live," she growled.

"Last night, you tried to die. I don't understand, 2657, this contrary nature of yours. What will it be, a life of prostitution, or death? Of course, I penetrate your thoughts at last. They are one and the same, a death sentence at the end of either road."

The cell door was opened and the lieutenant strolled in, to lift Mary Claire to her feet without effort. The weight of the manacles on her wrists threatened to tear her arms off. Immediately, the armorer knocked the irons from her wrists and she reflexively lifted her arms in relief.

"Time after time, I have offered you the opportunity to alleviate your discomfort, and time and time again you have disobeyed," Plowman sighed with exasperation. "Why do I have such patience with you, when I am not a patient man? Perhaps I am only being selfish, my dear, hoping to have another dance with you soon. And don't let me forget my good friend Lt. Wargrave. He was rather disappointed last night when you ended the ball at such an early hour."

A movement of her head and mouth was met with Plowman's forefinger applied to her pursed lips with some force. "If you spit on me, I will strike you," he said calmly.

"I despise you," she countered.

"Really? I don't despise you at all, 2657. And after all the problems you have created. Although every other man on this ship is doubtless unhappy with you. Everyone was having a lovely time, taking their minds off what is to come, and it was you, once again, who spoiled it."

"You cannot," she began, but he cut off her sentence with a booming guffaw.

"Oh, but I can," he said. With a courtly wave of his hand, he indicated that she was to exit. "I have the keys, you see, the keys to this cell. I have the leg irons and the manacles. I have the guns; I have the strength. All you have is what I cannot see. Can you appreciate that fragment of privacy?"

His philosophizing was too obscure for one who was too weak to think. "I have my heart and my soul. You shall never have them," she vowed.

"There is a woman's power over mankind," Plowman remarked to Scofield. "The only thing we want from a woman is her heart, and we jump through hoops and become a slave to claim it. Prisoner work detail in the galley, Mr. Scofield, and keep a sharp eye on her. She was convicted of stealing food, and there is no evidence that she has reformed."

Before long, Mary Claire discovered that she was not to be attached to the laundry detail, and she took it as a sign that her tormentor was withholding a favor because she had not knuckled under. Instead, she was given a task that amounted to hard labor for someone weakened by a lack of food. A muslin-covered plank was waiting for her in the galley, right next to the cook stove that was lined on one side with four very heavy flat irons. A basket stood at the ready, overflowing with Morse's table linens, sheets, shirts and petticoats. Margaret Atwood was brought in because no one knew where else to put her, and Mary Claire feared the consequences.

"If you please, sir," she said to Scofield when she caught sight of the madwoman. "She's a bit odd around fire, dangerous, sir. Can she be put elsewhere, sir?"

"Of course, my lady, when the convicts start to assign work details, I am sure she will be," Scofield said. "There's no houses here for the old witch to burn down, now, is there?"

"Please, sir, I haven't had my breakfast," she pleaded.

"This is not some yachting expedition, prisoner, where a lady can lie abed until all hours and be served after she calls for the cabin steward. Get to work, right smart, or I'll take a switch to you myself and make you move faster."

"*Go dtachta an diabhal tu.*" She picked up a chemise after expressing her desire that the devil choke the guard. Noisily bringing forth a glob of sputum, a difficult task when her mouth was dry, she deposited the spittle squarely on the linen fabric and stamped it fiercely with an iron. "And if I'm to press these, I'll need a bit of water. Or shall I spit them damp?"

With the heat of the stove, Mary Claire's wet clothes were emitting a cloud of steam. It was nothing when compared to the steam that she could imagine flowing out of the guard's ears. He could cuff her, she knew, or have the bosun give her a few swats on her bottom, but at the moment, she did not care. As long as she drew first blood, she would take whatever came after.

The way that Mr. Scofield's jaw clenched was a clear indication that he would not dare to strike her. Below deck were men who had nothing to lose, and to kill a guard to avenge a blow to Mary Claire O'Dwyer was quite possible. Without going that far, the Fenians could stir up trouble among the criminals that they were caged with, fomenting rebellion and unrest, and Scofield was wedged up tightly against a hard place.

Satisfied that she held the upper hand, Mary Claire soon came to regret her pique. Margaret was talking to herself, cradling her canvas sack like a baby, and Scofield took out his frustration on the hapless madwoman. Her filthy pretend baby was wrenched from her arms and sent sailing across the galley.

Another disgusting, guttural slurp arose from Mary Claire, drawing a scowl from Scofield. She spit on the fabric again, with a raised eyebrow that asked the guard if he was getting the water or not. "Willie," the enraged man hollered, "get the whore washerwoman a bucket of water. And you'll talk the Queen's English when you speak to me, goddamn you, not your Irish mumbo jumbo."

Under Scofield's fierce glare, Mary Claire dropped the irons on the board and then on the stove as she changed them. Her sarcastic smile was followed by a loud bang as she used two hands to clap the iron onto the board, returning the guard's scowl with a haughty toss of her head as she clanged the cool iron onto the stove. The steam rose from her dress as she smacked the board, pounded the stove, again and again, repeating the racket with glee. There were more creases pressed into the chemise than there had been before she started. The more Scofield fumed, the more she smiled at him. She added fuel to his burning rage by singing sweetly in Irish.

Margaret was walking back and forth, only a few steps in one direction before she spun around, and the ship's cook had to keep maneuvering around her. "I'll put this one to work, Mr. Scofield," the man finally offered, and he brought Margaret to a corner where he left her with a knife and a bucket of potatoes. She reappeared out of the dark shadows, to wander to the stove, pull open the door with the knife, and drop the potato into the flames. Her bizarre task completed, she returned to her corner and faded into the darkness.

"Here now, that's not," the cook began to say, but he never finished the sentence.

Mr. Scofield had become so irate that he had his rifle pointed directly at Mary Claire's forehead, the muzzle only inches from her face. She could be a contumely brat when she put her mind to it, and the guard had earned every twitch of his eyebrow and bead of sweat trickling from his temple.

"Go on, shoot, I don't care at all, at all," she said casually. "Are you man enough, John Bull, to shoot a half-dead woman like me? I'll turn my back, so, to make it easier for a coward to pull the trigger."

For a brief moment, she twisted around to retrieve a hot iron from the stove, and when she looked up, to sneer at Scofield, her eyes grew wide and she screamed louder than she had ever screamed before.

The report of a gun brought a crowd of guards and Marines, carbines and sidearms drawn and ready for a fight. Before they asked what happened, the Marines had wrestled Mary Claire to the deck. She came face to face with Mr. Scofield, who was writhing on the deck with a knife embedded squarely in the center of his back.

"God damn bitch," Scofield groaned loudly, repeating the phrase in time with the throbs of pain while he was lifted onto a stretcher and carted off to the surgery.

With her face held to the deck, Mary Claire could not turn her head away from the body of the cook, his neck splayed open like a butchered hog. The smell of his blood was filling her nose, drifting up from the sticky red halo that surrounded his head and trickled from his gaping mouth. In the background, she could hear Margaret babbling nonsense, repeating parts of words over and over in an insane monologue.

"What have you done, girl?" Brightfelt yelled at Mary Claire, but the terrified woman only stared at the cook's shocked expression, frozen forever in death, as she gasped for air with lungs that were filled with fright. "You'll hang for murder, do you hear me?"

"Hang me, please hang me," she pleaded, incoherent. Grabbing hold of Brightfelt's coat, she pulled herself to him, twisting onto her back and drawing him closer, as if she wanted to burrow under his skin and find a safe place inside.

"Did you stab Mr. Kettinger?" he pressed for an answer, attempting to extricate his tunic from her unbreakable grip.

"Why couldn't she stab me?" Mary Claire asked in reply. Tightening her grasp, she tugged at the corporal, asking her question again. Brightfelt lost his balance and fell on top of her. "Why must I be left here alone? Why me?"

"You aren't alone, love, don't be afraid," he said, his voice soft and soothing. "I am going to get up now, do you hear, and then I shall help you to your feet. We are going to go out on deck, and you can take some nice, deep breaths, and then you can tell me what you did."

Carefully, not moving too quickly as if he was afraid to alarm her when she was already crumbling, he got to his feet and handed his rifle to a guard. Getting down on one knee, and describing his actions so that she knew exactly what he was doing, he slipped his arm behind her back and lifted her to a sitting position. Standing upright, he helped her gently to her feet and directed one step forward, but then he heard the clank of the chain. Asking another guard to push a crate over, Brightfelt helped her to walk one more step, positioning the box and carefully setting her down with her back to the lifeless corpse that decorated the dark corner of the galley.

"Can you speak? Here, take a breath and drink some water." Brightfelt held her hand with great kindness, a gentle approach out of mercy to one who was going to be dead in a few hours time. He put a mug into her palm and closed her fingers around it.

Mary Claire guzzled the water, her thirst consuming her like a wild beast. Holding out the cup with a shaking hand, she silently asked for more, and Brightfelt could not deny her. Before the day was over, she would be swinging from the gibbet, and one more cup of water was the least that he could do for a condemned woman.

"He took her baby," Mary Claire blurted out, looking at Brightfelt with a puzzled expression. Suddenly animated, she went off on another topic. "Please, please, let me speak to the priest. I have to make a confession; I've sinned. God forgive me, I've sinned."

"Did you stab him because he took her baby?" Brightfelt asked, but Mary Claire was bawling into her hands and could not speak. "Did you kill him?"

"But it was my fault that he took the baby," she blubbered through her tears. "I made him angry, I was wicked, I made him angry and I knew it was wrong. Why wasn't I punished? I didn't mean it, I'm sorry, I'll never do it again."

"Calm down, love, that's a good girl," he lulled her. "Tell me who stabbed Mr. Scofield."

"He took Margaret's baby," Mary Claire enunciated, to make it clear. "He had no right to do it, she's mad, she can't help it. 'Twas wrong to torment her."

"Is that why you stabbed him?"

"I wanted him to shoot me," she stared at Brightfelt, only to grow hysterical again, asking to be shot, to make an end of it.

"You don't want anyone shooting you, love, don't be afraid. I promise, I'll stay by you start to finish so you won't be alone. Now tell me what happened, there's a good girl."

"Margaret's mad, sir, she didn't mean to kill or hurt anyone, but she can't know what she's doing," Mary Claire began to relax. "'Tisn't right, 'tis injustice to punish her for any crime when she's a lunatic."

"Did Margaret kill Mr. Kettinger and hurt Mr. Scofield? Is that what you are telling me?"

"But she's a lunatic," Mary Claire repeated. "He threw her baby on the floor. Mr. Kettinger didn't do anything to her, why did she kill him?"

"Well, as you say, she's not in her right mind and there's no logical reason for anything that she does. Can you collect yourself now, love? You are going to have to tell all of this to Captain Morse so he can conduct an inquiry. Speak calmly and don't ramble, or he'll snap at you," Brightfelt said with a brotherly smile. "Tell you what, I'll go find Mr. Plowman and ask him if I can have your leg irons removed, and while I'm gone, you can just sit here, nice and quiet. Willie can bring you a drop of rum to settle your nerves."

Willie appeared in no time with a sailor's mug that held a diluted mixture of rum and fresh water. Her thirst was deep as she threw her head back to experience the wonderful sensation of a mouth wet with fluid, gulping in one swallow the entire draught. Once it hit bottom, the rum threatened to come back up, and she fought the burning nausea. The drink went immediately to her head, and Willie watched helplessly as her eyes rolled back in her head and she pitched over.

Five

Having stood in the dock once before, Mary Claire had no respect whatsoever for the courts or British jurisprudence. With the rum making her a little light-headed, she discovered her somewhat inebriated bravado while walking to the captain's cabin in the stern. Under the force of an unbreakable will, it was the lady of the manor who sashayed into the room, coming to stand before the tribunal at the captain's table with her nose well up in the air.

Her eyes trailed down to examine the damask cloth. "I see that you are admiring Mrs. Morse's fine table linens," the captain said, puffing up with superiority.

"Pinchbeck," Mary Claire sniffed. "Mrs. Morse is to be commended for making do with such grace."

Men fought with weapons, they fought with fists, but women fought with words and Mary Claire gave no quarter. She had sized up the captain and his wife when they came out on deck to take the air, and she easily detected a bit of pomposity in Mrs. Morse's bearing. Captain Morse had his pretensions, and Mary Claire deflated his ballooning conceit with one word. Morse began to seethe.

"Prisoner 2657, you are here to provide testimony regarding the murder of Horace Kettinger, now deceased, killed in the line of duty to Her Majesty's Prison Service. Your neck is in the noose, my dear, unless you can prove that you are not guilty of this crime."

"Hang me or not, as you will," she spoke calmly. "I know that my words fall on deaf ears."

"Do you not care to speak up on your own behalf?" Mr. Wargrave asked. "If you have done nothing, you will be declared innocent."

"With my last breath, sir, I'll pray that God forgives you for such lies."

Wargrave grew rather huffy, until Morse very quietly mentioned that the girl was a passenger on the *Hellebore* because of false testimony. "Rathkeale case," Morse murmured by way of explanation. Setting a new course, the captain sought to gain her confidence. His threats would never work, not when she knew that she was blameless and would not be drawn into false testimony. Once he explained that he only needed a firm and legal reason to hang a raving lunatic, Mary Claire understood that he sought nothing more than an official story to put in his log, to cover his tracks when they arrived in Australia with one less convict. It was the Englishman's love of proper order that required her to state quite clearly what had happened in the galley, even though she had not actually seen everything that took place. Once he had what he wanted, he grew nauseatingly condescending.

"Mr. Plowman and Dr. Smith are responsible for assigning prisoners to their duties, but as captain, I have some discretion in the arrangements," Morse said. "Female convicts are known to benefit from education and proper training, to help them find suitable employment in Australia."

Morse sat back in his chair, smiling ever so pleasantly as he puffed up with self-importance. No light flashed in the girl's eyes, however, and he elaborated on his not so subtle suggestion. "One such as you, quite presentable, erudite, and very demure, well, there is no doubt in my mind that you have the makings of a fine lady's maid. My wife would be agreeable, I am sure, to assist in your training. To coach you through the day, that is, to bring you here to my quarters as her maid. There would be a very excellent reference provided at the end of the cruise."

Queen Victoria could not have displayed greater outrage, using such absolute restraint that the words had to be squeezed out through a gritted teeth. "You expect me," Mary Claire asked, "to serve her?"

Plowman put his hand over his mouth to cover his bemused grin. Captain Morse blew up. "I expect you to be confined to the punishment cell until you learn that you are nothing more than a convicted criminal bound for Australia."

"God bless Ireland," Mary Claire shouted as she was dragged out, "and a curse on the Queen who enslaves my people."

With a manly reserve that masked his pain, Scofield attempted to swing out of the hammock in the surgery, but Captain Morse excused him to lie on his side. "I am sorely tempted to hang her for sedition," Morse insisted. "She has given me just cause, Mr. Scofield, and if your testimony would also point to murder, it is an open and shut case. She'll swing by nightfall."

"Sir, if I had any doubts about her, but she saved my life by singing out. It would have been easy enough for her to stand by and watch, or even smash my skull with one of those irons when I was down," Scofield testified. "And I would like to add, sir, that she warned me right off that the woman was a danger. I didn't listen, sir, thought the girl was mouthing off, but she was honestly trying to warn me, sir, real polite like a well brought up girl."

"Not to be murder, then it shall be treason," Morse decided. "We have all heard her, and witnessed the agitation of the prisoners. She has fomented rebellion on my ship and now she will pay. It's mutiny, female mutiny."

"It's her nature, sir," Scofield came to her defense. "I've raised four girls, sir, and when it gets to that time of the month, it's hell on earth for a man. Back of your hand or a cook spoon on her ass is all she really needs, sir. Giving you a father's experience, sir. She's got a sweet temper, I'd say, the rest of the month."

"That time of the month," Plowman sighed with relief. "Thank God for that."

Still not satisfied but smelling the inevitable, Morse conferred with his Marine intelligence officer. "That leaves your bizarre scheme, Mr. Plowman," the captain grumbled. "Do you think that you can actually reason with such a creature?"

"With the wind shifting, sir, I believe that conditions will grow favorable in the next half-hour," Plowman said. "Frankly, Captain Morse, we have no other choice than to move ahead. If you were to sentence her to death, you would find no support for your actions when word reached Westminster. Despite Lord Derby's well-publicized convictions, foreign opinion and foreign trade take precedence over all. And may I remind you, sir, that my mission hinges on her arrival in Fremantle."

Cutting through the waves that were getting higher with every passing minute, the bow of the *Hellebore* was swooping through great arcs, rising majestically and falling deeply, up and down in a rhythm that was maddening in its tortuous circuit. Mary Claire was holding on to the cell bars, riding the waves and losing her sense of balance. The spray flew off the prow and splashed across her, the salt water filling her mouth as she gasped for air. Trembling, her head spinning, she lapsed into the despair of the seasick, a sensation that enveloped every part of her body in an unremitting misery.

"Am I your friend now, 2657?" Plowman had to shout over the roar of the waves beating against the hull.

"No," she rasped, her eyes rolling.

"Under my coat, am I your friend? What of the convicts who claim your allegiance? Under their masks, are they your friends?"

"Beat me with your fists, it would be more merciful than this," she groaned.

"You are learning, then, that is very good. Someone as perceptive as you must have realized that long before you reached this ship."

Nearly losing his balance, Plowman had to reach out and grab a cell bar to keep from toppling. A storm was approaching, and he wanted very much to conclude his business before he found himself getting soaked through on a pitching deck.

"Ah, there, I see the tears of self-pity. You are truly Irish, with their national fondness for self-pity. Wallow in it, 2657, anoint your head with the oil of injustice and weep for your misfortune. And when you have grown weary of that exercise, open your eyes and look underneath the surface of every person you encounter, for you are alone in this world. Whether you like it or not, you are completely alone."

"Then leave me alone," Mary Claire pleaded, reaching the end of her endurance.

"You sail under your true colors, a poor strategy for a wise sailor. You have shown my captain that you are his enemy, but you could have sailed into his cabin with the Union Jack on your mizzenmast and made an ally."

"I'll not lie, I shall not sin," her resolve sprouted anew.

"Not a lie, but a costume. Is it a sin to appear one way but hold something else in your heart? Look at me, 2657, can you not see through me? If you will let me be your friend, you can leave this cell and go below, where you will be safe from the storm. If you stay here, you are very likely to drown in the high sea. Do you wish to live, or do you wish to die?"

"Ask the priest, is it a lie?" she beseeched him.

Lt. Plowman could detect a note of panic that was reaching into her thoughts, but her request also told him that she was about ready to concede. "Is it a lie to pull your laces a little tighter so that your figure is made artificially more attractive?" he countered. "Is it a sin to sell your body to every man who puts a few shillings in your hand?"

Time was running out, and he knew that when he looked out over the horizon, where a black and ominous wall of clouds was skating toward the *Hellebore*. Sailors were scurrying across the yards to shorten sail, preparing for the coming storm that would throw mouthful after mouthful of seawater into Mary Claire's throat until it poisoned her. Drops of rain began to fall, fresh water drops spotted his red coat, and he bellowed once more above the roar of the wind.

"Is Mr. Scofield your friend?" he asked.

"No," she hissed, struggling to maintain her insubordination to the Crown.

"He finds a friend in you, the Fenian who saved his life. Is it a sin to prevent a cold-blooded murder if the victim is grateful to you, even though you despise him? Is it a sin, Mary Claire, to allow a man to believe what he will about you? Have you ever broken a boy's heart? Did you sin? Am I your friend, Mary Claire?"

"Yes, yes, please stop, please let me go." She was begging with desperation that he could almost taste, but beneath it he also heard a firm resolve to keep going, day after wretched day. He had won.

Released from the crazily swinging cell, Mary Claire was too dizzy to walk on legs that seemed to turn under her. The open hatchway had never looked so inviting, so welcoming, as she lurched along the deck. After a few days at sea, the deal board bed was home, her safe refuge, and she climbed in with joy, wet and shivering. She pulled her knees up and folded her head down, wrapped in a tight cocoon of oblivion, insensible and benumbed in the nothingness of sleep.

"I told you he's got it in for her," Bridie insisted, her loud voice scarcely penetrating Mary Claire's stupor.

"It's the political prisoners that get the worst of it," one of the pickpockets snorted. "All her talk of Irish freedom, a load of twaddle, and he won't let up until she's gone mad or she shuts up."

Bridie slid into the cot and held Mary Claire against her, to offer solace when there was no respite to be found. "He's closed up shop for tonight, love, with the storm that's shaking us. You sleep, and there'll be no one trawling in your waters tonight."

The lieutenant's report to his captain was received with a delighted hand clapping, as Morse felt a weight lift off his shoulders. The O'Dwyer problem was coming under control, and the madwoman was no longer a matter of concern. Finally brought to the surgery to get her out of the galley, the lunatic was close to the end, and the need to execute her was dripping away as her wound continued to ooze, her death precluding the need to hang her. Gleefully rubbing his hands, the captain returned to his earlier suggestion of training Mary Claire as a maid.

"A note of caution, sir," Simon warned. "In my estimation, it is quite possible that the prisoner will find fault with each and every object that Mrs. Morse prizes. It is a trait that we have seen often in the female sex; you are probably familiar with it. I would suggest, sir, that you spare Mrs. Morse any nagging doubts as to the quality of her possessions, and spare yourself the expense of improving them."

"Is this woman so disagreeable? I would be willing to issue her fresh water every day for bathing, and I guarantee you that my wife will find a dress for her to wear. Is that not incentive enough?"

Eyes downcast, Simon spoke in a hushed tone, taking Morse into his confidence. "Sir, considering her circumstances, how she came to be here, and what I have seen in her behavior, there is a deep pool of resentment that she may very well tap. A lady's maid becomes very intimate with her employer, sir, and it would be two against one."

"She has pegged my wife, that is what you are saying, Lt. Plowman," Morse sniffed. "And she has, too. My God, she is a clever thing. Good characteristic for an informer, though."

"Labors that require more physical exertion, in the unpleasant heat of the galley, would do more to reinforce the lessons which have been taught thus far. She would like nothing better than a daily bath and a pretty dress, sir, and we cannot give her what she wants."

"It's a pity that you cast your lot with the Royal Marines, Lieutenant, when we could use a sailor with your intellect. Not to disparage Mr. Wargrave's abilities," Morse commented. "Thank God you did not waste your time in the Army."

With characteristic beneficence towards his officers, Captain Morse hosted a dinner party on Saturday evening in honor of Lieutenant Simon Plowman, who would celebrate his twenty-ninth birthday on Sunday. From his sea chest, the guest of honor extracted a rum-soaked fruitcake, a delicacy given to him by his mother before he set sail on this cruise. The wine flowed, the after dinner liqueurs were savored, and Mrs. Morse offered her kindest compliments to the gentle soul who had sent her son off to sea twelve years ago. As he left the cabin at the conclusion of the festivities, the soft strains of the fiddle and tin whistle were drifting languidly on the warm air. Plowman felt his feet pulling him forward, to the impromptu concert that had arisen from a need to fill the endless hours.

Leaning comfortably against the rail with Lt. Wargrave at his side, Plowman let his mind wander to a far away place, guided back through the years by the lament that Mary Claire shared with her companions. It seemed odd for a group of transported convicts to ask for a song that told of a husband being sent to Australia while his wife was left behind in Ireland. Simon had never heard the song before, but the tune was the sweetest that he had ever heard when it fell from Mary Claire's lips.

"Can't we have a dance, ladies?" Wargrave suggested, his brain rather befuddled by drink. "Mr. Whistler, would you play a reel?"

Eager for male companionship, the women agreed. Plowman took Mary Claire's hand, nudging Wargrave out of the way in his haste. "Are we still friends?" he asked. Her smile was so sarcastically false that his eyebrows pinched together. "Determined to destroy your future?"

Her smirk was cruel, the reply of a human being who had seen everything taken from her. Her identity was destroyed in the Limerick County Gaol when they made her appellation a number, a cold string of symbols that denied her humanity. As for her dignity, that was crushed as well, from the first time that she had to set foot in a cold, filthy cell where male guards monitored her every move. In Dublin, her hair had been soaked in kerosene to kill the lice that she brought from Limerick, but never once did she receive a flake of soap to wash with. Cold water and her bare hands was all she ever had, like one of Padraig's cows in the creek. Her dress was so filthy that it was no longer gray but almost black, the sleeves frayed and the elbows nearly split open. Someone had worn it before her, and she had been wearing it day in and day out since March. Everything about her existence was disgusting.

Her jailers had taken everything from her, and she saw what she had become. Mary Claire was an object, a creature, but not a person anymore. She was alone, she had to help herself, and only the prostitutes had given her some concrete suggestions, some very clear guidelines to survive when her guards wanted her dead.

"You won't spoil the party again, will you?" Simon pressured her back to his control.

"No," she sneered, giving in to a moment of juvenile pettiness.

"Answer me. Am I your friend?"

"My friends help me. They've shown me a way to exist. Are you my friend? Bring me something to eat."

"What, steal from the ship's stores to hand over to you? Even I would be flogged for that offense. Ah, but you would enjoy the sight of my back being sliced to ribbons, wouldn't you? You'd swing the cat if the bosun would only grant you the honor."

"You are my tormentor," she hissed.

"As you torment me," came the reply, ominous in its intimidating tone.

Lt. Wargrave picked his partner for the next dance, gaily sliding across the deck as the strains of a waltz set a giddy pace. He looked at her, but Mary Claire was not looking at him, not with her eyes locked on Lt. Plowman's scowl. With a sigh, the sailor spun Mary Claire through a turn and cursed his luck, because it was happening again. In a feeble attempt at making conversation, he prattled on and on about Lt. Plowman's heritage, a long line of military men who had been richly rewarded for destroying the rebels in 1798 and crushing Napoleon afterwards.

Land that belonged to her people had been stolen and given to Simon's grandfather, land that made the Plowman family wealthy while the Irish starved to death along the boreens. When Wargrave mentioned the name of Simon's father, Mary Claire began to place her tormentor in the pantheon of English devils. Sir Peter Plowman was well known, the man who chased down the rebels of the Young Ireland movement in recent times. A man descended from cavalry and dragoons had chosen to be a Royal Marine. Something about Simon was odd, not fitting into Wargrave's long-winded saga.

"May I extend my personal appreciation of your actions earlier this week?" Wargrave said, veering off on a personal tack.

"You may howl at the moon if it pleases you," Mary Claire responded, her head twisted to glare at Plowman. He came from a family of blackguards and beasts, yet he was not following the same well-worn path as his father and grandfather. Somehow, she would get underneath his skin and take a good look at his heart, to find out what he was about.

"We take the threat of insurrection quite seriously, and I find the very idea of rebellion to be as odious as I find the rebels. My opinion of you has been completely reversed," he continued, struggling on in a rather clumsy courtship. The simple farm boys at the crossroads dances were more polished than this English version of a gentleman.

"My opinions remain unchanging," she replied with false sweetness. The song ended, and she wearily excused herself.

The frivolity and escape of the dance had vanished from Mary Claire's thoughts. She walked away from the gay throng and found a dark corner, up against the bulwarks behind a coil of rope. There were no more tears to shed, her eyes had gone dry, and she was certain that she had landed on the bottom at last. Her stomach was knotted with hunger but still Bridie could not seem to get enough to eat. All their combined efforts did not provide enough to feed one body, let alone two. There was only one solution, one final answer, and Mary Claire prayed fervently that night. She asked God if he would forgive her if she joined Mrs. Perkins, toiling under the supervision of a madam. She studied the option of turning herself out into the most repulsive trade on earth to alleviate the clawing of her empty stomach. Only Mrs. Perkins had given her an opportunity to survive, and while that did not make the old madam a friend, it certainly made her an ally.

"I concede," Wargrave chuckled, returning to the rail for a conference. "The sweet cherry is yours to pluck, you are the victor."

"The cost is too dear," Simon shook his head as he laughed. "I'll be left with nothing more than my drawers before she's finished negotiating a price."

"All those compliant peasant girls have warped your sense of value," Wargrave said. "She's a merchant's daughter, educated and capable of holding an intelligent conversation. The value of her pretty voice alone is something to consider."

"She's a thief, Dennis, a thief and an unrepentant Irish insurrectionist. Wrapped up in a grimy package."

"A thief who has stolen your heart, my friend," Wargrave observed, chucking his mate on the arm in an inebriated confidence.

In the wardroom that evening, the officers shared a bottle of brandy, anticipating a day of light duty on Sunday. The birthday celebration extended into the late hours, until the brandy was finished and the men bid their goodnights. As the younger men filed out, Simon could hear the sounds of loud, hacking coughs and snoring that filtered through the open hatches, drifting out of the prison deck. There was a warning shout from one of the Fenian prisoners, former soldiers who guarded their own through a series of military watches. Prisons were never quiet, only less noisy. He retired to his berth to stretch out, to contemplate yet another night of writhing and tortured dreams.

Drunken snorts echoed in the wardroom, an unexpected hubbub when it had grown quiet an hour ago. Plowman listened to his compatriots, off duty and drunk on a Saturday night, no doubt returning from the prison deck in a jovial frame of mind. At first, he pretended to be asleep, not answering the knock at his door. The visitor rapped again, more insistent and much louder. "Come," he replied, sitting up and running a hand through his hair to tidy up for company.

The door opened, and a woman was pushed rudely into the room, stumbling over her feet. "A very happy birthday, Lieutenant Plowman," Wargrave chortled, saluting and laughing at the wicked conspiracy. "It's a generous gift, so don't forget us at Christmas."

"What a joy it is to be blessed with considerate and generous companions," Plowman said, laughing uproariously as his friend slammed the door shut. He lingered over Mary Claire as she waited in his cabin, every muscle in her body as rigid as an oak plank. "So, you know why you are here. Get to work."

She sucked in a breath to steady her nerves while he snorted back another laugh. She perched lightly on the very edge of the bunk, completely forgetting what she had been told to do next, and Plowman tore into her again.

"Get off my sheets with that filthy rag you wear," he said, his tone blistering in its malice. "Take it off, woman, let me see what I am getting."

Fingers that trembled could not twist a button in a hole, and Simon did not hide his frustration over her incompetence. He did the deed himself, tugging with force so that she had a difficult time in keeping her balance. Roughly, he pushed the wool dress from her shoulders and Mary Claire obediently lifted her feet to step out of the garment when it hit the deck.

His manner was threatening as he towered over her, running a finger along the edge of her chemise, close to her breasts but never actually touching her. That same finger slid slowly down the center strip of inset lace, approaching her navel but stopping short just when she thought he was going to touch her in places that no man had ever touched before. It was suffering that he wanted to impose, and with every flinch of her lip or twitch of her head, he scored a point.

"Come, come, I am tired and I do not have all night. Hop up, let's get started," he said.

Her legs were shaking but she made them move, to take a step and lift her body into a strange man's bed, to do what Varena, Hettie, Cornelia and Bridie had told her to do. It was supposed to be so easy, but it was not easy at all.

Lieutenant Plowman wanted to laugh so badly that he had to bite the inside of his cheek to stop the snicker. His little gift had pulled up her upper petticoat and covered her face, cringing under the ratty fabric like a frightened child hiding under her blankets. Her knees were up and her legs spread, with one foot on either side of the bed to brace herself against some sort of onslaught. The overall image that she presented was not a seductive vixen but a woman in labor. Mary Claire reminded him of a lady who had popped in to deliver a baby, and she did not want to see what was happening down there.

Her under petticoat was a sorry sight, and he could imagine that the condition of her drawers was no better. An article of clothing that had once been changed daily was now washed only once each week and worn for seven days straight due to the limits of the prison ship. Dingy and threadbare, the hem of the petticoat was torn and a spot above her knee was so thin that it resembled gauze. To call the patches on her lower limbs stockings was stretching the word out of its true meaning, for there was little stocking left to cover her calves.

"Shoes, dirty shoes," he complained, and she quickly got up, unlaced her balmorals, and slipped them off. She promptly returned to her former pose.

In shirtsleeves and trousers, Simon eagerly leapt into his bed, squirming around between her legs until he could feel her quaking, actually vibrating like the ship's rigging in a windstorm. "Dear God, your scent is vile," he oozed disgust. "You don't have lice, do you? I'll find out soon enough, when I start scratching my crotch from your vermin."

He rose and called out to the cabin attendant for a bucket of water, claiming that he needed a bath. All at once, a wall of laughter crashed into the cabin as the drunken officers began to cheer their colleague. Crude remarks sailed through the wardroom, comments that she refused to hear. The fantasy of a wedding night was beginning to fade, to be replaced by regret and the realization that it was too late to go back. Mary Claire thought of her father, his death a blessing so that he would never learn of his daughter's fall from grace.

The bucket appeared at once and the cabin door was closed with rakish élan. Taking her arm, Simon tore her from the cot and positioned her in the center of the room, a rough flannel and a bucket of cold seawater at the ready. He began with her hands, rubbing briskly to clean them with salt-water soap that turned to slime on the skin because it did not lather. Working his way up each arm in turn, he nearly scoured the fine hair out of her armpits before he went at her neck. Forcing her to lift her hair up out of the way, Simon made thrusting movements towards her bosom, a never ending barrage that was met by a gasp and a flinch every time. After he had scrubbed her face, he stood back to assess the results. Mary Claire wore her mask, appearing like a rather blasé and somewhat grand lady of vast experience, aping Varena.

"In you go," he gave her a push and she lurched forward, to resume her position under the petticoat.

With a great deal of noise, he slid his suspenders off his shoulders and opened the fly of his trousers, commenting all the while about what he expected to find between her lovely thighs. It was vulgar, burning the ears of a girl who had never been addressed so harshly before.

"Let me check your hands once again, I want to be quite sure that they are clean before you lovingly caress my privates." She tensed up with that crude comment, and Plowman proceeded to plague her soul a little more. Speaking softly into her ear, he instilled pure terror. "What is the condition of your bottom, my beauty, is it somewhat clean? Shall I penetrate the soft flesh of your delightful ass? You could preserve your virginity, but not your innocence. I am told that women find the practice exquisitely painful. I warn you now, that if you scream out in agony I shall crush your Irish skull with one blow."

Soft whimpering came out from beneath the petticoat, an unstoppable reaction that showed he had inflicted some heavy damage. He was not done with her yet, and the menacing speech went on. "That will be your job in the future, now that you have chosen to follow the woman who would lead you astray. All the activities that are too despicable for a man to ask of a decent woman shall be your stock in trade."

Again, he sprawled on top of her, wriggling about as if he was searching for a comfortable position while her heart pounded in her chest. With his face only inches from hers, he resumed the assault. "A man enjoys a little kissing. You know how to do that, at least, don't you? Surely you kissed your sweetheart until his lips were falling off. Pretend you fancy me and give me your lips, as you did to him."

Ever so slowly, the hem of the petticoat slid down until her face was bared, her eyes shut as tightly as the grip she fastened onto her skirt. Her mouth was quivering in rapid time with every shaking fiber of her body, but she still would not break down.

"Lie on your side and face the bulkhead," he ordered.

Fighting back waves of nausea, she complied with his demand. Plowman curled up next to her, two spoons on a shelf. Tenderly he kissed her bare shoulder. "Go to sleep, Mary Claire, you are safe here."

Within minutes, his breathing grew deep and slow, a man at peace with a woman to share his night. "My God, my God," she implored, "why have you forsaken me?"

She waited, rigid and still, until she was convinced that he really was asleep and she was relatively safe. Free to let her mind wander where she wanted to send her thoughts, she had liberty to run from her captors, to escape the chains of the prison in her imagination. She walked across the green hills of Limerick, watching the dark line of Padraig's cows coming home for milking. Their bulk was outlined on the horizon as they crested a hill, their udders full and heavy. Padraig was with her, his blue eyes filled with stars when he looked at her, the queen of his heart.

"Taste this, Mary Claire, the first from the new milch cow," he said. He offered her a ladle of warm milk, dipped from the pail that rested in the greenest grass. Not just milk, but the cream had been skimmed into the ladle that he gave her, and she savored the richness that tasted of the grass and mist of Limerick, the marvelous flavor of the best cream in the world.

Her mouth was slick inside, the silky cream coating every surface and filling her tongue with sweetness. Padraig kissed her, with a kiss that tasted of ripe cherries, cherries and velvety cream. His hand was roaming but she would let him this time, in her happy reverie. Her arm wrapped around him, to hold him against her as they lay in the grass, the smell of the grass so soothing as Padraig kissed her. His hand was on her waist but it was sliding up, and this time she would not put her arm there to stop him.

Sister Loretta began to speak, invading the idyll with a mathematics lesson. The nun was counting, or telling Mary Claire to do a sum or an exercise in long division. She was kissing Padraig and she did not want to stop, but Sister was insistent, the numbers announced sternly, again and again. The nun whacked her on the knees with a switch for not responding.

The image faded as she opened her eyes, surprised to discover that she had even closed them. "Prisoner 2657, get on your feet," she heard the order, and it all came back to her then.

Both Plowman and Arkwright were staring at her, mouths agape, but Mary Claire had no idea what was so amazing. Her glance fell onto Simon's sea chest, which was now pulled away from its storage spot under the cot. A thick slice of fruitcake was looking back at her, happy to see her as it lounged on a piece of paper. Her legs rocked, to make a rush at the cake, but she only teetered.

"My God, sir, she really is asleep on her feet," Arkwright gasped. "I thought it was only a figure of speech."

For a long time, she was dazed, her weary head filled with dust and cobwebs. With great effort, she rose to her feet, her gaze fixed on the sticky confection of fruit and nuts. Just then, if he made her earn it, whatever it was he told her to do, she would have done it at once, if only to have that morsel for her belly. It was better than a beautiful dream, to watch Plowman wrap the cake in the paper and take her hand, gently setting her reward into her palm. He cleared his throat loudly, and Mary Claire heard a Marine clank away, to wait discreetly just outside the door.

He lifted her dress over her head, pulling her arms through the sleeves, as a mother would dress an infant. "I'm sorry I didn't let you rest, my sweet angel," he said rather loudly. "I couldn't get enough of you, and if not for my duties, I'd eat you for breakfast and ride you until dinner."

With a smile, he guided her to a sitting position on the sea chest and he put on her shoes, tying them carefully as he thanked her effusively for the best night of his life. Lifting her up, he turned slightly so that his back was to the open door. He wrapped her in his arms in a warm embrace that brought her lips next to his, but he did not kiss her.

"Am I your friend?" he whispered.

"Yes, sir," she replied.

"Yes, Simon," he corrected her.

"Yes, Simon, sir."

"Yes, my love," he pressed on.

"Yes, my love," she aped his words, but she was beginning to shake again.

"Yes, *mo mhile gra*," he added, speaking Irish and sending her heart racing until it began to shatter. "Yes, *a ghra mo chroi. An dtuigeann tu?*"

Panting in fear, she tried to look for the answer in his eyes but he held her head steady, their postures mimicking a lover's farewell kiss. "*Ni thuigim*," she choked out her response. "*Ni thuigim.*"

She pulled away and ran, ran as fast as her feet could go until she reached a ladder that went up, up and away from Simon Plowman. Bobby Arkwright chased after her, laughing over some imaginary events that had not actually transpired the night before.

Six

To be able to confess to Father McCabe and receive the sacraments was such a blessing that Mary Claire wept through much of the Mass, her voice cracking on every high note as she chanted the responses. Through it all, she clutched the fruit of her labor, something that she could not bear to eat at breakfast.

"Just to sleep next to him?" Mrs. Perkins asked, her eyes wide with amazement. "He paid all that for a warm body next to him? I knew there was something odd about him."

"Share it, Mrs. Perkins, so that everyone can taste a nibble of sweet in this bitter world," Mary Claire said.

"You worked for it all the same, lamb, now you get half at least," Moira insisted.

"Please, no, I won't be able to keep it down," Mary Claire begged off.

"Go on, just one cherry," Bridie said.

"Blood red cherry," Mary Claire murmured. "Paddy's blood."

"He did something to you, Mary Claire, I can see it in your eyes," Varena said, examining her friend's features. "Did he hurt you?"

"Only my heart, where the marks can't be seen," was her reply, and she burst into tears, running from the table and leaving behind a scrap of salt pork.

They were allowed to go out on deck in the late afternoon, when the sun was not as blazing as it had been at one o'clock. Mary Claire felt as if every ship's officer and Marine were looking at her, pointing and snickering, sharing lewd comments about Plowman's birthday gift, the girl he rode all night until she was so used up that she could not walk straight in the morning. The increased humiliation added to her deep depression, a malaise that was triggered by the words that Simon used to bid her a tender goodbye when he had finished with her. It was Michael's taunt, when he found her with Paddy before they left for Kilclooney Wood, Michael mocking Paddy who was all heart and precious little brain.

Towards the stern, the men were entertaining themselves with recitations of poems or Shakespeare's works, delivered from the depths of a schoolboys lessons recalled. The guards and warders enjoyed the show, and even the captain and his wife came out on deck with the assistant warders, looking like an audience in the boxes at the theatre. The only pleasure that Mary Claire found that afternoon was the uncomfortable and self-conscious skirt smoothing that Mrs. Morse engaged in from time to time during the performance. Those wrinkles were set into place by a convict who was not very skilled with a flat iron, but was an expert in petty aggravation and minor annoyance.

Lost in her deep sorrow, Mary Claire never noticed that Plowman and Wargrave were strolling the deck, the picture of two gentlemen at leisure on a Sunday afternoon. The southern sun was beginning to descend towards the horizon while the troubled young woman stared off into space, her eyes and her heart looking at Ireland. Simon gave her a nudge in the leg with his black leather boot.

"I've bought your services for the duration of the trip," he informed her, a cold pronouncement. "If she tries to sell you to anyone else, you are to refuse, raise a ruckus if need be and alert a guard. You've cost me one hundred fifty pounds, my dear, and I'd better get the full value of my investment."

"Did you torture him before you murdered him?" she asked, her voice seething with an absolute and total hatred.

"Torture and murder whom, my dear? You are such an odd creature; it is no wonder that I've grown so fond of you. By the way, I wanted to ask if you enjoyed the cake. My mother made it for me before I left on this cruise, for my birthday. Wish me happy birthday, my darling mistress."

"May it be your last," she cursed him.

"Now, when I returned from an engagement in Kilclooney Wood, all she had for me was a tin of tea biscuits. Came home unexpectedly and she hates to send me off empty-handed. I was a greedy boy, I'm sorry to say, and I ate them all in no time, or I would have given some to you last night."

"So it was you," she hissed. "You kill him and find a way to ruin me, was that your plan? Do your worst, for I swear on Paddy's grave that I'll give birth to a dozen sons, English bastards or freeborn Irishmen, and every one of them will suckle on the milk of revenge at my breast."

"Yes, I like you very much," he laughed before he turned and ambled away.

The Perkins contingent was chatting excitedly about their improbable windfall. They were on their way to setting up a new establishment, with a hefty sum at hand to fit out a new brothel in Perth. Mary Claire was not participating in their plans, in agony over the pain that Plowman inflicted without once hitting her.

"Words do not hurt like a man's fist, Mary Claire," Hettie said.

"He killed my Paddy," the girl moaned, her body rocking back and forth.

"How could he know who was your sweetheart in the middle of a battle?" Moira reasoned. "He's trying to get at you. His pleasure is derived from every ache he puts in your heart. Some men take their enjoyment in putting an ache in a girl's stomach with their fists. You can deflect his words easily, Mary Claire, by hiding the hurt until he finds another alley to chase you down. He doesn't strike you with anything that you can't fend off. You control him, lamb, but be sharp; please him but please yourself in the process."

"You've fallen into something grand," Varena hugged Mary Claire. "Look at you, taken up by a gentleman who doesn't make too many demands, only wants to make you cry, so you pretend you're sad for things that don't mean a thing to you."

"Do you think he even fancies girls?" Cornelia whispered, and all eyes wandered to the retreating figures of Wargrave and Plowman. "They say that men go to sea to get away from women and prying eyes."

A clutch of hens began to cackle, a silly sort of giddiness that raised Mary Claire's spirits. After last night's performance and this morning's blatant lies, she nearly believed that the man was rather repulsed by her body, and maybe he was longing for the arms of a strong sailor around him. The very idea of such abomination made her almost sick, as she briefly envisioned the kind of barbarity that a deranged Marine lieutenant could have inflicted on naive Paddy Cullen. That someone had talked in Kilclooney Wood was now quite clear, because Simon Plowman knew more than he should have, more than any man had a right to know.

After exactly sixty minutes, they were rounded up and lined out at the door to the hatchway, two by two, side by side. The warder appeared

96

unexpectedly, and all nineteen women feared punishment, retribution that was capricious in its delivery. "Prisoner 2657, step out and follow me," Mr. Hightower ordered, and a collective gasp went through the ranks, a concern that the brutal Mr. Plowman was up to something.

Bridie gave Mary Claire a reassuring squeeze of the hand before they parted, and that was a greater comfort than the warder's paternal smile. As she fell correctly into his column, Mary Claire noticed that the red-coated pensioner guards had their rifles slung over their shoulders, with not one weapon pointed at her head, and that was completely unnerving.

Streaming out of the aft hold were people that Mary Claire had never seen before, women and children who had no relation to any transport prisoner. The families of the guards and warders were also going to Australia, but they were settling as pioneers, to turn a prison colony into a country, expanding the reaches of the British Empire. Former soldiers were guaranteed a lifetime pension from the government if they would serve on a transport and then start a new life, and the offer was so generous that several men jumped at the chance. Just as Mary Claire gawked at the families, so the families gawked at the wretch from the forward hold.

"This is the prisoner, Mrs. Morse," Plowman made the introduction as Mary Claire was escorted into the captain's cabin. There was a tea party underway, with Mrs. Morse acting as hostess for the warders' wives.

"Thank you for coming. Mrs. Hightower and I heard of your bravery in the galley, and we wished to personally extend our thanks for rescuing Mr. Scofield from a dreadful fate," Mrs. Morse patronized grandly.

Mary Claire was the daughter of a successful tanner, a businessman and merchant, and her social position, convent education and prim manners were now on display. Lt. Plowman looked on with amusement, recalling the old tales of Queen Elizabeth and her graceful resolve in the face of Mary Tudor's pitiless torments. Anne Boleyn's bastard child could have been reborn in Mary Claire O'Dwyer, for such was the young lady's attitude. "Please, sit down and join us," Mrs. Morse spluttered.

Mary Claire sat rigidly in a chair, her back never touching the carved slats, her back never even bending. Mrs. Morse poured tea and slid the cup on the table, to rest under Mary Claire's nose. The look of bored disdain that came from the guest of honor made Mrs. Morse feel ashamed of the quality of her china. The tea would remain there, untouched, as if the Fenian prisoner would sooner die of thirst than touch such a cheap, vulgar cup.

Clearing her throat, Mrs. Looby fumbled for a topic to discuss, but seemed unable to think clearly when she looked Mary Claire in the eye. The warder's wife had been a fountain of words when the ladies were discussing the girl's case, the injustice of it all, the humiliation for Her Majesty's courts in far off America. She had plenty to say about Mr. Dickens and his assessment of British prisons, but now that reality was sitting in an upholstered chair, Delia was rattled and struck dumb.

"The, ahem, the lunatic murderess, ahem," she stammered. "Perished, thank goodness for God's mercy upon us. To have such a dangerous thing so close to us."

"You see now, Mrs. Looby, why bayonets are fixed and rifles loaded at all times," Mr. Hightower intoned. Captain Morse offered a "quite so" to punctuate the sentence.

"Would you care for a biscuit, my dear?" Mrs. Morse inquired.

"No, thank you," was the frosty reply of Her Ladyship in rags.

"But, surely, you must be pleased to receive a sweet treat," Mr. Hightower said. "A prisoner's ration does not include cream cakes and Charlotte Russe."

Light, polite titters followed, and Hightower gave his full attention to the genteel young lady perched daintily on the edge of the seat. "Through hard work and good behavior, sir, I have earned the privilege of picking through the ship's slops to supplement my rations," she spoke prettily, but her demure charm barely masked her bitterness.

Throats were cleared in extreme embarrassment. Retrieving edibles out of dustbins was common practice in London, but never before had the ladies shared a table with someone so desperate. Simon studied the face of each woman, finding in every one the sympathy and affection that he had hoped to unmask when he suggested that the girl from Rathkeale be invited to tea. They had given up their hearts to Mary Claire, the girl who placed the deplorable conditions of a British prison on Mrs. Morse's fine damask tablecloth, like a centerpiece crafted from a nightmare.

"Humility is a fine quality for a girl to learn," the captain said, too loudly. "Important in a wife, to be humble. And obedient."

"What will you hope to do in Fremantle, have you given any thought to a position that you might seek?" Mrs. Hightower asked.

"Other than that which has been offered to me in my cell?" Mary Claire inquired, casting a glance at Lt. Plowman. He shook his head ever so slightly, to negate the question. "Above all, ma'am, I wish to be God's servant to his children in Fremantle, to further the work of Jesus Christ in all that I do."

The sniffle came from Mrs. Morse, who dabbed at her eyes with her napkin. "To hear of such Christian charity in someone labeled a criminal merely confirms what we have been reading, ladies," Mrs. Morse sighed to her friends. They all agreed heartily, to the added displeasure of the captain.

"The town of Fremantle will be greatly enriched by her presence," Plowman noted. He smiled at Mary Claire, an affectionate glance that confused the girl. His final comment set her upright again. "Perhaps the governor can be convinced to extend her sentence to life so that the people of Australia might be blessed for all her days."

"Not the governor, Lieutenant, but a young man with a sizeable income," Warder Looby laughed. "That's a life sentence of domestic servitude that every girl jumps at."

For a short span of time, Mary Claire sat through the polite chatter until five minutes remained before the convict's supper. Mr. Hightower must have carried a clock in his head, because he broke into the conversation at that precise time. He thanked her for coming, arrogant but sincere, and bowed her off to her cell.

Simon swooped her up by the elbow and escorted her out the door, not sure if he should be angry or congratulate her on her prowess. "Divide and conquer, a fine strategy," he paid a compliment. "Captain Morse loathes you and now his wife has pitched her tent in your camp. You are learning quickly, 2657."

"Did you kill Paddy?" she insisted on an answer.

"No, I did not kill your Paddy," he said. "Tell me, do you receive any correspondence from your family to bring you a moment of cheer?"

"My letters have been withheld since my brothers arrived in America and began to spread the truth," she said. "There was one that arrived at Newgate; the superintendent showed it to me as punishment. Edged in black, it was, to be given to me in future if I behaved and followed orders. I suppose your captain holds it now."

"Do you not puzzle over the contents? If, as a sign of our friendship, I could convince Mr. Morse to give it to you, would you then give me your solemn vow to hold your tongue?"

"Bah, I know the contents. My mother's spirit came to me in Newgate to tell me herself that she was going to heaven to join my father. If it gives your captain such pleasure to withhold my brother's words, let him keep it and rejoice."

"Ghosts and goblins," he said. "Such foolishness. Yet it is one of your most charming qualities."

Again, his compliment had put her on edge and she seemed to be waiting for him to strike another blow, to catch her emotions off guard. "If your nose weren't so huge, you'd see past the end of it," she said, a bold gambit.

"You are in my debt, prisoner, and your sharp tongue will soon be dulled. Reimbursing my investment," he threatened, "will be hard work indeed."

The return of Mary Claire to the female mess had become a daily ritual of joyful expectation. Her ironing chores gave her access to the soft heart of Mr. McVickers, the former assistant cook who replaced the late Mr. Kettinger. He ran the galley with a sharp eye on the ship's stores, always on guard for thieves and pilferers. What was issued but not eaten was fair game, and McVickers gave to Mary Claire whatever was scraped off of Mrs. Morse's china plates. Lt. Plowman had ordered the girl to the laundry work detail every single day, and all the female convicts saw that as a sign of generosity.

Assuming that Mary Claire was getting a caning for scorching the captain's shirt, Varena roared with laughter over the tea party scene. Weaving a long tale, amusing her friends, the guest of honor mocked her hosts as a gaggle of idiots, full of idiot talk while she must surely have reeked of orange peels and chicken bones, the bountiful feast that she had hidden under her clothes.

Mary Claire unbuttoned her dress and reached down near the waist under her chemise, where the treasures of the scrap bucket had been hidden. Eager fingers pulled out the bones that Mr. McVickers had chopped in two so that the ladies could extract the marrow without breaking their teeth. Greedily consuming what she once looked on as slop for hogs, Mary Claire bit into an orange peel that still held a slip or two of fruity flesh. She fished out a few pieces of walnut, discarded by Mr. Morse because of some worms, but the destitute ate with blinders of necessity. Dinner that noon would be salted beef that had begun to rot in the heat of the hold, and the women had learned to pick out the maggots that floated in their dinner bowl. Worms on walnuts were nothing in comparison.

Over supper, Bridie revealed the glorious news. Her infant had quickened that very afternoon, fluttering inside her like a gentle butterfly. The baby became the only topic of conversation among the Perkins coven, as Warder Hightower had labeled the clan. Until the lantern was extinguished, they focused their minds completely on babies and infants, something that kept a body too occupied to feel the hunger and thirst that was a part of each woman, as much a part of her as her arms and legs. Excited about the infant, in need of the distraction, Mary Claire curled up in Bridie's bunk and shared a bed, to dream of another life, to dream of riding in a trap with Ed, Mike and Danny, bouncing on the road to the county fair where the tinkers told the fortunes of giddy, silly fourteen-year-old girls.

A bolt jangled, alarming Mary Claire, who was still worried that she would pay a price for being out of her bunk. "Prisoner 2657," Mr. Long barked, but mercifully he did not walk forward to the tiers.

"Present, sir," she answered, her teeth chattering with nerves.

"You've been called out," he snickered, and Mary Claire knew that she had to face another challenge. "Come on, don't keep a man waiting."

In the first hours of another Monday, the only sound that came out of the hold was the din of human beings penned up like animals, coupled with the blood curdling yelps of one man's nightmares. There was a muffled noise of feet tramping the wooden deck, the guards on watch or the restless convicts trying to escape their morbid thoughts. She was led through a maze of bulkheads and supply stores, taken through a circuitous route where she encountered few guards. Her master was waiting for her in the dimly lit wardroom.

"Take off every stitch of clothing and bathe," he told her quietly. "The basin contains fresh water, use that to wet the flannel and lather the soap. On the deck is a tub of seawater, use that to rinse. When you have finished, put on your undergarments, get into bed, turn on your side and face the bulkhead. Is that clear?"

"Yes, sir," she gulped.

"You may have five minutes to complete your toilette in complete privacy. The clock is running, my dear." He indolently slipped his pocket watch out of his trousers and tapped on the face.

She did exactly as she had been told, truly scared that he planned to barge in while she was nude, but too overjoyed at the opportunity to touch her skin with soap to think about a possible discomfort. Everything was cold, helping her to plunge in and move quickly, luxuriating in the aroma of sandalwood that lifted off her clean body. From the other side of the door, she heard his chair scrape on the planks, and she rapidly pulled on her drawers, her chemise, and the petticoats as fast as she could slide them over wet skin. He came in as she was sitting on the bed, struggling to get her stockings on.

"No, it's much too warm for wool," he said. "Lie down and turn away. I'm going to have a bath, but if you'd like to watch, I would be quite pleased."

With a gasp of embarrassment, Mary Claire flew across the bunk and pressed her body against the bulkhead, a pillow over her head to shield both eyes and ears from a man's naked body. She could not block out the splashing of the water, the scratch of the flannel on his skin, or the cheerful sigh that signaled his pleasure of cleanliness achieved. The door opened, the bucket of dirty water clattered slightly, and the door was shut again. The heat of his body reached her before she felt him lying next to her, her muscles already growing rigid as his bare legs touched hers.

"Turn your back to the bulkhead," he said. Rolling over on his side, he asked for her arm, which he draped across his ribs, his hand pressing hers to his chest. "Sing to me, Mary Claire, sing *Kathleen Mavourneen*. I'm very fond of it and I would like to hear it often."

"Why do you want to hurt?" she began to complain, but he quietly commanded her to obey.

Snuggled against his back, she lowered her tone to a tender shadow as she relayed the sad tale. The final verse spoke of parting from Erin, for years or forever. Her voice cracked on a sob as her torturer landed another blow, stoking an ember of homesickness until it grew into a blaze that burned her.

"Sir," she asked after she had swallowed the tears so he would not feel them.

"Simon," he corrected her.

"Simon, is it the boys that you favor?"

"I hope for a dozen," he mumbled.

Safe at last, she hugged her benefactor with warmth. Grateful for his protection, she was willing to overlook the abusive tongue that came with it. Eventually, she expected the wounds to give rise to scars that would be tougher, impossible to chafe or abrade. He held her hand a little tighter, twining his fingers between hers, and she nestled into the comfort of his gentle touch. Almost immediately, her breathing grew peacefully slow, her arm going limp as she fell into a deep and glorious sleep.

"I've turned thousands of men into warriors, Mary Claire," he whispered to her dreams. "Never did I love one of them, nor they love me."

Brought to him again the following night, Mary Claire was happy to go, to have someplace comfortable and quiet to lay her head for four hours at a stretch. She was ready to sing until her voice gave out, to listen to his insults until her ears fell off, all for four hours on a thin mattress in the arms of a man whose embrace was surprisingly tender and blissfully restful.

"You must ask Captain Morse for that letter," he told her when he joined her in bed.

"Let him keep it, I've no use for words that have grown stale with age," she sassed, bold now and at ease with the man who needed her to complete a disguise.

"For such an educated female, you are incredibly stupid," he said.

"It's you who's stupid," she countered, angry at his insult and giving vent to a tongue grown sharp.

"At least I know that a girl lifts all her skirts in bed."

"Hah, well maybe I though you'd like to do the lifting yourself," she spluttered.

"I would."

"So, not so stupid after all."

"Do you want me to?"

"Do as you please. Kiss the boys if it makes you happy, I won't speak."

"Can I kiss you?"

"Do as you please."

"Do you want me to?" he asked again, rolling over to face her. "Even before I met you, Mary Claire, I was in love with you. I will not touch you if you don't love me."

"Love me? Why should I believe you?" In the darkness of the cabin, she could not see his eyes or the way his mouth formed the words. His breathing was as rhythmic as the rocking of the ship, hypnotic if she let her mind drift away, drawing her in when she needed to maintain her distance.

"Have I ever deceived you? Everything I said to you, Mary Claire, every penalty you received, I told you what I would do and I did it. You asked me to be your friend and get you something to eat, and have I not done that without appearing to curry favor from you?"

"Yes, sir."

"Yes, Simon," he corrected her again.

"Say those other words to me and I'll kill you, somehow, I will," she hissed.

"I only learned a little Irish to turn a pretty colleen's head. You act as though your Paddy was speaking to you from the grave."

"You were in Kilclooney Wood."

"I did not kill your Paddy, I did not capture your brothers, nor did I hang Danny. He was thrown by a horse and dashed his brains out when he was sounding an alarm. It's probably all in the letter that is locked away in the Captain's desk. There may be other bits of important news as well. Wouldn't you like to read it?"

"No," she replied.

Holding her against his chest, he kissed the top of her head. "Dear, sweet, stubborn Mary Claire. I love you."

"So you said."

"Please, may I kiss you?" he asked gently.

Her mind made up, she tilted her head, to look him in the eye and see through him, to search for the truth in his heart. His kiss was warm, with soft lips that belied the strength of the muscles she felt through his shirt. His tongue was wet, moist with the water that she craved, and she drank his kiss to slake her thirst. His hand was on her waist, caressing her ribs and seeking her breast, but she did not move her arm to stop him. He fondled her breast, grown pendulous with loose skin like an old woman, the once rounded flesh melted away in Ireland's prisons. A twinge of vanity made her wish that he could have caressed her before, when she had a lovely bosom that curved gracefully.

Simon slid his hands under her back and she lifted her hips in acquiescence. The tattered fabric that covered her body slid off her legs as she let him undress her, gladly permitting him to put his hand between her thighs. She could not risk losing his power, his largesse, or his attention and protection. Mary Claire had fixed her mind on victory, and she sighed her lover's name like the whores did, softly cried his name as he took her greatest treasure, the one thing she owned and had fought to preserve, the reason she was sent to prison and her father broken. Simon Plowman took her virtue and he took her reputation, and she cried as she realized that if she had surrendered her virginity at the age of fourteen, her family would still exist in the green and mist of Rathkeale.

Seven

Table scraps were beneficial and life-sustaining, remainders that were the difference between life and death. Mary Claire could judge that easily enough when she looked across the deck at the male prisoners in the punishment cell, once burly men who were shrinking to bone at an alarming rate on a diet of bread and water. The rations that the women received were still inadequate, even with the slops added, something that the young woman was made aware of when she looked down at her chest to see her ribs beginning to poke through. Beyond that, Mary Claire could not bear to explore, having never lost the vanity that went hand in hand with pride. Besides, she had the company of eighteen other women to gauge her figure's changes.

Breakfast was always the same pint of chocolate, the taste getting more and more foul as the water cooked in the wooden barrels. Passively, the females accepted what was doled out, accepting what was given rather than complain and risk losing the small fragment of normalcy that they were granted. As Mr. Hightower had informed them, they should be grateful for a table and benches in their dining room, for it would be easy enough to feed them like barnyard animals if anyone caused trouble. He was looking straight at Mary Claire when he made mention of it, using her as an example of the benefits of prison, of discipline, and obedience to her master

About halfway through the afternoon, when the Protestant convicts who still believed in God were dragged off to Dr. Smith's religion school, Mary Claire dipped into her chemise and took out four squares of hardtack, a true bounty. With a merry smile, she whispered in Bridie's ear. "He is fully a man, one who fancies girls."

Bridie squealed with excitement, her happy congratulations drowned out by Cornelia and Varena, who peppered the girl with questions about the Lieutenant's preferences and style. Discussing a taboo subject that could not be more fascinating, Mary Claire gave a step by step report, asking Moira if it was typical for a man to tell a harlot that he loved her. Groaning, Moira explained about the romantic, soft-headed boys who believed in love, and who could be strung along for months with empty promises of undying devotion, given out expertly by the most successful courtesans. More and more, Mary Claire grew more confident in her ability to placate her lover, to flop on her back all day and every day if that was what it took to keep Simon's favor.

"Right you are, lamb," Mrs. Perkins cheered. "That's the spirit, by hook or by crook, we'll not be beaten by John Bull, not by his stinking prisons nor his stinking starvation."

When Scofield returned to duty he was a changed man, Mary Claire's ardent friend, someone who shared the gossip out of the pensioner-guard mess. His kindness was in direct contrast to Captain Morse's loathing, which had blossomed into full-blown detestation once Mary Claire wormed her way into Mrs. Morse's very tender heart. He had threatened to strangle his wife and the O'Dwyer girl together one evening, supposedly because Mrs. Morse continuously referred to the "poor little angel" and argued over Mary Claire's treatment. Morse had warned all the guards that there was nothing more dangerous than a pretty girl who was bright, but Scofield had no doubt that Mary Claire was keen to pay heed to her superiors, to reveal the sweet angel that resided in her gentle woman's heart.

On deck in the early evening, the female convicts searched in vain for a cool breeze, with the *Hellebore* steaming towards the coast of Africa. The warm woolens that had been issued in the British prisons were becoming unbearably hot and scratchy. When left on their own, the women stripped down to chemise and drawers as they lay in the airless hold, sweating and dreaming of water. The ration was one pint per day, and it had not been enough before, but the dehydration of the Southern Hemisphere was increasing their thirst.

"Walk with me, 2657," Plowman ordered his concubine, and Mary Claire jumped up with a childish eagerness, ready to please, ready to connive, to bow and scrape until she had a mouthful of water.

"'Tis a lovely evening, sir," she began, disheartened by his return to a cold and impersonal tone.

"Lovely? Nonsense, it is hot as blazes and it will get worse," he said. "I did not address you so that we could chat about the weather."

"Shall we chat about our nights together, my love?" she tried to be coy, to recall what sorts of things she had overheard in the racks, but her mind was foggy and the words kept getting caught in her throat. "Such, um, the greatest pleasure."

"Don't talk to me like a whore when you speak to me; it's repulsive," he barked.

"Yes, sir," she lowered her head, afraid that she was going to lose him already.

"Address me as a wife to her husband. Go on, what would you say to me if we were at home, taking the air?"

Pausing for a moment, she imagined that they were strolling along the lane to the church, and she asked after his father and mother. Without blinking an eye, he admitted that he rarely saw his father, had little to do with him in fact, but his mother was very well. She asked about his brothers and sisters, to learn of his immediate family, and Simon readily confessed that he had only one sister, and she was blessed with robust good health. Crafting her questions with innocence and guile, she learned that his mother and sister lived in Dublin.

"Are you Irish, sir?" she asked.

"When my father was a lieutenant-colonel, back in 1848, he slaughtered the rebels in Kilkenny. He is a major general now, slaughtering someone else who rebels against our Queen. So, darling, how Irish does that make me?"

His hard-edged tone was reaching her ears in some distorted way, bent in the heat perhaps, but she found him amusing. "Not nearly Irish enough, sir," she giggled.

"Will you maintain a confidence? Tell no one else, or I shall know that the word came from you. Within the next ten to fourteen days we will put into the port at Madeira to take on supplies. There will be fresh oranges, 2657, would you like to have one?"

"Oh, yes, sir, please, sir," she begged with wide eyes.

"Would you be willing to do anything?"

"Anything that you asked of me, yes, sir."

"Will you always be willing to do everything I ask of you, even if there is no orange in the offing?"

"I'll not lift a finger for free," she scoffed angrily.

"What sort of wife are you? Come now, we are playing a game, 2657, surely you played such games with your Paddy."

His words reignited a fury that could not be calmed, with his
continuous abrasion of an old wound that would not be allowed to heal.
"Who did you murder in Kilclooney Wood, if you have the courage to
confess your sins?" she said, her fists tightened.

"My activities were hampered by a blow to the head, darling. I
was ambushed during a reconnaissance mission, and lucky for me that my
skull was not bashed in. The battle was over long before I regained
consciousness."

"How did my sweetheart die?"

"How does any man die in combat? We take aim and shoot, and
sometimes the bullet finds its mark. Such is a soldier's death, and not very
glorious after all, is it?"

"How did you know of my brothers?"

"I am an officer, so I know a great many things. It is my duty to
know my enemy, to track him down and then kill him. Not very glorious
there, either, don't you agree? As a smart tactician, I also like to know
whom I can trust and who might betray me, which unfortunately for your
brothers was not a strong characteristic of the Fenians in the military. The
centers were riddled with informers; that is how those nine men came to
be here. In the military, trust is a requirement, for the men to believe in
their officer and the officer to have complete faith in his men. At the same
time, the enemy will always try to insert a pair of ears into the middle of
the camp. It's the nature of warfare."

"You know a great deal about things, don't you?" she said.
Crossing her arms, she leaned against the bulwarks, annoyed by his
flippant attitude.

"The Crown has informers in several American cities, listening to
the voices of the immigrants and monitoring the politicians. I probably
know more about your brothers' activities than you do. Would that foolish

husbands had such spies, and one of my colleagues would not have fathered his child without sharing his wife's bed."

His wink was conspiratorial, a man sharing a confidence with a woman who was entrusted with his secrets. "So it would be you who sowed the seeds?" she retorted in jest.

"Another man's wife? Never, my dear," he exaggerated his revulsion. "Not even another man's sweetheart. I till my own field, plowing in your furrow, my lovely colleen."

"And what of your wife, with her field left fallow?" Mary Claire inquired. With her back against the rail, Simon hovered over her, his hand on the rigging and his body close to hers, a courting couple in a flirtatious pose.

"What of you, wife, are you withering from a lack of my affection?" he asked.

"And your children?" she probed.

"Look closely in my eye, just there, can you see the twinkles in a father's eye? Boys and girls both, I hope."

Within four days she had learned the route that brought her to his cabin, and the guards paid no attention to Lt. Plowman's toy, barely noticing her and rarely wishing her a good evening as she quietly wandered through the hold. Just as quickly, she grew accustomed to him, to the radically different attitudes he displayed below deck as compared to his verbal battering above. It was something that kept her always on her guard, never quite sure what side of Simon Plowman she was going to encounter.

There were nights when he would sweep her into his arms, burning with desire and starving for a touch of her hand on his cheek or the sound of her voice. Many nights, she would find him in his bed, impatiently waiting for her, and then he would make love as if he had urgent business pressing. On those occasions, when he would roll over and go to sleep after he was finished, she felt hollow and insignificant, used like a prostitute and then ignored. But she was not anywhere near as hungry as she had once been.

Shortly before they reached Madeira, the clarion sounded, "Prisoners assemble to witness punishment," and Mary Claire gracefully put the bookmark into Mrs. Looby's well-worn copy of *Great Expectations*. The Irish prisoner had a new chore in the afternoons, since she was not required to attend Dr. Smith's Anglican catechism lesson and Captain Morse did not want her to be allowed to rest. Many an afternoon was spent with the Assistant Warder's wife when Mrs. Looby had one of her frequent spells. She quickly discovered that she was also a pawn between Captain and Mrs. Morse, drawn into their battle over the proper treatment of convicted felons. If she obeyed Mrs. Morse and continued reading, she was in for it. If she obeyed Captain Morse and went out, she was in for it.

The clanging of the metal rings of the triangle served as a warning that the prisoner was ready, roasting under the hot sun while everyone waited for the one prodigal convict to join the female ranks. Everyone knew where the girl could be found, just as everyone probably knew why she was missing from the assembly. Through the open cabin door, Mary Claire could hear the pounding of boots, the tramping of a guard, and the distinctive rattling of the armorer's chains

"When I order that all prisoners be assembled, Mrs. Morse, I do not exclude any prisoner, even one assigned to entertain you and your guests." The captain stood in the doorway, his voice cracking with tight control over his building fury. "And you, prisoner, I believe that you are cognizant of the rules, and you failed to leave this cabin immediately."

"Yes, sir," Mary Claire stammered.

"Apparently, it is up to me to train an insubordinate girl in obedience to her male superiors," he went on, only inches from Mary Claire's head.

"I did always heed my mother, sir," she replied in defense.

"No doubt, and at the same time you played on your father's heartstrings with your feminine confidence game, twisted him around with your charm and your sweet smile. Well, Prisoner 2657, before this ship drops anchor in the waters of Australia, you will learn to follow orders, and rue the day that you failed to heed your father's authority."

"I'm sorry I disobeyed, sir," she apologized.

"Too quick to run to my wife, that is your crime, prisoner," Morse continued, his tone beginning to soften. "I shall slow your pace until you learn that I am the captain of this ship, and you make haste only at my command."

A hard scowl thrown at the armorer was all the man needed to set about his job. A heavy chain of short length was swiftly attached to Mary Claire's bony ankles, the weight of the manacles falling onto the tops of her feet. Throughout the process, Mrs. Looby fanned herself with her handkerchief, flustered by the captain's angry tirade and more than a little sorry that she had instigated the entire spat by suggesting that her melancholia and headache would be relieved if Mary Claire amused her.

"Forgive me, Mr. Morse," Delia blabbered in her overwrought fashion. "But, to force a young lady to look at a man in a state of undress, without a shirt."

"State of undress?" Morse roared. "In a prison cell full of whores conducting their business in full view of everyone, Mrs. Looby, this girl has looked at sights that you will never see, things you could not even guess at in your most perverted daydreams. I envy the man that she marries, because she has learned more ways to gratify a man's lust in one week than a respectable woman would learn in a lifetime. This young lady has been taught by the most expensive instructors in Dublin, and within six months of her arrival in Fremantle you will see her draped in silks and diamonds, riding in the finest carriage in the country. And seated next to her will be a gentleman who follows her around like a lap dog, and he will have a very large grin affixed to his face because she will perform her domestic duties with a dazzling array of techniques that the majority of men can only wish for, and the wealthiest men pay a great deal of money to obtain. That, Mrs. Looby, is your young lady."

The leg irons were so heavy that Mary Claire could scarcely move, and her limbs ached with the effort it took to reach her assigned spot on the deck. She arrived, and Teddy O'Brien's flogging for stealing food could at last commence. One crack of the whip raised dark welts on the man's back, and in unison the nineteen women flinched, unable to watch such torture impassively even though they had seen it many times before. As the bosun's mate raised his arm for the next lash, a defiant Irish girl raised her voice in song. The beautiful sound that intoned the Ave Maria for the bishop when he came to Rathkeale to confirm the twelve-year-old children was heard now on the deck of a prison ship.

"Let Eireann remember the days of old," she trilled the unofficial song of the Fenian movement.

"Ere her faithless sons betrayed her," a few men picked up the anthem, and Teddy suffered each lash with the bold determination of an Irishman who had furthered the cause of freedom by accosting English soldiers in the Irish countryside and stealing their money, their weapons, and occasionally their lives. He never uttered a sound to betray his agony, and when he was released from the triangle he turned smartly and walked with pride to his cell. Mary Claire knelt and scoured his blood off the teak planks, singing her hymn lustily.

*   *   *

Supply ships came out to the *Hellebore* when it arrived at the port off the African coast. The hatches were shut up and locked, the cell doors were shut up and locked, and the guards patrolled the corridors and the decks to prevent anyone from making an escape. As quickly as possible, Morse got out of Madeira and away from the danger of pirates and Irish rebels. Back at sea, everything returned to normal on the ship, where every day would be the same as the day before.

"Mary Claire, Mary Claire," Simon clucked at her as she waited for him to finish removing her clothes. "Stubborn, pigheaded, obstinate, unrepentant Mary Claire. These leg irons are a tremendous nuisance; I can scarcely wedge myself in between your legs now. I cannot give you an orange, can I, when you disobeyed orders again."

"Keep your orange, and I hope you choke on it," she sulked.

"Bold talk for a young lady with her drawers at her ankles," he said.

"It's the costume of my chosen profession, and you seem to like the fashion," she retorted.

"The tongue has grown tart," he said, nuzzling the back of her neck while he cupped his hand over her breasts.

"I was so proud of the curve of my bosom," she sighed, almost to herself.

"It will return to its old form soon enough. I do not expect that your employer in Fremantle will follow Captain Morse's lead and put you on bread and water for two days, unless he dislikes your musical selections as much the captain did."

"I'm not sorry, either."

She began to pout, to relish the indignation that pulsed in her veins, but Simon disarmed her by running a hairbrush through her curls.

The seductive rhythm cut through her like a rapier, another reminder of something she had lost and could only acquire through his munificence. When she looked down at the floor, she discovered that her hair was falling out in clumps.

"What a marvelous black mane, like a wild filly," he said. "Were you proud of your pretty black locks?"

"Vain and proud, Simon. When the tinker told me I'd live in hell to pay for the sin, I thought that my father had bribed her to say it so I'd be more humble. Sure, but it's come true, and I'm in hell now."

"Don't you like being with me?" he asked, lifting her legs and heavy hobble chain into bed.

"'Tis the only joy in my life," she sighed, snuggling next to his chest as he embraced her.

"What would Dr. Acton make of you?" he asked.

"Bah, I'm not ashamed that I enjoy every night and I'm not ashamed that I like to share your bed. I'll not be ashamed of anything that I do. I am a fallen woman," she proclaimed, kissing his chest, moving her lips down to his belly. She left his cabin in the morning with six oranges.

Eight

The fresh water that had been picked up in Madeira was given to the officers and crew, while the rank scum of the old barrels was ladled out, a pint at a time, to a group of people who were fading into mere shadows of human beings. Bridie almost looked like a stick with a great hump, her infant growing inside her despite the meager sustenance it received. The heat was a never-ending torment that was increased by pregnancy, creating greater thirst, but water was not something that was easily exchanged in the women's mess. No one had enough to drink, and after so many weeks at sea, the will to survive took precedence over thoughts of mutiny or escape. The punishments doled out for fighting became rare, while the number of floggings for stealing increased.

Due to the relative calm that descended on the ship, Captain Morse allowed the prisoners to have nearly unlimited access to the deck, and a walk after sunset was relished. Although the air was relatively cooler, it was still miserably searing, but at least the sun was not blazing down and burning fair skin. Mary Claire was called on to sing, and she put on an impromptu musicale. At the request of a fellow convict she sang *The Water is Wide*, followed by *Kathleen Mavourneen* and *Lorena* for Mrs. Looby.

After finishing up with *The Last Rose of Summer*, she sat next to Bridie to listen to the fiddler.

"It's not moving anymore, Mary Claire," Bridie shivered, her hand traveling slowly around her belly. "For three days I haven't felt anything."

"Maybe it's sleeping in the heat," Mary Claire said.

"Mrs. Perkins thinks it's dead," Bridie sobbed. "They've done it, they've killed my baby and we can't beat them, no matter what we do we can't beat them at their game."

With no answers to give, Mary Claire offered a comforting hug, the only thing she had for Bridie's sorrow. Not willing to leave the red-haired girl alone all night when she was so distraught, Mary Claire climbed up to share Bridie's bunk, and Simon Plowman could think what he would when his lover failed to appear on time.

The ship's surgeon made the rounds every morning, purportedly to check on the health of the convicts, but everyone was marked down as healthy no matter how ill they were. He tore into Mary Claire for leaving her bunk without permission before he bothered to take a look at Bridie, even though all the women were in hysterics over the girl's fever. Discipline came first on the prison deck.

"Report to the surgery if this fever persists," he grumbled, but Bridie was so ill that she could not get out of her cot. Unable to walk to the infirmary, she stayed in bed.

Smith recognized his limitations, and he assigned Julia Ward, midwife's assistant and convicted abortionist, to act as nurse in the female quarters. He gave her access to his pharmacy, but all Julia understood were herbs and concoctions with bizarre names. He allowed her to use his surgical implements, but Julia was only familiar with sharp straws and long, thin needles. She stared blankly at the bottles of medicines and the shiny tools and shrugged her shoulders. There was nothing that anyone could do. No one actually uttered the words, but they feared that Bridie was doomed.

The circle of friends maintained a constant vigil, praying that Bridie's body would come around and fix itself, something that Julia said was a possibility. They brought the girl her meals and they brought her comfort, working in shifts to stay at Bridie's side. Mary Claire skipped the regular exercise period to sit with her dearest friend on earth, her closest confidante. Simon was alone for a second night, and then a third, but he never came in search of Mary Claire. She accepted the end of their tryst, while recognizing the need to start from scratch with another man, but that was something to worry about on another day, after Bridie was well again.

Sometime in the early hours of November's first Sunday, Mary Claire felt Bridie's last breath on her cheek. She began to sob, hysterical, screeching sobs, and the guard burst in with his rifle drawn, scared half to death at the outburst.

"Murderer," she howled, repeating a mantra. With all her strength she shrieked, her cries bringing in even more guards who had tumbled out of their cots near the female cell and come running with weapons drawn.

"I didn't kill anyone," old Mr. Long protested when his fellows looked at him suspiciously.

Brightfelt got a grip on Mary Claire's leg and tussled her out of the cot, catching her as she fell while extricating Bridie's corpse from Mary Claire's arms. He fought to wrap her up while she kicked and flailed, out of her mind with an anguish that had descended into madness. She clawed at his hands, she tried to scratch out his eyes and bite his arms while she twisted and turned, her screams never fading, and her energy to scream limitless.

In his official capacity, Dr. Smith turned up to record a prisoner's demise, right next to the notation in his journal that indicated the prisoner was not fit for work for the previous three days. A complication of pregnancy was so common that he was unfazed by the loss of a patient, particularly when he was only concerned with communicable illness and infection that might reflect badly on his care. His attitude fueled Mary Claire's insane rage, and she fought even harder as Smith forced her mouth open and threw a dose of laudanum down her throat. The effect was immediate; her contortions ground to a halt and her eyelids fluttered peacefully in a dazed stupor.

"Hysteria arises from the womb," the doctor informed the guards, offering a lesson in modern medicine. "The weak female mind is prone to such extremes, especially in the case of the distorted mental capacity of the criminal. Put her back in her cot and she'll be calm by morning."

The remains of Bridie Boyne were carted out without ceremony, to lie in the infirmary while the surgeon's mates prepared her for burial. The cell door was locked on the remaining convicts, who would not be permitted the honor of sitting with their lifeless friend out of respect for her brief existence. When the wailing started up, the turnkey retreated to the far end of his post to escape the heartbreak.

Sunday services went on as scheduled, with Mary Claire's voice resounding through the rigging, a rebellious tone that was unmistakably angry. After the breakfast was served and the utensils washed, the convicts were assembled on deck once again for the internment of mother and unborn child. Father McCabe officiated at a full-blown Roman Catholic funeral Mass and burial, with every part of the Catholic ritual intoned with solemn reverence. Mary Claire caught a glimpse of Simon, standing off to one side of the crowd, and she bellowed out the Pater Noster as if she dared him to silence her.

The disposal of the body was cold in its anonymity, with the corpse tucked into a long canvas sack that was hauled roughly by four male convicts who were assigned to the burial detail. By this point in their journey, they had barely enough strength to carry the weight, most of which came from the sandbags that had been tied to Bridie's body. McCabe's voice boomed out the prayers, Mary Claire warbled the responsorial chant, and the convicts heaved the bag up at the gangway. The earthly remains of Bridie Boyne, born in County Mayo seventeen years past, slid out of the open end of the sack and plunged into the churning waters of the South Atlantic, a burial as respectful of her life as the daily dumping of the ship's slop buckets.

"I am truly sorry," Simon mumbled to Mary Claire.

"For the savings to the Queen's purse you should rejoice, sir," she said with mean spite. "Not even a few pennies worth of canvas for a shroud, now that's economy, and Her Majesty's saving at least a shilling on Bridie's board. And don't forget Lord Cavendish, saved from the sight of his bastard child."

"It is a woman's lot in life, Mary Claire, not the Crown's will but the will of God," he consoled her. "There are three men serving as guards on this ship, taking their children to Australia to start a new life, leaving a wife behind in a graveyard. Blame no one for what happened, not when it was the hand of God that carried her home."

She would neither answer nor acknowledge him, a fire of retribution beginning to flare in her gut. "You starved us in '45 when my grandfather had to sell the last of his land to feed his children, and you starved us in '47 until people fled Ireland to save their babes," she said, her voice growing louder as she continued to express the rage of the Irish people. "But we'll rise up, as often as you knock us to the ground we'll rise again and fight against you. God bless Ireland, and curse the godless land that shackles her."

"You dared to deprive me of my comfort for too many nights," he glared at her. "Come to my bed tonight, or I shall drag you out of your cell."

"First you should hide your weapons, Lieutenant, for I'd happily swing from the gibbet in the morning if you were dead by sunrise."

"Curb your tongue, prisoner," he warned in a low growl. "The deck of this ship is no place for idle threats."

There was no other choice than to obey, and she meekly meandered through the hold and knocked at his door, discovering how distasteful the courtesan's life could be. Mary Claire was dependent on a man she had snapped at, forced to amuse him when she wanted to be alone with her sadness. To retaliate, she was haughty, putting on a strong front of casual disdain, but she fell apart when he welcomed her as a friend giving solace rather than as an insatiable lover.

Silently he undressed her and then he washed her body with great reverence, the atmosphere in the cabin one of quiet mourning and tender sympathy. Together they sat on the edge of his cot while he brushed her hair. With every stroke of the boar bristle brush, he pulled her grief out of her heart with a slow and caring touch.

"Turn your head away from me," he said, his fingertips caressing her black waves as he took the strands at the temples and tied them behind her head with a length of Kelly green ribbon. Playfully, he sang *The Wearing of the Green*, recalling how it outraged his father to hear the Irish mocking a law that had been properly enacted through the wisdom of Parliament.

"I'll never see Ireland again," she broke down into sobs, great wretched sorrow that he absorbed through a tight hug.

"You'll see Ireland sooner than you think, my little lark, sooner than you probably expect," he said.

"In my dreams, Simon, there's the only place that Ireland still lives for me," she choked out her words through a shower of tears.

Sitting side by side, he let her cry out her sadness in the only spot on the entire ship that offered her sanctuary. "In your dreams tonight, but the Emerald Isle will still be green in a year's time. I have another confidence to share with you. Your vow of silence again?"

"Who's to share these secrets with me?" she whimpered. "I'm truly alone now, to end my days in a friendless land."

"I bought this wine in Madeira. No glasses, though, we shall have to drink from the bottle like sailors on a spree."

Holding the bottle, he helped her to tip it up to her lips, encouraging her to take a big gulp. Again he lifted the wine to her mouth, coaxing her to drink again, to alleviate a little of her thirst. "Australia is not a lonely place, Mary Claire, not with so many Irish firebrands sown in her dry soil. Fremantle is a very fertile farm, planted with Fenian sympathy thanks to the prison service. All the poison concentrated in one place; not very wise, but in the overall scheme of things it probably matters little. Have another drink, this is very good wine; enjoy it. The entire country is an escape proof prison. In the water, the sharks are more effective than a hundred water policemen. Away from the edge of the coast, the land is so inhospitable that it is a brutal executioner. The natives are employed to track down the men who attempt to run, and they know every rock and every grain of sand in the bush. A convict has no chance at all, either he dies of exposure and dehydration or the Aborigines find him and he's back in The Establishment."

"Is it a colorless land?" she asked, and he felt her shiver.

"Drink, come on, another," he encouraged her. "Colorless, blinding white. Hot and dusty. Imprisonment is not meant to be pleasant, and it is not."

Pounding down another swig, she began to taunt him. "Ed and Mike O'Dwyer are free, free to fight with their pretty words and their American money. That's why I'm here, Mr. Plowman, and I'm proud of it. The courts tried to force my father into transportation, but he spent his last shilling on his bail. Better to wander the hills of Ireland a free man than rot in Fremantle Gaol."

"He was right, Mary Claire, it was better to lose all he had to escape a miserable existence in the colony. But if he had been wiser, he would have packed his family off to America and escaped the persecution."

"His family's land was stolen, taken by the English pigs who stole my country, so why would a man not take a stand and fight?"

He watched her gulp the wine, her mind beginning to relax. Finally, he took a mouthful, and they talked on. "Your family is scattered to the four winds, lass, and does an O'Dwyer still tan hides in Rathkeale?"

"Two boys live in freedom, to produce more boys who will fight, and they'll give rise to another generation. We'll not lay down like meek English sheep in the fold because of one battle, or two, or a dozen. As long as there are Irishmen, we'll fight on." Mary Claire's mouth was dry from so much chatter, and she put the bottle to her mouth and guzzled blindly.

"You have steel in your spine, Mary Claire, and it has been tempered," he said. "In less than two months you have grown old. I shall miss the girl who first came aboard, little Eireann go Bragh."

"And you shall be the first man that I'll seek out when I've served my sentence," she rose to her feet, swaying. "The man who ruined me."

"In the eyes of God, my dear, I am your husband. To kill one's spouse is a grave crime indeed."

"Then I'll slit your throat as you sleep and make a widow of me, to find a true husband and create an army of soldiers," she said.

"Let's toast to my death, then," he encouraged her to ramble, now that more than half the wine was pickling her brain.

"Tonight might be your last on earth."

"If it is, then I wish to die with the taste of this fine Madeira, and your sweet lips, on my tongue," he emoted dramatically. "By the way, it is very bad form to kill a naked man. You will have to dress me before you run me through."

"Mock me if you like, but there'll come a day when you'll be begging me to spare your life."

"Drink up, obey my command."

Brazenly, she tossed back her head and chugged the dregs, so drunk that her words were slurred. "You hold the power today, and you abuse that power," she snarled. "Beat a dog often enough and it'll turn on you and tear you to pieces."

"Let's play husband and wife again, I like that game," he said, patting his mattress to indicate she was to join him

Her eyes were swinging from side to side, to offset the bobbing of her head. As her body movements grew uncoordinated and her head rolled, he was overjoyed that she was oblivious, completely inebriated. She stumbled into the cot, giggling like a little girl. "Enough talking, it is time for us to engage in an act of sexual congress," he said, nuzzling her neck.

"Do I know how to do that?" she whispered.

"With uncommon skill. Have no fear; I shall guide you through the process, Mrs. Plowman, you have only to be quiet or Lt. Wargrave shall be driven mad with desire."

While his hips ground into her he whispered sweetness in her ear, even though he was not one to say much when he was in bed. Her back arched up to reach closer to him and he lowered his body down onto her, to become a fortress, an impenetrable wall that would hide her for a few minutes, fleeing from a nightmare of prison and homesick misery, running away into a dream. Holding her hands, driving into her, he made her one flesh with him, one being that existed in another place, where the hills were wrapped in the greenest grass and the cows came home across the greenest fields.

"Tell me, Mary Claire," he said. "Tell me that you love me."

With Bridie's death, Simon felt that the last remaining obstacle to his total domination of the Fenian supporter had been dumped into the sea. All that was left to Mary Claire O'Dwyer was Simon Plowman, and he moved to strengthen his position, the military man who could analyze his prey and come out the victor. Like her brother Danny, she talked freely when liquor loosened her lips, and he would never let her get drunk again. Like Danny, she made threats, threats that she was likely to act on as rashly as her hotheaded brother. The exacting calculation, a shrewd scrutiny of those around her, would have to be cultivated, to blossom until she was as sly as Michael and Edward. When they reached Australia, she would retain some parts of her O'Dwyer heritage, but she would be a piece of Simon Plowman, his right hand in Fremantle.

"Tell me," he urged her, his pace quickening. In his mind he could hear the rush of air as the club whipped through the air in Kilclooney Wood, he could hear the sound of his brains rattling in his skull, and he could hear Ed O'Dwyer.

"If I get word that you're riding my sister," Ed warned, and the wind whistled in Simon's ear as the forest floor flew up to meet his face

Simon kissed her roughly, with a force that was meant to be felt by the O'Dwyer boys. He rode their sister, rode her hard, rode her until she moaned.

"*Ta gra*," she sighed, "*ta gra agam duit.*"

Nine

Storms erupted, adding to the dismal melancholy that came to rest in the female quarters. Two empty bunks were always there, always reminding the remaining inmates that they were on a perilous journey and nobody much cared if they made it or not. Mr. Arkwright was broken-hearted, having fallen passionately in love with the girl who had shown him the many and varied pleasures of sexual intercourse. The Fenian prisoners found more ammunition in the girl's death, and a renewed sense of outrage rumbled through the ship. Simon had to quell the disturbance soon, because the *Hellebore* would soon be sailing through the Roaring Forties, surrounded by water and sky, where not a spit of land, a tree, or even a rock could be seen. It was enough to drive an ordinary man to the depths of despair, and a prisoner to the height of mutiny.

Six weeks out of Fremantle, Simon had gathered enough intelligence from his informers on the prison deck. He went straight to Mary Claire, at her post in the galley, where she jabbered with Scofield about the jobs that were given to the female prisoners when they arrived in Australia. She sighed over the loss of her respectability while the guard insisted that men were so desperate for wives that they did not care in the least if she was innocent or of a more experienced nature.

Simon pulled her aside, his cheeks hot with restrained fury. "You will keep your mouth shut, Prisoner 2657," he said.

"You bought my body, and now you think to possess my words as well," she said. She had been queasy for weeks, and the morning's dose of lemon juice had not improved her temper. "What business of yours, what I say or don't say?"

"You are a convict, 2657, and my job is to watch you, every minute of every day. When you reach Fremantle, someone else will watch you every minute of every day," he explained. "You make your business my business when you broadcast throughout the ship, and your business will be Fremantle's business if you carry on. Keep your mouth shut, or do not wonder why a guard or the prison superintendent himself knows who is the cause of his trouble."

The crash of feet pounding on the wooden deck put an end to Simon's frustrated outburst. He raced out of the galley to find that the guards were struggling to contain the fury of men who had been caged up for far too long. As many bodies as could be stuffed back into the hold, that many streamed out, to take their ration of meat and dump it overboard in a massive protest over rotten food. Never before had unrest grown this heated, this close to a full-scale riot, and Simon had to quell the uprising before his men lost control.

Using the power of his voice and his position, Simon ordered the prisoners below, calling out for one spokesman to state their grievance. John O'Reilly nudged one of the civilian Fenian prisoners, who boldly declared that the inmates would not eat food that was unfit for hog slop. Captain Morse worked his way to Simon's side, to hear the man out and find a workable solution that would not diminish the captain's authority.

"Coward." The taunt came from the clutch of Fenian soldiers.

"Lying bastard," said John O'Reilly through his teeth. "Made her a whore, did you?"

"Ruined her," another former soldier called out as the mob was herded back into their dark pens.

For the crime of not thinking like a soldier, for giving in to sentiment and an act of kindness, Simon had nearly sabotaged his entire mission. He was no coward, he was planning on rewarding his Fremantle agent when they made land, but there was no room for that sort of nonsense in this business. He had treated her like a proper soldier from the day that they set sail, and he should never have considered her soft, womanly feelings. There was one final detail that he had to see to, one last step to be taken so that Mary Claire O'Dwyer was inextricably bound to Simon Plowman, even if they had to be separated by miles of ocean. He would have to act now, and sentiment be damned.

Evening mess was a tense and chaotic affair, with only small groups given food and washing duties at a time, to avoid large congregations on deck or in the galley. The lower deck bubbled with dissension while the prisoners gasped in the cells, locked in with no hope of fresh air until their rage was calmed. A boiling cauldron of hatred had been stoked, and Simon moved swiftly to douse the fire.

The cell door was opened carefully, with bayonets leading the procession of men who entered. "Prisoner 2657," Plowman called out, his voice deep and commanding. His answer was a shrill barrage of accusations, as women swore at him and cursed his name. The female convicts came towards the door, churning in a hurricane of complete fury, ready to bar the way and save the life of one of their own.

"Mrs. Plowman, you are to attend your husband when he calls you," Simon proclaimed boldly, silencing the crowd.

"I have no husband," she cried out.

"Mrs. Plowman, come when I call you," he repeated, but it was an irate spouse who made the demand.

"Don't go," Varena said, taking hold of Mary Claire's arm.

"I have no choice," Mary Claire said. "Present, sir."

"Come out, Mrs. Plowman, I would like your company this evening," he said.

A convict's life was simple. She did as she was told to do, she went where she was told to go, and once again she followed an order to get out of her cot and drag her weary body to the side of her master. He placed her hand on his arm, as if they were going to take a walk around the park, and Simon led her up the steps and out of the rank air.

"You tell them but not me?" he asked.

"Night after night, Simon," she said. "Night after night, and God forgive me but I'm guilty, as guilty as you."

Captain Morse stared at Mary Claire, her head hung like a beaten dog, while Simon stood proudly at her side, a joyful smile tickling the corners of his mouth. "At your discretion, sir, such were your orders," Morse began, his tone both puzzled and upset. "Impregnating a girl is hardly discreet, is it? A dozen professional prostitutes, and you single out the one girl who was to be under your protection. I understand your antipathy, Lieutenant, I honestly do, and I do not fault you for seeking revenge. If we were not on a ship in the middle of nowhere, surrounded by the most dangerous criminals in all of Christendom, I would commend you, Mr. Plowman. I would give you a medal, praise you to Her Majesty and petition for a knighthood. Considering our situation, however, could you not have maneuvered her into position without giving her a baby?"

"From the start, sir, my intentions toward her have been honorable," Simon responded.

"Honorable? You put a baby in her belly and that is honorable?"

"Marriage was my goal from the first steps down Portland Hill, sir," Plowman explained. "On my word of honor, Captain."

"Have you lost your mind?"

"Only my heart, sir."

Morse groaned at the smarmy sentiment that was expressed, too concerned with a potential rebellion to appreciate the poetry of the moment. "Prisoner 2657, if I were your father, I would cast you off," Morse intoned with a patriarch's disappointment. "Are you ashamed to be enceinte and unmarried?"

Mary Claire thought for a moment, sorting through countless emotions that ran from love to hate. In Rathkeale, she certainly would have been ashamed, but on the *Hellebore* she was as nothing. In a world of prostitutes and thieves, the morality of her former life did not exist, replaced instead by the morality of animal survival. There was no correct answer to give to the captain.

With a sigh of exasperation, Captain Morse opened his logbook, turning back the pages until he reached the early days of the journey. A sheet of paper was placed over all but the bottom lines of the ledger. "Sign here," he said as he turned the book towards her, gesturing toward the inkwell and pen.

"What am I signing, sir?" she asked.

"Sign it," Simon cajoled. "Go on, nothing bad will come of it, I swear to you."

She made a move to shift the paper, but Captain Morse immediately slapped his hand onto the log. Turning to Plowman, he spoke as if Mary Claire were not present. "Do you believe that Dr. Smith, who is no friend to you, and I assure you he is no friend to the prisoner, do you really think he would witness such a fabrication?"

"The Irish Catholics who are stirring up the most trouble would not recognize an Anglican service as valid, and I have little doubt that Father McCabe would go along with the deception to protect the prisoner's honor," Plowman explained. "Indeed, he would be willing to state that we were married at birth to protect her honor."

"No, I'll not marry him," she blurted out, at last comprehending the meaning of the charade. "Allow me the use of your name in Australia, sir, that's all I'll ask of you."

"Prisoner, this is not a matter of choice. It is apparent that Lt. Plowman is in earnest and he intends to marry you, which is highly commendable on his part. You are most fortunate, though not deserving of any such windfall."

"I don't wish to marry him, sir," she said again.

"Have I ever lied to you?" Simon countered. "Have I expressed to you, from the very beginning, that my affection for you, my adoration, my love, are sincere? Can you deny that I love you?"

"I, I don't know, sir," she said.

"Did you mislead me when you spoke of your love for me?" he quizzed. "Can you deny that you have expressed your love to me on more occasions than I can count? In Irish as well as English?"

"No, sir," she said. He had manipulated her into a corner and trapped her, and Mary Claire knew that it was impossible to escape.

"Then you must marry me."

"'Tis a poor match, sir. You can find someone more suitable than a destitute orphan with no income or family," she said, hoping to sway the captain to her side. "Better than a criminal, sir."

"It's impossible, Miss O'Dwyer," Plowman said. "You vowed that you would love only me for the rest of your days."

"There, you see, you have given Lt. Plowman every indication that you were amenable to matrimony. You led him down the garden path, my dear. Now, sign the log and let's put an end to the rumors. Baseless, this talk of bastards and rape."

"Will you be baptized into the true church, sir?" she asked, hoping to improve an unavoidable fate.

"Are there to be conditions?" Morse thundered. "He is giving your child a name, young woman, and he is saving you from shame. I should think that was more than enough, and you are getting married whether you like it or not. You should have thought about religion before you hopped into his bed."

"Attempt to convert me for the rest of my days," Simon said.

"Are you satisfied now, Prisoner 2657?" Morse demanded.

"Yes, sir."

While they waited for Father McCabe, Simon pulled the green ribbon from his jacket pocket and tied it in Mary Claire's braid, draping the loose ends over her shoulders as if he were adjusting a veil. "I wanted to marry you in Fremantle, in a proper wedding gown. For that omission, I shall be forever sorry," he whispered.

"Why? Why must you do this to me? Will you set me free in exchange for my brothers' lives?"

"I'll never set you free. Now, sign the log, and it will be the last time that you will be Mary Claire O'Dwyer."

Simon conferred with Father McCabe while Mary Claire looked on, straining to hear the conversation but failing to learn anything more than what she already knew. The priest knew his catechism and he knew canon law, but he had a touch of the Jesuit that made him a very practical man, and Mary Claire never expected McCabe to turn away an opportunity to salvage her good name. Defeated, she mumbled through the service, her eyes as dry as sand.

"Congratulations, Mrs. Plowman," Captain Morse said, bidding farewell to a crisis. "You are now a member of a prominent family, and I expect that you will be a credit to your husband. Do not ever forget the vows that you made tonight, to honor and obey. Always obey him. You owe him that much at least for what he has done for you."

"Yes, sir."

"As for your wedding night, that is in the past, do you understand? You were married on the twentieth of October, and it has been kept secret because I ordered it so. Lay the blame on me; it is the most foolproof means to achieve this end. You will return to your cell and spread that story, is this clear? However you came to be with child, however you managed to be alone with him, continue as before and no one will be the wiser. I have given you the courtesy of addressing you by your name, but that will be the last time it is spoken on this ship. You are still a convict, and you will be accorded all the rights and privileges of a convict."

With one tug, she removed the green ribbon and returned it to her groom, agreeing to the deal with little more than a whisper of assent. She turned and went back to jail, escorted by Father McCabe.

Morse sat behind his desk, staring through Simon. There had to be no doubt that this was a genuine marriage, a lifetime commitment, and not part of a military campaign. It was critical that the captain understand that Mary Claire had not twined the Marine around her maypole. The only way to achieve those aims was to confess a little more of his mission. to take Morse further into his confidence. "I have no doubt that my strategy to monitor the Fenian prisoners in Fremantle will proceed smoothly, sir,"

Plowman assured the captain. "And at the conclusion of this mission, I shall have a lifetime of wedded bliss waiting for me."

"Either a lifetime of wedded bliss, Mr. Plowman, or a lifetime of looking over your shoulder, waiting for an Irishman to plunge a knife in your back."

"I am fully confident of the former, sir," Simon said. "Not only will my mission in Fremantle be fulfilled, but my life's goals can be realized. She will give me an army of sons, Captain Morse, and every one of them will enter Sandhurst and become the finest soldiers that England can create."

"The poor girl," Morse mumbled under his breath. Recovering his bearings, the captain smiled. "Congratulations are in order, sir. Your destruction of the O'Dwyer clan and their gang of armed marauders is now complete. I hope that you find revenge to be as sweet as it is rumored to be."

"Even now, I am savoring it." Simon grinned wickedly. "They are scattered and toothless, dead and buried, or bound for exile in the dry arse of the earth. Their vow to free their colleagues from the Establishment will be as futile as their vow to free their sister. Very soon, Mr. Morse, we shall witness the end of the Irish problem."

Like a good girl, Mary Claire obeyed orders and told her disbelieving cellmates that she was married all along to the lieutenant who delighted in her tears. As expected, Captain Morse came under blistering attack for hiding the fact, just so that he could be sure that Mary Claire received a convict's treatment at the hands of her unsuspecting jailers. No special favors, no concessions were to be granted, or so the female prisoners assumed. Before she could say more, Moira assured her that she would always be one of them, even if she was unable to join in their new enterprise. It was in her soul, the madam noted, and Mary Claire feared that it was indeed.

Ten

Christmas arrived, unnoticed by the inmates. They were roused from sleep by Mr. Scofield, full of holiday cheer when he informed them that it was a day of leisure, with a double ration of wine to toast a day that was not at all merry for those on the prison deck. The women asked Mary Claire to sing for them, and she treated her fellow prisoners to the joyful tunes she had once sung in Rathkeale. She could not help but recall days past, with a feast of roast goose and chestnuts, oranges and walnuts, coupled with the warmth of a peat fire. By the time that the women were mustered on deck for religious services, no one was feeling festive or happy. They ate breakfast in silence, morose and glum, the chocolate cold because it was served at eight and the Catholics could not eat before taking Communion.

Their holiday dinner at one o'clock brought more sadness with Captain Morse's reminders of home. As a magnanimous gesture, he had ordered spotted dick and orange-flavored sweetloaf be served with the usual salt pork and potatoes, but the rich pudding and delicate cake brought on tears of nostalgia. A few of the women had never eaten anything so grand, and they sobbed to think that they had to be in prison to receive a decent meal. At two, when they toasted to Christmas and drank their extra serving of wine, all eighteen women were feeling queasy with a heavy meal and heavy thoughts to plague them.

In the afternoon, Mary Claire joined her husband on deck, to hear his many plans and promises. "The minute we arrive in Fremantle, I shall have to contact my banker. When I think of the funds that I will need to equip a vain wife and a child to boot," he said. With silly gravity, he adjusted the blanket that she used as a shawl. "It's positively mind-boggling. What else can I do? I've snared a beauty in my trap and I have to show off my prowess."

"And won't I be the envy of all?" she spoke with merriment like a dutiful wife. "Promenading around town on the arm of a handsome man with a lovely round bottom, so grand in his scarlet coat and tall black shako. Tickling me with his moustache."

"You are a very wicked woman, Mrs. Plowman, to admire my rump. And those were secret kisses that tickled you down there last night."

On Christmas night, she asked him about his mother and his sister, but Simon was alarmed by the nature of her questions. She was overly concerned about Anna's interest in children, and if an unmarried spinster would be able to raise a child in the event that Simon's mother was too old to manage.

"All this gloom and doom, Mary Claire, you will stop it at once," he said. "Whatever else you may think of me, I am not so callous as to take a child from its mother."

"No, Simon, it's not gloom, not at all. I must be practical, if I'm to look after myself. I'm happy, filled to bursting. The tinkers, they told me, and it's so."

"Am I your tinker's prediction?"

"You are indeed. When I was a girl, sure, I never wandered more than ten miles from Rathkeale town. How could I ever imagine my husband would be a grand jackeen like you? I know you took me for revenge against my brothers, but I'll not hold it against you."

"You see through me at last," he said. "I regret that I have grown so transparent."

"But I'll not let you win," she continued. "I'll spoil your fun by being a perfect wife. Dress me in rags, lock me in your house, and never a cruel or unkind word will I speak."

"Well then, there is no point in ill treatment, I see. You would enlist every wife, mother and daughter in Dublin to your cause and I would look the fool. I could banish you to the countryside, miles from Dublin, where the ladies would never hear of you."

"You could banish me to Rathkeale."

"One day, I will build you a house in Rathkeale and buy you a herd of dairy cows so that you can bring me fresh milk every morning for my tea."

He closed his eyes, but she had more questions for him, questions about Fremantle and what she was expected to do every day. Simon was at a loss, given the fact that he had no idea what ladies did with their time, and his wife was one of those ladies. Struggling to recall his mother's activities, he suggested that she pay social calls among other members of Fremantle's polite society, or have friends around for tea. With a baby on the way, he envisioned hours of needlework, to produce a series of garments in ever larger sizes that kept pace with a growing child.

"I'll be a credit to your name, so," she boasted. "Is there a Catholic church in Fremantle?"

"Of course, there are Papists all over Australia," he said. "There is a priest, undoubtedly Irish, serving his Irish congregation. The convicts who are too sickly to work in the quarries or road crews are brought to Sunday services there. I hope that you will volunteer your lovely voice to the parish."

"Where am I to live?"

"In a house, living an ordinary life. That's preferable to a hotel room, more space and more privacy."

"You're just afraid that I'll meet a handsome stranger in a hotel and run off," she giggled.

"Naughty girl," he tickled her. "You must be in by nine at night, or the constable will haul you in for breaking curfew. If I get word that my wife is out until all hours, Mrs. Plowman, you shall be severely reprimanded."

"Perhaps the crime will be more pleasant than the punishment is harsh," she retorted.

"Then there will be no more of this if you misbehave," and he kissed her greedily.

Later, she woke him, asking about his father. His response was a groan and an annoyed grumble about waking at eight bells. She persisted, insisting on knowing his father's history.

"Dragoon, Fourth Irish, went to India after Balaklava, think he was still there when last he wrote. Please, let me sleep."

"Do you love your father?"

He was too tired to explain the whole story, and he was not sure that he could explain in words. Until Mary Claire entered his life, Simon had not truly appreciated how much he had learned from his father's life, and how much they were alike. "Yes, Mary Claire, I love my father," he said. "Thank you for asking. Sing to me again, I need to hear your voice."

Ever so softly, she sang to him as she had on many other nights, "Mavourneen, mavourneen, my sad tears are falling, to think that from

Erin and thee I must part. It may be for years, and it may be forever. Oh, why art thou silent, thou voice of my heart."

On the fourteenth of January, at three-forty in the morning, Lt. Plowman woke up out of habit when he felt the ship stop moving forward, all sails aback as the *Hellebore* came to a halt in the water. For the last time, he would have to wake her and send her away, back to the cell and the coarse deal board cot. The next evening could not come soon enough, when they would lie together as husband and wife, from dusk to dawn and before tea if the urge should strike.

"We've made port, love, wake up," he shook her gently.

Her reaction was one of slight panic, with a gasp of fear accompanying a desperate sort of embrace. He held her against his chest and felt her heart pounding.

"Must I leave you?" she whimpered.

"Not just yet, I can wait until they call for me. Let me tell you what to expect so that you are prepared and you won't be startled by what is to come. We will wait here for the port authorities to come out and examine Dr. Smith's bills of health, formalities that you won't see. After that, we will go into the harbor. The women are first on and first off, so you will have to wait on the quay for me. I'll be along as soon as I can."

"I can't do it, Simon, I know I promised to be brave, but I can't," she cried.

"Where's Miss Eireann go Bragh, the defiant Irish spirit?"

"I want to go home so badly, I can't bear it." Her tears began to flow, hopeless and longing for what could not be.

"We are home, do you see? You are an officer's wife, remember? Australia now, probably India or the Cape Colony on my next tour of duty. We'll see exotic lands and have great adventures while we travel from station to station."

"Promise that you'll take me back to Ireland, swear to me, and I'll be brave, so."

"When this child is ready for school, how would that be? Be a good girl, do everything that I tell you to do, and we'll settle in Dublin so our children receive the best education to be had."

"And when I die, bury me in Galway, Simon, in Athenry Parish with your mother's people. You won't leave me alone in Fremantle forever, will you?"

"I'm coming back, little Eireann go Bragh, I will never leave you. Let me brush your hair, and I'll make you as pretty as I can with your lovely green ribbon. By tonight, you will have forgotten all about this morning. You'll have a bath, to soak in the tub all day long if you want, and you'll have a new dress and be fitted for your Sunday best. We'll have our honeymoon trip and I'll buy you everything that you want."

"Buy me a thousand pairs of under drawers," she said. "I'm going to change them five times a day if I like."

"That's the girl I married," he said as he ran the brush through her curls. "Vain as Narcissus, vanity walking on high heels and riding in a jaunting car."

"When will you leave to go back to England?"

"Ten days, or twelve if I am very lucky and the shipyard is too busy to re-copper the hull right away. But remember, the sooner I go, the sooner I return."

For the last time, Mary Claire sat on the boards of a rough bunk in a dark hold. She folded the blanket, adhering to a rule that seemed pointless with the ship in port. Like a lady preparing for a weekend in the country, she checked the contents of her convict's duffel bag again, verifying that she still had the same prison issued clothing that she had been given in Portland. Then she sat, waiting nervously for a first glimpse of a harsh land.

When the hatches were opened, the women rose in unison and emitted a collective gasp of fright. Mr. Hightower appeared, strolling through the cell door with his revolver drawn, but the show of firepower was almost laughable to the weakened and submissive group.

"Prisoners, fall in," he ordered, obviously bored by the repetition. He observed carefully as they lined up in two rows, nine on each side. When the columns were as neat as women were likely to make them, he nodded to the pensioner guards.

Enfield rifles were raised, fingers as usual ready to pull triggers, and Hightower told his prisoners to forward march, smartly now. The shuffled, but then he could not honestly expect women to know how to march smartly, and they went up the ladder two at a time. When the first couple reached the top, they stumbled and forward progress ground to a complete halt. After months in a hold that was nearly pitch black, they were blinded by a sun that was impossibly bright.

Guards on deck jabbed at the women with carbines and firm hands, forcing the lines to keep moving, but it was the same blind stagger and rough shoving for every pair that tumbled out of the hatch. Mary Claire attempted to find Simon, but she could not see at all, squinting against the glare and unable to focus on anything. Her vision was a painful blur of the shining buttons and vibrant uniforms of the guards who lined the deck.

The women were kept forward while the men were released, everyone doing the same blinking and bobbing in reaction to the light. Shading her eyes with her hand, narrowing her eyes to slits to block out the intensity, Mary Claire peered over the rail and searched the land for green, but all she saw was flat and desolate gray, a colorless land. It was nine in the morning, but it was hot, arid and blistering as a furnace.

The ship began to move again, guided by a local pilot into the narrow channel of the Swan River. With her eyes held to the shore, Mary Claire began to wobble with dread. The closer they came to the port, the more colorless was the place, with sand and colorless buildings made of colorless stone, with dingy mountains far off in the distance. She had lived in hell for the past three months, only to arrive in a worse hell at the end of the trip.

Several local officials turned up on a steamer after the *Hellebore* dropped her anchor in the estuary. Two very distinguished and excessively pompous gentlemen came aboard, indicating a keen level of interest in the political prisoners. The taller man was grey-haired, his hands soft and scrubbed white, while the shorter official was as colorless as the town but for the dingy rust color of his beard. While the prisoners stood under a burning sun, the two conferred with Captain Morse and lazily scanned the crowd. For a long second, they looked over Mary Claire as if she were some prize heifer at the county fair. Embarrassed, she turned her head aside and closed her eyes against the glare that radiated from the water.

Barges crammed full of white-coated guards pulled up to the transport ship as Simon departed with the Fremantle officials. Gangplanks were shot up to the deck and just as quickly the guards formed an array, taking positions along the walkways, to menace the convicts with overwhelming firepower at close range. Sparkles and flashes sailed everywhere that Mary Claire looked, bouncing lights that flew from bayonets, water, buttons and polished boots. The *Hellebore* had been black misery; Australia's torments blazed.

Warder Hightower was calling out numbers and Mary Claire watched as her cell mates hastened down to the deck of a nearby barge, two by two, and suddenly it was her turn. Within minutes, she was standing on another deck, holding Varena's hand, both women shaking and on the verge of hysterical tears. As Mary Claire's eyes began to adjust to the light, the town before her grew increasingly clear, the stuff of nightmares outlined against a blank white-blue sky. The buff stone walls of Fremantle Gaol loomed up in front of her, perched on a hill in the middle of town.

The lighter waited for some mysterious signal to go, and Mary Claire took note of the crowd that was gathered on the quay. This was going to be the highlight of the winter for Fremantle's residents, because this last transport ship carried an infamous cargo, and everyone came out to see the sights, to gape at the circus sideshow.

With a lurch, the landing craft took off, only to bang into the stones of the convict-built jetty when it reached the final destination. The women stumbled to find their balance, but the guards were going after them again with rifles, bayonets and strong hands, goading the ladies into a single file line that was nudged off the barge and onto the dock. Every other barge was the same scene of haste, shouts and cursing. The single line on the quay grew longer and longer, until it stretched to the length of nearly three hundred people, with the women pushed ever closer to the town.

The residents of Fremantle were congregated largely near the head of the line, where the women were once again first. Some of the men in the crowd looked familiar, and Mary Claire recognized a few of the pensioner guards who had served on the *Hellebore*. They were huddled with their children, holding satchels and bundles with an air of expectation that seemed out of place. The ladies were ordered to right turn, and they faced the town, their backs to the water, while mounted policemen glared at with them with the threat of death if they moved a muscle. Dr. Smith passed in review with another man, probably the doctor who had examined the bills of health, discussing the robust good vigor of the prisoners with the amity of Rathkeale's leading cattle dealer. Fremantle's physician declared everyone fit, and the carnival swung into motion.

Mr. Ferrier stepped forward when Mr. Hightower called his name, bringing all eyes to the small table where the Assistant Warder conferred with a clerk who was outfitted with an open ledger, a pen and a bottle of ink. Ferrier perused the line of females very slowly, his three children following on his heels and exploring the ladies with equal intensity. Up and down, he examined Hettie, and then studied Mary Claire before moving back to size up Cornelia, while the youngest Ferrier stood in front of Varena, hopping up and down.

"This one, Papa, please, Papa, this one," the little blond haired boy pleaded.

"I'll take her," he made his selection, taking Varena's arm and tugging. "You remind the boy of his mum when she was sick."

"Prisoners to remain silent," the horse guard shouted when the women began to wail with renewed terror.

Heads began to swing wildly, seventeen women looking from side to side as mortal fear took hold of their thoughts. Going into domestic service had been their expectation, but this was not an interview with the lady of the house. Every woman now realized that her sentence was not to service, but to slavery.

Hightower's voice was booming in its official timbre. "Prisoner 2564. Varena Richardson. Servant to Pensioner Guard Willard Ferrier. Who is next, Mr. Chandler?"

No time was given for a final farewell, a wish of good luck or one last embrace. They watched as Varena was led away by her master, who was engrossed in telling his new housekeeper that he wanted dinner served by six every night, the children in bed by nine, and his shoes shined every morning.

"Indeed?" Varena was heard to scoff, a suppressed laugh in her inflection.

"I like her looks," Ted Carling grinned at Mary Claire, putting a hand on her arm. "2657, Mr. Hightower, and point me in the direction of the nearest church."

"I'm married," Mary Claire stammered, pulling away and searching frantically for her husband. All she could see were guards and guns, pointed at her head and ready to fire if she did not cooperate.

"Ship's officers were given first choice, Mr. Carling," Mr. Hightower said. With a friendly smile, he showed the ledger entry to the eager groom. "Picked her up almost before we left Portland, but we can see why he acted so quickly."

"Damn the luck," Ted winked at his lost love. Turning to Cornelia, he made his offer. "I'd break my back to make you happy."

Cornelia glared at the middle-aged fool who had never been married before. "I'll break my back to make your life hell," she mumbled through a seductive smile.

"Prisoner 2568. Cornelia Mears," Hightower called out. "Servant to Prison Guard Theodore Carling."

By and large, the sad-looking cargo went off with their employers, following meekly behind the Fremantle matrons who had come to the dock to select the less dangerous criminals for housemaids. Only the older women like Mary Jennings or Sarah Thorpe, along with the most haggard specimens from the streets of London, were left over at the end and made available to the different factories or local concerns in need of manual labor. There was a high demand for convict labor in Western Australia because so few people wanted to settle there. The dregs of England's prisons were welcome in Fremantle, to work day in and day out for no wages, with no hope of advancement or promotion. For seven years, or fourteen, or the rest of their lives, the women would toil for someone else's benefit, so that the British Empire could continue to expand around the globe.

"Prisoner 2569," came the call for Moira Perkins. "Geraldton Wool Factory."

"Look after the girls, Mary Claire," Moira called out as the factory foreman shoved her towards a waiting cart.

"Your husband will be along, Mrs. Plowman," Mr. Hightower said after the last of the female convicts were gone. "I expect to see you again very soon, under far more pleasant conditions. Until then, please excuse me, but I must attend to my duties."

Floating in a surreal world, Mary Claire felt hopelessly confused when she was left alone. Dazed, she stared at the strange looking buildings of the town, the style typical of British colonies but utterly unlike Rathkeale's cozy cottages.

"Mrs. Plowman, may we welcome you to Fremantle," came a voice over her shoulder, and Mary Claire jumped in surprise. Dr. Smith and the rust-colored gentleman were standing at her side. "Your husband is quite busy at the moment, and so I took it upon myself to make introductions. May I present Mr. Henry Wakeford, Comptroller General of Fremantle Gaol."

Like a mechanical contraption, Mary Claire lifted her arm and offered a hand to the rusty man. "I'm honored, sir," she said, afraid of doing or saying the wrong thing, and ready to drop to her knees and sob from nerves.

"Lt. Plowman has been given your papers, and when you have settled in, I hope that my wife and I may call on you," Wakeford said.

"Yes, please do," she said.

"Your husband has misled me, Mrs. Plowman," he said. Her lip quivered, and the gentleman quickly continued. "He told me that you were the prettiest creature to be seen, but like most husbands he gave a false impression. To say that you are pretty does not begin to approach your true beauty. Our quiet little town is greatly enriched by your presence."

She mumbled a thank you with downcast eyes and a deep blush, alarmed by Wakeford's rather forward approach. He dipped through a graceful little bow and took his leave, smiling like a hungry lion, licking his chops. Mary Claire stared after them, meeting four eyes as they looked over their shoulders at her, chuckling and shaking their heads in amazement or amusement.

"Are you fond of horses, miss?" the mounted guard asked. It was apparent that he was there to watch her, as if she had anywhere to run to if she had a notion to run. With a smile, she reached out to touch the snout of the gelding, glad of the chance to put her fingers on something that was familiar. "There's a livery stable in town that could fix you up with a gentle mare when you had a mind to go riding. Don't go off on your own, if you do head out. The bush is no place for a lady, not much of a place for a man, either, with the snakes. Mr. Wakeford rides nearly every day, he knows the roads if you were looking for a companion to show you around."

The uniformed guard, his white coat saturated with sweat, looked down at her rather closely, and Mary Claire had the peculiar sensation that he was there to explain the ropes in a most subtle fashion. With a polite touch of his hat he trotted away, towards the end of the column that was about to be paraded through the dusty town, to be fed into the gaping mouth of The Establishment, to be devoured by hard labor.

Eleven

A scorching sun had heated the air to a temperature exceeding one hundred degrees, a climate so unlike Ireland that Mary Claire felt woozy. There had been no time for breakfast on the ship, and now that it was approaching the dinner hour she was still without so much as a drop of water. Sweat soaked every stitch of clothing that she wore, making her wool dress even more uncomfortable and heavy. Dripping, she began to sink as if she were melting.

"Good girl, just where I asked you to be," Simon said, trotting down the jetty. "I've spoken to the proprietor of the hotel where we'll be staying."

Like any other polite husband, Simon offered his arm. Coercing her legs to move, Mary Claire began to walk, stepping along Water Street, wading through grit up to her ankles and looking at the cloud of dust that lifted off the feet of the condemned on their way to the gaol. "He's already asking after a house for us," Simon continued to jabber excitedly. "A cottage, Mrs. Plowman, to set up housekeeping, room for three."

Every building was glowing white, and Mary Claire was walking on the moon, with the glow reflected off the limestone walls and scorching the top of her head. Her gaze went up to the ominous stones of the gaol, like white teeth they appeared as the heat radiated into ripples across her eyes. "It's so hot, Simon," she murmured, and he caught her as she fell to the sandy street.

Inside the lobby of the Emerald Isle Hotel, it was much darker and cooler than outdoors, but the oven-like quality remained. Mary Claire woke up with her head spinning.

"Here, ma'am, sip a little water," the housemaid coaxed. Like a mother hen, the girl was hovering and exuding concern with her kindness. "The boy is bringing the hot water to your room right now, and you'll feel better once you soak in a warm bath."

"Can you walk, darling?" Simon asked. "Let me carry you up."

"I'm better, I feel, so much sun," she stuttered, still confused by such a curious place.

"Let's go up so you can rest. While you bathe, your faithful servant is going to find the nearest dry goods emporium and buy you a complete set of store clothes. I cannot wait to burn these rags."

She had never before seen the like, a room with a bed and two upholstered chairs, connected to a separate room that held a bathtub fixed permanently to the floor. The water in the tub was the perfect temperature, clear and clean, more like a dream than believable reality. "You look grand in your uniform," she mentioned while he peeled off her dingy and sweaty chemise.

"You, Mrs. Plowman, look grand in your skin," he replied.

He helped her into the tub and then he held her hand as she bawled, breaking down because she had not been immersed in a tub of water for over a year. Patiently, he waited until she sniffed and smiled again, and he could explain a few more things. He told her about her ticket-of-leave that allowed her to travel all over Australia, with the Tualap work camp becoming her destination every Wednesday. She was to assist Father Concannon, the bush priest, and if that meant reading from Scripture to the convicts, singing at Mass, or standing around, she was to be there.

As he expected, her main concern was that she be allowed to see her friends, to socialize with other women. Trying to find a way to describe the relative freedom of the female prisoners, he compared them to hired housekeepers, a suggestion that had both of them laughing. Mary Claire knew as well as he that every man would be in his housekeeper's bed that evening, making the women more like housewives than hired servants, with the same liberties as any other wife.

Mary Claire's social contacts, both free and felon, were limited by regulations older than Her Majesty's Prison Service. Whether employed to mind a pensioner guard's children or married to a warder, the women would move within their female sphere, chatting and gossiping over a bolt of linen at the draper's or exchanging recipes at the grocer's. All women were only as independent as the head of the household permitted, relatively free to roam around Fremantle as they went on about their business, no different than the wives in every other town in the world.

Taking a sponge, he plopped it on her head and squeezed a great gob of water onto her hair, eliciting a squeal of animal pleasure. She wanted to pretend to be just a housewife, but there was no need to play-act. In Fremantle, Mary Claire was nothing more than another married woman, one whose duties to her husband were yet to be fully detailed. Before he went off in search of ladies' drawers, he had to speak to her, to begin to set up his operations in Western Australia.

While she stroked warm water along her arm, he reminded her of the letter that Captain Morse had forgotten about until Simon asked for his wife's possessions. Her smile faded slowly, until he assured her that he would not read it, nor ask her to reveal its contents. The words on the paper would be meaningless, and Simon understood that. What mattered were the spaces, the hidden codes and the thoughts left unfinished, a covert communication between brother and sister. He knew what was written, with intimations of past conversations and the obscure words of a soothsayer's prediction, never forgotten by the young girl who believed that the tinkers were closer to God. Simon had read the letter before the ink was dry.

Stopping first at the local bank, Simon spoke at length with Mr. Cox, starting out with a conference about Mrs. Plowman's financial needs and ending with a confidential mention of Mrs. Plowman's complete dedication to her husband's cause, the destruction of Fenianism in Australia. In case anyone did not know, Simon reminded them that he was the only son and heir of a baronet, minor aristocracy but a glittering star in a remote corner of the world. Every respectable woman within miles would want the future Lady Plowman in her social circle. At the haberdashery, he said only enough to intrigue the shopkeeper's wife while learning that he was being lauded among the prison officials as a brilliant strategist, using every means necessary to keep the traitorous Fenians in prison.

Within an hour, Simon bounded into the hotel room, a large bundle under his arms, but he stopped short when he found his wife standing motionless in the middle of the floor, the letter in her hand. "Simon, *mo stor*," she said in a whisper.

Her love was given with a carefree abandon, an ardor more heated than Simon had seen in her before. As if she had washed away all doubt in a bath, she was a normal woman on her honeymoon, wildly in love with her groom. The horrors of the past were scoured away and she raced towards the future, at last understanding that they were inextricably bound together. She had surrendered to him, and no matter what he asked of her now, she would accomplish every task and perform every duty with untiring devotion. She had survived the worst prisons and come out whole, recast in a new mold, and she would carry out his orders without fail.

"I forgot to take my boots off," he apologized as he rolled over in bed. "I've soiled your bed linens, Mrs. Plowman."

"The dust of Fremantle," she grumbled angrily. "It's everywhere. I hate this place, I hate it."

"You'll feel differently when you have your own house to fuss over. The honeymoon trip is nearly over, and very soon you will be so busy coddling me that you won't even know where you are, you will be so exhausted with meeting my demands," he said.

"Is your wife to walk about so, Mr. Plowman?" she indicated a state of complete undress.

He stroked her belly, the firm mound adding a gentle curve to her figure. "Mr. Wakeford would doubtless find favor with this type of uniform," he chuckled. "Open up your gifts and see what I found for you."

It was a veritable avalanche of fabric, with a lace-trimmed chemise and three petticoats, some very frilly under drawers and a stiff corset made of a beautiful white cotton fabric. White cotton stockings, the material of choice for a Fremantle winter, complimented a pair of black shoes with French heels. Mary Claire laid everything out on the bed and stood back to admire and touch. She seemed disappointed that he did not bring crinoline hoops, and his attempt to explain the latest fashion of crinolinettes left her completely confused. It was a relief to report that the merchant's wife was on her way with the latest edition of *Godey's Ladies Book* and an eye for size.

"Does the corset fit?" he asked.

"Lace it tighter, Simon," she said, putting her hands around her waist to measure the correct degree of compression.

"Don't lace up the baby, you vain Irish lass," he chided. "I can permit the proper curves for the sake of fashion, but don't squeeze my child. You are going to be a mother, don't forget."

He gently turned her around to face him, so that he could look in her eye and make it clear that it was time to get down to business. If not for the woman coming with a delivery of clothes, he would have let Mary Claire relish the moment a little longer, but there was not a minute to lose. Panic and confusion cast shadows in her face. He had to detail her mission slowly so that his words were absorbed, but with every sentence that he uttered, he saw her fear grow, numbing her into silence. Silence would be her ally if she could not think of anything safe to say.

Mrs. Finch had offered to bring some items for Mrs. Plowman's inspection, although Simon could easily determine that Mrs. Finch only wished to inspect Mrs. Plowman. The most famous female convict to land on Victoria Quay was the topic of stories that had been spread all over town, via the large Irish population and several articles in the *Fremantle Herald*. The Martyr of Rathkeale had arrived, walking into town on the arm of the British Marine who had run down her brothers, and the shops were buzzing with the shocking news.

"Mary Claire O'Dwyer," Mrs. Finch whispered in shock.

Simon was not prepared for an outsider's view of his wife. For the first time, he noticed that Mary Claire was sickly-looking, due largely to morning sickness but exaggerated now by the rigors of disembarking. Her complexion was an ashen shade of grey, while her hazel eyes had taken on a haunted look. "I believe I asked you to fit Mrs. Plowman," Simon growled a warning.

A forced smile sprang up on the shopkeeper's face, and she pulled herself together at once. "Shall we begin with this one, madam?" and an outfit was lifted from the assistant's hands. "Are you fond of green?"

"She prefers green, Mrs. Finch," Simon answered for his wife. "I selected some yellow fabric for her Sunday attire; will you get that to a good seamstress? For now, she urgently needs something to cover her body. We have not eaten all day, and my wife's condition is very delicate."

With panache, the doyenne of fashion took a bizarre looking metal cage contraption that seemed to be making up the back half of a stiff petticoat. It was the newest rage, the crinolinette with a bustled rear, and Mrs. Finch tied it around Mary Claire's waist while Mary Claire gawked in awe at the fashion plates in full and beautiful color. Somewhat dramatically, to demonstrate the stylish volume of fabric, the merchant tangled with the yardage and lifted a skirt over Mary Claire's head, adjusting the waistband to accommodate an early pregnancy. The ruffles and flourishes were painstakingly laid across the bustle, the front was fluffed until it puffed over the stiff crinoline, and then the jacket was put into place.

The expert hand of a lady's haberdasher pulled tenderly at the excess fabric of the jacket. Mrs. Finch stood back and examined the fit, a tug here and a smoothing there, and at last she was satisfied with the Kelly green linen tricked out with lace and dark green ribbons.

"Stand in front of that mirror, Mrs. Plowman, and see what you think," Mrs. Finch suggested.

"No," Simon barked abruptly. "I will determine the suitability. Come here, darling, and let me inspect you."

While Mrs. Finch's convict employee held up various everyday outfits, Simon looked them over to choose a few things that he liked, with nothing white, even though that was the most popular color for ladies' summer wear in Fremantle. As the fashion show went on, Mrs. Finch offered to pin up Mary Claire's hair in a simple but becoming style, explaining to the husband about curling irons and cascades of ringlets. She spoke to Lt. Plowman, over and around Mary Claire as if the giddy bride were deaf and dumb, or possibly muzzled.

Mrs. Finch gushed over the Grecian Bend that was so popular. She carried on about the impossibility of hoops, which had mercifully faded quickly out of fashion, while the natural form of the female figure came to the fore of the fashion world. The amicable host, Simon nodded and put in his opinion occasionally before finally thanking Mrs. Finch for her kind, personal attention to his wife.

"This hat matches the green frock to perfection," she continued to babble, an awkward monologue.

"We will take the pink pelisse and that dark green linen skirt with the tunic, the lacy one that I liked," Simon decreed. "I have deposited funds with your husband to cover the cost, Mrs. Finch, you may go now. Thank you."

The way in which Mary Claire touched her new clothes proved that she could not fully comprehend that her nightmare was coming to an end. She studied the pattern of the lace cuff of her sleeve very carefully, as if she had seen something like this so long ago that she had to analyze the pattern to recollect some ancient era. He was bestowing gifts upon her, like a doting husband with a comfortable annual income, like a man who was flaunting his prized possession.

"Put on your hat, Mrs. Plowman, before your husband dies of starvation. You must be all in, darling, let's go down to dinner."

"Do I look pretty again, Simon?" she asked as he tied the flowing dark green ribbons that matched her jacket.

"My dear, you are so beautiful that my eyes ache to look at you. On stage, Mrs. Plowman. Rehearsals are over, and it is time for your opening night."

The couple was seated near the window of the dining room, on display behind glass for all of Fremantle to see. Mary Claire gracefully unfolded her napkin and spread it across her lap, admiring the cleanliness of her hands as she looked them over, back and front and back again. She began to touch everything. Fork, knife, spoon, cup, glass, each object was fingered to verify its reality. She sipped the water, a full glass that would be refilled as often as she wanted, and she looked out of the window to the hurly-burly of Water Street.

"A man can't escape unless he steals some civilian clothes," Simon noted. They watched a gang of old prisoners walk past, each one attired in the distinctive garb of the convict, a gray linen shirt flecked with arrows and gray linen trousers striped in red. The pants buttoned along the outside seam, so that a man could remove his trousers while bound in leg irons. "Once that is done, he next finds that there is no place to run to. The sharks are the most effective water police force on earth."

"He would have to fly," Mary Claire said.

"The water is wide, I cannot get o'er," he half-sang.

"But neither have I wings to fly," she joined in the melody. "Give me a boat that can carry two, and both shall row, my love and I."

Their laughter rang in the empty room, a warm and cheery note coming from a woman who had been reborn. "Mike's letter told me what I had guessed about my mother, and what you told me about Danny was true," she said.

"I have never lied to you, have I?" he said. "Is there anything else that you want to tell me?"

"My mother died of a broken heart, Simon."

"Heart break and grief both, nostalgia and loneliness." He took her hand across the table and kissed her fingers. "It is your duty to her to carry on as she would have wanted, as a loyal and dutiful wife. Here is our dinner, eat slowly; don't try to gulp everything down. It is going to take some time to recover your health, and you will have to be patient."

They were enjoying lemon cake and sweetened tea when Mr. Mahoney came over to greet his new guests. Without asking, he pulled up a chair and sat with them, something that Mary Claire found surprising but which Simon accepted as an everyday occurrence. He delivered his report with a broad smile, quite pleased to have found exactly what the Lieutenant was looking for. At the south edge of town, on a street that was little more than a dirt track, stood an isolated cottage that caught the air off the water and was only a short walk to St. Patrick's Church and the local markets. The key selling point was the fact that the kitchen window did not face The Establishment.

"You know the town, sir, and I put my full faith in your judgment. We will look it over tomorrow morning, but I expect that we will take it immediately," Simon decided.

"We're proud of your patronage here at the Emerald Isle, sir, and I'm sorry to see you two leave so soon. I understand; I know how the ladies like to have their own kitchen, especially the new brides. And there are plenty of young girls in town, willing to do a day's work around the house, scrubbing floors and such. When the time comes, let me know and I'll send a girl around."

The proprietor left without ceremony, and Simon did nothing more than urge his wife to finish her tea so that they could go out for a stroll to explore the town. "Walk out your sea legs, you promenade like a jack tar," he said

"I walk like my husband," she said. "We're well suited."

Arm in arm they perambulated, nodding politely to the shopkeepers and prison officials who did not know them by name, only by the tales that had already run through the city. A tall Royal Marine and a skinny little Irish girl were easy to spot, making them the target of friendly greetings from the newly arrived pensioner guards who were also trying to get their bearings on the frontier of the Empire. Mr. and Mrs. Plowman continued on their aimless excursion, and anyone passing by would have taken them for a prominent couple in a sleepy colonial backwater.

Birdsongs stabbed at Mary Claire's ears, sounds she had never heard before. The aroma of eucalyptus and arid vegetation attacked her nose, smells that she disliked because she wanted to smell Ireland. She thought of escape, intense reflection that marshaled every part of her conscious mind. Certainly, she was fully confident that Simon would do all that he could to secure her pardon. She did not believe that it was possible to withstand the wait in such a bizarre and horrible place.

"I scarcely recognized you," Mr. Wakeford greeted her, startling Mary Claire out of her meditation. She looked at the man whose prison was another circle of hell, and then she noticed Mrs. Wakeford, giving her a thorough going over.

"Prison gray did not do her justice," Simon replied. "She was meant to wear green."

"Do please come and call on me, Mrs. Plowman. I am at home on Thursdays," Mrs. Wakeford said. "If there is anything that I can do for you, any introduction to be made, please look on me as your friend."

Mary Claire glanced at her husband, not knowing if she should speak, or what she should say. After a very brief moment of contemplation, Simon nodded his assent, and only then did she answer.

"Thank you, ma'am, I'll be grateful for your help. In my condition, so," she said, touching her hand to her belly.

"My dear, how delightful," Mrs. Wakeford bubbled. Fremantle was so dull that the arrival of a new baby was a cause for much rejoicing, if only to have something special to look forward to. All of Ruth Wakeford's chirping left Mary Claire feeling weary, and she was glad to exchange farewells and leave the flighty grandmother behind.

"Plowman's puppet," she heard Wakeford snigger. Simon squeezed her hand to give her the reassurance that she needed.

"I am the envy of every man in Australia," Simon noted with a wry grin. "My wife is completely enthralled, or so she appears."

"'Tis the truth, so," she said, smiling back at him.

"Then I must be the most brilliant strategist on earth. Family trait, you know. My father crushed the Young Ireland movement back in '48, and now I've sent the Fenians scurrying. Plowman men are ruthless, Mary Claire, I warn you now that it is too late for you. I sent your brother Michael a cable today. Mrs. Simon Plowman arrived Fremantle Western Australia. My reputation for cruelty has been reinforced."

Just as Mahoney had promised, the cottage on the southern fringe of Fremantle was exactly what Plowman was looking for. Already furnished, it was comfortable and airy, shaded by sandalwood trees and cooled by an ocean breeze. Mr. and Mrs. Plowman stocked up on provisions and formally settled into their home near Spruce Street, just a few steps away from Dr. Hampton's convict built road.

Two days were set aside to travel the road to Tualap Work Camp, where Mary Claire was going to assist Father Concannon, to be his extra hands among the wretched. They rested overnight on the beach, making love while the Indian Ocean broke on the shore of a foreign land. She closed her eyes and refused to look at the strange arrangement of stars overhead, unwilling to admit that she was far away from Ireland.

"Shall I tell you how I came into this world, Mary Claire?" he said as she lay next to him on a pile of blankets, snuggled against his chest and listening to his heartbeat, to drown out the pounding of the surf and memories of the *Hellebore*. "My father wheedled and cajoled until my mother wavered, and then he seduced her so there was no turning back. He made me so that she had to marry him to save her family's honor, but by God he got what he wanted. Did he love her? Oh, yes, he loved her to the point of insanity, my dear, but a man cannot order a woman to love him in return."

"Are you any different?" she said.

"I told you I wouldn't touch you if you didn't want me, and I would have lain with you every night and suffered the torments of hell because I could not win your heart. But not so very different, you're right."

"And us, are we different?"

"A woman cannot be seduced if she is not already in love. Love can grow. Grow, yes, but it is easily poisoned, murdered and then mourned. Black '47, when Ireland became a wasteland, and then. And then. My father saw the sense in every emigrant ship that sailed out of Queensland while my mother cursed the Crown and cursed Trevalyan. There came a day when she locked the door of her bedroom and stopped speaking to him, until he was left a shattered and heart-broken man. There is my story, Mrs. Plowman, and now you know all about me."

"Are you more Irish than you let on?"

"My mother tried to turn me against him, against my own father. Suckled on the milk of revenge at my mother's breast, have you heard of that before?"

"Ah, will you not mock me? I was but a child when I spoke those words. I'm an old woman now."

Before the sun rose on the twenty-fourth of January, Mary Claire kissed her husband goodbye as they embraced on the Victoria Quay. The *Hellebore* was returning to England with a load of mahogany and sandalwood, the convicts' bunks torn out to make room for cargo. Cabins once filled with pensioner guards and families were packed with those who were returning to England, the passengers eager to board the ship that the convicts had been loath to enter. She stood on the quay, dressed in green linen, waving a white handkerchief as her husband waved back from the deck. Until the ship was a speck on the horizon she stood there, arm raised and handkerchief fluttering in the breeze. Mary Claire would never see Simon Plowman again, and she knew that as well as she knew her own name.

Twelve

During her first few days alone, Mary Claire kept largely to herself, so miserable, lonely, and scared that she did not want to even make an attempt at a false front of pleasantry. She attended Mass daily and made the acquaintance of Father Concannon, the priest to the convicts and a former resident of County Clare who was reputedly a Fenian sympathizer. She held her ears open and her mouth shut, at least until she found a comfortable spot to settle into.

Starting with tea at the Wakeford home on High Street on a Thursday afternoon, Mary Claire went into Fremantle society. Through Delia Looby's patronage, she spread out through the warders' wives, and soon became a familiar face on the terrace around the prison. Once she was introduced to Mrs. John Hampton, she was satisfied that her circle of female associates was sufficient, and centered largely in and around the seat of power in Western Australia.

Like any other lady of leisure, she took long walks to pass the time, and she made a habit of walking on the jetty every afternoon. "You're not to speak to the convicts, ma'am," the armed guard yelled.

"I'm so sorry," Mary Claire said, a little coy. "I've seen them at church, and I only wanted to ask if they'd be attending a service for the Feast of St. Blaise."

"That's a question for Mr. Wakeford, ma'am," the guard replied.

"May I walk on the quay while they're working, sir? My husband's at sea and I feel closer to him when I'm here."

"Walk where you like," he said.

Her gait was smooth and slow, the easy progress of one with no duties pressing on her mind. She hummed a bit, carefree, singing a few words with the absent-minded air of a woman going about her mundane routine.

"A ship there is, and she sails the sea," her voice barely carried over the sound of the convicts' labors. She hummed again, and then continued. "I know not if I sink or swim."

John O'Reilly listened very carefully, although no one would have guessed that he even noticed the Irish woman. A former sergeant in the 10th Hussars, he had a career soldier's ability to make his face a blank mask, to hear danger through the noise of battle. He was on Victoria Quay because he had not been aware of the informer in his ranks, a man who was planted in the Fenian center by Her Majesty's government.

As the singer continued her stroll, she stopped only long enough to stoop down and retrieve the knob of her parasol that suddenly popped off. Fiddling with the broken knob, she fumbled to replace the end of the handle while clucking in frustration at the bother and the nuisance. The scrap of paper that blew away had fallen at O'Reilly's feet as he bent over to pick up another plank. Only one word was written on it, "Speedwell", and the scrap was in the water before anyone else had seen it, the ink washing away as the fragment sank.

"Durham's in town, ma'am," the guard called to her. "He could put a screw in that for you, fix it right up."

"You're too kind, sir," she almost cooed.

At Sunday Mass, Mary Claire always sat in the front row on the left side, while the Fenian convicts sat on the right with the guards. The yellow shade of her Sunday best dress was a startling match to the yellow tunics and trousers that the prisoners donned for services, and some people found it unnerving to see her in unity with such a dangerous bunch. Her voice rang out during songs, easily the best sound among the other one hundred sixty participants. Father McCabe asked her to sing the Ave Maria while he distributed Communion, and Mary Claire was happy to oblige.

Each member of the congregation was greeted in turn as they filed out of the cool shadows of the church and returned to the bright sunshine. The prisoners came up at the rear of the queue; the first to arrive were the last to leave, and they waited for Mrs. Plowman to finish her chat.

"Will you be coming to dinner, Father?" she asked on the last Sunday in February.

"It would be my pleasure, Mrs. Plowman," he said, pumping her hand. "I'd like to discuss the distribution of ashes before you run off to Tualap with Father Concannon. And I'll be granting you a dispensation from fasting on Ash Wednesday."

"Lovely sermon, Father," John O'Reilly paid a compliment as he took his turn with the cleric's strong hand. "And it's a pleasure to hear the sacred word in such a lovely voice."

"We've been blessed with Mrs. Plowman's gift," McCabe said.

"'Tis a gift indeed," O'Reilly nodded, palming the note that had been passed. Blessing his forehead with holy water, he read the few words and smoothly stuffed the scrap into his mouth and chewed his correspondence to pulp. The prisoners were always strip-searched when they returned to the prison.

Sunday's dinner was a simple affair, but it was the only day of the week that Mary Claire put much thought into cooking, and only because she was entertaining Father McCabe. In the privacy of her own kitchen, she could speak freely to him, while he was just as comfortable lecturing her.

"You know their heartache, Mary Claire, it is no different than your pain and longing," McCabe said.

"Patience, Father, they must carry that word on their hearts. The Brotherhood in America is divided, with half thinking of us and the other half making plans to invade Canada like a bunch of idiots." She spooned a portion of champ into his plate, her thoughts fixed on escape and the best way to go about it. "Ah, sure there's the Clan na Gael in America, raising funds, but it takes time. The Irish Republican Brotherhood has little stomach for a fight; that's the truth of the matter. 'Tis the Clan na Gael that we'll turn to for help, but it takes time and the men must be patient."

"Patience is fine, my girl, for one whose labors are light and whose stomach is full. You'll get away from here because you've got yourself a husband who will go to the Queen if that's what it takes. These men have no such hope."

"They're not forgotten, Father, and you must tell them so. Father Concannon spreads the words through the camps, to put an end to nonsense and be patient. Can you not do the same here?"

Dinner was nearly over when the sound of a horse clattered and thumped in the dusty street. "And remember," McCabe warned, "that it is a sin for a married woman to look at another man. No matter how that marriage came to be arranged, it is still a sacrament."

"'Tis no sin on my part if a man looks at me, now is it?" she corrected him.

"The sin comes in enticing the looking," the priest said.

"Please come in, Mr. Wakeford, and join us," she called through the open kitchen door. "We've eaten already, but I'll gladly set a place for you if you'd do me the honor."

Henry Wakeford strode in, riding crop under his arm at a sporty angle. The man who was derisively called "Boots" by the convicts had been out exercising his horse, or so he claimed when he saw a Catholic cleric sitting at the kitchen table. He asked for a glass of water and sat through an awkward silence while Mary Claire went off to her china cupboard. The enmity between Henry Wakeford and Father McCabe was as palpable as the wooden table under their elbows.

"Well, if you won't eat my dinner you'll eat my cake and tell me it's grand," she said. Next to the water glass, she put a slice of lemon cake on a plain white plate. Taking her seat, she continued to chat. "I'll be in Bunbury for an extra day, Mr. Wakeford, should I stop at your office for a different pass?"

"As much as I would enjoy a visit at my dull office, it is not necessary. Your existing pass allows you to roam the continent freely, as long as you tell me where you are going and when you will return. I hate to think that you would ever consider leaving Fremantle."

Father McCabe's response was to slam his napkin to the table. "Her husband will take her from Fremantle soon enough."

"Of course he will. All the more reason for those of us who reside here to monopolize Mrs. Plowman's time before she must go," Henry said. "What is the nature of your business in Bunbury?"

"Oh, Henry," she said. "Mr. Wakeford, excuse me. I've a letter of introduction to the minister there, from Reverend Alsip himself. Mrs.

Richardson is extending her mission, invited she was, by the ladies of Christ Church. 'Tis my Christian duty, to bring the word of God to the fallen women, and Mrs. Richardson says I'm a great help to her."

"Distributing those tracts again?" Henry asked.

"And praying, Mr. Wakeford. We pray with the women to bring them back into the fold."

"The outpost at Bunbury is certainly blessed," Henry noted.

"If you would both excuse me, I'll be taking my leave." McCabe stood up. "Will I see you at Mass in the morning, Mrs. Plowman?"

"Yes, and I'll take the altar cloth home with me as well. There's a burnt spot, and Mrs. Doyle has enough to do. I can mend it as well as your poor old housekeeper."

Pouring tea for her remaining guest, the conversation became quite private. There was a newspaper discovered in a package of prayer books, purportedly sent to the colony by a friend of the Reverend Mr. Alsip. Mary Claire's job was to search for such things, especially when the paper that wrapped the books contained a scathing editorial about the Manchester Martyrs. The Fenian prisoners were forbidden any news that promoted their cause, and Mary Claire had uncovered several contraband broadsheets smuggled into Fremantle in seemingly harmless packages. The warder in charge of the searches, Mr. Rowe, was impressed by Mrs. Plowman's sharp eye and her ability to find things that the other guards sometimes overlooked.

"I'm wasting your time, Henry," she said when he asked about escape attempts. "I listen to the men, and 'tis nothing but despair. They must understand that their situation is hopeless. There are no plans to escape. Talk of running away was just that, idle talk to pass the time in dreaming. They're working in the bush all day, and they know 'tis a sure death to a man on the run."

"Mary Claire, you could never waste my time, even if you never had another scrap of news to share. Tell me, are you fond of riding?"

"In my present condition," she said, languidly placing a hand on her middle to draw attention to a pregnancy that was masterfully disguised through careful lacing of a maternity corset. "I did like to ride when I was a girl. So, there's another day to come for riding horses."

"Shall we make plans to go for a drive, perhaps?"

"Can I tell you what I really want to do, Henry? And don't laugh at me; 'tis silly, I know." She lowered her eyelids slightly, as she had done as a carefree young girl. Confined by the strictures of Catholic morality, Irish girls learned how to flirt. Mary Claire was an acknowledged master of the sport in Rathkeale. "I want to go out on the water and see a real shark. Everyone talks of them, but I've never seen one."

"We could go out rowing, you and I."

"That would be grand, Henry, and I could pack a picnic for us. Is Mrs. Wakeford fond of picnics?"

"If you and I were to meet by chance on the road to the work camp, it would not matter," he suggested.

"You're so clever, Henry, of course. Then Father Concannon could help you row. That's a much better idea, but then you're so sensible." She touched his shoulder, as lightly as a butterfly, and held his eye for a little longer than was proper for a married woman.

The Tualap work camp was a long way from Fremantle, requiring an overnight stay in a roadside camp. Concannon traveled a circuit and he was skilled at the sort of careful packing that was needed to survive the harsh climate. Enough water and provisions had to be brought along for both man and horse, to safely get from the middle of nowhere to the far edges of nowhere, riding along the convict built road that followed the coastline.

"Now wouldn't this be a fine spot for a man to meet his sweetheart," Mary Claire said when they stopped to water the horse. "Less than a day's drive out of Fremantle, a night on the sand, hidden by the scrub, and then home the next day with no one any wiser."

"Are you making a confession, Mrs. Plowman?" Father Concannon asked, a bit perturbed by her tone.

"I came here with my husband. If I come back any time soon, I'll confess what sins are done."

"Why would you do such a thing? Your husband may have taken advantage of you on that ship, but he married you, when most of them sail back to England without a by your leave."

Pacing next to the horse, she stopped abruptly and stared into the priest's eyes, daring him to reply with candor. "I asked Father McCabe, and now I ask you. Is it a sin to let a man think what he will? I sailed to Australia in a hold filled with harlots, and they taught me how to mold a man's mind. So, is it a sin?"

Completely disarmed by her blunt tone, the priest had to admit that he did not have an answer for her. All he could do was to pray for guidance, and when God showed the way, he would guide Mary Claire. In the meantime, he offered the privacy of the confession, where her words would be heard only by God. Climbing back into the buggy, she assured her confessor that God saw what she did, and He knew why she did it. At the end of her days, He would be the one to judge her, and she would find an honest court in heaven.

A crew of convict laborers shuffled by, chained to each other without end until death or disease claimed a man. As he recognized the faces of some of his congregation, the priest blessed them, his hand cutting through the air top to bottom, side to side. Drifting through the air was the strain of the Fenian anthem being hummed, but the voice was so low that it might have been the wind whistling.

"Mrs. Plowman, I didn't think I'd see you all the way out here," one of the guards shouted. It was Cornelia's so-called employer and ardent suitor, Ted Carling.

"We're off to bring the word of God to the very edge of civilization," she replied.

"Prisoners, halt," Carling barked. The clanking stopped and the entire crew collapsed in exhaustion to the ground. "Say, I feel all queer to be asking this, but I've heard rumors, Mrs. Plowman, about my Nell and other men while I've been out with the road gang. We're friends, ain't we?"

"I like to think so, Mr. Carling," she agreed. "Wish we'd see more of you, too."

"If it was true, that she had men in the house at night, would you tell me?"

Cornelia had vowed to make Carling's life hell, and she was succeeding beautifully. The guard's cottage in town was a bordello now that Ted was living in the convict camp in the bush. Duplicating the house in Dublin, Cornelia provided an expensive hour, but a client would find the highest quality of refreshments and the ladies were gracious hostesses. The atmosphere in the parlor was among the most refined in town, thanks to Varena's taste in furnishing.

Equal partners, Cornelia and Varena split the proceeds and put aside a fixed amount in the Fremantle bank, with a plan to eventually open a first-rate bagnio as soon as they could afford it, or before Ted came back to town. Mary Claire had loaned them a large chunk of her household allowance to get started, and she had even helped to make the heavy draperies and frilly bed linens for the luxurious boudoirs. Behind his back, the other guards laughed at Ted Carling and his mythical romance. The man who thought of Cornelia as his wife was now the biggest fool in Fremantle, an object of derisive gossip.

"I have never seen anything untoward at your home," Mary Claire said. "And what do you expect, Mr. Ted Carling, when you waltz into Fremantle with such a pretty bird perched on your hand? I'd sooner live with a woman's jealousy than a man's envy."

Ted tipped his hat, his smile running from ear to ear. "Afternoon, Mrs. Plowman, Father. Prisoners, stand. Fall in. Forward, march."

A confusion of dust drifted down the road. Mary Claire gazed at the sky, watching a line of dark clouds begin to form on the distant horizon. "Looks like rain," she said. "Bless me, Father, for I have sinned."

"Say a rosary with me while I drive, for the sin of bearing false witness." He growled out the prayer that began with a sincere hope. "May Almighty God have mercy on you, forgive you your sins."

Every week, Mary Claire joined the priest on his trip to Tualap, camping out near the road overnight and then returning to town on Thursday to call on the Wakefords. With Mary Claire conducting Bible readings and rosaries, Concannon had more time to counsel the prisoners, to hear not only confessions but act as a bulwark against hopelessness. Often, the men would confide in Mary Claire, seeking a woman's gentle word and sweet smile to heal a wounded psyche. Together, they carried on a highly effective ministry, one in which the convict parishioners seemed to accept their dismal fate.

"I have a boat, I think," Henry told her when she stopped at his office the following week. "Still interested in finding a real shark?"

"There's a quiet spot where I spend the night between here and Tualap," she said. "Father Concannon told me that he saw some fins out in the water, close to the shore. 'Tis a lovely spot, Henry, where I sleep under the stars."

"We could row out very far," he whispered, barely moving his lips. "Away from all this, you and I."

"Escaped convicts are caught and hanged, Henry," she said, showing a spark of anger. "With me a prisoner here, are you trying to entice me to my death?"

"Forgive me, Mary Claire, I promise you that I sincerely forgot your status. I am surrounded daily by the worst felons, until I see only two kinds of people. You are sweetness and kindness, not a criminal. You don't belong here, I know all about your case."

"But I'm a convict, whatever you might think of me."

"If there were some way to expedite your pardon, some way to secure your release," he said.

"Did you know that my brother sent me news? He's invested in a shipping concern, isn't it grand?" she went off on another topic. "Do you read my correspondence, Henry?"

Wakeford cleared his throat, uncomfortable to admit that he made it his personal business to censor Mary Claire's dealings. "Well, to be fair and consistent, your background and family," he babbled.

Touching his hand across the desk, she put him at ease. "I like to think that you read my letters, like a husband when I'm alone here. But, this one time, Henry. I've written to Mr. Plowman, and, 'tis intimate, so. Mrs. Wakeford would understand. Just this one time, would you ask Mrs. Wakeford to approve my letter?"

Henry sat bolt upright, keenly interested in intimacy. He hemmed and hawed about himself and his wife, in their younger days, admitting to a steamy correspondence that Mary Claire imagined to be as hot as snow. As much as he promised that he would not be shocked, indeed, would understand completely, she demurred, her color rising as she hung her head in embarrassment. She explained, as best she could, that she had written of a desperate longing to be touched by a man's lips, to feel whiskers brushing her cheek. Having elaborated on the reasons for her discomfort, she turned her eyes from his perspiring face to the floor, protesting that the very idea of him reading such things made her blush, while her gloved finger methodically stroked the top of his desk.

Nervously, he shifted in his chair, placing his hand on hers to stop the seductive rhythm of her hand fingering the pens that stood erect in the holder. The tone of his voice changed, growing accusing, putting her on edge. From his desk drawer, he retrieved a note that had been folded many times, smoothing out the creases as he watched her reaction. She recognized the page and her eyes lit up with joy. Before he could ask, she told him with a laugh that the missive had been given to him by Mr. Woolsey, the guard on the parade ground, and it came from a Fenian agent.

Clearly, Henry was not expecting the answer she gave, and he paused to stare at her, slack-jawed. "How did he acquire it?" he continued.

"A convict named Joseph O'Reilly received a message from a Fenian supporter." She winked at him. "If he turned it in to his guard, it must mean that he rejects the offer and wants to make the Comptroller General aware of a plot. Did I do it the right way, Henry, did I guess correctly?"

"How do I know that he submitted the original message to me? How can I tell if the convicts have uncovered the spy in their midst and are trying to silence her through imprisonment, by forwarding false information?"

"Because there's a secret code, something I invented. We'll be the only two people in the world who know of it. The Fenian agent has sent a message to you, a cipher that only you can interpret."

"Mary Claire, I recognize your handwriting," Henry continued, his tone growing threatening.

She picked up a piece of paper and covered the note, sliding the page off to one side to uncover the first words at the left margin. She picked up a pen, pointed at the exposed writing, and then slowly slid the end of the barrel between her lips. "What do you see, Henry?" she asked in a near whisper, her lips gently caressing the sterling silver pen.

Sweat beaded up on his rust colored temples as he stared at her, transfixed. He followed the line of her arm, his eyes running down her hand to the words that she pointed out with her white kid-gloved finger. "Be," he read aloud, his voice trembling, "My. Love."

"I know what a brilliant man you truly are."

"Be my love," he whispered.

"When next you intercept such a letter, you can search for our cipher." She looked at her jailer with starry-eyed adoration. "I wanted to create a plot for you to uncover, so the Prison Service would recognize you at last. Please, let me try again. Will Rogerson has been sniffing around, thinks I'm here to help the Fenians. Wouldn't it be grand if he tried to use me to ferry messages? You would know everything before it happened, and you could direct things through me to make a very dramatic capture."

"You did this for me?" he asked with surprise and buoyant joy.

"Sure, now I can't tell you when I contact Rogerson, but we have our secret code. Only you can know 'tis me behind it all. No man will ever escape your prison, but if they try, well, all the glory to you when they're caught." She put the pen away, giving it one final and languid stroke. "You deserve the praise of Her Majesty herself."

In early April, the temperature in Western Australia had begun to cool as autumn drifted into the Southern Hemisphere. Despite the balmy air, Henry Wakeford usually began perspiring when Mary Claire sat in his office, giving him a look that hinted at secret longings that could not be expressed with the Comptroller General's clerk only a few feet away and Mrs. Wakeford not much further than that. He cleared his throat, mopped his perspiring brow, and asked for news from the work camps. Her report was the same as usual, with the priest continuing to exhort his followers to wait for their heavenly reward and accept God's will. Due to recent Church dictates, Father Concannon was under a higher order than anything Henry could command. The bishops had issued a directive, threatening to excommunicate anyone taking secret oaths, essentially making Fenianism a sin. It was far better to be hanged than excommunicated, and Mary Claire assured Henry that the priest heeded his bishop.

"What of our local cleric?" he pressed on, making notations in his record book.

"Now, he's got a man he's keeping an eye on."

"An escape plot?" Wakeford bubbled over with excitement.

"The only escape that even you can't stop, Henry. He means to take his own life, desperate with his health broken. Much longer on the jetty and his heart will give out, and he'd rather do the deed himself. For the sake of his soul, can you not make him a messenger?"

"Perhaps. Some convicts can be put to lighter duties as their strength diminishes."

"He could shuttle your messages to the camps, and Father McCabe told me that he's skilled with horses. Can you use a man like that in the stables?"

"What a kind-hearted woman you are, to be concerned with such a worthless bit of human refuse." He put his pen down and gave her his undivided attention, which she sought to hold for as long as possible.

"'Tisn't the man I want to save, but his soul. Every soul is priceless, whether saint or sinner."

"If only my wife had a fraction of your consideration," he mumbled.

"Then you'd not come to see me, would you, and I'd be the poorer for it," she said. Her friendly smile evaporated at once, and her hand flew to her middle.

"Are you unwell?" he gasped.

"I must go home, Henry, will you excuse me," she stammered. Tears were rising in her eyes, and she fumbled for the handkerchief that she kept in her pocket.

"Let me take you home. I cannot leave you in such a state," he said.

"No, I must send a cable. I have to tell him, so he knows when he reaches Portland."

Only when he promised to send the cable would she allow him to escort her to his home on High Street, where Mrs. Wakeford took control of the situation. Cool compresses were applied to Mary Claire's forehead and neck while she lay on the parlor sofa, distraught and asking repeatedly about sending a message to her husband.

"Send the cable, please, you won't forget, will you?" Mary Claire pleaded. "Just say quickened, he'll understand."

Sliding a pillow behind Mary Claire's back, Ruth saw to the comfort of her friend. "Why are you upset, my poor child? This is a joyous occasion. Your baby is alive."

Taking a hand from each of the people who hovered over her, Mary Claire kissed them in turn and looked up with the saddest eyes. "If not for your friendship, for two such dear friends, I couldn't carry on. Thank you, thank you both."

"Yes, well, I had better send that cable at once," Henry said. He dashed off, holding Mary Claire's hand for about two seconds longer than necessary.

"Now then, this is a time of great peace of mind, to feel the child inside you," Ruth said.

"I'm so afraid, Mrs. Wakeford." Mary Claire said, tears falling. "I had a friend whose baby died after it quickened, but she died as well."

"Don't be afraid, you poor thing, without your mother's advice," the older woman said. "These things do happen, but so very rarely. You must not dwell on the fables and sad stories that you will hear from other women."

Memories of Bridie and Newgate, the *Hellebore* and hunger came back with their full force. Mary Claire was too exhausted to walk to church the next morning, and she sat in her parlor for a long time, not moving, paralyzed by her imagination. The sounds of a man rattling about in the kitchen startled her, making her drag her mind back to the present. She apologized for being so slow to greet a guest, starting to slice a loaf of bread as John O'Reilly took the knife from her hand.

"Here now, I can be captain of the mess for a change," O'Reilly offered. "My first day on a new job, and I'm delivering my first message from Boots to you."

"He's worried about me because I didn't keep our appointment today," she predicted.

"Will you be telling me why you're so eager to enter The Establishment every week?"

"No." She filled the kettle and put it on the stove before measuring tea into the china pot.

"Will you be telling me why a mason is out back, building a tall stone wall around your garden, so?"

"No," she said again, too busy setting a place at the table to pay any mind to his queries.

"Could you be thinking you'd best hide Boots' horse so it can't be seen?" the convict suggested.

"There's talk in the town," she said.

"And talk all through the gaol, talk on the parade ground and talk in the corridors. What will you tell your husband when he comes back for you?"

"Take me home, that's what I'll say," she said.

"Then why do you try to escape? You'll be set free, girl, and you speak of patience but don't show it in yourself."

"Must my child draw its first breath in a prison? I've patience, John, but my time will come in July and no man on earth can delay that. Where's my husband now? It's nearly four months back, and how long will he be in Dublin?"

"Arragh now. Arragh now. Where's the girl I knew in Rathkeale?"

"John Bull took her away and she'll never return."

"I'll not ask after your affairs. I'll go where I'm told and I'll do as I'm told."

Butter and sliced soda cake were put on the table, along with glasses of fresh water and buttermilk. While John sat down to eat, she busied herself at the stove, frying eggs and rashers while the kettle began to steam.

"It breaks my heart to see you so, John, like a scallcrow."

"And yourself? You're not well, lass; you're pale as a winding sheet."

"Ah, someone walked on my grave today. My door's always open to you, John. Take what you need, anything at all, whenever you can. God go with you."

In her bedroom, Mary Claire sat at the writing table that offered a view of the street, a quiet spot on the fringe of a quiet town. Opening her journal, she carefully wrote out the saga of Bridie Boyne, a tale of injustice and disregard for humanity. Day by day, the pages of the book were being filled with Mary Claire's elegant script as she recorded the story of her life. Episodes of a childhood in Rathkeale were interspersed with the wretched misery of a convict's fate, nothing in any particular order. As the tales came to mind, Mary Claire wrote them; day after day she created a textbook for the infant that had begun to stir within. One day, this journal would teach the child that she would leave behind, to be a record of Irish oppression and the struggle of a people to break free of England's shackles.

Thirteen

Easter Sunday was a day like all the rest, sunny and bright. What passed for a rainy season during February and March was utterly unlike Irish rain, with air so dry that the little moisture that did fall seemed to evaporate before it hit the ground. Mary Claire was left wondering if it ever rained at all. As for the heat, it might have diminished but it was still intolerable, and it made the weekly trips to Tualap even more grueling.

After Mass, the prison guard complimented her on her fine singing voice, with a timbre that put the felons in a more peaceable frame of mind for the day. The other prisoners shook hands with Father McCabe as Mary Claire asked after the guard's delightful little girl, interrupting the conversation just long enough to wish a good morning to the priest before John O'Reilly bid his farewell.

Even though Father McCabe was due for dinner, Mary Claire had an urge to stop at the telegraph office before going home. It was silly, when she knew that the *Hellebore* could not possibly reach England for another two weeks at least, but she had to check. In her dreams, she pictured a miraculous wind that always blew across the beam, to send Simon back to Portland at a record pace. Again, there was no news, only the listing of the ships that were docking at Fremantle to pick up wood or wool or wheat, delivering cargo to the far-away pioneers, or whalers who put in for supplies on the far side of the world.

"Are you not troubled by the rumors?" McCabe asked over dinner. Carving the roast chicken, he placed a thick slab of meat on her plate. "Surely it pains you to be spoken of as a woman of loose morals."

"Nothing can pain me, Father, I'm a prize fighter. Blow after blow, and I'll get back up on my feet and take another," she said. Queasy with the heat, she sipped her tea and left the chicken to grow cold. "Talk won't follow me around the globe, and all their gossip can drift in the dust of this miserable place."

"There's talk that Father Concannon is to be barred from traveling out to the work camps," he confided. "Have you heard of it from himself?"

"'Tis common knowledge that tales are carried out of Fremantle and everyone knows that news from the outside world is carried in. He's got a list, not only Father but a guard in the camp near Pemberton, and one or two men inside The Establishment. Sooner or later, the blame will fall on the guilty party. The men in the camps need a priest, and if Father Concannon is made to take the blame then I'll do all I can to get you out there for them."

In a serious vein, McCabe asked her if she truly confessed all her sins. She assured him, in the same tone, that her soul was pure and she sought God's forgiveness for every transgression. When it was time to confess, she was on her knees, and nothing was held back. The priest, however, was not satisfied, changing the topic slightly by suggesting that her solitary life left her open to temptation. The last thing that Mary Claire wanted was the Gaughan girl nosing around all day and night, with her big ears open and her big mouth running like a river. There was a reason that Simon forbade his wife from engaging any household servants, and Miriam Gaughan would never live in the cottage on Spruce Street.

"I know right from wrong," she said. "Some things can't be helped."

"Do you have any idea how this will hurt your husband? It's a betrayal, Mary Claire, and for no other reason than lust. It's a lifetime of penance you'll have, to live with a man you've deceived, a man who can never trust you again."

"Maybe he won't come back. Maybe he's gotten his hundred-fifty worth and I'll be left here alone."

"Spend more time reading your devotions and less time in the company of a man who would want you to believe such drivel."

"Bah, you'd have me in a habit if you could," she snickered. "Sister Mary Claire, dressed up for the Christmas pageant, portraying the Blessed Mother as she appeared on the twenty-third of December."

"A fine nun you'd make," McCabe said. "You'd be too busy eyeing the boys to keep an eye on your beads."

"Have another cup of tea, now," she said. "The longer you stay, the less mischief I can get into. Keep the *grogoch* out of the kitchen for another day."

With so much ocean, and with life confined to the coast, it made sense that the comfortable citizens of Western Australia would become enamored of sailing. The annual Perth regatta was held on Easter Monday, a local holiday, and Mrs. Simon Plowman joined her friends on the short trip to the capitol, where she was accepted as a guest of Dr. and Mrs. Hampton. Mary Claire was elegant and poised, her expanding figure adding an element of plumpness to her frame. Her day dress elicited reams of compliments from the ladies, who admired the unusual row of dainty chevrons, like little arrows, that ran down the sleeves and bodice of her grey linen jacket. The red color of the arrows was echoed by the stripes of red that ran down the sides of her grey skirt, the trim pulled together by the scarlet underlining that was folded back across the bustle. It was a masterful work of dressmaking and a unique expression of one woman's style.

To entertain the assembled dignitaries, the HMS *Conflict*, a gunboat that patrolled the coast, was steaming around in a display of royal might, and it was taken as a matter of course that Mrs. Plowman would be given a ride and a tour. While the steamer plied the waves, Captain Grady showed his guest the reefs, explaining their danger to navigation. When a whitish-gray triangle popped up out of the water, Grady slipped his arm around Mary Claire's waist to direct her vision to a real, live shark, an enormous creature whose size was far greater than one might imagine. With wide eyes, Mary Claire gasped in amazement and tilted ever so slightly until her weight pressed gently against the captain's gloved hand. As if responding to an unspoken invitation, he teased her, suggesting that the sharks might also be fond of such a tender morsel as his honored guest.

Noticing how the waves broke differently in one area, Mary Claire coerced a detailed analysis of the reefs, which were as likely to eat boats as the sharks were to eat a swimmer. With an air of great importance, Grady observed that he was dependent on his charts to avoid the rock-like masses, which would rip out the bottom of his boat without much effort. "This is a very difficult place to enter," he cautioned, "and just as difficult to leave."

"I used to enjoy boating, Captain, but I may never go out again. I don't want to drown," she said, "or be eaten alive."

"An experienced pilot could navigate around them," he said. "Do you head out with a party of knowledgeable sailors?"

"Well, Mr. Wakeford surely knows the water," she said, ticking off her mates. "Father Concannon is not much of a sailor, but he can pull an oar, and one of the convicts lends a hand but he's no more a sailor than I am. I should take you along, Captain, and leave those landlubbers behind."

"If only I were free, Mrs. Plowman, I would steer your little boat," the captain offered, receiving a pretty smile that implied more than sailing was desired. However, he was not free for some time, but he could give her a copy of his charts and show her exactly where the dangers lay, to protect her on her little outings.

From across the deck, Mary Claire could see an ember of jealousy begin to burn brightly. After asking Wakeford not to read her letter to Simon, she was confident that he absorbed every word at the first opportunity. At the very least, Ruth Wakeford could be counted on to spread every salacious detail, with a small town love of gossip and scandal. "A man of insatiable appetite," Ruth might have gasped, forming an impression of a certain Marine lieutenant whose wife wrote so longingly of that afternoon on the couch, that evening on the beach, in prose that dripped with lust and desire.

Before the sun was up on Wednesday morning, Father Concannon arrived from the eastern camps and went straight to the cottage on Spruce, where he would find a hot breakfast waiting for him. From there, it was a long drive on Dr. Hampton's road, south to Tualap for the weekly visit that was of great importance to the Catholics in the wilderness.

The priest had just finished blessing the meal when Henry Wakeford greeted the pair in the kitchen. Claiming that he was off to inspect the road crew, he invited himself along on their trip. Ever a good hostess, Mary Claire invited him to eat before they headed out, pouring a fresh cup of tea before Wakeford had a chance to decline her hospitality.

Going a step further, she suggested that he also join them for dinner where they stopped for the night, her voice oozing concern that the Comptroller-General might push himself too hard if he tried to hurry back to Fremantle in one day.

"Do you think I might persuade you to return with us, Mr. Wakeford?" Concannon asked. "We have a lovely spot that Mrs. Plowman sets up for our camp. She keeps an old crate there with a few extra tins of food, in case of emergency. If my horse were to go lame, or my old buggy break down, it's best that she have someplace to wait for me. In her condition, poor child, it's dangerous to travel, but she's a true daughter of Christ and she won't be dissuaded."

"A most admirable example of Christian goodness," Henry said.

"Well, I'm off," Concannon said, picking up the wicker food hamper that Mary Claire had packed that morning. "I'll just see to the horse."

"I'd like to see sharks with you, Henry," Mary Claire said. She was intent on washing the dishes, but Henry detected a note of annoyance in her posture.

"This place where you spend the night, is it secluded?" he whispered.

"Never a soul have we seen in all the weeks we've traveled the road," she replied. "The brush is thick there, where a man could hide a small boat, and take a lady out as often as he liked. Especially a man with duties that took him to Tualap."

The idea of such a scandal caused a fresh outpouring of nervous perspiration. While Henry mopped his forehead, Mary Claire teased and flirted, reminding him that the camp was far out of town, out of sight, where no one would see them. Speaking quietly so that Father Concannon could not overhear, her voice took on a seductive quality that made Wakeford's hand tremble with excitement.

"You saw my telegram yesterday?" she concluded, to further entice him.

"From such a prominent man, not to spy on you, and it was not a sealed letter."

"I'm not criticizing you, Henry, I'm proud of the way that you take your post so seriously. How can I expect my husband to return to me if his father wants to annul the marriage and pay me off with a small income to support the child? All my life, I was a good girl and I obeyed my father, and then I married and I obeyed my husband. I'm in prison because of it, forgotten and unwanted."

"I, ahem, do sometimes travel to Perth," he dithered. "Perhaps, one time when you go shopping you could go alone, without Mrs. Looby, or if there were some church business that would bring you to the capitol."

"Let's run away, Henry, let's go all the way to Sydney, just you and I," she said, taking his hands with her soapy, wet fingers. "No, let's go far away, all the way to New York City and we can start new lives together. To be Mrs. Henry Wakeford is my dream, far away from Australia where no one knows the truth."

"It's more than I ever hoped," he said. "And all that I could want."

In one swift lunge he had taken her in his arms, to claim a kiss from the woman who had inserted herself into his every waking thought and every dream.

"No, the priest," she protested, turning her face away while pressing her body closer.

He backed off, ill at ease but elated. "It will take time, but I will find a way."

"I have so little time," she said.

"No, there is time. Even if he were to come back, he cannot possibly arrive before September. I promise you, Mary Claire, that I will accept this child as mine, and when we get to America, no one will know otherwise. He can never find you there, can make no claim on our baby. I will give you more children, I promise you, the family that you dream of shall be yours."

"So very wise. Yes, we should wait until after the baby comes. I'll be patient, but you must be patient as well. Think of a lifetime of happiness, and the next few months will pass quickly."

Glued to Mary Claire's side, Wakeford was a nuisance to the camp guards, getting in the way as he showed off his public works project. Everyone was glad when Father Concannon finished up confessions at four, with the departure of the party eliciting a hearty farewell that was flavored with a sigh of relief. As it grew dark, the trio reached the campsite that Father Concannon marked with a red flag on a tall stick to make it easy to find. It was a festive little picnic that moonlit evening, with Concannon tending the fire and Mary Claire roasting potatoes as her mother had done on a peat hearth, long ago in Rathkeale.

While Mary Claire spread her blankets in a secluded clearing, Father Concannon made a point of showing Wakeford where they would be sleeping, well away from Mrs. Plowman's bed. The two gentlemen had little to say to each other, especially after they had engaged in a discussion of a uniquely Australian custom regarding female convicts. For decades, a woman was allowed to remarry even if her husband was waiting for her to finish her sentence and come back home, a casual sort of divorce that was accepted because it did much to populate the territory. The practice flew in the face of Catholic morality, and the topic never failed to infuriate Concannon.

Their morning on the beach had an innocent quality to it, not unlike a group of children at play. Mary Claire went wading barefoot in the surf, to ease the ache in her feet and ankles that reminded her of heavy shackles and the damage they had caused. With her hair down and floating on the breeze, she was an angel in pink, a gift from heaven to warm the bones of a man approaching the twilight of his life. She pulled her skirts up a little higher than necessary as a wave washed across her foot, casting an inviting glance at the man who would commit a crime, throw over his entire career, to set her free.

There were hard-boiled eggs, black pudding and an Irish bread that Mary Claire called soda cake, washed down with a very respectable tea that Father Concannon brewed over his blazing campfire. While the Catholics prayed, Henry looked around, his dull routine of riding to fill his days hanging like a weight around his neck. All he did was wander on inspection tours to work camps and quarries, to the jetty and to the building sites. As Mary Claire had suggested often, no one would notice if he was gone for a day, a week or even a month.

He strolled into the clearing, looking around carefully as if he were assessing the density of the scrub that hid the opening. While she folded her blankets, he walked back towards the road and studied the area, hunting for the best spot to hide a rowboat, to turn this section of ocean front into his personal love nest while he waited for the right opportunity to take Mary Claire and make a new start.

Riding north, they lapsed into a comfortable silence, with Mary Claire dozing off from time to time. The long ride made her tired, and the need to sit for hours made her joints stiff. Half way back, they stopped to stretch their legs and Henry snuck a discrete touch of her belly, a future father's tenderness for the child of his golden years.

One hour after another ticked by, and so another week passed with no word from Simon. Mary Claire began to haunt the telegraph office, stopping in at least twice each day to ask if she had a message, but no cable arrived from Portland. She scanned the list of ships that had docked, the ones that were scheduled to leave, and the ones that advertised available berths, as if she might find that her husband had returned and somehow forgotten to tell her. On the nineteenth of May, a runner from the telegraph office pounded on her door at three o'clock in the morning, to deliver something that was too important to be held for one minute.

"Buck up," he wired as soon as he set foot on land. "To Dublin immediately."

After Mass, she raced over to send her reply, to reach Dublin before the packet boat could make it across the Irish Sea. "Joy," she proclaimed, her one word that meant volumes of prose.

The convict road gang could not help but see the rowing party, a small group that went out across the waves towards the reef where the water boiled over the coral and the sharks swam lazily. Every time, John O'Reilly was pulled from his duties as messenger to lend a hand because Father Concannon wearied of rowing rather quickly and he would not permit the couple to be alone. Any man who looked up from his work would see the priest's black garb, which was in stern contrast with Mrs. Plowman's white parasol and colorful frocks. Boots was perspiring with the effort to please his fair guest, who could not seem to get enough of the bobbing waves and the shark fins that cut through the seas.

One day, however, with the cool breeze of late autumn wafting across the sand, only two people came into view, strolling along the strand with an easy manner. Mrs. Plowman wore gray trimmed with red satin ribbon, the uniform of the convict translated into a second best dress. The folds over the bustle were red like the stripe on the convict's trousers, the red and gray that made a prisoner so visible in the colorless expanse. John O'Reilly met her eye when he delivered messages to a guard, pausing for a moment to take a very close look while the chain gang dragged off down the road, heading towards Bunbury.

"I fear what's to come, Henry, but I know what it means for us," she said. "So very soon, we'll be one, the happiest of families."

"America does need a man of my caliber, you are quite right, darling, and not overly boastful of my knowledge. Their vast frontier, lawless, ready to be tamed by a man who understands the mind of the criminal. With you by my side, I can do anything." He took her hand, a hand that held all the promise of a glowing future. "My shining light, and I shall make you proud of your loving husband."

"Whatever you ask of me, Henry, I can do whatever you ask. A speaking tour would never tax my strength, because you are my strength. I exist to make you happy, you are my sun and I'll be the moon that reflects your glory."

Bless me father, she said to herself as Henry kissed her. It was their first kiss, and one that he sought to prolong. It was a sin, but Mary Claire gave herself up to the wickedness with nary a flinch of guilt.

"Are you quite certain that Dr. Greenleaf, no contact," he panted as his mouth tasted every inch of skin on her face.

"If only we could, how I long for you," she moaned. "June is nearly over, my poor darling, and I begin my confinement within days. July will race by, just wait and see. After that, a short period of lying in and then, Henry, then, I'll not be restraining myself."

He would have continued to slobber all over her if the sound of picks hitting rock and guards bellowing did not break through the crash of waves on the beach. It was time to go, to return to Fremantle and wait for the baby to arrive, to patiently dream of the grand and glorious life that was theirs for the taking. Henry checked the branches and brush that he used to cover the rowboat, to be sure that it was hidden from the road, and he escorted Mary Claire to the waiting trap.

"Afternoon, Mr. Wakeford," the guard tipped his hat.

"Good progress, Mr. Micklewhite?" Henry replied with jaunty authority.

"Mrs. Plowman won't find a single bump when she goes to Tualap for Christmas Mass," the guard said.

With an easy air, Henry flicked the horse's rump. There was plenty of male vanity involved, but he was sending a message as well. A Fenian had been rehabilitated, such was Henry's concept of Mary Claire, a former rebel had seen the light that emanated from the great Henry Wakeford and been converted to a loyal British subject. The uplift of his chin declared that the convicts who toiled to make Australia a better place were now looking at the world through his prism.

Certainly Will Rogerson had woken up, coming to Wakeford's office to alert him to a planned escape that was being organized by Mrs. Plowman. The secret note, in a woman's graceful hand, had been turned in to prove that a conspiracy was in the works, but Henry knew what the real conspiracy was. In a matter of months, he would be gone, with a new wife, a new baby, and a brilliant career in the New World. "I adore you," was the agent's secret message, and Henry could scarcely wait to spring the convict that he loved to the point of mindless worship.

"Patience is a virtue," he said, thinking of the next three months.

"Ever since I met you, I have set aside virtue," she said, looking up at him from the corner of her eye.

"Virtue, darling, is highly overrated in the female sex."

Mary Claire's confinement meant that her days of reporting on Father Concannon and his Fenian contacts came to an end. To be on the safe side, Dr. Hampton put pressure on the bishop to assign a new priest to the work camps, and Father McCabe switched places with his colleague. After months of incarceration, the Fenians were quiet, seeming to validate the dogma that The Establishment was escape proof, and that heavy labor, shackles and the lash could completely crush any rebellion.

Fremantle settled down to a peaceful winter in which the only excitement lay in the anticipated arrival of the Plowman baby. As he did every night, Sam Dooley made his rounds, verifying that all prisoners were in their homes by curfew. He strolled along the road to Spruce Street, cutting across waste ground until he reached the Plowman cottage, where Mrs. Plowman was in the habit of welcoming the foot-weary old man with a pot of tea and freshly baked bread that dripped with butter. On the evening of the twentieth of July, his routine was altered when he saw a lantern on the street in front of her house, something that signaled an alert, and he dashed to the open front door.

"Mr. Dooley?" her voice called, very weak. "Please, send for Mrs. Wakeford."

There was a tiny gasp and then silence, enough to throw Dooley into a panic.

"The midwife," Mary Claire groaned next, and Dooley took off.

He was too old to run, but he ran all the way to High Street, shouting "It's time, the baby," as if he were the town crier.

John O'Reilly had been crouching in Mary Claire's armoire for the past two hours, listening for any sound that was not typical of the house or the street. His horse, the one he used to ride along the road with his messages, was well hidden by the high stone wall that enclosed Mary

198

Claire's veranda. Sheets and petticoats hung on wash lines, enough screening to conceal anything in the yard. In his second hand civilian suit, one that had been tailored to fit a shrunken frame, he hunkered down among the lavender sprigs and waited for a signal. The armoire was flung open, and Mary Claire touched his shoulder.

"You know exactly where the boat is, are you certain?" she whispered.

He followed her out of the kitchen door and went to the fire pit that the mason had constructed last May. "I marked the spot with some rocks and sticks on the edge of the road," John said.

While Mary Claire put his prison uniform on the fire, he stayed in the yard for one more minute, to watch the despised Drogheda linen flare up and crumble to ash. With effort, he heaved the large copper wash boiler onto the fire, the tub already filled with water and lady's drawers. The pot was so heavy that he could barely lift it; his time in The Establishment had left him emaciated and weak. Finally, he added more wood to the fire, to make it burn hotter and consume every fiber of the gray fabric and its painted arrows.

"Come with me, Mary Claire," he begged. Taking hold of the horse's bridle, he offered her freedom. "Both shall row, we'll go together."

"God bless you, John." She embraced him, tears in her eyes. "God bless you."

Fourteen

Katherine Plowman inspected the wedding portrait and declared that the girl was rather thin. The bridal couple appeared rigidly formal, as they should, but there was a distinct suggestion of affection in the way that Mary Claire's hand rested on her husband's shoulder. It was more of a warm embrace than a nonchalant placement, just as the slight tilt of his head suggested that he was about to rest his head on her bosom as he sat in a chair while she stood at his side.

"She was just off a prison transport after months in Newgate Gaol," Anna said. "Quite pretty, Simon, I like her very much. When is the baby due?"

"July, middle or end, the midwife guessed. It's the coolest part of the year in that Hades on earth, thank heavens for that," he said. "I hate to think of her alone at a time like this, Anna; it's a nightmare."

"Oh, tish-tosh, she doesn't need you mucking about, getting underfoot," Anna said. "This is grand. We can take the old furniture out of storage and open up the spare room. I should have it painted, something suitable for a baby."

"Her sentence is probably seven years, my dear," Katherine noted. "The child will not need an infant's cradle. A convict, Simon, how could you?"

"Not just any convict, mother," Anna said. "The Martyr of Rathkeale, the story we were following in the American papers, do you recall?"

"Why did no one tell me?" Katherine complained. "I have not said one word to my friends out of embarrassment, and now I come to learn that my son married the O'Dwyer girl. Your impenetrable secrecy, Simon."

"Not everyone kept silent," Simon said. "I heard from father, the same message he sent to Mary Claire. Annulment or disinheritance. He's a fine one to talk about uniting with Irish rebels."

"Just ignore him, dear," Katherine advised. "That is the only tactic that works in a battle with the petty dictator. Wire your wife; tell her to ignore him. Insufferable brute, to torment the girl when she is all alone."

"Are you on leave, Simon?" Anna asked. "What do we do next?"

"Furloughed for a year," he said. "I start in tomorrow, at dawn if necessary. I must have my petition read and acted upon at once, and get her out of Australia before I lose her."

Within a week, he began to receive her long cables, all written under the watchful eye of Henry Wakeford and so they were bland and dull. Mrs. Simon Plowman organized a used clothing drive for the indigent of Perth and Fremantle and distributed food to needy widows and orphans. Dinner parties, tea parties, and card parties were her topics, a wife corresponding with her husband. The scorching love letter would be alarming, something that would make Simon wonder what his wife was up to on the other side of the world. He cabled her, to exert what little influence he had when he was half a world away. "Remember your name," he wired, "Be steadfast."

*　*　*

Two gentlemen rode peacefully through Dublin's quiet streets, two military men out for a night of drinking and carousing. They were a convivial pair, looking for a public house that would serve a man in a red coat. "So, you told her that you loved your father," Sir Peter Plowman said.

"It is the only lie I have ever told her, sir," Simon replied.

"Nonsense, my boy, you are not one to lie to a woman. Your mother saw to that, thank God. Not a scoundrel like your father, and I'm proud of you for it," Peter said. "You spoke the truth. It's no disloyalty to your mother."

"Is that why you joined me this evening?" Simon asked. "To earn my respect?"

"No, I must admit, I came with you to earn her forgiveness. I was out of line when I demanded an annulment, to speak before I heard the facts. Most of the Fenian soldiers were shipped off to India to get them out of Ireland and put down their revolution." The old dragoon shifted in his saddle, uncomfortable when admitting he had been wrong. "Naturally, I was only given one side of the story, and I presumed the worst. My view was distorted and based on the information I was given in Calcutta. I suppose you found it uproariously funny that I ascribed a political idea to your wife's sweet brain. As if a woman could possibly hold a care in her head beyond her husband's happiness."

"You are entitled to your perspective," Simon said.

"Paid a lot for her, though," Peter chuckled.

The sound of horse shoes striking cobblestones echoed off the facades, windows dark and shutters closed against the vapors of the night.

Simon did not care for his father's tone, with its backhanded insult. "Out of necessity, sir. It was not a business transaction."

"I'll take your word for it," Peter said. "Power of muscle or power of money, you're my son all right."

"I did not force myself on her, if that is your implication."

"No? The man who has spent half his income on women since he discovered them at the age of sixteen? Gave her gifts and treats for no reason?" Sir Peter shook his head in disbelief, grinning at his son as if he could irk him into a full confession.

"At first, yes."

"And after, when you thought your ballocks would explode, when your blood ran so hot you thought you'd catch fire, what then?"

Simon told him that he had sought permission and bedded a woman who was willing, that he had not used trickery, unlike the man who sought the upper hand in the discussion. Conceding defeat, Peter commended his boy's restraint, offering an explanation by way of apology. The threat of disinheritance had been a foolish act, impetuous, committed by a loving father who feared that his son was about to repeat old mistakes, with the same wretched consequences.

"You are a wiser man than I was, and I hope that you will be a happier one as well," Peter said. "We share a fine eye for a pretty face, you must admit."

"Thank you, sir."

"I've already sought her forgiveness. Sent two thousand pounds, a little wedding gift." Swinging easily out of the saddle, Peter flipped the reins to the stable hand. "The future Lady Plowman should be riding in a decent carriage. It's my name and my reputation, even if you don't give a damn about appearances."

From the livery stable they walked to the Major General's lodgings on Pitt Street, a short trip that ended in a tense moment. The estranged pair stood on the road, silent and uncomfortable, their eyes not meeting until Peter asked his son to come up for a drink. Breaking the chill, Simon noted that he felt a greater need for a bath, to clean up after the filthy business they had been about that night.

After Simon had dropped into a leather upholstered armchair in his father's study, Peter mentioned his plans for the future, which amounted to retirement from active duty, leaving India behind to return to Dublin for good. "You'll come by, won't you?" the older man asked.

"You don't intend to renew your harassment of my mother?"

"For God's sake, Simon, that was almost twenty years ago." Peter poured out two glasses of very good Irish whiskey and took a seat near the fireplace across from his son. "She'll come by, you know. Defy you if she must, but she'll come to call on me. Irish girls are so damned pious, she'll honor her father and mother in spite of you."

"You seem quite confident, father," Simon scoffed.

"Years of experience, my boy. You come to see me every now and again, write at least four times a year. It was your mother who sent you to me, and she put the pen in your hand."

The conversation grew increasingly honest as the bottle of liquor was drained, with inebriated confessions closing out their evening. He was his father's son, Simon finally agreed, and with that simple admission he became his father's equal. Their discussion took on a new tone, as if they met at last on level ground, speaking of things that were once unspeakable. For the first time, Peter rationalized a decision that he insisted was only a matter of duty over family, an act that Katherine should have supported.

"You were wrong," Simon argued. "You knew her brothers were there and still you kept silent when you could have requested a transfer out of Kilkenny."

"They would have thought me weak," Peter insisted. "Soft on the rebels because of my love of Ireland. Maybe I was wrong to place my career and reputation ahead of your mother's sentiments, but I had to make a choice and it was not her place to question me."

For a moment, Simon reflected on his father's words, the warmth of the whiskey soothing the chill of his heart. While he could not agree with the logic, he could accept his father's commitment, and in a straightforward, simple way, he forgave his father and reconciled with a man who was not such a stranger after all.

Until Simon made peace with his father, he found it nearly impossible to obtain a meeting with the Chief Secretary, who was enough of an acquaintance of Sir Peter to be aware of the Major General's thoughts on a certain marriage. While Sir Peter's change of heart may have opened the right doors, it was the scandal that exploded in Dublin that made all the difference in Mary Claire's case.

The two little girls found cowering in Reverend Wilkerson's bed insisted that their patron had been hanged by two men, gentlemen by the sound of their voices, two men who smelled of horses and leather. Although all of Dublin never heard of that particular detail, the residents were made aware of the Reverend's penchant for so-called French postcards, obscene photographs of children that he had scattered around his bedroom before he threw a rope over the door of his dressing room and killed himself. Nothing more was publicized, and the hearing into Reverence Wilkerson's suicide was a closed-door affair.

"It was not so much a suicide note as a confession," Mr. Wilson-Patten said, discretely revealing a few secrets to Lt. Plowman.

"Then he admitted that he lied under oath when he testified against my wife?"

"In explicit terms. He addressed his note, indeed, it was actually a petition to His Lordship, the very petition that you were hoping to obtain."

"Perhaps my repeated requests for a petition dislodged some guilt and sent his conscience tumbling," Simon suggested.

Leaning over his desk, clasping his hands on top of a stack of papers, the bureaucrat lowered his voice. "His actions alone, Lieutenant, would have been enough to plunge him into despair. He was found naked, and the girls who shared his bed were nude. What they told the matron would curl your hair."

"You did not send for me to discuss the Wilkerson case."

"We receive reams of petitions, and the mountain of clemency requests has risen higher by the day since the Fenians were transported." The subject changed, Wilson-Patten leaned back against the cushions, a politician's soft smirk creeping across his face. "Your wife, such a minor character, I'm afraid she may have been overlooked in the crush."

Simon leveled a knowing glare at Mr. Wilson-Patten. There had been an avalanche of petitions, from some of the most respectable residents of Fremantle, Western Australia. The Governor of the territory had lauded her meritorious and exemplary conduct; the Anglican minister had praised her Christian virtue and growing interest in the doctrines of the Church of England. Today's meeting boiled down to the fevered determination of Wilkerson's brother, Lord Dunbarton, to hush up the scandal as fully and completely as possible. It had already cost His Lordship a small fortune.

"In light of your record of service, Lt. Plowman, and your ability to enlist Mrs. Plowman...turned her around completely, it appears."

"In light of international outrage over the treatment of the Fenians, sir, I would think that such an egregious case of injustice would add little to Her Majesty's reputation abroad," Simon countered.

"Which is why we fully expect that this matter can be treated with great delicacy," the Chief Secretary said in a stage whisper. He handed over a portfolio with an air that suggested something illicit was trading hands. "You'll want to bring Mrs. Plowman the news yourself, I'm sure."

Out on the street, there was talk of the civilian Fenians being pardoned, with their rebellion relegated to history, just another uprising in a long string of unrest. In time, Mary Claire would surely have been released, but Lt. Plowman was owed something for his activities. While he could not be publicly lauded for his undercover work, he could have his wife back, and produce the little army of soldiers that he was so keen to create.

Simon booked passage on the *Linscelles*, leaving Southampton on Monday. Before boarding the packet boat in Dublin he wired Mary Claire to give her the details, and then he waited nervously for her reply. It was already late in Fremantle, nearly two o'clock in the earliest hours of Monday on the other side of the world, where the twentieth of July had not yet dawned.

"All haste," she urged. "God speed."

Simon boarded the *Linscelles* and passed the longest three and one half months of his life. The merchantman was not a good sailor, and foul weather added to the endless journey. Every night, Simon went to sleep in his berth below deck, and every night he dreamed of Mary Claire, of the great things that she would do as Mrs. Simon Plowman, moving through the highest circles in Dublin while holding an ear to America and the O'Dwyer boys.

The *Linscelles* arrived in Fremantle on the eleventh of November, a day that was as hot and dry as the day that Plowman left Mary Claire behind. With the volume of shipping traffic in the estuary, he had to wait patiently outside the harbor, sorely tempted to swim for it. It was after six o'clock when he finally set foot on Victoria Quay, but he did not waste time in town. Heading off along the beach, making his way to Hampton's road, he broke into a trot with his leather satchel tucked under his arm.

During the entire voyage to Australia he had pondered his greeting, thought about how he would tell Mary Claire that she was free, and how he should most dramatically present the official documents. He contemplated the best arrangement of words that would let her know that they were leaving for Dublin in three days. Breathing rapidly from excitement, he pushed open the front door and stopped in his tracks. He had to rub his eyes, to wipe away the gauzy film that he seemed to be looking through. It was not gauze, but a fog of Fremantle dust that filled the room, the dry grit that was everywhere.

The layer was evenly applied to every surface in the house; every step that he took stirred up a little cloud at his feet. From the parlor he walked through the dining room and into the kitchen, gray mist draped like crepe over every object he touched. Under the crepe was meticulous order, tidy housekeeping that had become shrouded in prison gray. He retraced his steps, back to the parlor to enter the bedroom. The candlewick bedspread was dingy, but the bed had been made without a crease in the sheets, the two sides of the coverlet falling evenly to the floor.

Moving swiftly, he pulled open the door of the armoire, afraid of what he might find. A section of shelves had been removed, a small empty space created, but the remaining compartments were neatly stacked. Two dozen pairs of under drawers lay peacefully within, Mary Claire's personal linens that she changed obsessively two and three times each day. A few dresses were folded and stored in their proper places, an exquisite evening gown carefully wrapped in an old sheet to protect the silk from Fremantle's dust. Gloves and hats were tucked into shelves and bins, handkerchiefs folded to reveal the embroidered 'P' that she had worked into a corner, and everything was coated with dust.

On the floor of the chest he saw two pairs of shoes, one a delicate evening slipper and the other a coarse walking shoe. He picked up the finely crafted balmorals, the black leather of the best quality. The tops were scuffed and marred by the abrasion of heavy iron manacles that had gouged scratches into the smooth hide. They were the same shoes that she had removed on their first night together, the same shoes that she had kept as a link to Rathkeale and her father's tannery. Saddened, he replaced the shoes in their spot with a reverence that suited a priceless artifact.

No matter how much he tried to deny it, he was aware that she had gone. He sniffed back a tear, hurt that she had run away rather than wait for him. It was not hard to picture her, grabbing at the first offer of freedom, unable to tolerate another day in a dry, dusty and colorless land. From the first day that he saw her, and every day on the *Hellebore*, he had turned her into stone, rock hard and unbreakable as a Royal Marine, but now he saw that she had finally crumbled. She was only a woman, and he had asked too much of her.

One man in town would know where she had gone, the only man in Fremantle who she would trust completely. Simon's steps were heavy as he made his way to St. Patrick's, picturing Mary Claire walking the same route every day to attend Mass. In his mind, he saw her striding along the track, passing the same trees that he noticed now, looking up to see the first few houses at the edge of town, the shops beyond, and the forbidding rocks of The Establishment that glowed in the light of the setting sun.

The old housekeeper at the parochial house was of no use. Father McCabe was in the bush, Father Concannon was the parish priest, but he had gone out to give the Last Rites to a group of convicts who were crushed in an accident at the quarry. Simon walked away from the rectory, lost, and he wandered through the churchyard in a daze.

It was jarring to abruptly be made aware of his selfish nature. He had married a woman and never bothered to ask her when she was born, something that was unimportant at the time but something that mattered to the ladies. He did not ask the date, not even the year; he thought only of her hair and her white skin, of being her lord and master. Aged nineteen years and three days, she was younger than she appeared in Portland Gaol, but prison tended to age a woman very quickly. Wife of Simon, he pondered the commonplace sound of it as he lay down next to her. With his satchel under his head, he stretched out an arm to embrace her through the mounded earth.

"You're free, Mary Claire, your name is cleared. I told you I would come back and take you home, and I have. You'll sleep in Athenry Parish, next to my uncles. They'll be great company, telling you the tales of Brian Boru and the sorrow of Vinegar Hill.

"My father is sorry about his cable. He can be cruel, like me, but we're soldiers and it is our nature. He bought our passage to Dublin, that's how he has expressed his regret, and he wants to settle an income on you so you can have the prettiest clothes that you choose yourself because it is your money that will buy them. When he takes you riding, he'll show you off, like a father, that's what he wants to do."

Salty tears soaked into the parched ground of her grave, absorbed by the dust as rapidly as they were shed. "If they killed you, Mary Claire,

I swear to God that I will avenge your death. Any man with your blood on his hands, I promise, I will kill every one of them. Your life belonged to me and no man had a right to take it."

Throughout the night he stayed with her, singing songs to help her sleep peacefully, to tide her over until she could rest in Ireland. He dozed off and on, waking to tell her about Dublin, napping and stirring again to laugh over the scandal of Wilkerson's possessions, forfeited to the Crown. Father Concannon found him in the cemetery at dawn on Thursday, dirty, confused and broken.

"Prison killed her, and they are to blame," the priest stormed, pointing towards the forbidding walls of The Establishment. Unclenching his fist, he wrestled his passion under control. "God forgive me, it's petty to speak so. She's not the first woman that I've buried just days after a new life was brought into the world. St. Patrick called her home, to sing with the angels, and it is not for us to ask why or rail at God because we don't want what he has willed."

"Did she suffer?" Simon asked.

"The fever came on quickly, and she slipped away very quietly, at peace with the Lord. Very peaceful, Mr. Plowman, she made her confession and took the Eucharist," Concannon lowered his voice. "I heard her confession, and anointed her as she was anointed in baptism. It gave her great joy at the end, and when she became delirious, she had peaceful and happy reveries."

Simon had to come to grips with the end of an idyll, the destruction of his dreams and plans. For a long minute he sat, struggling to maintain his dignity while his rage boiled unseen by Father Concannon. There would be no sons sent down to Sandhurst, not ever, because no other woman on earth would surrender her fate to him as Mary Claire had done. Life's simple pleasures and great triumphs were buried with her.

He was wrecked, cast adrift, lost without a star to guide him or a compass to chart his path.

"Have you seen the baby?" the priest continued.

His stare was vacant and uncomprehending. The baby was only a concept in his mind, a work in progress, a form in the making, and he could not grasp the reality of a living child. He allowed the priest to lead him into the parlor, to be served tea and to be consoled.

"The baby?" Simon finally asked.

"Your daughter was born on a Sunday, Mr. Plowman. Fair and wise and good and gay, the old wives say," Concannon said. "The night that John O'Reilly escaped, she thought it was her time and by morning the midwife decided it was beginning but still long off."

"O'Reilly?"

While Simon sat in the cool, shaded parlor, staring at his hands, the priest prattled on, sharing the gossip that had been running through Fremantle. Only a few words registered in the Marine's brain: a rowboat, the reefs, false labor and the water police. Simon did not care about the American merchantman that took John O'Reilly to freedom. He did not understand anything that the priest was talking about until he mentioned Boots going off to find Mary Claire when she missed Mass on Sunday.

"He thought she had run, but he was back in town in no time, his horse in a lather." Concannon paused only long enough to slurp a mouthful of tea, his throat dry from his long monologue. "Dr. Hampton, now, he's thinking 'tis a ruse, the same subterfuge, and he sends guards down the road towards Bunbury and he makes his headquarters in your house."

"Did he hurt her?" Simon started to rise, ready to kill.

"As soon as he walked in your door, he was feeling the fool. He told the midwife he had come out of respect for your position, to deliver the child. Maybe it was for the best, because she was torn inside and he stopped the bleeding." Concannon stopped, crossed himself, and murmured a brief prayer. "The fever set in the next day. He did all he could to treat her, but childbed fever and tropical fevers are two different things."

Looking up, Simon realized that the priest was studying him closely. He forced his mind to focus on Concannon's words, sentences that were of great importance to the cleric. "One day, when we were traveling on the road, she asked me if it was a sin to create shadows and becloud reality. I had no answer for her then, but I think I see now that we create illusions all the time." Concannon nodded at his own wisdom. "That is vanity, at its core, a woman creating an illusion of beauty and we accept it as a normal practice, one to be praised. Whatever you may hear in town, remember that she was faithful to you."

"And O'Reilly is gone?"

"Gone indeed. And Dr. Hampton before long, taking the blame for a plot that grew right under his nose and he never smelled it. Boots was nearly shown the door as well, but I'd not be surprised if London is advertising his position." The room fell into a deep silence as Concannon poured another cup of tea. A clattering of spoon against china was too loud, out of place, and the priest put the cup down without touching a drop. "Your wife made a fool of him, for reasons I'll never know, but she sowed the seeds of discord in that house."

"Where is my girl?"

Before he could answer, the priest had to stand and take two steps forward, then two steps back. "Listen to me, with a clear head and the tears dried. Your wife is with God, son, and you're left here on earth and there's no point in grieving for her when she's in paradise. The Wakeford woman took the baby and had her christened in the Protestant church, and they will take her for their own if you falter. Get your daughter back before you lose her."

"I'm taking them both home," Plowman said, going into battle. "I'll not leave her here to crumble into Fremantle dust. What do I do, where do I start?"

Placing a steadying hand on Simon's shoulder, Concannon offered advice to a man whose world had splintered. "Collect yourself, pull yourself together. Settle your accounts, take your family and get out of here. Turn your back on Fremantle, and never utter the name of this accursed land."

With new resolve, Lt. Plowman gathered his scattered thoughts and found a touchstone in the priest's advice. He had work to do, a lifetime of struggle left to him, and he set off on a new course with his jaw fixed and his stride unbroken. Barging into the Emerald Isle hotel, he glared at Mahoney when the man offered his sympathies. Simon pounded on the desk as he demanded a room, unable to stay at his house without Mary Claire.

"Ah, Christ, the funeral, Lieutenant, 'twas the biggest thing we've ever seen here," Mahoney said, watching Simon sign the register. "Four mutes followed the coffin, bells ringing at St. Patrick's and Christ Church together. Folks waiting outside, the church was so crowded. Fellow came from the *Conflict*, out of respect for your position. The captain himself, Lt. Plowman, acting as a pallbearer."

"What are they saying about my wife?" Simon growled.

"I'd rather not speak ill of the dead, sir," Mahoney said.

Grabbing the man's suit collar, Simon pulled Mahoney across the front desk and snapped in his face. "What are they saying about my wife?"

"That she'd be gone by now, and Boots the one taking her away." Mahoney gulped, braced for a punch in the mouth for slandering the woman.

"Go on, give me the rest," Simon commanded.

"Running off to America together," he said. "Helping a convict to escape is nearly as bad as the convict's punishment for running, and Boots was ready to smuggle her onto a ship leaving Sydney. I'd sooner say no more, if you don't mind."

"I want it all, Mahoney, every tale that has been told in your dining room and your lobby. I have a right to know."

Something that scandalous was not a fit topic for the entrance of a public building, so Mahoney brought his guest into his office. He poured out two glasses of whiskey, knocking his back before he could continue. Since Simon asked for it, he was given the unvarnished truth. Mrs. Plowman and Boots were lovers, keeping company in private and acting the innocents in public, out rowing with a priest and John O'Reilly for escorts. In the eyes of the Fenian sympathizers, it was surely O'Reilly's way to get even with Plowman for the disaster in Kilclooney Wood, to sit by and let Mrs. Plowman cuckold her husband. It was said that O'Reilly was never so happy as when he had spent the day with the lovers, exploring the reefs off the coast. The fact that the same rowboat was used for the escape made the entire episode that much more joyous, marred only by the death of Mrs. Plowman, God rest her soul.

"You knew my wife," Simon looked into Mahoney's eyes, warm gray and wet with tears as he spoke of the dead woman. "Do you believe any of it?"

"You know the truth yourself, don't you? She wanted to get out of here, and she used Wakeford to do it." Another drink was poured, a toast to Mrs. Simon Plowman made and seconded. "Wanted freedom bad enough to fall from grace. She would have put to sea with the devil himself to get home to Ireland. And to you."

With a swig of liquor burning his gullet, Simon thought back to days past, to etch a memory in his mind forever. In another mouthful, his glass was drained, and he fixed his gaze on his host. "She's blameless in my eyes. I'll never say a word against her."

"God rest her soul, Mr. Plowman, but she brought Hampton and Wakeford down, and for that they sing her praises in some parts of town. It's justice for all they've done to the Irishmen they've shackled, and I'm sorry if that insults you, but there comes a time when a man has to speak his mind."

For the rest of the afternoon, Simon went from shop to shop, paying up bills and withdrawing the funds he had left in the bank. Mrs. Finch gave him a complete rundown of all of Mary Claire's purchases, complimenting her frugal nature while pinning a black armband onto the lieutenant's left sleeve. Surrounded by shoppers, Simon was inundated with the respect and admiration that Mary Claire had earned in her time as a Fremantle housewife. As she had once promised, the reports of her time in Fremantle made him proud of her, an ordinary wife, a gracious woman.

In the secret world of the Fenians, and Fremantle was full of them, there were secrets that Simon would not be told, and secrets they would remain. No one had ever gotten away from Fremantle Gaol, and now the arrogance of Hampton and Wakeford, their confidence that their prison could defeat a man's spirit, had been utterly crushed, while their reputations and careers were diminished into near insignificance. Somehow, the ignominy of John O'Reilly's leave-taking alleviated a little of Simon's sorrow, offering a laugh at the pretensions of stodgy government officials who were not so clever after all.

Looking back, Simon could see that the O'Dwyer brothers had found freedom, and now O'Reilly was gone, leaving eight other soldiers still incarcerated but certainly not beaten. Perhaps the Fenian threat to Queen Victoria's dominion was dissipated now, scattered harmlessly in America or exiled to the most remote corners of the Empire. Perhaps it would rise up again. All that mattered to Simon was that Mary Claire was dead, his hopes for the future were gone, and he would not think about the Irish rebels any more.

He spent a restless night, tormented by memories, and his eyes were red rimmed the next morning when he looked out over Fremantle. Returning to Market Street, he bought a small suitcase and he walked back along Hampton's road with a renewed sense of purpose. It was left to him to pack up and get out, and there was little that he wanted to take.

Settled next to an overstuffed chair in the parlor he found her mending basket, with a pair of stockings rolled up inside. Near that she had stored her knitting bag, with a half-finished baby blanket hanging on the needles, all things that were useless to him now. The kitchen had been picked clean, by the ladies in town or the scrubwoman, with no scrap remaining that would have rotted in the heat. A tin of tea sat next to the dust covered cream jug, a piece of pottery that he flung at the wall in fury.

Wandering through the wash room, he touched her apron, left hanging on a peg and gray with dust. Soap for washing was there, far too much soap for one woman. An iron rested on some handkerchiefs, but he left them all behind and went to the bedroom, to think about an appropriate treasure to keep for a little girl who would never know her mother. Clothes were meaningless and he shut the door of the armoire on them. Finally, he saw it, placed on the table near the windows where she kept her writing supplies. The journal was coated with the dry grit that blew in through every gap of the window frame, and the Kelly green ribbon that tied it closed was dulled with dust.

Next to it was a copy of their wedding picture, enclosed in a beautiful and ornate silver frame. It was obvious that Mary Claire had left it there for their daughter, a pretty package that would be the child's legacy. Without opening the book, not wanting to see her words when he could not see her, he carefully lifted the journal from the table. Underneath, he saw the stacks of newsprint, single pages that she had saved from the Fremantle editions that mentioned Mrs. Simon Plowman at some social function or charitable activity, a record of one woman's ordinary life.

Everything was packed into the cheap suitcase, the case that Simon would use forever to store Mary Claire's memory. The task became impossible to complete; he had to get out. Guilt was beginning to grow in his heart, a realization that he had been too awash in his mission, and that he had mistreated her for the sake of orders. Others had used her as a pawn, and he was no better.

There were other tasks to attend to and Simon hurried back to the dock, to be assured that his belongings were transferred from the *Linscelles* to the *Northwood*. From there, he made his way up High Street, to the square and spare British colonial edifice that housed Mr. and Mrs. Wakeford. The wrought iron balcony on the second floor was the only ornamentation, a silly bit of fluff that was out of place, like a lace doily on a gun truck. It had been built on the backs of starving Irishmen, punished for the crime of being hungry.

A bent old woman ushered him in, looking like a convict who had served her sentence and stayed in her position because there was nowhere else to go. She brought him to the parlor, where the air behind the stone and plaster was ten degrees cooler than the sweltering climate in the street.

It was a very short wait before Wakeford appeared. Everyone in town knew by now that Lt. Plowman was back, and Henry was primed for the unavoidable.

"Lt. Plowman, we did not expect to see you again, that is, so soon," the disgraced Comptroller General stammered.

"I'll take my child and be gone," Simon replied.

"We've grown very attached to little Clarisse," Henry said. "We have come to think of her as our daughter, or granddaughter, and frankly, Lieutenant, I have given this matter a great deal of thought."

"You have thought?" Simon glowered.

"My wife and I can provide her with a warm and loving home. In your situation, Lt. Plowman, serving our country as a Royal Marine, on duty at sea for months, away from home. What sort of life is that for a child?"

"A better home, Mr. Wakeford, than one in which the husband has cuckolded the girl's father."

"Baseless rumor, sir, idle gossip created by weak female minds." Wakeford said, using an armchair as a barricade.

"Where would you have run to, Mr. Wakeford? Boston? New York?"

"We had considered New York, yes," Wakeford tugged at his collar.

"And do you know who lives in New York? Do you know who lives in Boston? Perhaps the names of Michael and Edward O'Dwyer have already passed into history and out of your thoughts." Step by step, Simon came closer, until he was inches away from Wakeford's face. "Here is a name that is more current, or have you forgotten Michael O'Dwyer's second in command? Is John O'Reilly forgotten as well?"

"O'Reilly was in Kilclooney Wood?" Wakeford croaked.

KATIE HANRAHAN

"Left in the safekeeping of the penal system, and the men I tracked, risked my life to capture, have been allowed to sail away as freely as business men on a sales trip," Simon snarled. "My wife's death was your salvation, you stupid fool, and that is all that saved your neck from a sharp blade. Do you know what Ed O'Dwyer said to me when I was ambushed in Kilclooney? He knew I'd run her down and chain her, and I did just that. Do you think they would have welcomed you as a brother?"

"It's not true," Wakeford said, circling away in a dance of fear. "She loved me, not you. I was going to give her a life of adoration, a life filled with love. You bought her as your whore; I know the facts from the women who shared her jail cell. We were in love, Lieutenant, Mary Claire and I were in love."

"I will be here in the morning for my daughter. If her nurse is a convict, God help you if you try to stop me from taking her along."

Plowman ambled to the front door, with an agitated man following behind. "What, the O'Dwyer, what did he threaten to do to you?" Henry finally choked out the words.

Simon did not answer, continuing to walk out the door until the hot air hit his face. He shot Henry a cold glare, a look that spoke of violent murder, and then he closed the door behind him. He never could remember what Edward had said to him.

Fifteen

Checking off a short roster, Simon finished his business in Fremantle as if it were a military campaign. The time came to return to the Comptroller General's house on Saturday morning, but Wakeford was ready for combat, with reinforcements to back him. Mrs. Wakeford welcomed Lt. Plowman into her parlor, where Mrs. Looby and Mrs. Hightower hovered like ravens in black mourning.

"Please, Lt. Plowman, is there nothing that I can say to make you change your mind?" Ruth sobbed into a handkerchief. "My heart is entwined around Clarisse. She is more of a granddaughter to me than my son's children. Don't take her from me, I beg you."

"My wife is dead, Mrs. Wakeford, and all I have left is my child," Plowman said. "How can you ask me to leave her behind?"

"You could start again, with another wife," Mrs. Hightower suggested. "There could be more children for you."

"My husband is planning to return to England soon, so that we can devote the rest of our lives to this precious child," Mrs. Wakeford went on. "A respectable home, mingling with the right sort of people. She would want for nothing and have every advantage."

"Is she ready to go?" Simon asked, unmoved.

"Think of the child, please, Lt. Plowman," Delia blubbered.

Unexpectedly, Henry popped in, leaving his hiding place behind the door. He saw the need to plead his case again, but this time he would not be cowed by the threats of a jealous husband. "Can you see now, Lieutenant, that my wife and I have lost a daughter, and all we have to comfort us is her child? When Mrs. Plowman was laboring, my wife was at her side, acting as a mother, to help her through a difficult and frightening experience. How can you tear Clarisse from her, when they were united at birth?" Wakeford said, seeking to curry sympathy from a heartless man.

Deaf ears heard nothing, blind eyes saw nothing as Simon strode to the foot of the stairs. "Nurse," he roared ferociously, "Bring my child to me at once or I shall come up after you and throw you down the stairs to make you move faster."

Every one of Henry's loud protestations was ignored as Simon waited, rigid and unbent. His vision was fixed on a young woman who was easing her way down the steps. Dressed in sober black bombazine and a crisp white apron, the lady had a firm grip on the sleeping bundle that she cradled warmly. Reaching the foyer, she stopped walking and waited for an instruction, the look of alarm unmistakable in her eyes. First at Mr. Wakeford, then at Lt. Plowman, her gaze flitted from side to side.

Focused on his task, Simon did not react, did not reach out to hold his daughter. This was not the time to look upon her face and search for Mary Claire reflected in a baby. He could see ahead to another day, when he would have time to shed tears and sink into sorrow. Tomorrow, he would have the rest of his life to be a widower with a tiny responsibility to care for, but that was tomorrow.

"Are your trunks packed?" he asked the nurse.

"Am I to leave, Mr. Wakeford?" she inquired with tension in her voice.

"There, you see for yourself, Nanny does not wish to leave. Clarisse cannot be taken away until she is weaned, at the earliest." Wakeford rejoiced at a hindrance. "No need for haste, Mr. Plowman. We can manage this affair at a reasonable pace and come to an agreement. Guardianship, while you remain on duty, why, a transfer to Western Australia would be most desirable for all parties."

"Outside the door, nurse, is a cart from the express office. Two men are waiting. Go out to them, now, and show them where your trunks are so that they can deliver them to the ship. Give the baby to Mrs. Wakeford so that she can hold her while you see that everything is made ready." Simon said.

The wet nurse moved swiftly, propelled by the threatening demeanor of a Marine lieutenant. Still not quite comprehending what was happening, Mrs. Wakeford held the infant in her tender embrace while her friends attempted to reason with Plowman. Two dusty convict laborers tromped up the stairs while two respectable matrons dabbed at tears and showered Simon with pleas. The convicts clomped back down with the nurse's worldly possessions and Mrs. Looby entreated the officer, begging for reasonable consideration. On a second trip, the laborers retrieved the infant's collection of clothes and toys, and the three women began to sink into a shocked silence.

"Everything that was purchased in town has been reimbursed to your accounts," Simon told Wakeford. "I shall, of course, pay all additional expenses that you incurred on behalf of my wife and child, if you would be so kind as to submit a bill."

The nurse took the baby and Simon took Mrs. Wakefield's hands in his. "My gratitude to you, for the love that you bestowed on my wife, is beyond measure."

"For the last time, Lieutenant, will you listen to reason?" Henry implored.

With an affectionate squeeze of each woman's hand, Simon nodded silent farewells. His grip was firm when he took Henry's hand. "Thank you for looking after my daughter in my absence."

Leaving behind a heartbroken couple and two stunned friends, he steered the nurse out of the house and closed the door quietly behind him. "What is your name, madam?" he asked.

"Barnhill, sir, Mrs. Ted Barnhill. Them in there, they called me Nanny Tessa, used my Christian name, sir, that's how it's done."

"Very well, Mrs. Barnhill. May I ask after Mr. Barnhill?"

"Died in Perth six months ago, sir, fell off a scaffold. He was a carpenter, sir, one of the best in Western Australia, if you don't mind my boasting."

"Where is your infant?"

"Liam's weaned last month, sir, and I put him up with a neighbor so that Clarisse isn't mixed with common people. Mrs. Wakeford says your father is a baronet, sir."

"Mrs. Barnhill, I am going to take my daughter to St. Patrick's Church and give her a name. Fetch your son and meet me there, and do not dawdle."

Not yet clear on what was happening, or where she was going, Tessa handed over the baby, dropped a curtsy, and tore down the street. With a single-minded purpose, Simon strode in the opposite direction, not fully aware of the blistering heat that radiated through the soles of his boots. His mind was consumed with his last few tasks.

Kicking on the door of the parochial house, Simon shouted out for Concannon, ordering him into his vestments. There was no time to waste. Standing at the baptismal font, with old Mrs. Doyle acting as proxy to Miss Anna Plowman, the cleric asked for the name, not hiding his joy at rescuing a soul from Anglican hands.

"Eireann," Simon spat out angrily. "Eireann go Bragh Plowman."

"But wouldn't a name to honor one of our saints be more suitable for a Catholic girl?" Concannon suggested.

"Her name holds those of every saint of Ireland, St. Patrick, St. Brendan, St. Brigid, and all the rest. Anyone who shed blood for Ireland is honored in that name. She's to be Eireann, Father. Baptize her into the Catholic faith."

Just as Father Concannon was pouring a trickle of Holy Water onto the head of a screaming infant, Mrs. Barnhill returned with a dirty little toddler of twelve months in one hand and a tattered bag of clothes in the other. At that instant, Simon sensed the life that squirmed and wailed in his hands as he held his daughter. For the first time, he looked at her face that was growing red with anger. Her thin curls were brown, coiling like her mother's but so wispy they could have been soft clouds. Her eyes opened and he saw the blue of the Plowman line, with fair skin that had come to her from the Kenneally clan.

The inexperienced father rocked and cooed, soothing the unhappy little girl, and as she calmed down her tiny mouth puckered into a pout, a moue that was all inquisitiveness and wonder. Her unblinking stare, her curious seeking, they were all the unique features of Eireann Plowman, a new person. Only now did Simon understand that he had created a human being and he was holding her in his hands. His daughter had been conceived in the horror of the *Hellebore*, but Eireann was as beautiful as

Mary Claire's love, the love that grew out of a lieutenant's berth on a prison ship.

The Barnhill boy began to fuss, reminding Simon that he had work to do before the *Northwood* sailed on Sunday. Rounding up the party, he carried a rather unhappy Eireann to the Emerald Isle Hotel. He ordered food, then asked that his bill be tallied and his bags brought down. Simon was nearly ready to go.

Brought to a table, Mrs. Barnhill sat dumbly with her jaw dropping, completely confused by the day's goings on. She had never eaten in a hotel before, never expected to do so, and now her overwhelming sense of social inferiority made her choke on a sip of water. A pair of businessmen came in for dinner, their summer linen soaked through with sweat, and Tessa wanted more than anything to dash back to the safety of her little room in the house on High Street. One of the gentlemen was Irish, prosperous by the look of him, and he embarrassed Tessa into a tizzy by complimenting her on such a sturdy lad as her son.

If not for Mahoney's intercession, Tessa would have melted into a pool of shy discomfort. The two businessmen were playing with Liam, hiding behind their napkins and then popping out, all to make the little boy giggle.

"Can't you always pick out the men with a dozen babies at home?" Mahoney chided his clients. "He's a little boy himself, ma'am, pay him no mind. Go on, Quigley, let the woman be."

"Say, Mahoney, is it true what I heard in Melbourne? Someone escaped?" Quigley asked. "John O'Reilly?"

"Every bit of it, and it was the Fenian Brotherhood behind it," Mahoney confided. "I didn't say anything to a fellow earlier, not when I think his wife was sweet on John O'Reilly, and a few other gentlemen as well. O'Reilly got pulled off the jetty crew and made a messenger by her say-so, and he was always stopping at her house, bringing love notes they say. He saw his chance, I guess, as soon as he was out of the chain gang, had his fun in her bed and took French leave."

Eavesdropping, Tessa learned for the first time that a naval gunboat was somehow involved in all this, steaming north looking for Fenians who were trying to cut the telegraph cable to Java. According to Mr. Mahoney, the captain had made up the excuse because he was off on a shopping trip, looking for something to entice the late Mrs. Plowman. As if she needed to stop up the little girl's ears, Tessa settled her hand onto Eireann's head, stroking the soft curls.

"There's always a woman involved," Quigley's partner shook his head. "People in Canberra are saying that Wakeford and Hampton both took the oath."

"Nothing could be proved, but Hampton's been given the boot and Wakeford's next in line," the innkeeper continued. "Wakeford denied all along that he was a sympathizer. Didn't deny that he had booked passage out of Sydney for him and his wife and child. Going to New York City, except the wife wasn't actually his wife, and the baby wasn't actually his baby. Made plans to sneak a convict out of prison, and he's the man running the prison."

With the men preoccupied with their randy gossip, snickering rudely over the recently deceased, Tessa settled into a moment of peace. She nursed Eireann and kept an eye on Liam, casting glances out of the window from time to time as she searched for her new employer. Her nerves were on edge with the fear that Liam would break something, and she was aching with discomfort over the plush surroundings that were not suited to her station in life.

One last time, Simon braced his nerves to return to the house and finish his task. The home had sheltered him for the most blissful few days of his life, but somehow he could no longer capture an impression of happiness in the dusty, hazy bedroom. He was never coming back, and he forced his mind to analyze, to find and take away the mementoes that Eireann would come to treasure.

A last walk through the parlor, made this time in daylight, did not reveal anything more than a pamphlet with a series of devotional prayers. On the bed in the adjoining room he found the open valise, just as he had left it, and he scanned the room once more. There on the small table next to the bed was a book that he had nearly overlooked.

The dust of Fremantle obscured the Celtic cross that had been embossed on the leather cover. Inside were words that had once been banned in Ireland, by order of the king. The pages contained a record of practices that had been condemned under the old Penal Laws, and Mary Claire had suffered because of the contents of her missal. Because she was a Roman Catholic and Irish, she had been persecuted, hounded to her death by an Anglican government. So much of Simon's life became distilled into the essence of that observation. It was all that he would look for, the last item worth keeping, because it was a reminder of subjugation and the cruelty of transportation, the roots of Fenianism and rebellion.

He came back at six, after Tessa had essentially given up on him. She was settling her mind on staying at the hotel if Mr. Mahoney would give her a hand-out, and the arrival of Lt. Plowman elicited tears of relief. The officer was less bellicose at supper, which he ordered for them all, and which he ate in the company of his hired servant. The nurse wished that he would ask, so that she could tell him that she should be eating in the kitchen with the hotel's maid, but Tessa was learning fast. Lt. Plowman did not ask, he ordered.

After they had eaten and the children cleaned up for travel, Simon paid his bill, took his bag from Mahoney and shook hands. There was a touch of sadness in his voice as he said goodbye, but the time had come to move on, to leave Western Australia and never look back.

"If you please, sir, where are we going?" Tessa screwed up her courage when they were standing on Victoria Quay.

"Dublin," he grunted.

A Marine could be expected to scale the shrouds and take in the view from the ship's rigging, and the merchant master of the *Northwood* paid no heed to Lt. Plowman. The officer in the scarlet tunic and the tall black shako, black armband precisely attached to his sleeve, climbed aloft with Eireann held tightly to his chest. Wrapping a leg around the ratlines, he faced the southern edge of Fremantle and told his daughter all about her mother, what her parents had done together, and what he hoped Eireann would do some day.

He showed her the flames that were beginning to lick the frame of the kitchen window of the house behind Spruce Street, where a pair of leather balmorals had been filled with whale oil and put into a hot stove. Together they admired the conflagration that spread across the floors, feeding on the rivers of lamp oil and coal that trickled throughout the cottage. Nothing would be left of the funeral pyre, not a stick of wood, not a scrap of fabric. Nothing remained to mark Mary Claire's term of imprisonment.

Sir Peter and Lady Plowman were both at the North Wall on a miserable February day. They maintained a suitable distance from each other, standing like strangers in close proximity. Anna had not bothered to come, apparently preferring to avoid her father at all costs and miss a first glimpse of Eireann. Katherine wore full mourning and Sir Peter sported the requisite black armband, appropriate for two people who had lost a daughter. As passengers disembarked, they moved forward, competing to be the first to greet their only grandchild.

Peter extended his hand, giving a welcome that was formal but rimed with sorrow for a young mother's tragic death. Katherine embraced her son, kissed his cheek, and fumbled for a handkerchief while Peter laid claim to the bubbly little girl who had learned to roll over on the deck of a rolling ship.

"Half a minute, Katherine," Peter protested. "My opportunities are limited. Welcome home, my sweet, grandfather's precious angel."

Simon introduced the Barnhill family while his normally staid father babbled foolishly. With that done, and everyone ready to get out of the cold and damp, Peter returned his granddaughter and prepared to take his leave. He needed some assurance that he would not be separated from his granddaughter, willing to go through Katherine if necessary. Simon shook his hand again, promising that Eireann and her grandfather would not be divided, and without saying goodbye, the lieutenant chased after the heavy wooden crate that had been off-loaded from the *Northwood* and transferred to a packet boat. The final leg of his journey would take him to County Galway.

He kept his own company on the trip, making frequent forays into the hold to visit with his wife, who would lie in St. Agatha's verdant churchyard, next to the Kenneally brothers who had given their lives for Ireland nearly twenty years before. The internment would be very quiet, with only the husband in attendance as the lead coffin, nestled into a carved mahogany box, was slipped into the field in Athenry. Mary Claire, wife of Simon, aged nineteen years and three days, was returned to the green hills where she belonged, and Simon was satisfied that he had kept every vow and every promise.

Even though the Fenian uprising had been put down nearly two years ago, the violence and fear that was generated had not been forgotten. Perhaps that was the impetus that stirred Parliament out of its doldrums, but the punitive laws that punished the Empire's rebellious subjects were ever so slowly beginning to change. For seventy years, Irish Catholics were forced to pay a tithe to the Protestant Church of Ireland, and when Simon came home with Mary Claire and Eireann, that vindictive practice had at last been ended. Simon saw that as a sign, but he could not yet read the message, could not interpret the marker that pointed to another road. After he buried his wife, he was not quite sure which way to go.

With a few months remaining in his furlough, Plowman meandered through Galway, a county he had never seen even though it was the home of his mother's family. When his uncles were buried, his father had forbidden him to attend the funeral, and this first trip to the ancestral homeland was profoundly depressing. From Athenry he made his way south, drawn to Rathkeale in search of Mary Claire, aware that he would not find her. All he hoped for was something to soothe his heart, as her songs had once comforted him. At every house, every shop, he asked if any O'Dwyers remained, but the landless peasants had no words to share with a man who wore the Queen's colors.

All that the local people would confess was that Lord Dunbarton's agent was on edge when he got wind of a stranger in town, a Royal Marine with a glazed expression and a far-away look. His Lordship was hiding out at his country estate, where he had run in humiliation after his brother had thrown a rope over his dressing room door and put an end to his perverted existence. Following the deathbed confession, Dunbarton was terrified of retribution from the men who had once been his tenants. The violent clan who had taken up arms in Kilclooney Wood were on the loose, somewhere in the world, and when His Lordship heard of a military man asking questions in Rathkeale, he sent his agent out to collect some facts.

The estate agent found Plowman in the public house, drinking himself into a stupor. "I may have information for you, sir," Mr. Boland offered.

"And I have information for you," Simon sneered. "They've all been evicted, run off to America, or died. I've finally seen what she saw, every day, the green of the hills, the mist, the cows, everything alive, everything that she saw in vivid color."

"Yes, well, that was my information, that the O'Dwyer family is gone from these parts." Boland remained stiff, leaning towards the door as if he meant to run for the bailiffs.

"That's the true torture of Australia." Simon gesticulated with his glass, a thin layer of whiskey sloshing across the bottom. "Break her spirit with gray and dust. A weak woman, punished by proxy because it is so easy to do."

"Sir, if you intend to stir up trouble, I can have you hauled off to the local prison," Boland declared.

"I'd like to see it," Simon said, rising unsteadily to his feet. "Make a pilgrimage, that's what I'd like to do. From the county gaol, to Mountjoy, to Newgate, to Portland, and finally, to The Establishment. And I'd like to take every damned landlord with me, and count the minutes until they crack."

"Lieutenant, I would strongly recommend that you make yourself absent from Rathkeale by dawn," the agent blustered.

Rational thought crept in through a crack; the answer to Plowman's quest to avenge his loss was attempting to glow in his muddled mind. The battle had to be fought elsewhere, not just in Rathkeale, and one day he was sure to find the right place. He grinned devilishly at Boland, chuckled a bit, and staggered out. Simon made his way to Limerick City and boarded a packet boat for Dublin.

Sixteen

Over the course of the next five years, Simon Plowman was nothing more than a Royal Marine, performing his duties with the level-headedness that marked a man with no other purpose in his empty life. He rose to the rank of captain because of his dedication, serving through a period of relative peace and madcap expansion of Queen Victoria's kingdom. His seniority provided for a better station, steaming around the Mediterranean on a warship, keeping watch over the newly opened Suez Canal and the all-important route to India.

Life ran smoothly until he attended an official function in Alexandria, where he ran into Dennis Wargrave. The dinner became nothing more than an unpleasant reminder of Fremantle, and Captain Plowman put in for a transfer the next day. He was sent to the Cape Colony, to cruise off the coast of South Africa where the recently discovered diamond fields had been annexed to the British Empire. The Royal Marines were ready to do battle against those who would like to claim England's jewels, drilled to perfection by a captain who thought of nothing beyond men and munitions, military evolutions and battle tactics. It was the only way that Plowman could get through each day, one day at a time.

Simon had fooled himself into believing that Eireann would automatically accept this separation as the way that they lived, before she was born and on into the future. Hidden away in the darkest corner of his mind was the knowledge that the girl would eventually ask questions that he did not want to answer because he did not want to dredge up the buried past. He left his daughter in the care of her extended family, those who did not have the answers, and so Fremantle and the *Hellebore* could rest in peace.

Attention and affection were showered on the child, along with an occasional burst of discipline from Anna. Eireann had her aunt, she had her grandmother and grandfather, and she had a picture of her parents for company. The wedding photograph was kept in her bed every night and studied during the day, hugged warmly while her grandmother sang the songs that Mary Claire O'Dwyer had once whispered into Simon Plowman's ear as they lay together in the bunk of a small cabin. Eireann had shadowy images for parents and nothing more than reassurance that the woman in the picture had been as real as her aunt, as alive as the mothers of her friends.

Claiming his grandfather's rights, Sir Peter had custody of Eireann for two Sundays each month. They did the sorts of things that well-off grandfathers did with their pampered granddaughters, often riding through Dublin on horseback with Eireann perched on her grandfather's lap like a fairy princess in a storybook. After dinner, there were more amusements and ice cream and afternoon tea, where Eireann resided at the very center of her own blissful world.

"Grandfather, is a major general more important than a captain?" she asked when she was five.

"More important?" Peter thought for a moment. "It is a higher rank, with greater responsibility."

"Can you give orders to a captain?"

"Yes, depending on the circumstances. If we were at sea, the captain of the ship is superior to me." Thinking her satisfied, he poured milk into his tea, relishing their time together.

"Oh, at sea." She fell silent for a moment. "But what if the captain left his ship and was on land, then could you order him about?"

"You ask so many questions, Ireland," he said. "Very much like your auntie."

"Why don't you come to St. Mary's with me on Sundays?" she asked, mashing her slice of jam cake into sticky crumbs.

"Because I am Church of Ireland and you are Papist," he said.

"If you are really married to grandmother, why do you live in a different house?"

"Too many questions, Eireann go Bragh," he corrected her.

"Like auntie," she said.

In the afternoon, they perambulated along the Liffey, dropping stones into the river and cheering on the ripples as the circles raced to the banks. "Can a major general order a captain at sea to do anything?" Eireann asked.

"Why are you worrying this question into shreds?" he said.

They stopped at the confectioner's, Eireann's favorite shop in all of Dublin. She licked a spoonful of ice cream with a frown on her sweet face, and she began to ask questions again. "Can you order a captain at sea to come home?"

"Sea captains are under the command of the Royal Navy, not the army," Peter explained. "If I were planning a military campaign, and I required the assistance of the Royal Navy, I could speak to the admirals and they could then order a captain to make port. We must adhere to a chain of command."

"Can you ask the admirals to send my father home? He has to do what they command, doesn't he?"

As a career military man, Peter never considered the effect that a man's duties could have on his children, especially a little girl without a mother. His son had seen Eireann no more than three times over the past several years, but such was the nature of military service. The child had never said a word about her father's absence before, but her convoluted inquiry indicated some very long and profound examinations of the issue.

"Your auntie may write to your father and ask him to come home," Peter suggested.

"She said she could not, sir, because Papa is broken-hearted."

"Soft-headed more likely," Peter grumbled. "So, you would like your father to come home. And what shall he do to earn a living, Ireland?"

"Could he be the Lord Lieutenant? Auntie says that Earl Spencer does nothing all day and bleeds the treasury dry in return. Papa could do that," she replied.

"Very well," Peter said, "I shall write to your broken-hearted Papa and order him to come home."

In his cluttered library on Pitt Street, Sir Peter composed a scathing missive, dripping with indignation over Eireann's treatment, which amounted to exile from her only remaining parent. A successful tactician, Peter could attack Simon where he was most vulnerable, going after the corner of the heart where memories of Mary Claire were flourishing. A mention of Eireann's fear that her mother had run away and abandoned her was worth relating, to make Simon think about what he was doing. Wisely, Peter chose to put his greatest emphasis on respect for Mary Claire's legacy.

The old soldier saw a love that was elevated to mythic status, an adoration that remained because the couple had not been together long enough to have quarreled. All they had was the joy of a honeymoon, when a new bride was her husband's willing slave, before everyday life had a chance to tarnish their shining ideal. For Eireann's sake, Peter would inflict the most lethal wounds, to shake his son out of his pathetic and self-centered gloom.

The ultimate bait for the hook, however, was a mention of the conference on Home Rule for Ireland that had been held the previous November. "You could do more for the memory of your late wife, and the Irish people, by taking a seat in Parliament. You are wasting your life, and Eireann's childhood, if you remain in the Cape Colony," he closed the letter.

It was a bold gambit, for the father was suggesting that his son become actively involved in the disgusting morass of politics. As much as Sir Peter referred to Home Rule as 'Rome Rule' and decried the Papists, horrified at the prospect of the Catholics running Ireland, he accepted the inevitable and hoped to insert the Anglo-Irish elite into any new government. To make Eireann happy, Peter asked Simon to give up his military career, the glory and achievements, to cast his hat in the ring. Between the lines, Peter called his boy home before Simon, too, lost the love of his only daughter.

Having completed his tour of duty in February of 1875, Simon returned to Dublin, to make amends with the child he had ignored because he put Fremantle behind him, and Eireann was caught up in his rush to run away. She waited on the dock as the packet boat steamed into the harbor, dressed in forest green with Kelly green ribbons on her hat, a captivating beauty. The minute that the gangplank reached down to the quay, she ran full tilt onto the boat's deck, calling for her father as rudely as a wild savage.

"Don't cry, Papa," she consoled Simon as he squeezed her against his chest. "Your broken heart will get better."

As the son of a prominent British officer, and with his own stellar service record, Simon Plowman was a darling of the Anglo-Irish set. Before he had been home for a month, he took advantage of an opportunity to increase his property holdings when Lord Dunbarton fell into some financial difficulties relating to the resurrection of an old scandal at a most inopportune time. From that simple business transaction, Simon found himself standing for a seat in the Commons. The solution that Simon had peered at in Rathkeale, submerged in a sea of Irish stout, appeared before him as he stood on the hustings outside the public house extolling Home Rule.

Looking out over the faces of the electorate, Simon saw that he had the respect of the powerful, and he garnered the support of the Irish Catholics who quickly learned that Captain Plowman's daughter was being raised in the faith. Somehow, although the source of the rumor was never pinned down, the word was spread throughout Limerick that little Miss Plowman was the daughter of Mary Claire O'Dwyer. The former Marine won in a landslide.

"Will I go to London, Papa?" Eireann asked.

"No, you will go to school," her father stated the facts. He kicked a pebble off the quay, slowing his pace to watch the ripples run to the other side, only to fade half way.

"Auntie will take me," she said.

A touch of belligerence caught Simon's attention. "Auntie will not take you to London, and if you go behind my back, miss, I shall cane you," he said.

"Then you should take me, sir, so that I do not misbehave and make you angry."

"God bless Ireland," he sighed. "You are as stubborn as your mother."

Rarely did Eireann hear a single word about her mother, making the woman a grand mystery. No one ever said much, and the child's questions were usually brushed aside. Today, strolling along the Liffey on her father's arm, she tried to extract something, a short story or even a brief sentence.

"Was my Mama very stubborn?" she asked, waiting until her father was busy tipping his hat to Mr. Darragh.

"Terribly stubborn," he mumbled.

"And was she pretty?"

"You have her photograph, what do you think?"

"Was she born in Dublin like me?"

"Your mother came from County Limerick," he said after a pause. "From Rathkeale, in the district that I will represent in Parliament."

"Why did grandmother and auntie not go to your wedding? Did they not like Mama?"

"There were no railroads back then, not like today. I did not want to wait, because I loved your mother so much. We were married about ten days after we met."

"Did she have a pretty white dress, like Miss Callahan?"

"No, there was no time for a dressmaker to make something pretty," Simon said. "She wore a pretty green ribbon in her hair."

Sir Robert and Lady Carlyle interrupted the interrogation, to Eireann's displeasure, but to finally learn a little about her parents was pleasant enough to make her smile agreeably when Lady Carlyle patted her cheek. She was thrilled to snag those few sentences, but there were so many other questions that she had stored up in her head. Her father was a bit of a puzzle in his own way, going to meetings most nights and then not saying where he went or whom he met with. When Eireann asked, Simon snapped at her so sharply that she burst into tears.

"Your papa is an important man," Anna had explained. "And it is none of your affair to inquire into his activities. Good girls do not plague their fathers with such impertinent questions."

* * *

By the time that Eireann turned six, she had said goodbye to her baby days with the departure of her governess, Miss Hoban, and the arrival of Naomi McDermott, the lady's maid that she would share with Anna. At the same time, she was introduced to the adult world by a dedicated group of nuns who were showing her how to take the letters that she had learned at the age of four and make them into words. The magic and wonder of literacy were presented to her, and Eireann discovered the universe. She never tired of showing her skill, and Simon indulged her wish to read the newspaper to him after dinner. There were times when she would pronounce a word and he would hear Mary Claire in their daughter's voice, a painful recollection that he endured silently.

"Drapers," she proclaimed as she promenaded with her father near Trinity College. She pointed at signs in shop windows, calling out words she had learned in only two months. "Fine, that word is fine."

"Aren't you the scholar," Simon said. "Is that why you have been given a reprieve from your studies today?"

"No, Papa, I am to buy you a gift for your birthday today."

"Can I be given what I want most of all?"

"I only have one pound, sir."

"What I want is quite inexpensive. I would like a slice of peppermint cake, and a kiss from a pretty Irish colleen."

He smiled at her, and she smiled back, as happy as a child could be. When Simon looked up, to see where he was walking, he noticed a woman staring at him. It was a visual inspection, as if they had met before, and the lady gazed intently at Simon's face to identify him. Ever since he became involved in politics he had seen countless new faces, but the very elegant woman on the street was not familiar.

Her clothing was in the latest style, expensive yet understated, and the veil that covered her face added to her allure. As she approached, Simon cringed, hating to chat with people who knew his name when he could not recall theirs.

"Lt. Plowman?" the lady inquired. "Are you Lt. Plowman?"

"Captain Plowman, ma'am," he corrected her.

"You sailed on the *Hellebore*, did you not?" she asked.

His cheeks flushed. "Yes, at least seven years," he began to say, but his words caught in his throat.

The veiled lady crouched down and kissed Eireann's forehead with a tenderness usually reserved for a sacred relic. "I kissed your head when you were only one day old," she said to the awestruck girl.

"Did you know my mother?" Eireann asked.

"She was my most true and beloved friend," the woman said.

"Was she very pretty?" came the child's favorite question.

"We were five chained together, and your mother was the most beautiful light that blazed among us."

"I am afraid that I do not recall your name, my apologies," Simon stammered.

"You knew me as 2564," the woman stated. "Mrs. Plowman knew me as Varena Richardson."

"You are back in Dublin, then," he said. "You look very well, Mrs. Richardson, you have prospered."

"Yes, Captain Plowman, I have indeed prospered. Your wife was of great assistance to me when I first entered into a business venture." Varena reached into her handbag. Holding Simon's hand, she draped three banknotes across his palm, pressing and crumpling the paper as if she meant to embed the money into his body. "For many years, I have hoped to repay my debt to her, not only the money that she lent me, but the generosity of her heart."

"If you please, Mrs. Richardson, did you know my mother in Rathkeale?" Eireann broke in.

"No, dear, I did not meet her until she came to Newgate."

One word was all it took to bring Simon to his senses. "You must have mistaken me for someone else," he spluttered. "My wife lived in Rathkeale and then came to Dublin."

The glare that Varena leveled at Plowman was vicious, brutal in its cold accusation. "You seek to erase the past by changing it, sir, but it will rise up and burn you. She will learn, some day, from some mouth not shut as tightly as mine is today. Perhaps my lips will part and she will know you for the beast that you are."

"The time will come," Simon whispered, "and she will be told what must be hidden now."

"What is your name, little girl?" Varena asked, casting a loving glance on the child.

"Eireann, ma'am," she said proudly. "Eireann go Bragh Plowman."

Again, Varena bent over and kissed the girl, but as she turned to go she gave up a wan smile. "That was your father's pet name for your mother. Ireland forever, Mr. Plowman."

"Mama must have been so beautiful," Eireann said. "That was the most lovely lady I have ever seen, and she said that Mama was even prettier than she is."

"They were lovely, Mama's friends," he agreed. He glanced at the banknotes in his hand, but when he looked up to see Varena's retreating figure, she was already out of sight. "Lovely birds of prey."

When Anna grew agitated about Simon's meetings, Eireann had a sense that things were not as they should be, but she was too young to understand the world of grown-up people. The men who came to the house on Merrion Square were always nice to her, and a man with bushy auburn whiskers usually brought her a peppermint stick when he called. Mrs. Richardson came once, but Katherine and Anna refused to be in the parlor when she spoke to Simon, and Eireann was furious that she was kept out as well.

"The most notorious madam in Dublin," Katherine had hissed, but the remainder of her horrified harangue was whispered away from the little girl's hearing.

Simon celebrated Christmas with his entire family, including his father who acted the part of guest in what was technically his own home. Shortly after the New Year began, Captain Plowman took his seat on the back bench in Commons and quietly studied the art of the M.P., glad to be free of the social scene that revolved around Dublin Castle. He struck up a friendship with Charles Parnell, an Anglo-Irish landowner who shared Simon's desire to win home rule for Ireland. As the session dragged on, they also reached a surprising consensus on another issue, something that settled around a shared disdain for Sir Michael Beach, and a respect for the military Fenians that Plowman had once pursued.

At the very end of April, reports of a Fenian escape from Fremantle reached London, nearly two weeks after the six prisoners made their getaway. News was delayed; the telegraph wire between Australia and Java had been cut. It was obvious that the plot was huge, well planned, and flawlessly executed, and the furor in Parliament was beyond measure. Bits of information and unsubstantiated rumors reached Captain Plowman, the former Royal Marine who had safeguarded those same scoundrels on the journey into exile in 1867. The authorities in Fremantle were so busy pointing fingers that the whole story did not get to London until the beginning of June.

Mr. Percival shared his information almost apologetically with Plowman while they sat in Simon's chambers. As if he were in the dock, he was grilled by his colleagues, all eager to know about the beach near Fremantle where six Fenian prisoners had boarded an American whaleboat under the very noses of a group of dockworkers. Having only been there for a short period of time, Plowman had little information to contribute to the discussion, and urged his friends to read aloud from the reports they had, to share the gossip and the news from official sources. Surprisingly, he was not as upset or angry as Mr. Percival would have expected, particularly since Simon had expended a great deal of effort in pursuing the military traitors and seeing that they were put away for life.

"The world is full of bunglers, Mr. Percival," Simon said, displaying a sportsman's sense of gracious defeat. "I did my duty, and I must be satisfied with that."

Sir Richard Selfridge burst into the room, waving an official dispatch. "Two warships intercepted the Yankee whaler," he fumed. "Two of our own Royal Navy gunboats, and they turned tail and ran. Afraid of an incident in international waters, so they held fire. One blast and that American pirate would have been blown to bits."

"Disraeli should demand that the United States return the felons," Percival declared. "This is an outrage, to abscond with such fiends."

"I am afraid that our government's concern for the textile industry during the American civil war is going to have repercussions now," Simon said. "In the last few months of that conflict I was attached to our embassy in Washington, and I can state today with some confidence that the very government that you wish to pressure, Mr. Percival, is the same government that was less than pleased with our support of the Confederacy. Gentlemen, we can expect a very polite refusal, while every Irish immigrant in America laughs at us behind our backs."

Simon reached over and retrieved a copy of a long telegram, containing almost the entire editorial from a recent edition of *The New York World*. He handed John O'Reilly's mocking prose to Sir Richard, a wry grin on his face.

"All talk about demanding redress is nonsense," Selfridge steamed as he read the nasty and sarcastic tone. "They dare to equate blockade running with picking up...and how dare they call these brutes political prisoners."

"Two of the eight that were left after the previous escape did not get out, as I understand," Simon added.

"They shall taste revenge, Captain," Sir Richard gloated. "All tickets-of-leave were cancelled, and now those two are confined to cells, well within the walls of the prison."

"That proves how despicable those Irishmen are," Percival said. "To coldly abandon two of their own."

"It's quite ironic, actually. They were promised reduced sentences if they cooperated, and they had a lot to say." Plowman spoke with resignation. "When it came time for sentencing, Whitehall found it convenient to forget the deal, and now the men who were of the greatest use to us are the ones who are suffering the most. Who is despicable, Mr. Percival?"

Some of Simon's closest colleagues were aware of the tragic story of Mrs. Plowman, who repented of her family's sins and then gave her life to prevent an escape from The Establishment. Her sacrifice was wasted, and that explained the legislator's burning disdain of the British penal system. Not only had the O'Dwyer boys run from the noose, but the military Fenians had all fled from Fremantle, as if those who created rebellion did not have to pay a price. The man who lost his life's partner and watched his enemies fly off to America would be forever embittered, or such was the only explanation that could be offered for Captain Plowman's bizarre speech a few weeks later.

Only a few of the men who aided the O'Dwyer brothers' escape had been caught, and the three who were hanged had not fired the pistol that killed the police constable during the melee. Their death was elevated to martyrdom for the freedom of Ireland, but to men like Sir Michael Beach, their death was the end of three murdering dogs. On the thirtieth of June, with the break-out from The Establishment still a fresh wound, Captain Simon Plowman rose in the House of Commons and came to the defense of the "Manchester Martyrs." Having opened a breach, he stepped aside and allowed Mr. Parnell to wax prolific on the injustice of their case, the injustice of their sentence, and the justice of their cause. In a roundabout way, Parnell was preaching in favor of an independent Irish Parliament, but the fury that was created did little to make the members more amenable to Home Rule. What the long harangue did was to make Charles Parnell the biggest hero in Ireland. No one knew quite what to make of Captain Plowman.

The uproar in Parliament was broadcast in Dublin, and Parnell's passionate defense was the sole topic of conversation. Eireann's Sunday outing was marred by constant intrusions as Sir Peter's friends and colleagues stopped to talk.

"They threatened your son and he speaks out on behalf of the very men who freed them," Sir Charles gasped with goggle-eyed shock. "He's gotten mixed up with the wrong crowd, Sir Peter. There are too many radicals representing Ireland, and they're working on your son to sway him."

"Not at all. My son is keen on a fair fight, and nothing gets his hackles up like a slapdash trial and summary execution. The penal system has fallen short in every way possible, Sir Charles, and I for one cannot fault his criticism," Peter said. "The Manchester murderers were more deserving of mercy than the Fenians, and they executed one group while the other took French leave. Even I find it preposterous."

"Did Papa do something bad?" Eireann asked after the gentlemen had argued to a draw.

"No, Ireland, he did something well," Peter explained. "He stood up for his principles, independent of popular opinion and unconcerned with my approval. We are very proud of your father, you and I."

The doting old man hugged her closer, guiding his mount with one hand in the elegant style of the dragoon, a master horseman. Awash in a sense of absolute security and safety, Eireann resumed her interrogation. "Grandfather, where is Newgate?" she asked next.

"The gaol, do you mean? That is here in Dublin, on Green Street next to the Courthouse."

"Was my mother in gaol?"

"Whatever gave you that idea?"

"Her friend said they met in Newgate."

"Ladies often go into women's prisons to bring the word of God to the convicted criminals. Your mother was very devout. I would not be surprised if she had done that sort of charitable proselytizing."

Despite the impression that she was content with everyone's fractured answers, Eireann remained a profoundly curious person. For many years, she had roamed through the townhouse and made the garret her personal treasure trove, where she explored the old and forgotten relics of her family's past. When she uncovered Anna's dolls in an old trunk, it became a festive time of play and pretend with her beloved aunt. Anna regaled her niece with stories of her childhood, a life so much like Eireann's that the little girl could not seem to get enough of the anecdotes. The forays into the garret became great fun, something that Anna and Katherine enjoyed through Eireann's eyes.

The expeditions eventually moved down to the bedrooms, where the child found amusement in poking around dresser drawers and trying on the shoes and hats of her aunt and grandmother. She played dress-up with her father's riding boots, making Katherine laugh until the tears were running down her cheeks. Simon's dress uniform, reserved for formal occasions, was as fascinating as any lady's frock, and there were many afternoons when Eireann donned the scarlet coat just to admire the lovely gold braid and shiny buttons.

Given such freedom, it was inevitable that she would find a small suitcase, tucked away in a bottom drawer in her father's dressing room. Hidden under some old shirts that were no longer worn, the cheap valise was intriguing, so unlike anything that Simon carried to London. The latch opened easily, lacking any sort of lock, and Eireann was confused by the dusty and dirty contents.

The small book looked exactly like the missals that all the ladies brought to church, but this one had an ornate cross worked into the leather cover. She ran her finger over the pebbled tooling, and found that she had picked up a quantity of yellow-gray dust. Opening the cover, she recognized a Catholic prayer book, but she could not interpret the handwriting on the flyleaf.

She did not know the cursive alphabet as yet, but she could recognize the last word because it was her surname, scribed in the same way that her aunt and grandmother signed their correspondence. Long, thin colored ribbons attached to the spine were tucked into different pages, and she turned to a section to explore.

The words were too big to read sentences, and picking out the small words did not give her any sense of what she could not decipher. It looked like her grandmother's missal in its arrangement and illustration, but this was a secret thing and that was very odd. Eireann wondered for a moment if it belonged to her father or grandfather, imagining that they were actually covert Catholics who had to hide their faith. Bored rather quickly with the commonplace book, she looked into the case and found a collection of yellowed newsprint.

Pictures looked back at her, images from a fairy tale translated into a newspaper illustration. On one side was the beautiful princess, and right next to her was the haggard and frightening witch. There were few words that she could read, but she studied her discovery until her father came in to dress for dinner.

Never had the girl seen him as insanely livid as he was just then, catching her with the hidden box. In a rage, he pulled her to her feet by her arm, flailing at her bottom with his free hand and screaming at her face. Terrified, Eireann began to screech hysterically, bawling and crying from fear rather than pain. Somehow, she ended up in her aunt's embrace, her head smothered against the perfumed serge of her aunt's bodice.

"You mustn't go into anyone's private things," Anna said. "Never, never do such a thing, Eireann."

Anna pulled her out of the room, but when Eireann looked back, she saw her father on his knees, closing the case but wailing at the same time, sunk into an impossibly deep grief.

"I'm sorry, Papa, I'm sorry," she cried out. "I'll be good, I'll be good, I'm sorry."

She was led away before she could say more, but with bright perception, she understood that she had done the wrong thing by discovering her mother. Whatever secrets were hidden in the old suitcase, they were things that her father did not want to share. After searching for her mother for so long, Eireann now had every intention of revealing those mysteries one day, in spite of her father.

Their excursion to Galway was a grand and unexpected adventure, taking the Great Western train and then renting a pony and trap to drive from the city to the peaceful backwater of Athenry. The stone marker in the churchyard matched the cross on the missal, and Eireann knew then that it was her mother's book that was concealed in the case. For some unknown reason, her father was trying to reveal some of his secrets, but his broken heart was still not healed, and the pain kept him from telling her as much as she wanted to know. Considering this trip as a beginning, Eireann determined to accept what little her father could give now, to do her best to be patient with him.

"This is a Celtic cross," Simon told her, rather like a lecturer. "The Fenians used this as a symbol of their movement."

"Like my uncles in America?" she asked.

"Exactly like them, yes."

"But they are wicked," Eireann said. "Grandfather said they had to run away from Ireland because they were traitors."

"They are not wicked, but that is not something to debate with your grandfather. A lady does not discuss politics." Simon smiled, looked off into the distance for a moment, and then continued. "A person cannot be a traitor to a government that is not his. Eireann, you are growing up, and perhaps you are old enough to share some of our family secrets. Your O'Dwyer uncles are outlaws, and I am a government official. Your aunt writes to them and has another friend post the letters because of that. No matter what they have done, they are still a part of your family and they have a right to be informed of your well-being."

"Was my mother a Fenian? Is that why this cross is here?"

"This is a traditional form of Irish art as well. Do you see how beautiful this is, compared to the simple cross over there, or the dull slab of stone next to it? That is the best reason to choose this to mark your mother's resting place, and mine when the time comes."

For now, she was satisfied, and they spent a few days in Galway as a lark, enjoying a holiday before Eireann returned to her coursework at the Dominican convent in Dublin. Somehow, actually seeing where her mother was buried was comforting, for it proved that her mother had not gotten lost someplace. Eireann was not abandoned as she had once feared, and the Celtic cross gave her a strong sense of security. Even so, she still possessed an ember of curiosity about the papers she had seen, and as soon as she mastered reading, she planned to return to the bottom drawer in her father's dressing room.

Seventeen

For a man accustomed to the military's plodding pace, Simon found the ponderous stupor of Parliamentary debate to be as frustrating as the monotonous routine was narcoleptic. The Ulster contingent, battling fiercely to maintain the status quo, drove him mad with their droning. He wondered if he had done the right thing by getting into politics, until the annual session that opened in the winter of 1879. The atmosphere in Commons bore a distinctive stench that year, reeking of deep-seated hatred and a bitterness that recalled Black '47 in its danger.

Michael Davitt, a Catholic and militant member of the Irish Republican Brotherhood, found a welcome among the poor peasants who supported his call for land reform. Due to the crop failure of 1878, the hardships of the famine years returned, pushing the cry for Home Rule into the background. It was replaced by Davitt's cause, and the homecoming of the civilian Fenians from Australia provided a ready army of agitators.

Farmers with no crops to sell could not meet their rent payments, and the brutal practice of forced eviction plagued the countryside. Davitt fought for restraints on the absolute power of the landlords, and Simon practiced what he preached in Commons. His tenants in Limerick found that their rents were reduced, and their landlord informed them all that they were welcome to stay on and try again next spring. Financially, Plowman was not hurt by his generosity, not when he owned a large parcel in Hampshire that had belonged to his grandfather. He raised the rents of his English tenants.

Simon discovered what tactics Mr. Davitt was using to bring the landowners to the bargaining table when Lord Dunbarton lodged a complaint with the Member of Parliament. Fodder for His Lordship's stables was suddenly not available locally, nor was the butcher supplying meat to the estate. One local merchant after another refused to do business with the Wilkerson family, not one vendor was interested in the lucrative trade that poured out of the manor house, and parlor maids left their positions after making feeble excuses. To make matters worse, any land that had been farmed by an evicted tenant was lying fallow. New leaseholders were driven away by rude treatment, the practice of shunning, or threats of violence that had been carried out more than once. His Lordship was losing money, through exorbitantly higher prices or lack of income.

Standing as a Conservative in the general election of 1880, Plowman had the full support of Lord Dunbarton and his Anglo-Irish colleagues. Despite the landlord's hatred of Parnell and Captain Plowman's support of land reform, the well-healed electorate of Limerick felt that Captain Plowman was a man of reason and someone capable of subduing the most belligerent terrorists. On the other hand, Plowman's handling of the economic crisis endeared him to the poorest voters. With a reputation as a sensible diplomat, he was returned to his seat.

Just as Ireland was beginning to change, Eireann was beginning to change, maturing into a young lady who was too old to ride on her grandfather's lap when they went out on their Sunday excursions. Much to Sir Peter's disappointment and sorrow, his little granddaughter sat a mare and rode next to him, like a mature woman, because she was too big for a baby's perch. Her curiosity was developing as well, with her burning desire to find her mother ripening into an obsession.

To commemorate her First Communion, Simon had given his daughter the missal that she had discovered. The act of handing over the book had reduced him to tears, and he fled from the parlor while Eireann puzzled over his overwrought reaction. Running her finger over the leatherwork cover, she found that it had been cleaned thoroughly and polished, to remove every speck of dust that had once coated it. Turning the pages, she was awestruck by the connection that she felt with her mother, holding a book that her mother had held, reading the prayers that her mother had read. Eireann pictured her mother at Mass, with her missal open to the Offertory, but the little girl imagined St. Mary's Pro-Cathedral as the setting.

In bed one night, touching the pages, looking at the Word of God, Eireann discovered a tightly folded scrap of paper concealed in a section where the binding had been worked loose. She was unsure if she had missed it before, or if someone had put it there recently. The paper was dry, and must have been old. Carefully, she worked the note out of its spot and smoothed out the brittle creases.

"Dearest Little One," the greeting was penned by a man's hand, and her eyes went straight to the signature, to find out who had sent it. There was no name, just a bizarre appellation, "The First Brother."

"The door of the tomb stand ajar," the letter read, "Your deliverance is at hand."

Turning over the sheet, she touched the ink marks that spelled out her mother's name, followed by three words that made no sense. "Mrs. Simon Plowman," she understood, but the note that was dated April 4,

1868, was forwarded to Fremantle, Western Australia. Eireann was only eleven, and she feared that her father had lied to her.

Anna declared that Eireann was old enough now to attend adult parties, and her first experience was a dinner in October. There were be various Irish politicians in attendance, men like Mr. Parnell whom she had met before, and she expected to be extremely eager to leave the table because it was going to be as boring as all the other times that her father's colleagues came to call. On this grand day, shortly after her father had turned forty-one, Eireann sat in the parlor and greeted the guests, all the people who would jabber endlessly about land and farmers.

"You will never suffer as your mother's people suffered," Mr. Davitt said, his first words after he was introduced. Indulging Eireann's curiosity, he delayed speaking to Simon so that the little girl could examine the empty sleeve of his suit coat. Davitt had lost his arm in an industrial accident as a child laborer, and he was not one to shield a little girl from the real world outside her door.

"Auntie, that man said my mother's family suffered," Eireann said to Anna, seeking clarification.

"Yes, dear, they were evicted by a petty and cruel landlord. Mr. Davitt and your father are working very hard to put an end to such practices," Anna said.

"Where did they live after they were evicted?" the girl asked.

"A different place," Anna stated with confidence. "Your uncles went to America to live."

"But Papa told me they were outlaws and that is why they had to run away."

"They were outlaws because they had no home, and being a homeless vagrant is against the law."

"But if they were evicted, they could not help being outlaws."

"Exactly, you begin to understand," Anna said. "That was injustice, do you see? Because of such injustice, your father must struggle against those who hold such terrible power. He works tirelessly in your mother's honor."

Normally, Eireann sat quietly through dinner, having the companionship of her grandmother and aunt as they instructed her in the feminine art of making conversation. Tonight, however, she was captivated by the very eloquent prose of Mr. Davitt. Like her American uncles, the man had been a supporter of the Fenian movement, and he had been in prison for seven years at hard labor because of it. Such qualities made him a most fascinating character.

"My uncles are also members of the Irish Republican Brotherhood," the little girl piped up, to the amusement of all the guests.

"I heard one of them speak when I was in Philadelphia," Mr. Davitt said. "And while you should be proud of them, you would do well to keep tight-lipped."

"Yes, sir, I know, because they are bad men in Dublin," she said.

"Only in Dublin?" Mr. Parnell joked.

"All over the Empire," Mr. O'Connor put in, raising an eyebrow at Mr. Parnell.

Once again, the topic went deadly boring, and Eireann kicked her legs under the chair as she waited for the adults to disperse. She kissed her father goodnight, joined the ladies in the parlor for an hour, and then politely left the party. Just as Naomi had finished tucking her into bed, Simon came in to have a word.

"Do you understand a part of what we discussed this evening?" he asked, sitting at her side and holding her hand.

"Auntie said that my O'Dwyer grandfather was evicted," she said.

"Our land in Rathkeale includes the parcel where the tannery stood," Simon began. "I bought it so that the Wilkerson family could never again force another innocent person out of their home or business. But I cannot buy up all of Ireland, lass, and so I have come to agree with Mr. Parnell and Mr. Davitt."

"Am I not to speak of my uncles?"

"No, you are not. You must learn to be cautious before you speak, to mask your true feelings when they serve no good purpose. Don't be quick to tell all, but always be fast when it comes to listening. Keep in your heart what others do not need to see."

She was about to ask about Fremantle when her father kissed her, putting an end to their intimate conversation. Still, she did not comprehend all the mysteries of the adult world, any more than she could appreciate the need for secrecy and silence. Perhaps it was only to appease her grandfather, who thought very poorly of her American uncles. Slowly, Eireann's eyes closed and she gave up her thoughts and queries, to dream of her mother riding in a carriage with a dotted-Swiss veil over her face, an enigmatic figure shrouded in shadows.

Over time, Eireann had subconsciously imprinted an image of Varena Richardson on her brain, intermingling it with the wedding portrait that was kept on the bedside table. Her mother became an elegant woman in the child's mind, someone so incredibly attractive that men turned to look at her face. That pleasant picture did not allow any room in a girl's imagination for another, less happy, view of her mother's life. The graceful belle with a wan smile never appeared on a country road in Limerick, in rags and without a home. Eviction was too esoteric a concept for a child of privilege, and gradually Eireann came to think of her mother's eviction as an inconvenience, having to move to another house and carry heavy bundles that made her arms weary.

Even though Eireann never spoke of her uncles to her many friends, some of their parents seemed to be aware of the O'Dwyer name. Molly McNamara's mother was particularly fawning when Anna and Eireann came for tea every so often. One quiet afternoon when the adults thought that the children were not listening, Mrs. McNamara clucked sadly and remarked that someone had escaped persecution in death. Anna's reply was a firm denial, and Eireann was pleased to learn that her father was so deeply in love that her mother's death shattered him.

"Do you think that she was influential in easing his strong convictions?" Mrs. McNamara whispered.

"Little more than intense guilt," Mr. McNamara grumbled. "To avenge one's self on a weak female, even he saw how despicable he had become."

"I assure you, your suppositions are utterly unfounded," Anna insisted. "If you had seen him when he returned…he went mad."

"Now he has infiltrated the Land League," Mr. McNamara intoned gravely. "Ireland for the Irish, he claims, and land for the people, but who can believe him with his record?"

"His conduct as a father has been more than exemplary," Anna said.

"While he denies her any knowledge of her history. That validates my opinions."

While Mr. Gladstone assailed the Land League and their underhanded efforts to bring down the landlords, Lord Dunbarton followed Captain Plowman's lead and lowered rents by nearly twenty percent. His Lordship was immensely grateful to his neighbor for his intercession with the leaseholders, and Lord Dunbarton found no harm in agreeing to ban eviction without just cause, as Plowman had urged. Lady Dunbarton had a full staff once again, the expense of running the household declined, and the threat of violence against new tenants simply evaporated.

Sir Peter expounded on the inner workings of negotiation while Eireann struggled valiantly to comprehend, and she nearly caught on to the concept of economic pressure applied by the weak on the powerful to level out the playing field. What she did understand quite clearly was the delight that her grandfather took in his son's political maneuvers.

"Point of order, Mr. Speaker," Peter said, repeating a recent debate. "And then all the right honorable gentlemen must stop running off at the mouth and get back to business, which your father makes Irish business. The speeches, Ireland, you would never guess that he was so long-winded. Classic siege warfare, and those dim-witted politicians are as frustrated as can be."

Strolling through Dublin, Eireann believed that she was gaining a little knowledge of Parliament's inner workings. "I think I see, sir," she agreed to the point, but a sudden vision of radiance distracted her.

"Good God," Sir Peter mumbled. The lady in the open carriage looked at him, smiled, and nodded in recognition.

"Mrs. Richardson, good afternoon," Eireann said.

The carriage stopped, and Sir Peter tipped his hat but slightly. "Varena." He acknowledged the passenger as if she were a disease.

"Sir Peter, how delightful to see you again," Varena greeted the gentleman. "You have grown, Miss Plowman, I scarcely recognize you now that you are a young lady."

"Thank you, ma'am," the girl said, pretending that she was, in a way, talking to her mother.

"Has your father ever told you how he came to meet your mother?" Varena asked.

"No, ma'am, is it a very lovely story?"

"Good afternoon, Varena," Sir Peter huffed, pulling Eireann away.

"Be sure to ask," Varena called over her shoulder. Her carriage rolled away, while Sir Peter doubled his pace in the opposite direction.

"Ireland, you will tell me exactly how you came to be acquainted with that creature," the grandfather fumed.

"She is one of my mother's friends," Eireann said. "They met in Newgate, where they spread the Gospel."

"That woman, child, was not spreading God's word," he said.

"You spoke to her very informally, sir, do you know her well?"

"I know her intimately, Ireland, very intimately," he said. Already close to running, Peter picked up the pace. "If your grandmother knew that I allowed her to say one word to you, she would forbid me to ever see you again, and I would not argue with her because she would be correct."

"Because Mrs. Richardson is notorious?"

"Precisely, because Mrs. Richardson is notorious. One of the wealthiest women in Dublin, I might add. A wise investor in real estate and bonds, and she extracted advice from the best men in town."

"She borrowed money from my mother once," Eireann continued. "And Mrs. Richardson paid Papa back, too, that's how I met her, when she gave him the money that she had borrowed."

To hear of borrowed money stopped Peter cold, his mouth agape. "The woman is notorious, Ireland, but she is an honest businesswoman." He recovered his composure. "However, you are not to ever speak to her again, do you understand?"

"But, sir, if my mother spoke to her," the child protested.

"When you are grown up, and you wish to further the work of your priests and bishops, you may speak to her," Peter said. "Until then, do not even so much as recognize her on the street."

"Yes, sir," Eireann replied.

The answers to her questions resided in Mrs. Richardson, she saw with complete clarity. Such an elusive woman was not easily found by a young girl in short skirts and pinafores, but Eireann knew that she would not be forever a child. One fine day, she would dress in corsets and her hems would fall to the floor, and then she would seek out Mrs. Richardson. Then, she would unlock the treasure chest and set her mother free.

Eighteen

Violence erupted across the Irish countryside as the supporters of the Land League used brute force to subdue the landlords. To those in power, the issue was not so much about the rights of the landless as it was a call to rip apart the Empire. Many in Parliament felt that the Land Act of 1870 provided adequate protection to the Irish peasants, but the worst agricultural season in thirty years managed to bring out the countless flaws in the old legislation. Blinded by an insatiable appetite for income, the propertied class could not see what their renters had been looking at for decades, not when most of them had never set foot on their Irish property.

Members of the Land League fought to protect the poor, and they had plenty of financial backing from the Fenians in America. Through the efforts of Parnell and his colleagues, tenants organized rent strikes, battled against evictions, and waged war against the estate agents who tried to enforce the law. Some of Simon's colleagues pleaded for appeasement of Parnell's supporters to put an end to the violence, recognizing that those who had emigrated during the debacle of the Great Hunger were paying back the country that had failed them. Under the influence of fervent anti-

Irish and anti-Catholic sentiments, the majority in Parliament saw the need for tighter control and more intense suppression.

"He's done it." Anna quoted the newspaper at breakfast. "Gladstone has made the Land League illegal."

"Will Mr. Parnell become an outlaw?" Eireann asked.

"I hope your father does not become too deeply involved with them. They have certainly tried to bring him into their sphere of influence," Katherine said.

"They have decided that a man can be jailed without a trial. That's what has become of British justice in Ireland; eliminate due process when it becomes convenient," Anna said.

Not sure where her father fit in the tangle of politics and legalities, Eireann was often on edge, worried about what would happen. So often, her aunt would brush off her fears, but when Anna was speaking with friends, her message was not quite so comforting. The problem for Eireann lay in the fact that she did not know which side her father favored, his actions seeming rather contradictory to a girl who did not comprehend the machinations of the powerful. Day by day, the news grew more dire, the situation in the countryside more desperate, and she grew more confused.

The wrangling became so chaotic in Commons that Mr. Davitt, elected in 1880, was arrested while a large block of Irish M.P.'s were ejected from the chamber. Simon was nearly caught up in the bedlam, saved by his many friends on the Conservative side of the aisle who would not allow one of their own to be tossed out, not when the law was the work of the Liberal Prime Minister. "He'd support the devil himself if it served his purpose," was heard often, repeated by men who knew Simon Plowman for what he was, the eyes and ears of the Admiralty in Commons.

Tampering with the heart of British law caused Gladstone more trouble politically than he cared for, and the law was allowed to quietly lapse. Out in the Irish countryside, the violence continued to escalate, and with every new eviction, the incidents of retaliation climbed. The feared Captain Midnight rode through Ireland, maiming cattle and burning hayricks. Land agents were assaulted and some were killed, and Parliament acted to bring law to a lawless land, to a land that the old Fenians were determined to claim for the Irish people through bloodshed and brutality.

Eireann's perfect little world was shattered just after her thirteenth birthday, when her beloved grandfather became ill. Katherine welcomed him home to die, in return for Peter's past consideration. He could have forced her to be his wife, taken her to court to seek reinstatement of his conjugal rights, but he had never done anything but admit defeat. No one in the house on Merrion Square could tell if Katherine despised her husband or held a touch of affection for him in her heart. She was dutiful to the end, cheerful and kind, and Sir Peter Plowman left the earth as he had hoped he would when he first set eyes on Katherine Kenneally in the wild expanse of County Galway.

On the day of the funeral, Eireann lashed out at her aunt and grandmother. They were the only available targets, the people who had forbidden her from entering the Anglican church to attend the funeral service. By all accounts, Simon attended for the sake of appearances, not being a religious man and generally considered a dedicated agnostic. While he was in Christ Church with his father's numerous colleagues and friends, Eireann stole up to his bedroom and began to systematically rifle through his belongings, searching for the valise that would reveal the truth. Her grandmother found her, furiously opening drawers and pushing clothes aside, flinging shoes everywhere and behaving like a savage.

"How did my parents meet?" she screamed, shocking Katherine with her tone.

"I have no idea, but you will stop this childish behavior at once," Katherine ordered. "Get dressed this instant. We will not be late for your grandfather's burial."

"He knows," Eireann said. Running down the hall to her room, she wailed, "He knows but he won't tell me."

A new Land Act in 1881 sought to provide greater rights to tenants, and Gladstone prayed for an end to the violence through his philosophy of conciliation. By the time that Parliament took action, the rockslide had become an avalanche and it was too late to stop it. Simon realized that the act failed to consider the right to own land, to buy a few paltry acres and grow enough potatoes to live on, and that glaring omission was fuel to the Land League's wrath. Once again, Gladstone saw to it that the Land League was made an illegal organization, but that did nothing to stop the unrest.

In October, with turmoil and vandalism still rocking the country, Dublin Castle decided to act, and they used the new Coercion Act to squeeze Mr. Parnell and his associates. He was hauled off to Kilmainham Gaol, along with a few close colleagues, in a bid to apply pressure from the top down. On a peaceful Sunday night, the reach of the law extended beyond Parnell to the outer ring of Irish politicians who were on the fringes of land reform.

Eireann had been asleep when she heard loud voices in the foyer, and she snuck out of bed and inched silently to the top of the stairs. A policeman was standing guard at the open front door, and when she craned her neck she found another constable at the entrance to the parlor. Quickly, she went to her room and threw on some clothes, ready to go even though she had no idea where she would be going, or if she even needed to go anyplace.

"I've been arrested, lass," her father called over his shoulder when she ran to the entryway.

In the confusion, no one noticed that Eireann followed the men out the door, but she was stopped from joining him in the Black Maria.

"Kilmainham's no place for a little lady," one of the officers chuckled as he pulled her off the step.

"Don't be afraid, Eireann, everything will be taken care of in no time. Be brave, be as brave as your mother," Simon told her, but then the door of the van was shut and locked before she could ask him anything.

News of the arrest of Sir Simon Plowman, Baronet and former Captain in the Royal Marines, fanned out through the city as the police wagon wound its way through the riots. Near Dublin Castle and City Hall, the protest were more loud and aggressive, the crowd more dense as Eireann tried to keep pace with the van. She had no idea where Kilmainham was as she followed the police wagon that raced down the streets, making its way to Inchicore Road through a war zone.

She lost sight of the gruesome black box as it disappeared into a milling crowd that churned and boiled with rage. "Please, sir, where is Kilmainham?" she asked a bystander, but the man did not hear her, one child's voice drowned out in the cacophony of a mob bent on destruction. The constabulary appeared, a wave of clubs and horses that tried to break up the disturbance, but the people of Dublin would not be stopped. Pushed and jostled, the young lady grew more frightened, lost in Dublin and surrounded by madness.

A woman took Eireann's hand and tugged, nearly dragging her into a doorway. Looking up in surprise, the girl recognized the wife of one of her father's associates, an agreeable lady who smelled of lavender and violets. Her ire was unmistakable as she spoke. "Your father will get his comeuppance tonight, my dear, and your mother will be dancing in heaven."

"Where have they taken Papa?" Eireann asked, overwrought and scared witless.

"To Kilmainham Gaol, where they took the others," Mrs. Cosgrave said. Finding an opening in the crowd, she plunged in and took Eireann with her. "And he'll taste his own bitter medicine."

Half-trotting and sometimes running, the two figures worked their way west. Eireann had never walked so far before, and her legs were weary, but she thought of her father's advice as they hurried to the building that had come to represent Ireland's fight for freedom. It was no place for any human being, lady or gentleman, but Mrs. Cosgrave wanted Eireann to see what happened to those who did not go meekly or peacefully.

"Why would my mother be happy to see my father in prison?" she asked, puffing with exertion.

"Because of what he did to her on the prison transport," Mrs. Cosgrave replied, her dislike of Plowman not masked.

Eireann stopped in her tracks and Mrs. Cosgrave nearly lost her balance as she was tugged backwards. "They were in Rathkeale," the girl said.

"Is that what he told you?" the woman scoffed. "He bought your mother on a prison ship for one hundred fifty pounds, and I heard the tale from a woman who was chained to Mary Claire O'Dwyer from Newgate to Fremantle."

Sickened, Eireann pulled away from Mrs. Cosgrave and ran, blindly and fast, until she reached the quay along the Liffey. The mystery was uncovered, her father's filthy and revolting secret had been revealed and Eireann hated him. Her tears obscured her vision but she stumbled along, keeping the river on her left hand until she saw the Gothic splendor of Trinity College.

The house was in tumult, with Simon under arrest and Eireann missing. When the girl finally turned up, soaked through from the drizzle that was falling, her grandmother lapsed into hysterical sobs. Tearing out of Katherine's embrace, Eireann ran to her room and ripped off her wet clothes.

Anna came up to console her, to give some assurance that life would go on. "This will be cleared up quickly, angel, don't worry about your father," she said.

"I don't care about my father," Eireann said, rejecting Anna's solace.

"He did nothing wrong, Eireann, and you have no reason to be cross with him."

"I hope he dies in prison," she blurted out, but racking sobs prevented her from saying anything more.

"That is a terrible thing to say," Anna said. "How can you wish your father dead? I am ashamed of you, Eireann Plowman, completely ashamed."

The gas jet was shut with fury and Anna stalked out of the darkened room, slamming the door behind her. When the outer door banged close, the thump echoing up the stairs, a strange quiet descended on the house, as if a thick fog had settled down to the foundation. From the street, the muffled sounds of breaking glass and outraged voices penetrated the very walls, along with an aroma of burning wood that could be arson or bonfires that blocked the intersections. Every drop of mist was hung with smoke and shouts, filthy with anger that had no other outlet. Eireann wanted to throw open the sash, to inhale the madness and make it a part of her very being, to become burning rage.

Anna's damp coat smelled of wet wool and soot when she marched back into the room an hour later. "Your mother was arrested on trumped up charges," Anna said. "She was convicted on lies. When your father saw her in Portland Gaol, when the prisoners were being mustered for transportation to Australia, he fell in love. He did not know she was an O'Dwyer when he fell in love with her. That is the truth, Eireann, plain and simple. They were married on the ship and you were born in Fremantle, in Western Australia. Your mother was pardoned. She did not live long after you were born. Never say again that you hate your father, do you hear me?"

"He paid money," she said through tears, "to buy her."

"He paid money to some bad people who only understood the language of currency. He paid them to protect your mother from harm. On that ship, miss, life was topsy-turvy and your father did what he had to do to safeguard your mother."

"It's shameful, that's why he never told me," Eireann sobbed anew.

"No, dear, it is not shameful. It is horrible, what happened to your mother. Injustice because of our religion, because we are Irish. Your father sits on a bench in London to change the laws that allowed it to happen. He is sitting in Kilmainham Gaol now because of it. When you are grown, I hope that you continue the fight that your father has begun."

Alone in his cell, Simon thought of Mary Claire and their daughter, pondered his father's life and the tenets that he held dear, and he worried about his mother's frail health. Injustice was all around Sir

Simon Plowman, and he chuckled out loud as he pictured his illustrious colleague, Mr. Parnell, comfortably ensconced in the matron's office. The ringleader had a soft setting, but his cohorts were being punished in a way that was true hardship for well-bred gentlemen. A common criminal had a cell that measured seven feet by four feet, quite a contrast with the rooms of a fine Georgian mansion on Merrion Square.

There had been countless nights passed on a cold and windy ship's deck, and Simon was prepared to face a cold prison cell. The damp began to seep into his bones, bringing back fond recollections of his younger days, mingling with the Irish brigades in Virginia, crossing the lines and sleeping in chilling rain as he gathered information from both sides of the conflict. The only aspect of Kilmainham that was punishment for him was the lock on the door, the loss of freedom. He was a soldier, by breeding and training, and he almost laughed as he imagined the authorities in Dublin Castle, expecting a baronet to cave in while forgetting that they had a Marine Captain under lock and key.

"By a lonely prison wall, I heard a young girl calling," he warbled the newest tune. "Simon, they've taken you away. For you stole Trevelyan's corn, that your babes might see the morn."

The door was opened a crack and the turnkey made a request. "If you please, sir, the prisoners are to be silent after lights out."

"Now a prison ship lies waiting in the bay," Simon continued. "Come in, sir, and you can sing harmony. Do you know the song?"

"Know it well, sir, but I'd rather not have to make you be quiet, sir," the guard said.

"Member of Parliament incarcerated and beaten," Simon thundered. "A fine headline for tomorrow's late editions. Won't the American press be pleased to learn that British politicians are treated like criminals for the act of representing their constituents?"

He did not need paper or ink to send a message, not when so many willing messengers were hovering at hand, keen to spread every syllable that he uttered. Simon returned to his tune, to finish the chorus and second verse before the door was opened again.

The prison superintendent came in with stealth, and Simon offered him a seat. "Sir Simon, due to your apparent support of the Land League, you have been brought in on a violation of the Coercion Act."

"Why do you think that I am here?" Simon let his lip curl into a sneer, one eyebrow slightly raised

"Sir, it is not up to me to judge your case. I was told," the man stammered, uncomfortable under Plowman's hard stare. "The warrant, you see."

"Will you kindly inform Mr. Gladstone that I remain committed to my duties as a Member of Parliament? I intend to continue representing my constituents in accordance with the laws, and if the Irish Republican Brotherhood comes calling, I would be remiss if I did not entertain them. My late wife's brothers, after all."

Every word that Simon spoke was a lie, except when it was the truth, and never had a man been able to tell which was which. The superintendent nodded a farewell, his posture that of a man who suspected that something was going on far over his head. Comfortable that Dublin Castle, and then Whitehall, would get the message, Plowman stretched out on his cot with memories of Mary Claire and a lieutenant's berth to lull him to sleep.

The highly respected barrister Mr. Charles Lytton, a long-time friend of Simon, was ushered into the solicitor's room in Kilmainham on Monday morning, to meet with a client whose followers were still up in arms over his arrest. He acted like a man with a simple mission, to urge his friend to speak against Parnell, a man whom Simon despised, making no secret of his utter lack of respect. Everyone knew that Parnell cavorted with a married woman, an act so despicable to Simon Plowman that he publicly condemned Parnell's conduct. There were some things that were more important than politics, and morality was paramount.

Trying to force Simon to agree that violence was pointless, undermining the peasant class that the former Marine was oddly attached to, Lytton grew more frustrated when Simon countered that argument with an observation. If not for the recent violence, the Land Act would not have been passed in Commons. The peasants in need of protection from the landlords were not so stupid as Gladstone seemed to think, and Simon used the lack of consideration for those whose rents were in arrears to drive home his point. He refused to cave in to Gladstone's demands until Gladstone took his paltry act as far as was needed. A mention of a return to convict transportation showed Lytton that he was well off course and would have to find a completely different tack.

"All of Dublin is in turmoil, my friend, while your home is unguarded," Lytton said, seeking a new angle.

"My home is safer than the Lord Mayor's, I'd wager."

"Can you take this matter seriously, Simon? There is no doubt that Gladstone will work towards a compromise with Parnell; we both know his style. In the meantime, I would like your cooperation in seeking your release."

"My defense is simple, Charlie. I am an elected representative, and I pursue an agenda that benefits those people. Let the Crown prove that such an activity is illegal, and they upend our entire system of government."

"They can hold you without trial, and there is no desire to bring anyone to trial on this issue. Until a settlement is reached to put down the riots and vandalism, you can expect to stay here."

"Criminals are housed here, and my government has labeled me a criminal," Simon folded his arms across his chest, closing out the discussion.

"Just what are you up to, Simon?"

"You know that I can't tell you."

Confined to one small room, Simon paced for exercise, not unlike the way he had exercised as a young Marine corporal many years ago. His life in the military had prepared him for the rigors of prison life, and his career at sea had accustomed him to limited space and poor food. He was allowed visitors, out of deference to his rank, and he passed a pleasant afternoon with a few friends who regaled Captain Plowman with news from the street. The rioting was continuing unabated.

Using the rather mean-spirited tactic of heartstring tugging, Lytton returned on Tuesday afternoon with Eireann. In her convent school uniform, she looked absolutely Catholic, and her green hat ribbons added the requisite Irish touch.

"You wish to bring her in here, sir?" the guard at the gate asked.

With great apprehension, Eireann looked up at the cold face of the prison, the heavy door at the entrance a dark and terrifying entry to the sheltered girl. Her knees trembling, she had an image of her mother facing a door just like this, perhaps worse than this. "I was born in the penal colony of Fremantle, Western Australia," she proclaimed. "I am not a stranger to an English prison."

"Rather outspoken, miss," the guard said with a condescending grin.

"I shall speak out, sir, before the Crown's injustice takes my father as it did my mother," she shouted. Abruptly, Lytton and his guest were ushered into Kilmainham as the mob began to percolate with fresh vigor.

A stern woman examined Eireann in a hunt for contraband, something that the girl found humiliating. Mr. Lytton grew outraged, accusing the woman of stripping an innocent child down to her skin. His speech overflowed with indignation, implying something repulsive or disgusting, judging by the deep blush that burned on Matron's cheeks when Mr. Lytton finished. The search ended immediately, before another button could be undone on the dress.

With grace, Eireann donned her jacket and replaced her hat, picked up her missal with her right hand and took Mr. Lytton's arm with her left. Walking though the gallery of the prison, she found it surprisingly light, but the reality of the building was made clear when she was escorted into the foul, dank solicitor's room. A picture of restraint evaporated instantly when she saw her father. Like a child, she ran to him, threw her arms around his neck and wept.

"Mr. Lytton, how could you bring her here?" Simon grumbled, but only after he had hugged her to his chest.

"Do you see how she suffers?" the barrister intoned with melodrama.

"I don't suffer at all, Mr. Lytton," she said, wiping her eyes and putting on a cheerful face.

"Good heavens, Eireann, you have become your aunt," Simon said.

"I'm very, very proud of you, Papa. We pray for you at chapel every day, and Mother Superior wishes to extend her personal hope that you are released soon. I have a prayer to share with you, sir, here, in my missal."

Opening the book to a page where the binding had been worked loose, she picked out the note that she had folded like the old memo, a small scrap that easily fit in her palm. As she held the missal close to her father's hand, she slipped him a message.

"Who showed you," Simon whispered, but he could not complete his thought.

Before long, Lytton discovered that his ploy to bring Plowman to his senses was having the opposite effect. Miss Eireann Plowman was not quite like other girls, but then other girls did not have a grandfather who taught them how to shoot a Colt revolver and an Enfield rifle. Other girls did not have a father present at target practice who chided them for flinching at the percussion of a gun. Other girls did not have a father who had engaged in the dark and secretive practices of espionage and intelligence, as Captain Plowman had done throughout his military career.

"As I predicted, the case has been delayed," Lytton reported. "And it will be delayed until Ireland is at peace."

"It will be delayed until Parnell's paramour has given birth," Simon confided, his hands over Eireann's ears. "He'd rather be in Kilmainham and pretend the child is actually O'Shea's offspring. He'd rather bed his mistress than focus his energies on Home Rule. He'd rather mollify Captain O'Shea than worry about the loss of control over the Land League."

"For that, you are willing to risk assignment to the stone-breaking yard?" Charles Lytton asked. "Your treatment has been restrained, but if law and order are undermined, they may apply some pressure, and you are not a young man anymore."

"If Gladstone thinks that the Irish people will be subjugated because I am breaking rocks, he is a bigger fool than I thought."

Simon and Eireann closed their meeting with a prayer, with the father performing his Anglican duty as head of the household in leading the devotions. By Tuesday night, the manifesto that was smuggled out of

Kilmainham Gaol was being broadcast throughout the land. "No rent," was declared all across the country, and the rent strike was on.

Naomi McDermott was a nondescript sort of woman, the type who blended into a crowd because she looked like any average Irish woman. Like many others in her situation, she had gone into service because it was the best job she was likely to find. A quiet country girl, she could easily walk into a telegraph office and send a wire to family in New York, and like most Irish servants, she had plenty of family abroad. Her action was not at all unusual, and it caused no alarm.

Michael O'Dwyer was roused from sleep at four in the morning, to receive an important message from Dublin. "Sir Simon in Kilmainham," Naomi informed her so-called cousin. "Violated Coercion Act while acting as M.P. Fear for my position."

The last sentence was gibberish, added by Anna to hide a news item in a plea for help. By Tuesday afternoon, newspapers from New York to San Francisco carried the story, and Irish-American editors had a grand time lambasting Her Majesty and Mr. Gladstone. If the Americans had fought against taxation without representation, their Irish counterparts had representation, except their representatives were in prison instead of the House of Commons. Members of Parliament were being jailed for attempting to improve the lot of the downtrodden, and London was growing embarrassed by the mocking. London was also growing enraged over the rent strike and the never-ending violence, which was made worse rather than made better by Gladstone's ham-handed efforts.

On Sunday, Anna paid a call, bringing a bundle of clean clothes that was thoroughly searched for hidden messages. Anna was also thoroughly searched, but she tolerated the invasion with her pride intact. Escorted to the meeting room, she kept her chin up despite her agitation.

Like many women, Anna opened her visit with a prayer, turning to a missal for a Gospel reading to share with her brother. Taking the prayer book, Sir Simon selected the passage that would bring him comfort, something that suggested that the gentleman was finding God and would soon return to the straight and narrow path that followed the law.

"Eireann knows," Simon murmured. Touching the cover of the girl's missal, he looked his sister straight in the eye. "And I did not teach this to her."

"Yes, she does, she knows how her parents met and where they were married. Do not dare to be cross with me, Simon. I was left in charge and I had a problem to deal with. Someone told her that you bought Mary Claire," Anna whispered. "I had to set the record straight, and she is perfectly happy now. It is her mother's missal, Simon, and I have no idea what you are talking about."

Plowman folded his hands, almost in prayer, let out a sigh, and put his head down for a moment. He thought, a careful deliberation, and then he raised his head. "Give her the old newspaper clippings, then. Let her know how her mother came to be in Portland Gaol, how our meeting came about. Anna, I don't know how long I must stay here. If it becomes necessary, you are to go to Boston, do you understand?"

"Statements have been made by American politicians with large Irish followings," she assured her brother. "Mr. Lytton does not think you will be here much longer. Something is happening, Simon, between Dublin Castle and London, a conflict over strategy."

"I shall miss my Sunday afternoon coffee with Father O'Malley," Simon changed the subject. The guard looked over, carefully watching all meetings between prisoners and guests. With only two eyes, he could not look everywhere, and Simon used volume to draw the man's attention.

"I don't understand why he gave you that bizarre contraption, only to call once a month so he can drink coffee with you. He could have kept the thing and made his own coffee."

"It was a gift, Anna," Simon said. "I never cared for coffee, but once a month I can enjoy the flavor because our conversation is so delectable."

"You are becoming a poet in here," Anna said.

"Don't give her the journal." He returned to the previous discussion when the jailer looked away. "Don't touch it, please, swear to me. Leave it exactly as Mary Claire had it, tied up in a ribbon."

"Of course, but it does not seem right to withhold Mary Claire's most intimate thoughts. She meant for Eireann to read it."

"What happened on the transport, Anna, what Mary Claire did for me in Fremantle, I don't want Eireann to know it yet."

"It only illustrates a wife's submission to her husband and her duty to follow his orders. Eireann will see that a woman gives up her past life and her family to create a new family under her husband's command. It's not as if Mary Claire went against you. Or did she?"

"Be sure to give Father O'Malley my regards," Simon ended the chat, raising his voice.

Simon passed ten dull weeks in Kilmainham, light duty for a Marine, and he was released on Christmas Eve as a gesture of the Lord Lieutenant's good will. Captain Plowman was not considered much of a threat, not a man who had served his nation for so many years. So went the official story, but the Home Office at Whitehall had put pressure on Dublin Castle to keep Sir Simon incarcerated until they asked for his release. The Home Secretary assured his colleagues in Dublin that Sir Simon was a trusted confidante of Parnell, the one to whisper in the man's ear while Captain O'Shea acted as mediator between Gladstone and

Parnell, something that he could only do if the gentleman had daily access to Mr. Parnell. Captain Plowman had been arrested under order of Whitehall, and Whitehall would let Dublin Castle know when he had completed his mission.

Although never proved, it was firmly believed that the messages to the press that were smuggled out of the prison came from Plowman. Those who knew him best saw a clever man who used any means necessary to achieve his goal, someone so devious that he would not hesitate to undermine Parnell and Davitt through false propaganda. Few tenants in West Limerick were withholding rent, having reached agreements with the landlords, and the call for a rent strike was obviously a sly bit of business. Plowman was the kind of strategist who would use his enemies for his gain, and the time of his imprisonment proved that to be a fact.

On Christmas Day, Eireann took the portfolio of clippings to her father's library and sat with him, to review the stories and verify that all she read was true. "It was the last time that criminals were sent to Australia," Simon explained while they looked at the Fremantle *Herald*. "Your mother was infamous at the time. But after the reporter found out that she had married me, they lost interest in her and she became just a lovely lady whose comings and goings were put on the society page."

"But how was she brave?" Eireann puzzled. "You told me to be brave like Mama when you were arrested."

"She was alone because I had to return to sea. I had to go to Dublin to press for her pardon. Your mother was as brave as a soldier, all alone in Fremantle, and she had to make all new friends to help her while I was away. Mrs. Wakeford, here, she is mentioned in this article about the Easter Monday regatta. She took care of you until I returned. In fact, when I came back to Fremantle, Mr. and Mrs. Wakeford were in mourning, as if your mother were their daughter. At her funeral, the most prominent people attended. Her pallbearers were the governor of Western Australia, Mr. Wakeford, and Mr. Cox, the banker. Captain Grady was another one; he was the captain of a Navy ship. To become so loved, Eireann, it takes a great deal of courage."

Leaning against her father's leg, sitting on the floor near the fire, Eireann tried to picture her mother stepping onto a strange dock, without familiar faces there to greet her. "Did her brothers write to her?"

"It's possible, but all the letters that were sent to the convicts were examined by the warders. Your mother's correspondence was censored by the Comptroller General of the prison, Mr. Wakeford, because of her importance."

"But what if she received a love letter, Papa?" Eireann asked.

"From another man?" Simon said, pretending to be aghast.

"From you, of course." The girl rolled her eyes at her father's silliness.

"I was at sea and could not get a letter to her. Now, if some other sweetheart was trying to court her, I don't think Mr. Wakeford would have stood for such nonsense."

"What if Uncle Michael wrote in some secret code?"

"Well, I am sure that Mr. Wakeford was screening your mother's mail to search for such secret messages. He was also concerned that your uncles would try to turn your mother against me."

"They dislike you so much?"

"We don't always agree on everything, that's all. It's funny, about falling in love. You will see one day, Eireann, before too long. One never knows who will be the one that catches your heart and won't let go."

The voyage of the *Hellebore* was completely forgotten that afternoon, skipped over in a choppy sequence of events that avoided the truth. Sitting in a comfortable room on Christmas Day, warmed by a coal fire, the former Royal Marine covered up the journey through terror that transformed a simple Irish girl into Simon Plowman's agent. The journal, still bound in its Kelly green ribbon, was hidden away to gather even more dust.

Nineteen

The military veteran fought on when he returned to his seat in Commons. Plowman's duties were interrupted in February when his mother died, her nerves strained by Simon's incarceration and the upheaval that she watched unfold all around her. The paroxysm of bloodshed continued, culminating in the brutal stabbing of Lord Cavendish and his undersecretary in Phoenix Park. Only a cold-blooded homicide seemed to move the new Chief Secretary, who set about fulfilling the promises that had been made in Gladstone's Kilmainham Treaty, reached after months of bargaining with Parnell. Those whose rents were seriously in arrears were given some aid by their government, and once again the issue of Home Rule was brought forward.

Plowman fell out with Parnell over his machinations to enact the Home Rule bill. Parnell threw the support of the Irish Nationalists behind Gladstone because the Prime Minister promised Home Rule, but Simon saw the true key to success in winning his fellow Conservatives. He knew who the enemy was, and it was embodied by Randolph Churchill, Duke of Marlborough and fervent empire-lover who worked both sides of the aisle to defeat Home Rule and the Liberal government as well. The bill failed, and Gladstone resigned, turning over the government to Lord Salisbury.

Simon began to wonder if he would live to see the Irish have a voice in the management of their country.

It was Anna's influence, and Simon's acquiescence to his sister's control of their home, that sent Eireann to university when few women furthered their education. What had begun as a childish curiosity had developed into a love of learning. Even though Eireann did not expect to enter the working world, as much as she would have liked to become a barrister or a banker, she pursued her liberal arts studies with giddy pleasure. It took a great deal of steely resolve to tolerate the heckling and condescension of her male colleagues, but she stubbornly refused to be scared off from a quest for knowledge. Growing older, becoming her own person, Eireann grew further away from her father, their political leanings so opposite that she did not see where they could possibly meet.

"Are we not going to London for the Jubilee?" Eireann asked her aunt in the early days of June.

"Hardly something to celebrate, don't you think?" Anna replied. She continued to rifle through her wardrobe, choosing outfits for an annual summer excursion to Athenry.

"I can't believe my father would miss the Golden Jubilee," the young lady said. "He spoke of a weekend at Althorp with Earl Spencer. Thank God I won't be required to kiss His Lordship's bottom."

"Vulgarity, Eireann," Anna corrected her collegiate niece. "And a weekend with Lord Spencer is purely political. He is on the outside with the rest of the Home Rule crowd now that Churchill's gotten his way. Your father won't be attending the conference anyway. He is coming with us, just as he has every other year."

Whitehall's secret police were overworked that Jubilee year, chasing after Irish bomb plots against the Royal Family. Sir Simon had been of some use to Mr. Jenkinson, the former chief spook and confidante of Earl Spencer, but he was not a close friend of James Monro. The new head of the internal security cabal had his suspicions of Sir Simon because Plowman favored Home Rule and greatly disliked the new Secretary for Ireland, Sir Michael Beach.

Plowman warned Monro that the most violent Irish separatists were experimenting with dynamite bombs, but Sir Simon's information resulted in a flurry of wild goose chases all over London. When a bomb ripped through the House of Commons on a quiet Sunday, Sir Simon sent a cursory note to the gentleman's office at Scotland Yard. "I told you so," Captain Plowman quipped, and Mr. Monro would never forgive the M.P. for his cheek.

"I have sold my tickets to the grand festival," Plowman notified Monro as the day approached. Queen Victoria would enter Westminster Abbey in a great display of pomp and pageantry, and Scotland Yard was terrified of an assassination by dynamite. It had been done in Russia, and the evidence was clear that the Irish Republican Brotherhood was planning to replicate the deed in London. Sir Simon's mean prose added to Monro's tension. "Who is attending in my stead? Clan na Gael? I.R.B.?"

"You found it humorous, no doubt, that I wasted the time of a detective to determine that you sold the tickets to Lady Edwina Penley," Monro complained to the M.P.

"I should have given them to her, is that what you mean to imply?" Simon parried, flippant mockery in his tone. "After our tryst at Maplewood last March, I suppose that would have been the honorable thing to do."

"Tossing four farthings on her bed after you'd had your way," Monro spluttered in outrage.

"Lord Salisbury's lovely agents cannot worm their way into my heart," Plowman said, "because I have no heart."

Rumors about Sir Simon always seemed to find their way back to him, as speculation about his true motives became the topic of gossip between political camps. Plowman learned that Monro was making inquiries about his duties in America during the war, his activities regarding the Fenian movement shortly thereafter, and his actions in the Cape Colony and the Suez. No one knew anything, or at any rate no one claimed to know anything. Lord Salisbury butted up against a solid stone wall, unable to penetrate the secrecy of Her Majesty's military leaders. It gave the impression that Their Lords of the Admiralty were keeping an eye on Lord Salisbury, who became convinced that Simon's support of Home Rule was a charade. Few of the Conservatives believed that their colleague was any more in favor of Home Rule than his father before him, spewing rhetoric about a restoration of the Irish Parliament that was pro-monarchy at its core.

On the day of Queen Victoria's Golden Jubilee, a very industrious Detective Soames observed the Misses Plowman attending Mass at St. Agatha's Church in Athenry while Sir Simon sat in the graveyard and chatted with a tombstone. Much to the man's humiliation, he was coerced into joining the Plowman family on their return trip to Galway, where he was bullied into sharing Sir Simon's room at the inn where the family stayed, and then intimidated into dining with them. Sir Simon also had the gall to order the detective to accompany them on their return to Dublin, sending him back to Scotland Yard with a rather nasty note.

"Thank you for amusing my daughter," Simon tormented Monro. "She found Mr. Soames' attempts at shadowing us to be wildly ridiculous. His table manners, however, are lacking, and in future I would request that you assign a more well-bred gentleman to follow me about. I ask this, not for myself, but in consideration of the ladies."

James Monro had once been secretary to the prison superintendents, and he was well aware of Sir Simon Plowman's obsession with a mistake that had occurred nearly twenty years earlier. It was apparent that the M.P. would go to any length to embarrass the Criminal Investigation Division, and a career bureaucrat would not willingly tumble if the house of cards fell. Salisbury's spymaster did not know how much Plowman knew, any more than he realized that Plowman was an expert at the espionage game. Out of fear that Sir Simon would flagrantly publicize anything that made the Metropolitan Police look foolish, Monro tried to find a few Plowman skeletons as counterbalance, but his search was maddeningly fruitless.

Crushing the Home Rule movement became the credo of Lord Salisbury, returned to the office of Prime Minister as the Conservatives took power. He saw a grand opportunity to eliminate Parnell, the ringleader of the faction, when Mr. Parnell called for a special commission to clear his name. A purported link between the murder of Lord Cavendish in Phoenix Park and Charles Parnell had been broadcast in *The Times*, and Parnell was determined to set the record straight. Sir Simon was caught in the Home Rule net along with almost every other Irish M.P. who had ever called for a separate Irish Parliament.

"I'm sure that I make him nervous, sitting behind him in the chamber." Simon poured out another drink for his attorney. "He only wants to be rid of Parnell, and he's put me in the same bed because I insulted his lady spy. My God, she was a ninny."

"His rationale has nothing to do with the issue of Lady Edwina," Charles Lytton advised his client. "He'll crush you if Home Rule is buried with you. My job at this point is to collect evidence for your defense, if there is anything that you can reveal without divulging classified information."

Lytton's law clerk, his son Roger, sat poised in the Plowman library, ready to take dictation. Eireann knocked quietly and slipped in, delivering tea because the parlor maid was never allowed to interrupt Sir Simon in his lion's den. Observing the young man's dreamy gaze, Simon graciously made introductions. The way that Roger admired Eireann's figure was unsettling for a father, who was aware that such inspections were inevitable but preferred not to know about them. For his own peace of mind, he suggested that Eireann accompany young Mr. Lytton on a stroll of St. Stephen's Green, for fresh air and an opportunity to stretch out his legs after a long afternoon of legal briefing.

"But, the tea?" Eireann protested.

"Roger, Miss Plowman would like to be taken to tea," Charles said. He obviously had brought his son along for more reasons than work, and Simon had to put his hand over his mouth to cover a smile that he pretended was a slight yawn.

"It is not necessary, Mr. Lytton, we can retire to the parlor if you are seeking privacy," Eireann said, reading her father's mind.

"There you go, Roger, off to the parlor and do say hello to my sister," Simon dismissed the clerk. "Eireann has a very poor opinion of men due to her experiences at university. Try to bring her around to a more positive outlook, but I warn you that she is skilled at debate."

When the couple was gone, Simon looked intently at his old friend. "I know, in some detail, who is behind the dynamite plots of the Jubilee year. Lord Salisbury knows, and he suspects that I know as well. Why do you think this libel case has been turned into a spectacle, to be paid for by *The Times*? The Prime Minister was warned, by me in fact, that the letters he relies on to link Parnell with the dynamitards are all forgeries. It will come out in the end, Charlie, but the newspaper will pay the price and Salisbury will still be able to discredit Parnell."

"Is our Prime Minister engrossed in demolishing Home Rule or demolishing Parnellism?" Charles asked.

"Both, and more deeply than I can explain to you." The tea that Eireann had left earlier was poured out and improved with a little whiskey while a tired silence crept into the room. Deep in thought, Simon stirred a generous spoonful of sugar into the cup, swirling the liquid and staring intently at the vortex of the whirlpool. Many times before, he had come close to being exposed, but never before had he had such powerful enemies, intent on uncovering his true identity. There was a card to be played, a trump that would save his skin but spell the end to his career. "If there is ever a need to examine me in the course of this expedition, you are to ask me what I know about Frank Millen."

"That name does not appear in any document that I have seen," Lytton said.

"I pray that his name is never uttered. Lord Spencer would be burned in that fire. Michael Davitt knows the man as well, and he will guide the defense counsel by feeding him bits of information until Salisbury backs off. His Lordship won't come after me, in all likelihood, because I know too much."

Charles stared at his dear friend, someone he knew to have been involved in military intelligence during his years of faithful service to the Crown. With a very slight nod, Plowman implied that he had never really left the Royal Marines or given up the part of his life that no one ever saw. He used people to achieve his goals, just as he was about to use an old friend to carry a message. Sometimes the people he used were put into danger. This time, Lytton was the unsuspecting, harmless messenger, passing along a threat that he could not see, as safe as any other barrister in Dublin.

"Through unofficial channels, Charlie, you are to get word to Salisbury, remind him that Captain Plowman was active in anti-Fenian actions within the armed forces. We are both men obsessed, but he is blind while I have kept my eyes open. He won't tie me to Parnell, but if he makes any attempt to rope me in, I will testify to the Commission. Let him stew over that."

The inquiry dragged along, and Simon went on about the business of government, sitting behind Lord Salisbury with the Conservatives. When the opposition shredded the Home Secretary following the revelation of forged documents used to discredit Mr. Parnell, Captain Plowman did nothing to staunch the flow of blood. Neither did he join the Liberals' attack as they tore into the Assistant Police Commissioner, who had apparently shared secrets with the editor of *The Times*. Salisbury heard the message, loud and clear, and he lived in fear of Sir Charles Russell's defense, while he was kept awake at night by thoughts of Sir Simon's potential testimony and the unseen hands that pulled Plowman's strings.

Salisbury ran into Plowman at the refreshment bar one afternoon, a chance encounter that Simon recognized as carefully planned. His Lordship rarely showed his face in the room, and Simon responded by becoming the most chatty representative in all of Whitehall. "My late wife's brothers have been mocking me for years," he mentioned, bringing up the incident of the Fenian escape and coupling it with current unrest. "Lately, however, I find their jibes to be acutely painful, as do your associates in the front row. If you can't repair the damage, I expect that Her Majesty might be looking for heads to roll."

"The heads of those who wish to break apart the Empire should be sliced off first, I believe," Salisbury warned.

"What of a man who could be charged with treason?" Simon countered. Eye to eye with a man who could bring him down, the Royal Marine leaned forward, taking advantage of his height to appear towering. Sensing that he was gaining the upper hand, Simon allowed the slightest suggestion of a friendly smile to appear as he shifted his weight, creating a comfortable space and giving Lord Salisbury a little room to breath. "And may I remind Your Lordship that previous monarchs saw fit to acknowledge an Irish Parliament at one time. Would you paint them with your brush as well? The Empire did not crumble then. Just as the Empire did not crumble when the Hindu were allowed to practice their religion while the Irish were banned from their faith. Sauce for the goose, Your Lordship."

"I am aware that Ireland has been largely ignored," the Prime Minister said by way of an offer, intimating that he would bring Plowman into his camp if the former Royal Marine was willing to deal. For his part, Simon would not ask for too much, preferring to keep Salisbury under his thumb but not overly pressed.

"Every summer, I return to my wife's grave to pay my respects, and every summer I must go through the most absurd routes to travel from one side of the country to the other. Lack of railroads, quite unlike England. Inadequate funding of the universities, inadequate public facilities. When that is what passes for good governance, what would one expect from the citizens?"

On through Eireann's final year of schooling, the Commission investigated but never quite proved fatal to either side. Parnell did himself in, enveloped in the messy divorce of his mistress and her husband, with the disgrace of immorality finishing his political career completely. The

Catholic Church equated support of Parnell's ideals with support for adultery, preaching bitterly against the legislation. The Home Rule movement went down with Parnell, whose vindication seemed pointless in the end.

"Oddly enough, the assassination of Her Majesty would have benefited either side," Charles noted as they relaxed after the verdict came down. "Kill the Queen and blame the Irish, and there goes Home Rule. Kill the Queen and mount a rebellion, and Ireland could potentially have split off from the Empire. It's a wonder anyone would try to stop it."

"Did you hear that James Monro resigned?" Simon asked, a note of triumph in his voice. "He's a policeman to the tips of his shoes, and when he finally realized that Lord Salisbury was playing politics and not crime prevention, he surrendered. It's rather tragic, in a way. He sincerely wanted to do well, and he worked like a demon, but he was in over his head and never knew it. Decamped for India to find solace in charity work, poor fellow."

In the spring of 1891, a time of grandiose public works projects and far-reaching railroad construction that was meant to placate the unhappy subjects of the Emerald Isle, Eireann married Roger Lytton. Lord Salisbury sent a wedding gift, counting Sir Simon as conservative enough to publicly acknowledge their political alliance. Even so, the cry for an Irish Parliament did not go away, although the voices were disjointed and no leader had emerged to replace Charles Parnell.

Mr. and Mrs. Lytton took a honeymoon trip to London, an abbreviated journey when Roger could not spare more than two weeks away from the family's law practice. Eireann's first choice was a long sojourn to America, to finally meet her American relatives and see New York City, but there was not enough time for a transatlantic cruise. The doting groom thought his bride would enjoy London, since she had never been there before, but all she wanted to see was Parliament, and only because her father spent so much time there.

After the honeymoon, they rode through Dublin on their way home. Between the North Wall and Merrion Square lived Dublin's poor, a population of wretches who were more ragged, more hungry, more destitute and more numerous than their counterparts in London. Lost in her own thoughts, Eireann was startled when Roger took her hand and held it to his chest.

"This cannot be tolerated, dearest," he said. "We must make it better. Surely it is our duty, to not sit back in our comfortable homes and allow this to continue."

"How, Roger? There are no leaders; the movement is in chaos," she said.

"Out of chaos comes order. The old Fenians are past their useful time. It is up to us to take their places and move forward. You'll support me, won't you, if I cast my lot with the Irish Republican Brotherhood?"

In all their discussions of politics, Eireann had never been able to convince him that she was walking the right path. In the span of two short weeks, her hatred of England grew hotter, while Roger discovered the truth of her beliefs and he accepted her views as his own, using them to create a new purpose in their lives. The need for violence, the use of the gun, became apparent; a last resort, of course, but the only way to achieve freedom.

Mr. and Mrs. Lytton settled into the Plowman home on Merrion Square, no longer the most fashionable address in Dublin but Eireann could not imagine being separated from her beloved aunt. She could not give up the family's habits and customs, including the monthly Sunday afternoon with Father O'Malley. Her first social occasion as a married woman was not the same as usual, because Simon made a great fuss about presenting the silver coffee service to his daughter and his son-in-law, the new holders of Plowman's valuables.

"I have deemed this a treasured artifact," Simon explained, in jest.

"But sir, you only drink coffee when Father O'Malley calls," Roger said.

"He's a good man, Mr. Lytton, and not one to make a priest drink alone," O'Malley said. "I developed a taste for the vile brew when I was in America on a fund raising drive, and my old friend indulges my whims because I give his agnosticism a thorough going over in return."

By New Year's Day, Simon had begun to think of retirement, to leave the house to Roger and Eireann. "What do you say to a move to Limerick?" he asked his sister as they sat in the parlor. Two life-long companions, they enjoyed the privacy that they gained while the newlyweds were off making their rounds of social calls. It was not as easy as Anna had thought, to share the house with a fourth person who was still a bit of a stranger. "It's something that I have been thinking of for a long time, and when Eireann became engaged I made up my mind to do it. I want to build a summer house, just a little cottage, near Rathkeale."

"That would be lovely," Anna said. "Dublin is too crowded for me now, too noisy and dirty. It's our time, isn't it, to plant our roots in Irish soil."

"This house will be full of children one day. Just as our father had wanted all along, with all his grand plans that came to nothing," Simon said. "Eireann shall be able to do as she likes with this place, and I'll give her free rein when they're ready to change a bedroom into a nursery."

"There was so much unhappiness under this roof." Anna wiped away a tear. "It's time for all of that to be changed as well."

With a new year came a new trend, a period in which all things Irish became fashionable. While Simon's architect drew up plans for a cottage that was inspired by the simple structures of rural Ireland, the Lyttons joined their friends in the study of the Irish language. Every Tuesday evening, they gathered in the parlor with a tutor who had come from Galway, and they studied with patriotic fervor. Eireann was surprised that her father wanted to join them, but Sir Simon only made it through one lesson when he abruptly gave it up. As soon as the tutor translated *"Ta ocras orm"*, Simon fled from the parlor, mumbling excuses.

"Ta ocras orm," Eireann repeated, shrugging off her father's departure. "I am hungry."

Twenty

The Gaelic revival left Roger and Eireann increasingly dissatisfied with Irish politics. Without a doubt, the many nights of debate with Sir Simon worked on Roger's thoughts, along with the radical thinking of his wife. Somewhere between the birth of Michael and Peter, he decided that the Irish Republican Brotherhood was not moving fast enough for him, and he joined Sinn Fein to explore a political solution to the crisis. The drive to give Ireland its own Parliament had long been steeped in militancy, an aggressive dynamism that had been building since the Fenian uprising of 1867, and Roger became an expert marksman under the tutelage of Sir Simon. Eireann encouraged her father to teach her two little boys how to handle guns as well.

The Home Rule movement had no leader, and the lack of progress showed on the streets of Dublin. Labor unrest had become commonplace, with an undercurrent of violence that left Eireann in fear for her children's safety. Despite Simon's protests, Roger abandoned Dublin to the teeming masses and bought a house in Rathmines, to escape the pestilence that was the expanding tenement districts edging closer to Merrion Square. Eireann spent hours riding the trams, looking in on her aging aunt while her father spent more time in Rathkeale. In her mind, he had abandoned the urban centers because he saw the solution to Ireland's problems in land, in granting ownership to the rural poor. His stubborn refusal to acknowledge a single idea or carefully crafted opinion from Eireann's sharp mind did little to bring father and daughter closer.

Taking to the hustings again in 1910, Simon was returned to his seat by his Limerick neighbors, a duty that he accepted despite his age. Approaching seventy-two, he was getting tired of argument, and the short voyage across the Irish Sea was becoming a dreaded chore. A Home Rule bill had passed Commons, only to be killed in Lords, and it was coming up again. Simon felt that his obligation to his country took precedence over his personal comfort, and he wanted to be in Parliament to finish a task begun long before.

He knew it was coming because the northern Protestants had organized a militia, the Ulster Volunteers, to wage war against a Catholic government that many thought was inevitable. Before long, the Catholics answered with the Irish Volunteers, a group of men ready to defend their Home Rule state from the Anglicans they had been fighting for hundreds of years. The battle lines were drawn, crystal clear and sharp.

Roger approached his father-in-law one night after dinner, to press the old man yet again on accepting the hospitality of a person Sir Simon considered a son. He opened with a reminder that Anna was being run ragged, at her age, with a house to keep and a brother to look after. Four grandchildren longed for their grandfather's company. The Rathmines home was spacious and Eireann would be much happier if she was confident that her father was being taken care of and her aunt did not have so many duties. Before long, the conversation turned from one of concern for the elderly to a probing of political boundaries.

"I made a commitment long ago, Roger, and I have stood by it for over forty-five years," Simon said, in reply to a question about loyalty. Wishing that Roger would go away, he sat and stared into the fire. He missed the smell of the peat fire that they had in the country, just as he longed to get back to the cottage in Rathkeale.

"At this time, Sir Simon, I must remind you that, upon my marriage, you assured me that this home was to be my home, with all the privileges that are inherent in a man's place of residence. In turn, I will offer you the same consideration if you would come to Rathmines with us."

Like a dog worrying a bone, the young man would not let go. With a sigh, Plowman turned to face him, to speak as honestly as he could when he could not be completely honest. "Roger, I expected you to be your own man." It struck him then that forty-five years had gone by. Mary Claire had lived to be nineteen, and no more. "Good God, you are nearly as old as my commitment. How could I have lived so long?"

"I trust that our arrangement would continue, sir. What is said in my house by my guests is confidential."

"Worried about informers in the ranks?" Plowman said, a somewhat distant look glazing his eyes. "Silence and secrecy are hard to maintain. So, what side do you think I am on, anyway?"

"In the event of armed conflict, with the Crown," the younger man stated.

"With the Crown," Simon repeated. "If the Crown is wise this time around, they will abandon the Ulster contingent and we shall all be united."

Month after month, new social groups sprang up and Eireann spent more and more time at meetings. There were groups demanding female suffrage; there were organizations promoting the Irish language, Irish crafts and Irish independence. The Lytton boys joined Fianna Eireann and the group's founder became a family friend, yet another woman who was tipped towards the more radical side of politics under Eireann's persuasive influence. A corner of Rathmines grew into a locus of revolutionary ardor, while the Merrion Square house became a convenient gathering spot that was close to the heart of labor unrest.

On a warm August morning in 1913, Eireann shuttled between her new home and her old residence, where Anna was staging a debate about Home Rule and the wisdom of forming a nationalist army to fight Edward Carson's proposed Unionist forces. Shortly before ten in the morning, her journey ground to a halt. The tram stopped in the middle of the street and the driver walked off, stranding the passengers.

Riders sat in stunned silence for a few minutes before a group of gentlemen determined that this was the very industrial action that the nefarious Jim Larkin had been threatening, right at the start of Horse Show week. Amidst the grumbling, Eireann felt a slight urge to join the men in cursing the inconvenience. She was supposed to drink tea with Connie Markievicz, and she would never get there on time if she had to walk. Even so, there was a certain excitement in knowing that the fledgling union had done something concrete and solid, that the country was no longer sitting on the side waiting for London to move first.

Before she could decide what to do, a fresh driver arrived and the car continued along its route, getting as far as Dame Street before another stopped tram blocked the tracks. Eireann got off the car to see what was going on, but a milling crowd of constables and curiosity seekers blocked her view. By the time she made it to Merrion Square, she had puzzled out a new course of action. Irish freedom could be found with the very men who kept Dublin alive with transportation and coal and cartage. They earned less than their colleagues in London or Glasgow because of an unfair government that made rules from afar and never wandered over the Irish Sea. Such an arrangement had to end, and she would join their fight.

With talk of the military being sent in to quell unrest, Eireann sent her husband a message to let him know that she was safe and would not risk the return trip to Rathmines, not when the trolleys might be attacked by strikers. Instead, she joined Countess Markievicz on a short drive to Beresford Place, to hear Jim Larkin speak to the workers who had walked off their jobs at his order. Never before had Eireann heard a man deliver oratory that stirred so many. She had found a cause that she could support, a route to independence from British rule that would bring dignity and fairness to the poor while wiping out the class structure and intolerance that kept Roger's prospects in check. Until the strike was settled and the workers satisfied, she would follow Mr. Larkin's demand and never set foot on one of Mr. Murphy's cars.

Eireann wrote to her father, to fill him in on the changes that were erupting in Dublin, but she also wanted to warn him of her steadfast determination to support Larkin and the union. She received her response within a week, when a boy delivered a new bicycle to her, compliments of Sir Simon Plowman, for his tram-less daughter. If he wanted to show her any more clearly that they were in complete disagreement on the matter, he could not have done any better. Her response was equally barbed as she thanked her father for the practical gift that came complete with useful panniers for carrying her bundles in waterproof security.

All that anyone could talk about at the Markievicz party on Saturday was the situation in Dublin, but it would not be until the next morning that Eireann would learn about the rioting that took place. "Mr. Larkin still intends to speak," she told Roger over breakfast. "Despite the threats of the police."

"Casimir offered us a lift last night. I'll just ring him up and accept, shall I?" Roger said.

Seated in Connie's motor car, Eireann felt the power of the milling crowd pulse through the vehicle, as if she were on a ship that was rocking in a gentle swell. There was an excitement to the mob, an air of expectancy that washed away the trepidation she had felt earlier. She was here to join in a general defiance of Dublin Castle, to support the same people who had been clubbed by drunken policemen when all they wanted was the same right to assemble that was granted to their Protestant countrymen in Belfast.

"It's Larkin," came the cry, and the crowd surged forward. Eireann scanned the facade of the hotel and saw him standing at an open window.

Responding to the press of people, the police pushed back. Somewhere behind her, a large pane of glass shattered and so did Eireann's composure. Only hours ago, she had been laughing as one of Connie's theatrical friends dressed up the labor organizer in one of Casimir Markievicz's old coats and a false beard. They had all giggled at the plan to spirit the disguised Mr. Larkin into the hotel so that he would not be arrested before he kept his vow to address the workers. The deed was done, the chain of events played out, but no one had thought about what would occur afterwards. The scene had no ending, no final curtain.

Excitement filled her heart until Eireann was made deaf by her own pulse. The car moved but she could not tell if Casimir was driving or the police were pushing them towards the alley. In a burst of inspiration, Connie stood up and called for three cheers for Mr. Larkin, which brought even more policemen and attracted the attention of onlookers who drifted over to see what new excitement might be found. This was no longer a lark or a Sunday afternoon drive to take the air. Uniformed officers brandished batons, more men ran down Sackville Street towards the hotel, and Eireann saw that it was time to flee.

In the confusion, she was separated from Roger but managed to find Connie near the hotel entrance. If they could get inside, they could find refuge until the street was cleared, but as soon as Eireann made her plan, a group of policemen pushed through the doors with Mr. Larkin in their grasp. Connie hurried forward and grabbed Larkin's hand, wishing him good luck as if he were a barrister off to tackle an important legal case. It was foolish, but Connie was prone to theatrical gestures when discretion and silence would have been more appropriate.

Perhaps the outburst infuriated the men brandishing their batons. It was equally likely that they were as panicked as Eireann at that moment, when the throng moved as a whole towards the Imperial Hotel to get a better look at Mr. Larkin under arrest. She managed to locate her friend's hand and grip it firmly, to pull them both away from obvious danger. Connie stumbled under a blow from a detective, dragging Eireann into the melee. A wave of noise, screams and shouts and chaos, drowned out all other sound. The fist that struck her cheek moved so fast that it was nothing more than a blur of flesh and white knuckles. A sharp pain creased the back of her thighs, followed by a kick to her head. She scrambled to her feet and took a few shaky steps, thinking that she could make it to the General Post Office across the street, but just as soon as she stood she was on the ground again, a tremendous pain beating through her skull.

Strong hands took hold of her arms and lifted her, but the men who rescued her were unsteady, not powerful enough to resist the force of thousands of frightened people running for their lives. Groggy from the beating, Eireann was not sure if it was Roger holding her in her arms or some stranger who carried her away from the madness. She closed her eyes for a moment, but when she opened them again she was in her bedroom in her father's house, a cold compress on her forehead.

"The doctor assures me that you will recover," Simon said. He patted her hand, as if she were a child afflicted with a slight cough. "Roger is cleaning up. Beaten almost to a pulp, poor man. Whatever were you thinking, Eireann, to put yourself in the center of such danger?"

"I won't sit idly by in my parlor. Not all of us are Members of Parliament who can make or change the laws," she said. Every bone and joint and muscle ached, from her toenails to her teeth.

"Even M.P.s are hard-pressed to change the laws," he said.

"We never considered," Eireann said. "The whole thing was concocted at a party last night."

"The Markievicz theatre of high drama?" He sat on the edge of the bed, no longer mocking her with his bemused smile. "She's as substantial as a butterfly, flitting from one thing to another and never sticking with one of them to conclusion. Not the stuff that leaders are made of."

"But at least she moves and doesn't sit still like a rock in a field."

"I wish to point out, my dear, that every plan requires a strategy for retreat as well as advancement. To charge in without thought is an exercise in futility."

"As I discovered after the fact," she said, forced to admit that her father was as observant as ever. "And I wasn't brave, father, so I failed on two counts."

"Bravery is a facade. Screaming in fright, running to and fro without direction, that's another matter. Roger thinks that you charged into the riot to rescue Mrs. Markievicz, which is quite a brave thing for a soldier to do." His eyes twinkled in a way she had not seen since she was a little girl, begging for tales of her mother and Fremantle. "You are brave, and your mother would be proud of you."

"Will you tell me about my mother?" Eireann asked. "You're holding back, I know you are and I've always known that you're keeping secrets from me."

Simon smoothed the flannel on her forehead. "However, she would have scolded you for a lack of thorough preparation before taking action. There will be more of this, Eireann. Don't let Mrs. Markievicz run amok and take you with her. You have a fine, level head and the makings of a leader." He touched her cheek and clucked at the nasty bruise that had been left behind by a detective's hairy-knuckled fist. "Battle scars marring the faces of upstanding citizens. They shall be felt long after the pain has faded."

"What's to be done to stop this?"

Simon got to his feet and shrugged in reply to her question. "There are many solutions, of course, but who is powerful enough to force any of the involved parties into a concession? Anyone at Dublin Castle? Surely not Lord Aberdeen."

"Mr. Larkin has strongly suggested that we take up arms. Kill two of them for every one of us."

"And do you have as many guns as Carson's brigade? Or even the money to buy weapons? He's skilled with words, your insurrectionist friend Larkin. No one's died from a tongue lashing, have they?"

Her father never failed to catch her off guard, to lull her into a sense that he was bending to meet her, only to feel the sting when he snapped back to his normal position. Eireann tested her balance gingerly, one foot on the floor at a time, until she was standing on weak limbs. "What brought you to Dublin, might I ask?"

"The Horse Show, of course." He kept on walking down the hall, making for the stairs. "Deadly dull, as usual. Lady Goulding sends her regards, by the way. Hopes to see you next year."

"How can you associate with the very leeches who feed on the blood and misery of your own people?" Eireann asked. The pain in her head increased along with the volume of her voice.

"I've had word from my grandson. Holding up magnificently at home, no need for you to worry. You and Roger are welcome to stay until you've both recovered." With his hand on the banister and one foot on the step, Simon turned to her. "He is armed, by the way. With instructions to shoot every one of them before they can shoot one of ours."

Tucked into the privacy of his library, Simon fired off a blistering letter to the *Irish Times*, lambasting the outrageous and uncontrolled behavior of the Dublin Metropolitan Police. He set his pen on the holder and rubbed his eyes, weary to his bones. There were too many factions doing battle on the island, with too many leaders going off in different directions. They all wanted the same thing, in their own way, but they all insisted on their theory leading the van and triumphing in the end. London did nothing, and by doing nothing, the government encouraged the disunity of the opposition to British rule. Divide and conquer was accomplished without a single bullet being fired.

He could hear Eireann pacing in front of his door, waiting to pounce. She would berate him for failing to support the striking tram drivers, and then she would explain why every Irish citizen should shun Mr. Murphy and all the other landlords of industry. In his head, he imagined their argument, in which he would point out that the parsimony of the average Dublin homeowner contributed to the over-all problem because no one was willing to pay more in taxes. How often had Roger sighed over the rates, while tenements collapsed on top of the tenants and slum landlords sat on the very boards that were meant to regulate them?

The hall outside of his door grew quiet. Eireann had given up for the moment, but she was not through with him yet. Ever since she had learned to think for herself she had been on a crusade to win him over to her side. Simon missed the days when she was impressionable and thought that her father was brilliant. He picked up his pen, to finish his letter. No matter how tired he might be, there was still some purpose in his life and he would stay in Dublin for a few more days, to gather whatever intelligence he could. Who could say if the events of Sunday afternoon were the beginnings of an earthquake or merely slight tremors that cracked a facade but brought nothing down.

Twenty-One

Be a leader, he had said, but events were unfolding too quickly for Eireann to find the front of the line. Within days, the women who toiled away making biscuits for Jacob's were locked out of their jobs, and only because they joined Mr. Larkin's union rather than one approved by Mr. Jacob. Tedcastle's coal company had locked out their men as well, and while the Lyttons could survive without the trams or Jacob's biscuits, they would be hard-pressed to boycott coal if they were to make it through the coming winter. What could she do, as an ordinary woman, when the men who governed were incapable of doing anything? How blind must they all be, to put that many disgruntled men on the streets? Her father must have been thinking along those same lines, since he gave her his old Enfield rifle and a box of cartridges to take home "in the unlikely event" that she might need it.

Protest marches became a daily occurrence, just as a steady rise in the cost of goods marked off the days. The children returned to school, Roger focused on his legal practice, and Eireann returned to her former routines. The newspapers were filled with editorials and articles that centered on talks between the strikers and the merchants. The Chief Secretary had finally crossed the Irish Sea and had great hope of solving the crisis, while Carson's Unionists drilled like soldiers and no one said a

word about a politician's private army that threatened war against the will
of the Irish people. Those in authority were headed in the wrong direction,
hunting the wrong prey, but Eireann had no idea how to channel their
energies.

"Simon, don't go," Mary Claire said. "I beg you, don't go."

"Mary Claire?" Simon shot up in his seat. Cold sweat trickled
down his face and his heart pounded until he feared it would burst.

"Are you all right, sir?" the train guard asked.

Simon mopped at his forehead. "Quite all right, thank you. I
expected to find Belfast much colder than London." The last wisps of fog
floated out of his head and his mind cleared, bringing him back to the
Belfast-bound train and the scratchy upholstery that prickled his thighs.

"Not so very different here than London, you'll find, sir," the guard
said. "We've arrived in Belfast, sir, your destination."

As if nothing were amiss, Simon reached up to retrieve his grip
from the overhead rack, but he had to pause to catch his breath. He
dreamed of her often, but the images had become more real recently, to the
point that he sometimes was unsure where he was. The rocking of the train
carriage had done it, in all likelihood, with the rhythmic movement and
the clatter of the wheels. From the minute that the engine's whistle blew he
had Mary Claire on his mind, picturing her on the platform, begging him
to stay home. An old man had no business traveling for miles, to offer
military advice to a group of young men who probably had never heard of
the Fenian Brotherhood or knew the reputation of Sir Simon Plowman.
Perhaps on the journey back to Rathkeale he might stop and have a talk
with her, to explain why he could not be confined to a cottage while the
nation was on the verge of crumbling.

By the time he found Sir George Richardson in Great Victoria Street station, Simon had pulled himself together in preparation for the rest of his grueling mission. They did not know each other except by reputation, with their new relationship forged through mutual friendships in the military. Simon was tired, but seeing Sir George in uniform sparked a little of the old vigor, with its reminders of days he once thought were long past.

Sir George was, as Simon expected, intensely interested in the state of Dublin, where the army had just been sent to maintain order. During the short walk to the hotel, Simon provided as much information as he could about the attitudes of various factions towards Larkinism, Home Rule and Unionism. His host was generous in sharing his own opinions about the Chief Secretary's dithering and the message that was being sent to the striking workers. Both men agreed that it was all based on politics, at its core, and Prime Minister Asquith would support the devil himself to remain in power. The inconveniences of strikes and lock-outs, the dangers of rioting, did not touch them directly and so there was no incentive to deal harshly with those most in need of harsh treatment.

"Yes, I have a staff of fine officers, but I need someone who can train a small contingent of specialists," Sir George said. He followed on the heels of the boy who was almost too small to carry Simon's bag, and then continued to chat about his plans within earshot of all the strangers who crowded into the hotel elevator. The lieutenant-general saw no need to maintain secrecy, apparently, or he had enough confidence in those around him to talk openly. "Your reputation led me to seek you out, to offer you a position. Teach these men how to infiltrate, how to gather intelligence without being as obvious as a police detective."

"My oath binds me for life, as I see it," Plowman said. "Yet I am nearing the end of it, and I would not be comfortable in making a commitment. It is very taxing, to whip bright young men into shape."

"At least listen to what we have to say this afternoon." Sir George continued his sales pitch. "Once you've seen our men on parade, your blood will be stirred and you'll be begging me for a post."

Before the Ulster Provisional Government meeting got underway, Simon explained to Sir George that he did not wish to be pointed out or spoken of. A man who made his way in the background was most comfortable with anonymity, the better to gauge the abilities and talents of those who would plunge Ireland into a civil war in a determined effort to preserve the kingdom. He took a seat near the back of the hall and listened as the call went up for donations to an indemnity fund that would aid those who would be injured in a battle that was deemed unavoidable and necessary. By the time that Simon sat down to dinner with Sir George and several other retired officers, the fund had collected a quarter of a million pounds.

He had come with a purpose in mind, and Simon spent most of Friday with a group of volunteers who demonstrated a particular enthusiasm for getting the better of their nationalist enemies. To the disappointment of many, Sir Simon culled the ranks over the course of the day, as one man after another failed in the different scenarios that Plowman constructed. Sir George came to collect him for dinner, and was delighted to meet the makings of his counter-intelligence unit. Not one of them was well-educated, but Plowman put little stock in books when it came to the sort of work that called for insight and common sense.

"The ferry leaves at eight and I'm sorry that we must rush," Sir George said. He could not help but notice that Simon was exhausted after skulking around Belfast half the day, sneaking up on the lads who were supposed to be following him, and then turning the tables on others who thought they were extracting vital information from an enemy agent. "Have you ever been to Balmoral?"

"Near there, but Her Majesty never saw fit to invite me in," Plowman said. "Can't imagine why, can you?"

Richardson roared with laughter. "And after you kept her from being blown to bits by the Irish. I'm sure your wife has asked you that same thing on a regular basis."

Simon sipped at the one whiskey that he allowed himself every night before bed, even though there would be little sleep on the ferry from Belfast to Stranraer. "I lost her many years ago." And there was the extent of Richardson's investigations into Sir Simon Plowman. Clearly the man was a fool, and there was nothing more dangerous in battle than a fool for a commander. "But there are four grandchildren to keep me well-occupied, and the girls are far too young to badger their old grandfather about presentations at court."

"Children are a great comfort to us. However, we see our future in our sons."

"Don't take your eye off the daughters. They are possessed of a hidden strength that, if exposed to the air, could reduce our self-esteem to insignificance." Simon cleared his throat and leaned closer to his companion. "In the past, I have used that feminine strength to accomplish several of my missions. The man I've left in place to train the undercover operatives is quite capable, but I wouldn't recommend that he be encouraged to recruit women. It's not so easy to judge their characters. The ladies manage to convince us rather easily that they're madly in love with us, even while they're assuring some other swain that he's their one and only. Inconstancy is acceptable in the parlor, but not in the field."

"That's why we need you, Sir Simon."

"As I said, I'll review the troops and see what material we have to work with. It's one thing to be needed, and quite another to be able to play a role. Ten years ago, I doubt I'd have wavered."

"You were there fifty years ago, when you were needed, and your country can't fault you for sitting out this one." Richardson raised his glass in a toast. "Whatever you can do will be appreciated by all of us."

Simon bowed his head, uncomfortable with accolades when he preferred to go unnoticed. "To the best of my abilities, then, and thank you for understanding my limitations."

He was groggy from a lack of sleep when he arrived, hours later, at the train station. His joints ached from sitting so long, but stretching his limbs was not as easy as it had once been. A car took them the last length of the journey to the show grounds near Balmoral and Simon dozed off, to open them upon a fluttering of Union Jacks. He regretted not wearing a warmer coat.

Richardson guided him to a reviewing stand that was already growing crowded. Some of the gentlemen had met Sir Simon before, passing back and forth in the corridors of Whitehall, while others had no idea who he was or why he was important enough to be given a prime spot. Simon collected names and attached them to the faces, making small talk about the weather and what a man should be sure to see on his first visit to Scotland. With planned nonchalance, he worked his way to the back of the stand, to blend into the clutch of old soldiers who turned in unison towards a growing noise.

A contingent of motorcyclists puttered past, forty-eight in all, and Simon could not picture that many vehicles in all of Dublin. Behind them, an open car followed. "You've met Sir Edward Carson, surely?" Richardson asked.

"Indeed I have." Simon observed the angular face, hardened with steely triumph. For all his talk about the tragedy that a partition of the island would bring, Sir Edward appeared to be prepared to split Ireland. They disliked one another, Plowman and Carson, although they had occasionally found something on which to agree, to the chagrin of their party leaders.

Carson mounted the steps of the viewing stand to thunderous applause, the clamor of fifty thousand Unionist voices ringing through the highlands. Then came Carson's army, the volunteers who would shed blood to preserve the United Kingdom. There was no doubt that they had been drilled like proper British soldiers, taught the manual of arms and put through the evolutions. Simon swept his eyes over them, making a quick count. Ten thousand, perhaps fifteen thousand, were as ready for a fight as any recruit to His Majesty's armed forces. No one here was playing at being a soldier. They were soldiers.

"Very impressive," Simon murmured.

"Didn't I tell you that we had the makings of a fine corps?" Richardson boasted. "What say you, Sir Simon?"

He swayed a little, dizzy from standing still when he should have flexed his knees. Fellow soldiers reached out to steady the old man. Fellow politicians cast concerned looks at him. "You don't need me. The seeds have been planted and now a younger man must cultivate the abilities that sprouted in Belfast these last few days."

A hand touched Simon's shoulder and he turned to find the cold face of Edward Carson, unsmiling sharp angles that knew no mirth. "The last man I might have expected here," Carson said. "Changed your tune, have you?"

"Not at all," Simon said. "Had you been to Dublin of late, you'd be singing the Home Rule chorus."

"I'll grant you that Birrell's the most worthless Chief Secretary that Ireland has seen in my lifetime. But he has arrived and London has matters in hand," Carson said. "Rather than argue, as we have done so often, I would like to extend my thanks for your condolences on the death of my wife. Your letter was a great comfort."

Simon adopted the air of a man who might admit that he had been wrong in his opinions until that very moment, but he knew that Carson was not going to believe a word of it. The leader of the Ulster Volunteers was one of the most brilliant lawyers in all of England, a native of Dublin who feared partition because he would have to choose between relocating to Belfast or exile in his home town.

Despite the cold wind, Simon felt beads of sweat prickle his temples. This reviewing stand was more like a courtroom and he was in the dock, being sized up by a master who could locate any weak point that would yield to sharp words and piercing rhetoric. Simon was too old for the game, too tired to summon the strength to counter and parry. He had seen all he had come to see and it was time for him to go home.

"Would you be shocked if I were to introduce an appropriation in Commons, requesting arms for our volunteers?" Carson asked.

"I would be shocked if His Majesty's government gave you a single bullet," Simon replied. Not a single bullet, but the entire Royal Navy might very well steam into Belfast's harbor. The Churchill clan were at it again, the second generation this time around, foaming at the mouth over Home Rule, Young Winston, First Lord of the Admiralty, was in a position of power and he was brash enough to take advantage. All that kept him in check was Carson's deep antipathy to partition. "However, if you were tried for treason I would not be at all surprised. It is treasonous, in my opinion."

"Can I be blamed if the politicians fail us? Don't bring up Birrell again."

"Isn't that the sort of disinterest that has brought us to this point?"

"But to throw the baby out with the bath water, as it were. No point in changing the form of government when all that's required are some new cogs in the machine."

He needed to sit down and the only place available was in Richardson's car. Simon shuffled down the steps of the stand, leaning heavily on the railing. "It's gone too long, Sir Edward, the cogs are toothless and the machine no longer operates." He paused on the last step, to take a breath. "If only you were in government twenty years ago, and I were twenty years younger. We might do something then, would you say?"

"I understand that you worked your magic in Belfast. If you weren't in agreement with me, you would not have set up the skeleton of an intelligence unit." Carson took him by the elbow, to assist an elderly comrade. "You don't fool me for a minute, Plowman. You talk up Home Rule in Commons to please your constituents, but it's a bargaining chip for you. Just another politician, holding on to his seat and winning prizes to take home."

"Flatter me all you like, but if you want guns for your volunteers, you'll have to obtain them on the open market." Richardson's driver pulled open the door and helped Simon into the back. "Find someone who would like to tweak the King's beard and you'll get the best bargain."

Exhausted, Simon closed his eyes and leaned his head back, wishing that he had heeded Mary Claire's advice and not gone off gallivanting. This was the last time. He was going to retire from everything, from politics and war and the world that existed outside of the cottage door in Rathkeale. Until he was back there, however, he would be upright, composed and excited by the day's events. While he rode to the station with Richardson, he spoke of nothing but the brilliant display of force and the impressive number of troops.. London could not fail to take notice now, and bend to the unionists. The situation in Ireland could only improve, with the government trapped in a corner and held at bay by fifteen thousand fighting men.

Dublin was ninety miles away, a short ride that would bring Simon to what felt like a different country. As was his custom, he bought a seat in a second-class compartment, sat next to the window, and watched the people of Belfast scurry like mice about the terminal. He would not be back here, he decided, and he would never see any of these sights again. For the first time in days, he relaxed and let his old bones sink into the horsehair upholstery.

The young gentleman who shared the compartment reminded him very much of his grandson Michael, who was in love with a rather pretty girl from Dalkey. As if on cue, a young lady walked in and took the seat next to the man, creating an image of youth and romance. She lifted a book out of her satchel and pretended to read, but her nervous tics suggested that she was only play-acting. The gentleman uncrossed and then crossed his legs once, twice, before finally putting both feet firmly on the floor. Simon watched the show's mirror image, following the reflection of the couple on the pane of glass.

He was sure that they were the same two people who had been standing outside of the station in Belfast, doing a very poor job of spying on him as he exited the hotel after a trying return trip from Balmoral. His contacts did not entirely trust him, but Sir Edward had said as much and so it had been throughout his career. Simon oftentimes did not trust himself, and the thought of it brought a tinny rumble of laughter to his throat. The couple looked up at him, alarmed. He would play along with them, a harmless charade, rather than embarrass them with exposure. Surely he had been just as clumsy when he first started out as an earnest young man, thinking that he knew it all. Having reached his advanced age, he could afford to be indulgent to the third generation.

After a perfunctory nodding of heads, the trio lapsed into a silence that remained unbroken until their tickets were collected. Legs crossed left, then right, then left again, and Simon turned his full attention to a man who clearly had something to say to him but could not seem to find his tongue. In reply, the man's head swiveled to his left, to read over his friend's shoulder as if Simon were not there. Either they were too young or too inexperienced to know that an unmarried couple who were clearly not related would not act like sweethearts one minute and transform into mere acquaintances in the next. There was a great deal of nuance in the espionage game, especially for women. They had to forget who they were, abandon their morals if necessary, but few ladies were such skilled actors. Eireann lacked that particular quality, the result of a pampered life, and that was Simon's fault. He had wavered too much when she was growing up, trying to instill a little steel in her backbone but then easing up because he wanted her to have the comforts that had been stolen from Mary Claire.

The girl spoke to her companion, asking about the stops that the train was scheduled to make. These two would probably shadow him all the way to Merrion Square, to see who he met with along the way. He had a little bit of energy left, enough to play a game that would amuse only him. Before he arrived at home, he would stop at Mr. Murphy's offices and make a generous donation to the Loyal Tramway Men's Fund. And then he would stop at Liberty Hall, to match his gift with one for the striking workers. Eventually, word would get back to Carson and the unionist could ponder the meaning of Simon's actions. The man deserved a dose of aggravation. His wife's body was barely cold, and he was courting a woman half his age.

Twenty-Two

Their bruises faded, but their outrage grew. Michael joined his father's law firm, and together they donated hours of time to represent children who were hauled into court on charges of stealing, when the little ones were guilty only of hunger. The lock-out was intended to starve the workers into submission, and Eireann came to believe that the tactic would work.

After centuries of colonial rule, her fellow Catholics were not the ones holding Dublin's great wealth, and so the school dinner fund suffered from a lack of contributions. The industrial aristocrats were not going to donate to a charity that would undo a key component of their strategy to bring the strikers to heel, and if Lord Iveagh could not dip into the enormous profits he earned from his Guinness stout, what hope was there for the innocent children?

Three days each week, Eireann went to Liberty Hall to assist Mr. Larkin's sister in the preparation and distribution of meals. At the same time, she drifted away from Constance Markievicz's sphere, growing disillusioned by a woman who was adept at putting on a show that was all stage dressing and little substance. Connie was present, she was ever ready to strike a pose as a skivvy if a news reporter or photographer happened by, but she was not one to peel potatoes or stir a soup kettle. Eireann much preferred to ease back into the shadows, to be active while keeping a low profile. In the process, she listened and learned and was able to move about the place without attracting anyone's attention.

It was commonplace to see Dublin's literati serving up stews from morning until night, a collection of artists and poets and writers who penned volumes for the daily papers. Their sympathy contrasted with the hard-nosed attitude of the business owners, proving to Eireann that she was on the right track. She was not alone in the belief that the lock-out was headed towards a resolution that would be cemented in blood. Life could not follow the same track, not when thousands were going hungry and the truth was exposed for all to see. This was bigger than a strike for more pay, it was a struggle for a voice that had been stifled for hundreds of years.

Her father continued to entertain, as he always had, hosting dinner parties that were guaranteed to erupt into heated argument. Serving after-dinner coffee to the ladies, Eireann kept her ears open and her mouth shut, using the opportunity to uncover the sentiments that hardened their hearts. They would not contribute to relief funds that were supported by the Archbishop, they were relatively unaware of what life was like for the man who delivered their coal and they had no idea how much it cost to live in a city tenement as compared to a country cottage. If her aunt had not begged her to attend the dinners, to stand by a woman who struggled to hold a civil tongue in her head, Eireann would have avoided Simon's house. She found it nearly impossible to keep her thoughts to herself when surrounded by those who shared their own empty words with giddy and empty-headed abandon.

A peat fire blazed in the parlor hearth, chasing away the October chill. The women chattered on and on about the high price of coal, about the rising cost of food and the possibility that the rates would have to go up as well. They seemed untouched by the rioting that took place daily on the docks and the streets, keeping safely behind the walls of their suburban homes. The subject that they kept returning to, however, suggested that these ladies of the leisure class were growing aware of conditions on the other side of the Liffey.

"If their fathers aren't working, how are they to provide heat?"

"Mrs. Montefiore's scheme is the best solution I've yet heard."

"It's no use trying to feed them here. They've either refused to accept charity or their priests have ordered them to steer clear."

"We cannot allow the Dublin kiddies to starve because their fathers are enthralled with Larkin."

As if she hadn't heard a word, Eireann asked if anyone would like more coffee, and she busied herself with pouring out a hot liquid that she would have loved to dump on several well-coiffed heads. Ever since the Famine, there had been a push to convert Catholic souls and finish the work that Cromwell had begun. Old habits were resurrected during the lock-out, when there was plenty of food to be had, at the price of one's immortal soul. The cruelty was so appalling that Eireann feared her cheeks would burn red with fury and expose her real feelings about the cynical ploy. Protestant missionaries walked the streets of the Liberties, promising to turn the paving stones into bread if the starving Catholics would bow down and worship a false god. Even Jesus Himself had once been tempted, but not everyone was possessed of such divine strength.

"Some of the British homes that have offered to take in the children are said to be Catholic," Eireann said. She was startled by her own utterance, a sarcastic bite that could have come from her father's mouth. Was she becoming him in her middle age?

"By Monday, after that Montefiore creature spoke at Liberty Hall, there was a crowd all around, eager to sign up," Anna whispered to Eireann. "They're calling it a holiday, of all things."

Mrs. Dillon squeezed into the empty space between Eireann and the armrest, seeking solace among her own kind. "If I hear one more person use the term "Dublin kiddies" to refer to the poor children, I shall wring her neck."

Condescension washed over the room, dripping into Eireann's ears. The guests spoke of what was best, as if they were the superior beings and the downtrodden needed someone wise to tell them what to do. They were the aristocracy, noses held high above the filth around them, dispensing their advice and expecting it to be followed. Mrs. Montefiore had come from England, as had her assistants, and this plot was hatched in England. The message was plain. England knew best, and England would take care of things because the Irish were too lazy, too stupid, too incompetent, or too what-have-you to cope. Hence, they were utterly incapable of governing themselves, and Home Rule had to be quashed.

"This cannot be allowed to stand," Eireann said.

"What else can be done?" Mrs. Dillon asked. "The children will either freeze or starve to death."

"Why has no one thought to find homes in Ireland?" Eireann said. "How many big houses are empty right now, while the landlord resides in England? They'll spend money shipping the little ones off, but will they part with a shilling to buy that child a crust of bread without a dose of proselytizing thrown in?"

"That poet I met at the canteen, Joseph Plunkett," Anna said. "His mother would be willing, but she's a rare one."

"As rare as the Irish Catholic who can afford to take in another family," Mrs. Dillon said. "We're at the mercy of the industrialists."

"What we lack in financial strength, we make up for in numbers. Mrs. Dillon, if you speak to ten friends and they speak to ten friends and so on, we can have every parish in the county with us." Eireann was not blind to the fact that the Catholic Church had done little to help, and anyone applying to the St. Vincent de Paul Society for relief could not avoid the humiliation of begging. She never heard priests demanding that the faithful donate food or clothing for the strikers' children, that they boycott locked-out businesses, at least not since the British government had provided funding for the construction of the seminary at Maynooth. None of that mattered, if she could make use of Catholic outrage to achieve her goal. "I'll pay a call on Dr. Walsh. Aunt Anna, can you stir up your friends in the Catholic Defense Association?"

Every Dublin daily reported on Dr. Walsh's condemnation of Mrs. Montefiore's proposal after his letter hit the morning paper. As word got out that the notorious Lady Warwick was involved in removing children from their homes, Catholic Dublin became more incensed. Not only was the plan questionable from a religious stand-point, it was labeled as immoral, with one of the King's former mistresses front and center. The lessons of history were recounted, tales of the Famine and the soupers resurrected, and the priests took a stand. The Archbishop's plea for labor peace was lost in the swell of emotion.

Eireann and Anna were at the Tara Street Baths on Wednesday morning, moving through the crowd and voicing their objections until the women around them took up the call. By the time that the priests from St. Andrew's arrived, the mob was agitated and the mothers whose children were scheduled for passage were having second and third thoughts. Once the fire was ignited, it spread, and the irate mob that followed the procession from the baths to the train station sparked another crowd that blocked the station's entrance. Eireann tasted a drop of victory as she watched Mrs. Montefiore and her little "kiddies" retreat towards Liberty Hall. The priests were skilled at wielding the cudgel of Catholic guilt, and the poor mothers who had given in to temptation would be on their knees begging for God's forgiveness before the day was over.

One front had been conquered, but the reserves were ready to move out and Eireann took the fight to Liberty Hall. The place was a madhouse, with Mrs. Montefiore shrieking in her shrill little voice while dozens of children wailed and mothers wept in confusion. Labor agitators went from father to mother and back again, trying to restore order when chaos reigned.

"They won't let the children leave," Mr. Connolly said to Eireann, as if he expected her to have the answers. So many times, she had goaded someone to make a donation when money was most needed, and she was the person he turned to when volunteers required guidance or a daily schedule of chores. The labor leader was lost within the confines of a building he once knew well. "This scheme worked so smoothly in Birmingham."

"Birmingham is in England, Mr. Connolly," Eireann said. He stared at her, confused by an answer that was too subtle. "We, I remind you, are in Ireland."

"Are you suggesting that we find host families in Belfast?" he asked.

"This whole notion to tear apart families and rend the fabric of society is unacceptable," Anna said. "Do they not suffer enough without separating generations of families who live close by? Provide decent housing and assist with the purchase of food, that is all that is needed.."

"How much does it cost to export one of our children?" Eireann asked. After hearing the sum, she continued, "And how much food could we purchase for that same child for that same ten shillings? Enough to last two or three weeks?"

"But Mr. Larkin has committed to this," Connolly said, "and he's not going to back down. You know that well enough, Mrs. Lytton."

"I've supported you every step of the way, but I won't give England another hair from an Irish head. We cannot stand by and let one of our own take the King's shilling because we cannot counter the offer," Eireann said.

"We can't have the priests dictating to us," he said.

"We cannot allow England to siphon off even more of our treasure. During the Great Famine, ships pulled out of Cork's harbor laden with food, while the people who grew the crops and churned the butter were allowed to starve, " Eireann said. "I see no difference today, and no priest has influenced my opinion."

Nothing more could be done and there was no point in arguing, given the tension that reverberated off the walls. Ready to leave, Eireann found her aunt in the kitchen, slicing bread and commanding distraught women to sit down, creating tiny pools of serenity where small mouths were quieted with a morsel to eat. Just as they reached the entrance, a window above them was thrown open and the churning masses gave their attention over to Jim Larkin, who began to speak. He lambasted the clergy for interfering, he accused the priests of colluding with the industrialists, and then he criticized Lady Plunkett, an esteemed Irish woman who had offered the use of her country house rather than permit the export of Irish children.

"Horse's ass," Anna mumbled. "As if he discovered the slums when he graced our shores with his presence. Just another Englishman, telling us ignorant Irishmen what to do."

For the first time, the great Jim Larkin failed to move the people. The speakers who followed him were rudely heckled. With a sigh, Eireann turned to her aunt and suggested that they go. It made no difference to her what was said about the children or Mrs. Montefiore or Countess Plunkett. These were distractions that she would ignore, her vision focused on the ultimate goal of ridding Ireland of English influence. It did not matter who might be used to further the cause, even a demigod like Larkin. In war, nothing could be taken personally.

Police hovered on the fringes, keeping an eye on the unruly and no doubt taking copious notes on the sour reception that Mr. Larkin received. Anna slipped her hand into the crook of Eireann's arm, a gesture that spoke of a close bond forged over a lifetime.

"Ever since you were born, I did my best to be a mother to you," Anna said. "Every day, I find myself praying that I have done the right thing, that I have guided you as she might have."

Her aunt was the only mother she had ever known, and she had never thought of Anna living in the shadow of a strange woman, second-guessing every choice made. Who could predict what one person might have wanted for a child, and never before had Eireann considered the sort of pressure that her aunt took upon herself, in an attempt to mold a girl into an undefined but specific shape.

"Our politics, our religion, all these things I have instilled in you were things that must have mattered to her," Anna continued. "Of course, times change and new situations arise that call for a different course of action. Still, there are far too many poets and writers, and no soldiers, at the forefront."

"We are on the cusp of something," Eireann said. "I felt it tonight. The average man has been beaten down too many times. Our poets and writers give them dreams, and the right man will come along behind and build on that foundation. There is no hope for a peaceful settlement. Blood must be shed."

Anna squeezed her arm in a gesture of solidarity, an indication that Eireann had been made into her mother's daughter, in spite of her father's political leanings. Not that she was barren of Simon's qualities. Like her father, she was discrete and cautious, never leaping without first studying the terrain. She had an insight into human behavior, had a sense of how individuals might react in certain situations, and she made it a point to listen well, then speak only as much as was necessary. Eireann wished that she could know if her mother had been the same way, but her father had walled off those days, buried them as deeply as her mother's body was buried in the cemetery in Athenry.

"Dreamers, and I fear that you've become captivated by them," Anna said. "Be careful around men like Pearse and Plunkett. They think with their hearts while wars are best fought with the head."

Wary of the police after the riot on "Bloody Sunday", Eireann observed everyone on the street, from clusters of women loitering in doorways to pairs of men hurrying home from meetings. The darkness played tricks on her, made her believe that the two figures tucked into the shadows near Liberty Hall were her father and James Connolly, deep in conversation. She admired men like Mr. Connolly, but she saw action in the words of a school teacher and a poet. In their different ways, they exposed the injustice of British rule and puzzled out ways to change Ireland. Sentence by sentence, stanza by stanza, strike after strike, they were heading towards the road that Eireann walked, the path to a pitched battle.

The fog rolled up the river and their coats snagged tiny droplets of mist as they crossed the Liffey. Below her feet, Eireann heard the slap of water against the hull of a barge, the supply of Guinness continuing to

move from St. James's Gate to the hundreds of pubs that provided refuge
to men with no other comforts in life.

"Who can say what the future holds?" Eireann wondered aloud.
"What kind of Ireland will my children inherit?"

Anna slowed her pace as they crossed Dame Street. "Your father
and I came into some land, but that's all gone now. Don't tell him I told
you about it as he frets over the debts and doesn't want you to be
concerned." She looked up when a motor car breezed past, but carried on
when they were once again alone. "After the Land Act, as I recall. The
farmers who worked the estates could not afford what the acreage was
worth. Your father believes very strongly in the stability that comes with
ownership. He holds mortgages, for our inherited property and countless
other small farms. Desmesnes opened to cultivation, walls and barriers
torn down."

"I shouldn't be surprised that he's kept his seat for so long. The
electorate owes him their ability to vote," Eireann said. "The more men
who own land because of Sir Simon Plowman, the more men who will cast
their ballot for him."

Anna chuckled. "Yes, he'd like you to see it that way."

"No wonder, then, that he's in favor of women's suffrage. Even
more votes."

"On that, you are mistaken. He respects us, you and I. He knows
from experience that women are intelligent beings, as cool and analytical
as men if they've been educated in the same manner."

Eireann saw Roger's car parked on the road in front of the house.
He was waiting for her, eager to take her home and show off his newly
acquired skill. The tram strike faded into insignificance for men like Roger,
who could afford to purchase their own transportation. Even Eireann had
managed, thanks to her bicycle and her own strong legs. They were two

people whose coins did not drop into the Dublin Tram's till, and they were not the only people in the city who supported the boycott. It might take a month, it might take a year, but sooner or later, the industrial aristocrats were bound to notice that their pockets were no longer bulging.

Her father was in his library, chatting with Roger about Larkin's upcoming trial and the suppression of the strikers that would inevitably follow. To Eireann's surprise, her husband was in complete agreement about the failure that loomed. "They were too quick to go out, too hasty," Simon said. "A man who's a firebrand is not the man for cool logic, and a leader needs a cool head."

"The union is bankrupt," Roger said. "What little reserves they had for strike pay is used up, and no end in sight. The owners have so many more resources to draw on. It's impossible, as far as I can judge."

"So you've played into Murphy's hand," Simon said to her. "The children will serve his purpose with their hungry presence."

"Is that your solution, to ship them off?" Eireann said. She had been proud of her accomplishment, but her father was intent to snatch away her happiness because she had won and his side had lost. "Why not pack them into coffin ships and send them to America while we're at it? Why not parcel them out to loving English homes so that they can have a wonderful English life? You'd wave good-by at the North Wall with a cheery smile on your face."

Simon shot up from his chair, his eyes blazing fire. "Never accuse me of," he said, his fists so tightly balled that his knuckles were white. "Never accuse me."

He had not been this angry with her since she was a child, poking her nose into his private papers in an effort to uncover her history. She had touched on the rawest nerve, had inflicted pain to an open wound that had never healed. Eireann trailed after him as he stormed out of the room, her apologies bouncing off his back. "I'm sorry, Papa. I didn't mean it. Please don't run away from me."

He was too old to outpace her and she caught him at the foot of the stairs. She grabbed his arm, the muscles more sinew than solid flesh. Simon shook off her grip but she would not relent. His reaction to her taunt was not his usual sarcasm or keen observation, but an outburst that demanded explanation. Let him try to keep his secrets and take them to his grave, but Eireann would wring some small memory out of him before he left her alone.

"How can you criticize what I did when you know my mind?" she asked. "You have no cause for anger."

Her father turned his face to her, his cheeks flushed. "They tried to take you away from me," he said through clenched teeth. "All their best intentions, knowing what's best for someone else's child. They would have taken you if I hadn't stopped them."

Eireann could only shake her head in wonder. Nothing made any sense. One minute, Simon was in favor of transporting children and the next he was furious that someone had attempted to steal her. Who would have wanted to take her away from her father, if that was even true? "I'm here; I've always been here," she said. A tear trickled down her cheek, a child's pain uncontained. "Why do you always push me away?"

"Because I must." Her father wrapped his arms around her, holding her as if he could shield her from the dark. "God forgive me, but I have only done what I had to do."

"You talk in riddles," she said. "You will tell me the plain truth."

Simon patted her cheek with paternal affection. "Go home to your children and be the good mother that you've always been."

"You will tell me the plain and honest truth," she said to his retreating back.

"Good night, Eireann. I'm quite proud of you. You've done well. I shall tell your aunt, in fact. I owe her more than I could ever repay." At the landing, where she had once watched him being arrested, he paused. "Ignore my ramblings. Whatever I might have said, or what I might say in the future, don't abandon me."

Roger called his farewells up the staircase and helped her into her coat. "He's quite an enigma, your father," he said. "My own father was his closest friend and even he couldn't get a grip on that wily old soldier. Still waters run deep, my dear, and we may never plumb his depths."

"He's nothing more than a bitter man who is reaping what he sowed," Eireann said. "What could he have meant, do you think, when he said someone tried to take me from him?"

"You know how the priests are when it comes to mixed marriages. My mother was brought to grief for choosing a solid Church of Ireland man and there was no peace until every child was baptized at the Pro-Cathedral." Roger climbed into the car after he had gone through the lengthy procedure to get the machine started, and then picked up where he had left off. "Who knows if his monthly visit with that Augustinian priest isn't part of some deal that was made. You must admit, he's not very fond of Roman collars, your father."

"I don't think he's fond of anyone."

"My dear, he dotes on you and our children. How many grandfathers would traipse up and down the boreens, playing at soldier? I wish my father had been less formal. All my shooting had to involve hunting in a gentlemanly fashion."

The car sputtered for a moment as Roger shifted gears. Eireann watched the scenery change, from congested city to airy suburb. "Never have I known where I stand with him," she said. With that, she rested her hand on her husband's thigh, finding comfort in the security he represented. "At least I have you, dearest. I know where I stand in your world."

"I rather like where you lie in my world," he said.

Her spirits were lifted by his wit and the suggestive nature of his quip. There might have been a time when she feared that she had married Roger because her father influenced her decision, but if that was the case, he had done her a good service. Her years with her husband had been the happiest of her life.

With all the resources she had at her fingertips, she could afford to be generous with her father and his cold temperament. Of course she would not abandon him, no matter what he did, because she was bound by God to honor him. At the same time, she would not allow him to hold her at arm's length until his arm dropped in death. Like Larkin, she could not give up or give in, but had to persist until Simon unlocked his heart and let her in.

Twenty-Three

No one was surprised that Jim Larkin was found guilty of seditious speech and packed off to Mountjoy, but Eireann was somewhat shocked to stand outside of Liberty Hall and hear James Connolly, the de facto leader of Larkin's union in his absence, boldly declare that the export of children was ended. The ten shillings that it cost for their passage, he told the assembled crowd, would feed them for three weeks. Her father sent her a brief telegram, declaring Mr. Connolly's insight to be brilliant. Somewhere in those few words was a message, she was sure of it, but a man accustomed to ciphers and subterfuge could not fathom that everyone else lacked his ready skill.

While the warring parties each declared victory, Eireann was paralyzed by uncertainty, not sure if she had done the right thing. People whose views she admired were castigating the priests in the daily papers, and groups whose views she found appalling were taking credit for a stellar success. Her oldest son, Michael, debated the issues with his father, and Eireann grasped a central truth from their dinner table discussions. She had a core value, one single goal that was not to be gained by walking towards it in a straight line. There were those she disagreed with, but if some other organization's activities could further her aims, she would be foolish to not take advantage.

By the beginning of November, her faith in herself was renewed. The blockade that kept the hungry children in Dublin did not bring the strikers to their knees. Rather, the mighty sultans of industry bent to what must have been a crippling pain in their bank accounts. No matter any more that the kiddie scheme fiasco brought joy to the Ancient Order of Hibernians or the same priests who sided with management in the lockout, not when things were coming right in the end.

On the way to Liberty Hall to prepare stew for the canteen, she walked past motorized lorries delivering coal, accompanied by soldiers and guns, their bayonets glistening. Dublin was no longer the down-at-her-heels capital city, but an armed camp in a British colony. Tensions were running high, and the men who spent their days organizing strikers on Beresford Place were preparing for a real battle. Information floated across the Irish Sea, carried from British union men to their Irish brethren, and before the first boat load of scabs arrived from Manchester, the unemployed men of Dublin knew they were coming.

Overcast skies greeted the imported labor, who went about the business of unloading Lord Iveagh's malt. For all of Mr. Connolly's attempts to create an army of picketers, relatively few men showed up at the quays, and those who pleaded with the replacement workers to walk out with them were preaching to the deaf. A caravan of motorized lorries chugged away, making for St. James's Gate. "There go jobs, Eireann, into oblivion," Anna said. "One by one, the drays and horses will be replaced by those machines and there'll be no need for these same men who are fighting for decent wages."

"Surely such a fleet of vehicles would be cost-prohibitive," Eireann said. "What Roger paid for our automobile could have purchased a very nice coach and good horses."

"Your automobile does not need a stable hand, or oats, or water, or a veterinarian's services. It does not get sick, it does not spook, and a man can drive a lorry more easily than he can manage a skittish horse. Over the course of a year or two, I'd estimate that it costs far less to operate, and we know how keen these pinnacles of industrial virtue are to pare costs to the bone."

"Would you like to go to Liberty Hall tonight for the fireworks?" Eireann changed the subject. "Mr. Connolly is celebrating the defeat of the Liberal candidates in the by-elections in England."

"A political victory in the face of the working men's defeat," Anna said. "Thank you, but no. I shall remain indoors tonight, in front of a warm fire."

Afraid of unruly crowds and the armed soldiers who walked the streets, Eireann was hesitant to permit any of her children to witness a piece of history being made. In the end, Roger prevailed. Michael was on the cusp of adulthood and was already reading the law, while Peter was at university and no longer a child to be coddled. It was time for them to prepare for their future, a future that could be radically different than anything Eireann envisioned.

Speakers chortled over the stab to Home Rule that had been handed to those in power. Peter listened to less than half of what was said, too busy was he in scanning the crowd. "Isn't that grandfather over there?" he said, and he hastily excused himself before slipping between bodies and disappearing into the throng.

One of the feminists encouraged the people to smash the trams and march on Mountjoy, to free Jim Larkin. Another faced down hecklers who mocked her family's connections to the Liberals, but she held her own and gave as good as she got. Just as Eireann lifted her arms to applaud the woman's courageous retorts, Peter was back at her side, looking thoroughly puzzled.

"Was it him?" she asked. Peter shook his head, unwilling to meet his mother's eye.

"No, mother, you are mistaken," Michael said. "It wasn't *her*."

While the two boys traded sharp elbows and fierce looks, Roger took Eireann's arm. "Perhaps he was so intent on coming with us tonight for reasons unrelated to politics," he whispered, a conspiratorial twinkle in his eye.

Simon had planned his monthly dinner party well before Larkin was abruptly released from prison, but his guests took it as a celebration. It was the Liberals who had been so insistent on prosecuting the labor organizer, and it was the Liberals who paid the price at the polls. The point was proved with Larkin's freedom, the seven month sentence shrunken down to seventeen days. That evening, however, the men who sat around the table were not so interested in the Irish question as they had been a month before. Their eyes were turned to the east, to Germany and the Kaiser. The war that they spoke of was not in Ireland. The army that they feared was not Carson's Ulster Volunteers but the hundreds of thousands of German troops who were rattling sabers.

Her father was unusually animated over dinner, as if a war with Germany would be a good thing. Eireann was appalled as he spoke of the strikers and the hordes of casual laborers who could find steady work shooting a gun. What made Simon's quip particularly unpleasant was the fact that it was true. An army of unemployed men had long been a source of bodies for His Majesty's armed forces. This time around, unlike the past, those same men might be waging their own battle for liberty. The locked-out and the underpaid were being recruited by James Connolly to form a Citizen's Army.

Young men, hired to lift empty plates and tote platters for the evening, went about their labors with faces as blank as if they were deaf. For all his support of the Crown and his Conservative colleagues, Simon was a generous man who employed those most in need of work, and it was not the first time that Eireann had been served by a man who had been served by her at the Liberty Hall. She wondered if these strikers understood that it was their lives these honorable gentlemen were talking about, sending them to front lines far from home, to die for a cause that had nothing to do with them.

She watched them bending over and slipping between diners, impassive but listening. Their ears were open and they were absorbing every word that was said, every indiscreet remark or harsh criticism. After the last of Simon's friends had departed, Eireann stood at the kitchen door while her father paid off the temporary workers. He shook each man's hand, gave them a packet that was too thick to hold only a few shillings, and wished them good luck.

"Did you know that those men are with Larkin?" she asked.

"I know that they need work of any kind," Simon replied. He guided her to his library, where Roger was waiting with a decanter of whiskey and two glasses. "My guests are accustomed to hired help, Eireann, and they aren't likely to be indiscreet. I have no doubt that some comments might have been directed to the footmen, to remind them of who is superior to whom."

"And they can have no doubt that Sir Simon Plowman would not mourn the demise of Winston Churchill," Roger said.

"Mark my words, Roger," Simon said. "Carson will land a cache of arms, not in Belfast, mind you, but at a minor port, and the Royal Navy will stand by and do nothing. Let Connolly's group try the same thing and every customs agent in the Kingdom would be after them. Nothing infuriates me more than such blatant unfairness."

"You often told me that a fight was rarely fair," Eireann said.

"You remember?" Simon lifted his glass in a toast to an enjoyable evening, filled with talk of war in Europe and very little said about the lock-out and the strike. Larkin's actions were fading away into the past. "This one will be painfully lopsided, I'm afraid. Mr. Carson has a contingent of former and current officers to train his troops. Mr. Connolly has Countess Markievicz to design elaborate costumes."

"What if Germany should declare war?" Roger asked. "The troops that are protecting the lorries would be busy overseas, and if there were some sort of uprising, who would Birrell call on to put it down?"

"So the Fenians thought, all those decades ago."

"The Ulster Volunteers will be happy to step in," Eireann said. "Some of our own neighbors have been spending their Sunday afternoons drilling with a retired Army colonel who would overturn Home Rule legislation and consider it a favor to the Crown."

"There's where the old Fenian Brotherhood had a slight advantage over Larkin's crowd," Simon said. "They were armed and well-trained. If Mr. Connolly wishes to round up his own army, he will have to follow Carson's lead. A gang of unemployed coal carters won't stand a chance against men who have some inkling of warfare."

Roger nodded but kept his mouth shut up tight. Over the course of the previous week, he had met several times with a group of gentlemen who were organizing a proper army, led by the highly respected Captain Jack White. The strike was going to collapse sooner rather than later. Any man trying to picket a work site was beaten or arrested by the police, who backed the employers, and the country was filled with the unemployed who were willing to work as scabs rather than starve. Improvements in living conditions had to come from somewhere else, beyond the level of the business owner. Those in power meant to keep it, by force if necessary, and Mr. Connolly understood that force was the only way to overthrow British rule. Men like Roger Lytton had accepted that fact.

While her father and Roger examined the threat of civil war over Home Rule, Eireann stared at the man who had made his name by crushing the Fenian Brotherhood. She had heard that he was seen in Belfast with one of Carson's old soldiers, and there was a rumor that he was in league with Carson. She knew that her father despised the unionist hot-head and all that he stood for, but her sources were trustworthy. Simon Plowman was a sly fox, a man who had taught her to master games of secrecy, ciphers and codes. Let him support his side, and she would put her training to good use for the benefit of her people.

She stirred in her chair, tired after a long day and longing for the comfort of her warm bed. Taking a cue from her signal, Simon tipped back the dregs of his drink and went to his desk, where piles of correspondence waited to be opened and answered. He shuffled through one pile, and then another, an intense scowl on his face.

"There will be a war. It's inevitable." Simon handed a slip of paper to Roger, who passed it on to Eireann. It was a name and address of a woman in Boston. "I am not speaking of Europe, you understand. Captain Jack White is an old colleague. He thinks very highly of you both."

A hot flush reddened Eireann's cheek. Her father knew everything and everyone. "Are you suggesting that we run?" she asked.

"Should it become necessary for you to leave Ireland, you will find a safe haven." Simon spoke to the fire in the hearth. "Your American relations continue to support Clan na Gael."

Having never corresponded with people she had never met, and who had never tried to contact her, Eireann was stunned by her father's announcement. She was speechless, but her husband found his tongue. "The courtesy that your father failed to extend to his wife's brothers is now to be extended to us?"

"My mother's brothers lacked opportunity," he said to Eireann. "Your mother's brothers were given the opportunity and took it. *An dtuigeann tú?*"

"Have you been practicing your language skills?" Eireann asked.

Her father sighed and slumped into his chair. "Your mother didn't understand either."

Uncomfortable under Simon's probing gaze, Eireann got to her feet and paced the room, pausing when an opened envelope on the desk caught her eye. American dollars were tucked inside. A bank draft was peaking out from under a letter that had been turned upside down, as if the reader wished for privacy when he was not alone. She had heard about the vast sums of money that were flowing to the unionists, all money that could have served a more worthy purpose in the form of higher wages and decent housing for the common man. Simon was up to his old tricks again, playing at soldier like the rest of them.

"Then we would extend the same offer to you," she said. "Safe passage to England."

"I'd prefer America," Simon replied, "where I might lay a wreath on your Uncle Michael's grave."

He had gone too far with his sarcasm and Eireann blew up in anger. She stormed out, with Roger on her heels, and hastily breezed past her aunt who was waiting to be kissed good-bye. A perfunctory hug was all that Eireann could muster, so furious was she with Simon's cheek and the sense of superiority that marked his class.

"Whatever have you been arguing about this time?" Anna asked.

"He's so sure of himself," Eireann said. "A politician to the bone, talking out of both sides of his mouth. A champion of Home Rule, and now that it's about to be made law, he's hopping into bed with the very men he faced down in Commons."

"No one is ever sure where he stands, are they?" Anna said. "He finds footing on the shifting sands."

"You don't need to stand up for him any more," Roger said. "There are limits to family loyalty. Suggesting that we run, like criminals."

"He thinks that this is all for the best, Roger, and I have disagreed with him since Eireann was a little girl, but it is his decision," Anna said. "I shall always support him, and I hope that you will as well. You did not live through those days, when the Irish Republican Brotherhood was ascendant. Experience is a harsh teacher, but an effective one."

"Please, Aunt, now you're talking in riddles."

"Here's something plain, then. Will you join me next Friday? Lord Iveagh is hosting Mr. Carson and the ladies are planning to greet him, shall we say, with great heat and little warmth."

Her father might be in league with the unionist devils, but Eireann could let it be known that they were on opposite sides. Had Sir Simon ever once tried to convince Carson and his cronies that women were deserving of the vote, or were his own words merely rhetoric without a foundation of truth? If he would not speak for his only daughter, then she would speak for herself. Perhaps then her father would find the courage to stand up for what he believed in, if he believed in anything at all.

* * *

The Citizen Army passed in front of Liberty Hall, but Simon's two grandsons were not among the ranks. He knew that they drilled, but they traveled to Rathkeale, where nationalist, Catholic eyes watched the junior officers with hope rather than hatred. This ragged band was not the most formidable force he had ever seen, but they had potential. The Irish Republican Brotherhood had wormed its way into Connolly's circle, and the lock-out was proving useful as a recruiting tool. After hearing enough speeches and lofty rhetoric, many a young man could be swayed into believing that it was time to shed blood rather than live as a slave, to overthrow the bosses and destroy the old order. Given time, the Citizen Army might be up to the very task.

Such an obvious display could not go unnoticed by the anti-Home Rule crowd, and Simon's schedule for the rest of the week was full. He sat in on a meeting of Union businessmen, who laid out a very cogent argument against the pending legislation. They were the same men who had sung the praises of the lock-out, but Simon wondered if they had managed to tie up the threads that linked unemployment and rebellion.

In essence, the speakers wanted the status quo. Nothing should be made to change, but the world outside the doors was spinning more rapidly than any of the business leaders realized. In Russia, socialism was taking hold of the hearts of the poor peasants, and Larkin's success in Ireland was rooted in the same discord. During the course of the afternoon, he never heard a word that addressed the deep-seated anger.

Edward Carson paid a call on Thursday afternoon, satisfied that Sir Simon Plowman was amenable to switching sides if he was suitably rewarded. With war imminent, however, Simon was not expecting London to find the money for new corporation housing, as Lord Salisbury had once managed to locate funding for better railroads in return for Plowman's silence. Back and forth, the debate flowed, point made and then countered. Unlike the former Prime Minister, Carson had no skeletons in his closet that would rattle. The fact that he was involved in a plan to ship in arms made no difference, not when those in power were going to look the other way when boats stuffed with munitions arrived in a quiet Irish harbor. Simon was in a weak position, having only his military background and reputation to trade for concessions. He would have preferred to have the upper hand, but he had long ago learned to make the best of what he had rather than wish for something better.

"All I seek is justice and fair play for all British citizens," Simon said.

"Fair enough. You have been consistent during your time in Commons," Carson said.

"Then you understand my position, one from which I do not waiver."

"Come to the conference on Friday, Sir Simon," Carson said. "Listen to the words of your colleagues. I have no doubt that if you give us a hearing, you will see that we are seeking the same thing. That'll knock you off that fence you're riding and land you where you belong."

"How can I say no?" Simon asked. "If I am a champion of equality, I would be remiss to ignore one side of the argument. Convince away, Sir Edward, and I will listen to your barrage of unionist prose with an open mind."

Surrounded on all sides by prominent gentlemen of his social class, Simon settled into his seat in the Theatre Royal and scanned the crowd. An enormous Union Jack provided an impressive backdrop, to boldly proclaim allegiance in case anyone there present had forgotten who ruled the island. In the dress circle, the ladies held sway, a sea of bobbing feathers and silk flowers that contrasted with the dark hues of gentlemen's suits. Two hats stood out, two large confections that he had seen many times before.

"Are you well, Sir Simon?" asked the man on his left when Plowman failed to suppress the bubble of laughter that tickled his throat.

In response, Simon shared an anecdote that he claimed had made him laugh to himself, rather than reveal that Eireann and Anna had turned up for a spectacle that they would later describe as appalling. He trusted that neither one of them would repeat the suffragist's stunt from earlier in the day, when Sir Edward Carson and Bonar Law were practically assaulted by women who were demanding the vote. With his usual charm, Simon replayed the incident in great detail, describing the scene that he witnessed outside of the Conservative Club that afternoon. Over lunch, Mr. Law vowed to see the miscreants sent to prison for a good long time, so upset was he that the little ladies had dared to approach him.

After that, the esteemed gentleman unleashed a torrent of abuse on the press photographer who had been so vile as to capture the scene forever. The poor man was accosted after lunch as well, by the same group of harridans, with the Dublin Metropolitan Police coming to his rescue. The last thing that any man wanted was to be photographed in the act of striking a woman, especially one as petite as the suffragist, and chivalry only added to Law's outrage. Pointing his head at Mr. Law, who had taken the stage, Simon wondered aloud if the man was so handsome as that, to have such a large coterie of female admirers dogging his heels.

One speech after another sounded the same note that Simon had heard before. Unionism was good, Home Rule was bad, and where were the Irish Party Members of Parliament when things grew hot at home? Lord Iveagh reminded them all that their personal liberty was at stake, that their Protestant influence would be lost in the three Catholic-majority provinces. Simon watched his daughter's head, as still as if her hat were perched on a mannequin. They buy his Guinness stout, he wished that he could whisper to her. They buy his products, they pay his way, and this is what he thinks of his clients who lack the will to boycott beer. Not much of a foundation for an army, Simon wanted to tell her.

He left before the last words were intoned, to get out of the theatre before Eireann saw him. Later, he could speak to her and not let on that she was spotted where she did not belong, obviously spying for the opposition. She had done a superb job of blending in with those around her, never letting on that she was not a fellow traveler. It gave him hope, that it was possible she would manage through the war that was to come, and she would never have to follow her uncles across the Atlantic. Losing his daughter and his precious grandchildren was too much of a sacrifice for an old man, and Simon had sacrificed more than enough already.

Twenty-Four

While her friends moaned the lack of British luxuries in the shops, Eireann witnessed the effects of the lock-out on families who could not afford a loaf of bread. Her own finances were strained by the high prices and the shortages that drove costs up ever higher, forcing her to cut back on the amount she donated to the various relief funds. Many of her social set slipped her what they could from their household allowances so that their husbands did not know, but they were hard-pressed to come up with extra shillings.

By Christmas, the strike was falling apart, with desperate men returning to work under the same wretched conditions, while others were blacklisted as troublemakers and could find no work at all. The British trade unions had grown tired of Larkin and his fire-breathing speeches, and support for the workers was slipping away. Shipping was back to normal, with boats coming and going from the quays and plenty of men available to handle the cargoes. Soldiers in the Citizen Army had little to do besides attacking scabs when they were not marching through the streets of Dublin, on their way to drill at Croydon Park. The call for arms grew louder.

Eireann arrived early at Croydon Park on Christmas Day, to donate what little time she could spare from her family. As usual, Constance Markievicz was there, bustling from one marquee to another without doing much physical labor. Con was more of an organizer and leader, not a worker, but she was a person Eireann could use without fear of discovery.

"A case of the Privy Council closing the barn door after the horse has run off," Con said. The decree that banned the import of munitions into Ireland was enacted after Carson's volunteers had built up their arsenal, but before the Citizen Army had a chance to raise enough funds to supply its troops with guns.

"It's a case of blatant discrimination against Catholics," Eireann said. "Is it any different than the sentences that have been handed down in the courts? The working men are sent up for months at hard labor for so much as looking at a policeman, while the scabs are let off with a slap on the wrist for murdering innocent women."

"We can complain all we like, but words will not turn a hurley into a rifle," the Countess said.

"When you find a crate from America on your doorstep, Con, don't question the delivery man," Eireann said.

"Whatever are you talking about?"

"Can you do that; can you not ask questions? You know as well as I that Mr. Connolly, Liberty Hall, and everything around here is watched. Will you make use of your automobile? Will you travel when asked, go where you are told?"

Constance's eyes lit up. She would be helpful, but she could yet prove to be dangerous if she did not manage to control her enthusiasm.

The day after her father handed her the American contact, Eireann wrote to a complete stranger as if they had been corresponding for years. She detailed the dream of the Citizen Army, to have weapons equal to the enemy's force. Not sure if spies in Dublin Castle might be intercepting the letters of anyone seen at Liberty Hall, she could not come right out and ask for what she wanted. In the hope that she had painted a picture for her Irish-American comrade, Eireann suggested that supporters of the Irish worker might consider sending supplies, rather than money, which could not buy what was really needed. She asked questions that were disconnected by small talk, hoping that she managed to make it clear that she wanted rifles hidden in crates of horsehair. Shortly before Christmas, a telegram from America promised the arrival of a donation from the Winchester family.

The year ended and a new one began before the box arrived. Roger pried it open in the back garden, disappointed at first that it looked like a shipment of horsehair bundled in a large sack. He reached into the itchy mass and felt gun barrels, ten in all. It had slipped past the customs inspectors, an innocuous box being sent from a lady in Boston to her relatives in Rathmines. After closing up the bag, he pounded the lid shut and chipped away the paper address label. In the middle of the night, Roger drove to the Marcievicz house with Peter, and together they slipped the crate into the Countess's car.

Within days, another gift arrived and Roger repeated his performance, depositing a set of Libby Glass tumblers, and one thousand rounds, at the Markievicz kitchen door. Eireann quickly realized that she needed to spread out the material, to have camouflaged munitions delivered to other places before she drew attention to herself. Afraid that she would be inundated with cartridges and bullets, she sent an urgent telegram to Boston. In reply, her overseas relations asked if other needy

Dublin residents would like to receive gifts from their Irish-American brethren. The question was, who would be willing to take the risk of being caught and imprisoned for violating the ban on importing weapons?

The guns were intended for men in the tenements, but sending crates of munitions directly to the Citizen Army soldiers would be met with raised eyebrows by the authorities, and raised eyebrows translated into police raids. Con Markievicz had friends who would be willing to accept contraband, but Eireann would not trust one of that flighty crew to keep a secret. The girls who worked in the Lytton house were in the Home Rule camp, but they were religious as well and the Catholic Church's policy was anti-Larkin and very much anti-violence.

The non-descript building on Moore Street was available for rent at a reasonable rate, after Roger dripped guilt into the landlord's ear. Mrs. Lytton was opening up a center to provide work for unemployed women, a charitable enterprise that would provide fresh mattresses for those living in vermin-infested slums. No one was doing it to make a profit, but to do good deeds as Christ would have all men do for his lambs. Besides, the place was filthy and on the verge of collapse, like the tenements on Church Street that had crushed seven people. Mr. Lytton was a respected barrister who had only to make the request and the Inspector of Dangerous Buildings would be paying a call and making a report.

When she volunteered at Liberty Hall, Eireann selected a few women who appeared trustworthy, but she interviewed them carefully just the same. Her questions were indirect, circuitous, so that she could assess the level of commitment to the Citizen Army without being obvious. She purchased a few basic supplies to set up her work house, to paint a complete picture that was nothing but a facade, and then offered piecework employment to ten young women who knew every laneway and street in the city. A small army of jobless men arrived in the morning with piles of ticking that passed for beds in the slum rooms, and they returned several days later to retrieve and distribute the rifles that were hidden in freshened mattresses.

Before the next shipment of rifles could be sewn up in the ticking and disguised with horsehair, Eireann was entertaining a stoop-shouldered old woman who insisted that she wanted to help. Dressed in the latest style, she appeared to be well-off, but she had a manner that suggested someone low-born who had come into riches without mastering the finer points of being a lady.

"When I heard that a respectable woman was accepting bedding from houses in the Monto," the visitor said, her eyes downcast at the mention of Dublin's notorious red light district. "My curiosity was aroused."

"I make no distinction," Eireann stammered. She never considered the source, but only the end result. "I'm sorry, but I must have missed your name."

"It makes no difference who I am, if we are not to become colleagues."

Anyone could be in the pay of Dublin Castle, even harmless, grey-haired ladies. On the other hand, there were several women like this one who were supporting the strikers and were happy to give of their ample time. Eireann looked closely into her guest's eyes, and found a reflection of a difficult and unhappy life. Such a person could support either side.

"We have suffered greatly from injustice at the hands of our masters," the woman said. "My dear friend and I, two spinsters traveling life's road together until she was called home. Before she passed on, she asked me to look after you."

"Did I know her?"

"I believe she was acquainted with your father. Or your grandfather perhaps. Not important. She did follow your comings and goings. When you married, and when your children were born. Oftentimes, she would ask me if I thought that you were happy, as your mother would have wanted you to be happy."

"Did she know my mother?"

It had been years since Eireann had asked the question. When she was younger, she had put it to everyone in Rathkeale, every farmer and tinker who passed by the cottage, but there was no one left who recalled much about the O'Dwyers. No one in Dublin had any answers, besides her father, and he was certainly not going to open his mouth.

"Knew that she had been taken from you too soon," the lady replied. "But then, anyone who encountered your father in those days would have been well aware of that tragic turn of events."

"I don't know that there is anything that you could do here," Eireann said.

"Perhaps I can do something for you," she countered. "When I was young, I invested my savings in a sheep station in Australia."

Eireann leaned forward, every muscle in her body growing tense. "Did you," she said, but paused when he realized that the lady had not given her name. "I'm sorry, we haven't been properly introduced and you must think me very rude."

"Miss Mears, my dear. I never married. Never wanted to, either. You would like to know, I take it, if I knew your mother? Everyone knew of her, of course, by her kindness and charity. And the wrong that was done. I was well aware of that. But how much do you know of her?"

"Her false imprisonment, yes, I am very familiar." Eireann's heart was pounding, her palms clammy with nervous sweat.

"The same prejudice endures to this day, growing more oppressive with every passing year," Miss Mears said. "As a woman whose own mother was made a victim, I wonder if you would care to join another member of that sad little club in an effort to put an end to it."

"Do you know of her life in Fremantle?"

"We are separated in age, you and I, and you will not think it proper, but if you would call me Nell. My Christian name is Cornelia, but I have fond memories of another who thought I was more of a country Nell than a prissy Cornelia. I wouldn't feel so old if we could be on familiar terms. May I call you Eireann?"

"Yes, of course. Excuse me, but what did you have in mind?" It could be a trick, a cruel game that was played regularly by the authorities. The information that Nell possessed could easily have been culled from Simon's conversations. Nothing that was said was new or revealing, and Eireann had to be very cautious. "Our little factory here can always use donations, of course. Besides the cost of material, we have to meet the price of tea and buns, and there is a dinner provided."

"Time I have in abundance. Days and weeks of it, since my dear friend passed on. I looked after her in her final illness, and now that I am alone, I find that time weighs heavy." Nell looked down at her hands, folded in her lap. The veins stood out, dark blue against pale skin that was mottled with age. "Business in the Monto is booming, as you might guess. Having soldiers in the city is beneficial for one element of Dublin, and not the one that supports working men's families."

"I suppose that the mattresses are getting excessive use," Eireann said.

"Wearing out quickly, my dear," Nell said. "In need of refurbishment. The girls would be willing to pay, of course, but one of your men would have to see to the pick up and delivery. I am trustworthy. I have references."

From under her skirts, Nell retrieved several letters that had been written by leaders of the Citizen Army. Mr. Connolly, Captain White, and Mr. Partridge all said much the same thing. Miss Cornelia Mears was one of them, and Mrs. Lytton was judged clever enough to find a place for an old woman of limited physical strength and moderate wealth. Eireann held each letter up to the gas light, to verify that they were not forgeries. The cipher written under each signature popped out, the lemon juice becoming visible in the heat.

Whatever Nell had done in her life, she had mastered the art of organization. Even though the factory was not operating every day, she spent each afternoon generating business and stoking the fires of burning rage among the men who had followed Larkin and now had no jobs at all. Judging by newspaper stories, the employers were pleased with the results of their tactics, confident that they had smashed Jim Larkin's union, but Eireann found a different atmosphere. Only the union was put down; the movement was stronger than ever, and there would be no going back to the old ways, even if the men had gone back to work under the old terms.

There were more able bodies than guns, however, and as much as Clan na Gael in America donated to the cause, it was a trickle when a torrent was needed. Boxes of ammunition arrived at the Markievicz home from time to time, and Eireann had her small shipments every week or two, but at such a slow rate they would never outfit an army.

By February, her father reported that all was back to normal in Dublin society, based on the gossip he took away from Lord Aberdeen's annual levee and the first state ball of the 1914 season. There was no doubt among the gathered politicians that Home Rule was guaranteed to bring war with Ulster's Protestants, based on the Prime Minister's dithering and

Carson's intransigence. Eireann understood one thing. The Citizen Army had to build an arsenal, without delay, or face a civil war with nothing but hurleys and stones against Unionist steel.

Roger worked behind the scenes with Constance Markievicz to write a formal constitution for the Citizen Army, to provide a skeleton to an organization that had been fairly loose until the His Majesty's officers stationed at the Curragh vowed to resign rather than do their sworn duty to uphold the law and fight against the Ulster Volunteers. Home Rule would be voted in, and British troops would stand down so that Carson's men could sweep across the island and put an end to a legally binding decision of Parliament. When word came from London that the Ulster provinces would be excluded from Home Rule to appease the unionists, Eireann turned to Nell Mears and her shadowy network in the tenements. The Citizen Army was against a clock that was running at break-neck speed.

While Larkin and Mrs. Markievicz spoke to the Trades Council, seeking recruits for the Citizen Army, Eireann met a man who had a boat and a crew that was willing to smuggle just about anything. Thanks to her father's inability to keep a secret to himself, she was told all about Carson's clever bit of business in Antrim. Over two million rounds of ammunition had arrived at Larne, a quiet port in the Ulster county, along with thirty-five thousand rifles, and the authorities had stood aside and done nothing to stop it. The Citizen Army would require far more secrecy, but they would have their weapons. Eireann was fully confident of success.

"The Ulster Volunteers are a full-fledged militia now," Simon had said the night before. "God help Ireland if the army officers follow through on their vow to resign rather than fight back. It's treason, you know. As traitorous as the Fenians in my time."

"Only Protestant rather than Catholic," Eireann had said.

"That sums it up, doesn't it?" Anna had noted, and Simon got up from his chair to walk around the library, as if he wanted to turn away from a very accurate observation that did not square with his views. The back of his head gave no clue to the thoughts swirling inside of a man who believed in duty and adhering to one's oath, even if those vows should grow distasteful. Men like her father had long since ceased being made in the United Kingdom, substituted by men like Carson who would overthrow Parliament's decree when it was not to their liking. She was grateful to have found something she could still admire about him.

Nell had a cottage near Clontarf where the meeting was to take place. Eireann had no idea who she was speaking to, but her contact looked every inch a weather-beaten old tar who knew every inlet along the Irish Sea. Unfortunately, he was of more conservative stock and he was not willing to lift a finger for Larkin and the socialists who were condemned by the priests. He favored John Redmond's views of the Irish question, and he would be happy to run guns for the Volunteers, but not the Citizen Army. At once, Eireann transformed into a solid Redmonite, a woman with family connections to the Irish Republican Brotherhood. Only half of her claim was a lie, while the rest had been the truth at one time in the distant past.

Using his law office as cover, Roger carried out the next phase of the plan. He made arrangements with an IRB man to provide strong backs and whatever motorized vehicles could be rounded up, to cart the contraband from a fishing pier in Howth to the city. With delivery routes organized, it was a simple matter for Eireann to cable her friend in Boston and request a delivery of fresh supplies, using a code that had been carried across the ocean under an Irish immigrant's skirts. As soon as her request was acknowledged, Eireann paid a call on Con Markievicz.

"The Volunteers will be at the pier to take delivery, but you know as well as I that they wouldn't know which end of a rifle does the shooting," Eireann said. She stole a glance at the mantel clock, hoping that Con would not be long-winded. Anna was always ready to run down to Rathmines so that the children were greeted by someone other than the maid when they came home from school, but it was taxing and the poor woman was being run ragged. Balancing gun-running and mothering was not as easy as Eireann had hoped.

"It's an absolute waste, you're quite right," Con said.

"The shipment will travel along the Clontarf road. I will send a messenger to Croydon Park when the ship arrives. You will be drilling the troops, who can then march up the road and intercept the convoy. Train them, Con. Get a motorized lorry out to the grounds and practice so they can unload and disappear into the fields before the Volunteers know what happened."

Eireann examined every foot of the road between Howth and Dublin, travelling the route countless times until she decided on the best place for the Citizen Army to meet up with the Volunteers. She reconnoitered the route one last time before she drove to the North Wall to pick up her father and Michael, who returned early from London. Simon had gone to take part in the ongoing battle over Home Rule, bringing Michael along as his aide, but the journey was short-lived. The legislation was amended, to exclude the six northern counties, as Commons bent to the will of Winston Churchill and Edward Carson. Her father came home in a foul mood.

"Mr. Redmond made a sensible point, sir," Michael said, continuing an argument that must have begun in London and sailed with them on the ferry. "All Irish men, united against the Hun, would be clear proof that the island is equally unified."

"Irish men. Irish cannon fodder. Shot to pieces, united in rot in a single grave, and the Ulster Volunteers will lay down their arms." Simon stared out of the car's window, arms folded across his chest. "Naive. Naive as newborns. Redmond is a fool, Michael, and I brought you with me so that you could see what an imbecile looks like in the flesh."

"Any talk of the lock-out?" Eireann asked.

"The lock-out? Oh, yes, you are referring to that slight disagreement that shut down Ireland's industry for five months. We in Commons only discuss current events, my dear, not ancient history."

"So it's partition?" Eireann continued.

"Grandfather believes that the set period of partition, at six years, is significant," Michael said. "The Ulster Volunteers wouldn't sign on to fight in Europe if they thought that they were needed at home."

"It's a variation on a peace treaty," Simon said. "Peace in Ulster while blood is shed elsewhere, and if half of the Ulster Volunteers fall on the battlefield, so much the better for keeping the peace in the northern counties."

"While the Catholics in the three southern provinces drive out their Protestant neighbors," Eireann said. "These brilliant men who advise the King, do they think they can draw a border on a map and ring-fence the people?"

"If it comes to war, I would fight to hold this island together," Michael said.

Eireann shushed her oldest son, before he said too much in front of his Royal Marine captain of a grandfather. The family's history was peppered with conflicts between opposing sides, and the outcome had always been tragic. Simon's uncles dead, her own uncles exiled, and if Michael could not keep his own counsel, he would be the next generation to pay the price.

"Hold it together under Home Rule?" Simon asked.

"As an independent nation," Michael said.

"Is this what he learned at Patrick Pearse's school, Eireann?" Simon asked. He leaned back against the upholstery and closed his eyes. "Peter's the one who's most like Danny. Impetuous. Too free with words."

"Danny?" Michael asked.

"Rattling on and on in the pubs as if everyone present was a Fenian," Simon mumbled. He opened his eyes and blinked, as if he had forgotten where he was. "I gave politics my all, but I don't believe that I failed. There is only one solution. I wanted there to be another way, but I was chasing a fantasy that I knew was not real."

"No, you didn't fail," Eireann said. "You were outnumbered."

"If war breaks out, you won't let your sons be swayed by Redmonite nonsense," Simon said. "I shall speak to Roger. I shall make it quite clear this time."

If he did as he said, it would be the first time that he was clear about anything. Eireann smiled to herself, recalling all the years of verbal games, of obfuscation and topics changing abruptly. He did not have to be clear with Roger, if he was worried about the boys signing on to fight for England. Not one of her sons would ever consider anything so pointless. They were preparing for a different battle altogether, one that Simon had sought to avoid and his daughter was actively seeking to meet.

Twenty-Five

The messenger on the motorbike took off at high speed as soon as the steamer signaled to shore. A few automobiles filled out the ranks of men on foot, lining the dock in anticipation of a well-choreographed maneuver. Knowing her limitations, Eireann had Michael at the wheel, more capable than she could ever be at high speed driving. The Volunteers swarmed over the boat as soon as it was tied up at the dock, joined by a few local fishermen who bore no love for the Royal Irish Constabulary, the Royal Navy, or any other form of royalty. With so many people and so much heavy material, it was impossible to off-load quietly. Eireann checked her watch repeatedly, praying that she had been accurate in the timing.

A giddiness took hold of the Volunteers, which in turn led to chatter as they began their march along the Clontarf road, the Plowman automobile at the end of the line. They moved in darkness, past houses that were closed up for the night, along the coast towards Dublin. Off in the distance, one cottage stood out, lit up as if for a grand party. It was Nell's signal. "They're on to us," Eireann said. "Get ahead. They'll know to scatter."

The authorities might have been on guard when their spies noticed the Citizen Army at Croydon Park, drilling into the late night. Likely as

KATIE HANRAHAN

well that someone in Howth had sounded the alarm, and Eireann had considered such a possibility when she plotted out the mission. Soon, if the messenger had gotten through, the Citizen Army would appear out of the darkness and start a fight, if one was not already in progress, to distract the police and the military while some of the men grabbed the guns and retreated.

A tide of dark shadows washed towards the road, men who were almost invisible in the black of a moonless night. Harsh voices called out orders, to attack, to stop them, to confiscate the guns. Eireann's skull met the door frame as Michael veered off to the left, accelerating and then braking as a policeman appeared in front of the car, inches away from being struck. Dirty fingers coiled around the edge of the open window, a figure clung to the automobile, and Eireann did not hesitate to smash the hand with the butt of a contraband rifle. A sharp cry, a thump of body meeting soft ground, and Michael was back on the road, the tires finding every rut and divot, throwing Eireann up out of her seat and into the hard roof.

They were traveling in the human current, flowing steadily towards Dublin. Irregular shapes suggested men carrying rifles, clumps of strong dockers toting crates of ammunition, all moving away from the melee that was just behind them. Michael was off the road again, into a field, to use the vehicle as a weapon to frighten off a policeman with a truncheon. The person who came close to being clubbed grabbed onto the car, like a barnacle clinging to a moving ship, while Eireann reached out to brace herself and keep from flying through the windscreen.

The angry noises, the sound of fear and alarm, all brought back a memory of Kilmainham, of a little girl who boldly stood at the door and demanded to see her father. Despite the warm July air, she felt a chill deep in her bones, the same cold that permeated the stones of the jail. Her mother's missal, the pages yellowed and brittle with age, still held the last note that her father had tucked away in the secret hiding place. "Your papa loves you always, in his heart where none can see," Simon had written in tiny letters on a tiny scrap. Would he love her still, a grown woman fomenting war against his government? Would he come to visit her in Kilmainham if it came to that?

Sound rushed through her ears, unintelligible noise that she realized was her own pulse, pounding with fear. Michael slowed down and the barnacle jumped off, to head west across the fields with several rifles slung across his shoulder. The car roared through the night, speeding towards Croydon Park, where Michael pulled over to wait. Eireann mopped beads of sweat from her lip, wiped the clammy chill from her palms, and prayed that her family would be safe that night. She turned her head, to see if Michael was all right, and found the face of her mother and father, blended into a young man who was too inexperienced to know that he should be quaking in his boots. Be brave like your mother, her father had advised, but her mother was younger than Michael when she was transported to Fremantle. Eireann was too old to be brave, too close to fifty and old age, too aware of the world and its cruelty.

"Well done, old girl," Michael said, his eyes bright with excitement. He was so much like Simon at that moment, giddy almost, as if he were drunk on danger.

The rattle of metal and the scuffle of feet rose behind them. Eireann leaned out of the open window and saw a motorcycle come up rapidly, leading a large lorry. From the opposite direction, the headlamps of another car swept across a stone fence and then went dark before the vehicle slowed and then stopped nearby. With her knees trembling, Eireann stepped out of the car, her ears tuned to any sounds of danger, ready to flee and escape the threat of prison.

Heavy boxes of ammunition were tossed into the lorry and the men who carried them scattered, gathering up rifles from their colleagues who were overloaded with weapons. In groups of three and four they set off through the grounds of Croydon Park, moving to the northwest or to the south, to deliver an arsenal to the men who had lost the strike but had not lost the will to fight. Michael lent a hand at the lorry to speed up the process while Eireann watched with Connie Markievicz as the boot of the Countess's car was stuffed with guns.

"Never was the arrival of the police so timely," Eireann said. "I don't know how much we retrieved, but the Volunteers did a fine job of keeping the authorities busy while our men gleaned the field."

"We'd best be moving out," Michael said. "The soldiers didn't confiscate much, and they'll be heading to Dublin to finish their night's work. The sooner we get out of their path, the better for all of us."

"You're the daughter of a fine soldier, Eireann," Con said. "Only someone with a military mind could have planned this down to the tiniest detail."

"A chip off the Plowman block," Eireann said. The two women embraced, not certain that they would meet again if something went wrong, and went their separate ways, heading in opposite directions. The lorry and the motorcycle were to wind through streets and quiet laneways, to run in circles rather than head directly into the city where more Citizen Army soldiers were waiting, to divide up the cache.

Troops on foot had little chance of catching up to a speeding car, but a speeding car would attract attention. Michael slowed down to a leisurely pace, acting the part of dutiful son with his kind-hearted mother at his side, returning from a mission of mercy. Dear Aunt Nell was feeling poorly, if anyone in uniform were to ask why they were out in the middle of the night. Dear Aunt Nell would verify the story, if needed, and no one would say otherwise.

"When we were in London, Grandfather mentioned that he was sorry that I never went down to Sandhurst," Michael said. "Do you think he was hoping that one of us would carry on the tradition?"

"You never lacked for training as a boy," Eireann said. "His idea of suitable play for boys and girls involved drilling, shooting and general mayhem. He re-created Sandhurst in Rathkeale, I'd say, and didn't he put me and your father through his course as well?"

"He made us ready for what's to come."

"In a way, I suppose. A case of things working out for the best." Eireann reached behind, to verify that the blanket she had thrown over the back seat was covering every barrel and stock. "My poor father. He snooped and spied for his entire life, and he never realized what was happening in his own house. I'm sorry that we have to keep secrets from him, but it cannot be helped."

They picked up Roger at the little mattress factory on Moore Street, where he had taken possession of a portion of the Howth arsenal. In the morning, Nell would open the doors and the ladies would stitch the rifles into ticking. Men without work would arrive by the end of the week, to deliver the goods to tenement rooms overcrowded with starving, ragged people. Nine hundred German rifles would be issued; tens of thousands of rounds would be parceled out. The Citizen Army would be a real army, ready to fight on equal terms with those who would deny Irish Catholics the right to equality.

Her first attempt at gun-running had been a success, and her friends in the Volunteers never guessed who had tipped off the Citizen Army. Eireann went back to work at once, planning the next delivery by scouting a different harbor when she suspected that Dublin Castle would mind Howth more closely and take an eye off other small ports and suitable inlets. Whoever she could convince to ferry the guns to the port would have to be a Larkinite, since the Volunteers weren't likely to fall for the same ruse twice, and that would take some time. Before she was barely getting started, a madman fired a gun in Sarajevo and the entire world was upended.

England needed men to fight the war in Europe, and the Crown-loving loyalists of Ulster signed on in droves. The Ulster Volunteers, already accustomed to the ways of soldiering, formed the backbone of many Irish companies. Ready to fight for King and Country, they marched off to France, joined by Irishmen who had no love of royalty.

"It is a job; we all understand the situation." Eireann paid off the woman who had apologized to the point of tears because she had to give notice. It was the second time in three days that one of the mattress makers had abandoned the mission, and all because their husbands had signed on for the sake of the separation pay that would fall to the family. London was buying soldiers out of Dublin's slums.

"We've managed to get a few donations from some of them," Nell said. "They come home on leave before shipping out and misplace their guns, so to speak. But it's not enough. Not nearly enough."

"Nell, we'll have to shut down. I don't have many workers left, and the ones that are here," Eireann said. "They're not about to talk their men out of leaving. The Citizen Army can't pay its members and we simply cannot compete."

"Move with the times, my dear, move with the times. Find another way. They will go, of course. Their children are starving." Nell permitted Eireann to help her into her coat, acknowledging a growing frailty. "Pity that Mr. Larkin wasn't starting up his union now. The strike breakers are gone for soldiers, and the aristocrats of industry would have to yield or go out of business."

"Home Rule has been put into mothballs until the war is over," Eireann said. "At least we have that on our side, to keep the flame burning."

By November, the Moore Street facility was shuttered. Con Markievicz received one last shipment from Boston, a crate labeled 'Tombstone. Fragile" that disguised a small cache of rifles, but it was the final contraband that the Irish-Americans in Boston would ship. Their country was determined to be neutral, and to be visibly neutral, which resulted in greater diligence at the ports. Smuggling arms had become impossible for the duration.

Eireann lost her strongest ally when Nell slipped on a carpet and broke her hip. The old woman was made comfortable by the Lytton's family physician, and nursed by a girl who was paid by Roger, all in return for Nell's devotion to their shared cause. Every day, Eireann drove out to Clontarf to sit with the dying spinster who was otherwise alone.

"I am aware that this isn't the way to Grafton Street," Eireann said to her father. His acerbic observation required an especially sweet response, to let him know that she was in no mood for his temper. Christmas shopping with Sir Simon was no garden party. "This won't take more than an hour and you'll have a lovely cup of tea to warm you while Nell and I chat."

"And we shall all knit cozy stockings for the boys in the trenches who won't be home by Christmas after all."

"The families will have a better Christmas this year than last," Eireann noted.

"Remarkable men, aren't they? To go to their death, sacrifice their lives, so that their children can survive. I can't imagine being that desperate. Can you?"

"Yes, I can. I've seen it."

"I wish you hadn't."

As was his habit when he did not care to discuss a topic, Simon changed it. He mentioned a list of items that might suit Grace, but he seemed to forget that the youngest Lytton was no longer an infant and she had stopped playing with dolls some time ago. For Maura, he would find earrings set with emeralds because she had the coloring for green gems, while the boys might like something modern and mechanical. Having done all that, was he then expected to give some token to Michael's sweetheart? Before they finished debating the proper etiquette for giving to girls not yet engaged but nearly so, they arrived at the cottage.

The nurse showed them in and gave them both a complete run-down on the patient's condition, which Simon understood was not good. People of his age did not recover from shattered bones that were too brittle to ever mend. He ignored the details, instead wandering through the cluttered parlor that would have been all the rage fifty years ago. Heavy velvets and lace were everywhere, while the tops of every flat surface were littered with porcelain objects. The air was heavy, too warm and too close, too much like a sick room for his liking. To let Eireann know that he expected her to be true to her word, he made a show of checking his watch and reminding her that she had fifty-nine minutes remaining.

The upholstery was threadbare, but in a genteel way, as if the owner's wealth had trickled away, keeping pace with the decline of the body, until the armchairs were as broken as this Nell character. She was respected in the area, that much Simon had learned, and had purchased the cottage with a bequest from another old spinster. He got to his feet and paced in front of the fire, but it was too warm and he retreated to the far corner, in search of something to read. Not a book was to be found among the curios; neither was there a single photograph. The parlor spoke of a solitude so absolute that Simon shuddered.

"She'd like to see you as well, Sir Simon," the nurse said. He checked his watch and found that another ten minutes remained.

The frail creature in the bed was tiny in comparison to the size of the carved mahogany headboard. Her eyes were glazed, the result of morphine administered freely to stave off pain without regard to the side effects on breathing. Her bony finger beckoned him forward, and Eireann evacuated the chair at the bedside so that her father, nearly as fragile as Nell, could sit down.

"You and I are much changed with the years, Captain Plowman," Nell said.

Simon leaned closer, as if he might focus beyond the wrinkles and the white hair, but he did not find a familiar feature in her face. "Have we met earlier, Miss, um, Miss Nell?"

"More important that we meet again, sir, in God's heaven," she said.

Eireann perched on the edge of the bed, to take Nell's hand in a gesture of comfort. "Perhaps you shall have to bribe St. Peter," she said with a wink at her father.

"My daughter is very fond of you," Simon said. Not even the voice was recognizable.

"Eireann, dear, will you be so good as to put the kettle on?" Nell asked. Her eyes followed Eireann's every step, across the room and out the door. "Very fond, yes. I am blessed in my last days. As her mother was blessed with faithful friends who held her hand as she gave up her last breath."

No longer spry, Simon's attempt to jump to his feet was thwarted by Nell, who managed to grasp his arm and pull him down towards her. Her cheeks flushed from the effort, but she held on as if she were clutching her last few minutes on earth. "You are much changed since your days in Fremantle," he said. Sweat beaded and then rolled down his temples.

In a flash, her hands found the lapels of his coat and she pulled him closer, until he feared he would topple over onto her. "I know you are not who you seem to be, Captain Plowman. I know because she loved you. Body and soul. Body and soul she loved you."

Eireann extricated him from Nell's grip and nervously fussed over the old woman, rearranging arms grown limp, smoothing sheets and plumping pillows. "Body and soul, Eireann," Nell repeated the mantra. "Body and soul. I see through him. Like a pane of glass. Make him tell you."

He lifted her hand, cold and white, and touched his lips to Nell's fingers. "We are much changed over the years, Nell, and we remake ourselves many times over. What we were in the past does not need to follow us."

"Some secrets are best taken to the grave," Nell said. "Only some."

"What secrets would a kind and gentle lady have?" the former Marine officer said. "My daughter has been fortunate to have known you."

As if she was falling through air, Nell seemed to sink deeper into the mattress, her muscles growing slack. Exhausted, she fell asleep. "Poor thing," Eireann cooed as she stroked Nell's forehead. "The doctor said she might appear confused because of the morphine."

Simon rose and touched the gnarled fingers that had once gripped Mary Claire's hand when she lay dying in a strange land. "I suppose that's it. Confused. She doesn't have much longer."

"No. Not much time left."

"I'd like to pay for her funeral."

"Where is this sentimental drivel coming from?" Eireann said with a chuckle.

"Can I not perform an act of kindness without you coming down on me?" he barked. Simon apologized at once, regretting that he had allowed a reformed prostitute to get a jump on him. She had been decent, at least, to trade her discretion for his. Let the world think that Nell was a lady of impeccable reputation, let her die with some dignity. "She has an Australian inflection in her voice and I sometimes find it painful to recall."

After she had tucked a lap robe around his legs and gotten behind the wheel of the car, Eireann turned to him with a hard look in her eye. "Are you going to say anything this time? I haven't asked for ages, but don't think I haven't forgotten."

"Why must you plague me with this nonsense?" Simon asked. "Nothing will change. Drive on. Let's go to the Imperial Hotel for lunch."

"Will you answer my questions?"

"No."

"You're ashamed of her. Did you get her in trouble and have to marry her?"

"You ask too many questions, Eireann go Bragh."

"So that's it. You were a cad."

"A cad would have left the lady to her miserable fate." Simon adjusted the collar of his coat and tugged at the wool scarf around his neck. "You haven't been to visit her grave for years. You have a family of your own to care for, and a husband, and your charity work. That's as it should be. It's all right for me to dwell in the past, but you must look forward."

"There has always been an empty place in my heart."

"Of course there is. You never knew her. You never can know her. So make an end of it."

Confronting Fremantle had worn him out and he wanted to go home, to sort through the scraps of those days. He thought he would outlive them all, find peace at the end when he was the last one standing, but Nell's existence had served as a harsh reminder that there might never be a time when he could stop looking over his shoulder. Nell's silence came cheap, but what price would he pay to keep Eireann's love? How his daughter would despise him if she heard the bits and pieces of other people's memories, a hatred so deep that she would never accept his version of events. Easier by far if the past died with him and rotted under the sod of Athenry.

Twenty-Six

Within days of Nell's funeral, Eireann realized how important her colleague had been to the Citizen Army. Mr. Connolly was in touch, demanding to know what progress was being made on procuring more arms, and she had no answers. It was Nell who knew the fishermen and merchant masters, not Eireann, and having lost a key player, the entire organization was collapsing.

In an attempt to re-group, Eireann made inquiries through her American correspondent, thinking that someone could get word to Jim Larkin who was raising funds for the union in New York. She never heard back from Mr. Larkin, but she did receive a note from another Irishman who was in America to seek donations from the sons of immigrants. His mission fit seamlessly with Eireann's needs.

Before proceeding, she had to make inquiries about Roger Casement, and she did not like everything that she heard. The son of a dragoon, born in Dublin, he had been knighted for exposing the misery of the rubber plantations in Peru. Some called him 'Congo Casement', a reference to his work there in the Foreign Office, while others lauded him as the savior of the Putamayo Indians. On the surface, he would seem to be the sort of respectable gentleman who could find his way around a business transaction without stumbling. The very career that had brought him accolades had opened his eyes, and he was an ardent advocate of Irish freedom.

Casement's allegiance, however, was to the Irish Volunteers, and Eireann was warned by her friend in America that not everyone in Clan na Gael trusted the man. He was not a member of the Irish Republican Brotherhood, and he had run afoul of many nationalists because he let Redmond take over the movement and wreck it. The radical element found him too moderate, while she felt that Casement was overly emotional, and that made him dangerous when the game required cool heads and steady nerves. There was the element of the crusader about him, a fool who would rush in. Even though she had qualms about pinning her hopes on a person who failed to win her confidence, she had no other choice.

Word came that Mr. Casement was in Germany, touring the prisoner of war camps in search of Irishmen who would sign on to his madcap scheme. Many of the soldiers who had agreed to fight for England were there because Redmond convinced them that they could win Home Rule by shedding their blood, and to seek recruits from men who thought they were accomplishing their goal was nothing short of idiocy. As for the rest, if Casement had spent so much as a day with the striking dockers he would understand that they were fighting for England because it was a paying job. Offering them more of the misery that they had lived for five months was hardly an incentive. Glory and liberty never put food in a child's mouth.

Not only was the notion ridiculous, but Casement's folly was drawing unwanted attention to his actions. As far as Eireann was concerned, he might just as well have issued a bulletin to Dublin Castle, and she considered cancelling the venture. Considered, and then reconsidered; Mr. Connolly kept asking about landing munitions and they were running out of time. The Citizen Army had formulated a battle plan, had chosen locations to be seized and held. A date had been selected and all units were prepared to mobilize. Mrs. Lytton would have to deal with the hand that was dealt to her, and make it came up a winner.

Using the same strategy that had worked so well in Howth, Eireann chose a little used fishing port near Tralee, in Kerry. Five days before Easter, she drove across the island with her son Michael and checked into rooms above a pub. To create a cover for their presence, she made inquiries about farmland for sale and toured some properties that were on the market. Using the ruse, she was able to meet local members of the Citizen Army and distribute orders without attracting the least bit of attention from the Royal Irish Constabulary. Two days before Easter, mother and son drove out to the coast under cover of darkness and waited at the appointed spot.

Men stood ready to emerge from the shadows when the signal went up, Con Markievicz was waiting to be called forward with her car and a motorized lorry, but Eireann was uneasy. Casement insisted that the use of a German submarine was a brilliant strategy, that he could ship in thousands of guns without being seen, but he had broadcast his business all over Berlin and even the dogs in the street knew that the British had spies there. The people who were going to off-load the submarine were arrayed at a distance for safety. Better to waste valuable time in bringing them forward when the submarine arrived than to have them all gathered near the pier.

Afraid to light a match, Eireann could not check her watch and it felt as if she had been waiting well past the rendezvous time. She paced along the side of the road, keeping her field glasses trained on the water. "I don't like it," she mumbled. "Something doesn't feel right."

Michael crouched next to the car, which he had left idling in case they needed to move quickly. In one hand he cradled a match and in the other he held the vesta case, hovering over the petrol-soaked rag that he had stuffed into a glass bottle filled with fuel. One word from his mother and the signal would be lit, to warn their comrades to flee through the fields and across the boreens to safety.

Far in the distance, a cluster of light moved and then stopped, bobbing in the swell just outside the mouth of the bay. Eireann fell silent and stood perfectly still, listening for sounds beyond the splash of waves that lapped at the hulls of the shipping boats and the pilings of the pier. There were too many lights to be one vessel in one spot, too many different patterns of movement that suggested several small ships congregating at a single point.

"We're done for," she said to Michael, and turned to jump into the car.

The flame took and cast a glow all around, enough illumination to blind her vision. She heard the cars roar up before she saw them. Her eyes adjusted at about the same time that two men, armed with pistols, raced forward. One grabbed her and hustled her into one car while Michael was hauled off to the other. Someone jumped into her car, revved the engine, and was gone.

Eireann fell against someone in the back seat, someone who wrapped her in his arms and pulled her head down to his lap. She smelled her father's familiar aromas of wool and bay rum and sandalwood soap, heard him give an order to move out, and felt his hand, comforting, remove her hat and cradle her cheek. He instructed someone to get word to Connolly, to send the motorcycle rider to the city to pass the word, and then the car jerked forward, away from Tralee.

With her heart beating hard enough to beat out of her chest, she said nothing as they bounced over the rutted road. No one spoke and she had no idea who might be driving. There was no point in struggling, in attempting to jump out of the car. If she was to be arrested, if she was to be shot for a traitor, she was now helpless to stop it.

On and on in silence they traveled, for what seemed like hours. "Knockeen," Simon murmured. He put an arm around her shoulder and helped her to sit up, so that she could watch the little farm town pass by outside of the window. From Tralee to Knockeen meant they were traveling east. Had he been following her all week? Had he come so that he could do his duty to his King and take her in?

"I've taken the oath, Mother." It was Peter, her son, who was behind the wheel, a broad smile on his face.

"And didn't I tell you what became of your great-uncle Daniel for speaking so freely?" Simon chided the boy.

"Amongst ourselves, sir, would hardly be a breech of security," Peter said.

"How do you know your mother is one of us?"

"I'm not," Eireann said, regaining her composure and her fighting spirit. "How could you, Peter? After all that's been said and done in our home, how could you be turned?"

"Well done, Grandfather," Peter said. "You're right, she has no idea."

"Don't crow about it, it's shameful what I've done." Simon handed her back her hat. "I have never been proud of it, not for one day."

"Shameful indeed," Eireann spluttered.

She glared at her father, whose face remained as impassive as ever, the slightest hint of a grin playing at the corner of his mouth. "We can stop in Knocknagashel to rest," he said. "Roger and the girls should be in Rathkeale before us."

"Why are they not at home?" Eireann asked. She was confused, and her fear increased with every passing mile. If only she could read his face, find some clue as to his state of mind, but he was a Royal Marine yet, unyielding, without emotion.

"Change of plans. You decided to spend Easter in the country with your father and your aunt."

"I'll be in Dublin on Monday morning," she countered.

"About that." Simon shifted on the upholstered seat. "Peter was supposed to be serving under your friend the Countess, but I spoke to Mr. Connolly and had the orders changed. She'd shoot herself in the foot before she'd manage to shoot the enemy."

"Have you turned us all in, is that it? Done your dirty work, like you did when my uncles tried to," Eireann said, but Simon cut her off with a hand over her mouth.

"Enough. Take the main road to Castleisland, Peter. No need for us to go skulking about the laneways."

With a firm jerk of her head she escaped his grasp. Her family's pathetic history was playing out yet again. Just as her grandfather had chosen his military duty over family ties, so too was her father adhering to his oath. All the rumors and tales she had heard as a child were proving to be true, all the intimations of dirty dealings and double crossings that featured her father in a starring role were accurate after all. "You're a cruel man," she said, a point to which he fully agreed. After that, not another word was spoken until Peter turned into the road that led up to the cottage in Rathkeale. All was quiet, but lamps were glowing in the kitchen and the parlor. The Lytton automobile was parked near the front door, and Michael was stepping out of the vehicle that was stopped behind it.

Her oldest son reached back through the open window and shook the hand of the driver. As she stormed towards the door, she heard him say something about God's grace and Monday, but she was too bewildered and angry to make sense of anything. As soon as she entered, she found Roger waiting for her, a glass of whiskey in his outstretched hand.

"You're safe, thank God," Roger said. "Drink this to settle your nerves. I've had one. I could use another."

Anna appeared at the bottom of the stairs. "Not sleeping, but at least they've gone to bed," she said. She took the empty glass from Eireann's trembling hand. "And so it begins."

After hanging his coat on the newel post, Simon took Eireann's arm and led her up to his room, his pace slowed by stiff legs after a long ride. She asked him what was happening but he had no answer, not yet, not until she had calmed down and was amenable to reason. "Sit," he commanded, and she plopped onto the edge of his bed, as obedient as she had been when she was a little girl. With some difficulty, he bent down to retrieve the valise that was tucked in the bottom of his armoire. The case had grown heavier with every passing year, and it took all his strength to lift it onto the bed.

The locks sprung open at his touch and he lifted the lid on his precious treasure, the legacy that he had once planned to leave behind after his death, but which could no longer rest in peace. "Since 1865 I have waited for this time," he said. "The Fenians have been waiting for England to be pre-occupied with a foreign war, and that day has come."

Carefully, Simon slipped his fingers under the book that was tied with a faded ribbon. With tears in his eyes he set it into his daughter's open hands. He then turned back to the suitcase and removed a thick bundle of miscellaneous pages bound together with rough twine, and put it on her lap.

Her fingers touched the ribbon lightly, fear tinged with reverence guiding her movements. She examined her fingertips, coated with a yellow-grey grime. "That's the dust of Fremantle on your hands, Eireann go Bragh," he said.

"To my child, the story of my life," Eireann read the label on the cover, the ink faded with time.

He tipped her chin up, so that their eyes met. "Read every word, Eireann, don't turn your eyes away when you imagine in your mind what I did to your mother before we reached Australia. When you finish her story, you must read mine, in these letters that I wrote to her. And then, you must forgive me."

He left Eireann alone, to meet Mary Claire O'Dwyer and Simon Plowman for the first time. She had suffered a tremendous shock, and there was no better time to present something more shocking. He had learned that, when he was training recruits, and he had used the same technique on Mary Claire. A person had to be turned inside out before they were pliable, melted down before they could be poured into a new mold and hardened into a soldier.

The lamp was burning in the bedroom where Maura and Grace were waiting for Grandfather to finish his story. Roger had gone to check on his daughters, Michael had followed on his father's heels in search of his bearings, and Peter had taken a seat on the floor, afraid perhaps of being alone in the face of an unknown and frightening future.

The girls scooted over in the bed to give Simon a spot to rest his old bones. "Where was I? I told you about the O'Dwyer tannery, and how the tumbled down walls of that building were put back up to make our cottage here?"

"Where was our grandmother's cottage?" Grace asked.

"Somewhere out there in one of the fields. The bailiffs knocked the walls to rubble, after Thomas O'Dwyer was evicted, and I never could find where it stood," Simon said.

A brief review of the reign of the Wilkerson clan drew Roger into the lamplight's circle, a tale that wound through days of wealth to a modern era of much reduced fortunes.

"All three O'Dwyer boys took the oath and went to Waterford, near Cork. They went there to fight, to free Ireland from tyranny, but the uprising was nothing but a scattering of armed resistance." He had not thought about those days in Kilclooney Wood for so long that Simon was surprised at the clarity of his recollection now. Maura asked a question, pulling Simon out of his reflections and dragging him back to 1916.

"After their defeat? They were wanted men, condemned to death. Danny, the middle son, died in a fall, but Edward and Michael survived, to escape to America." His mind went back again, working of its own accord to play the day over again. As if he were there, he smelled the damp of the cold mist that lingered over the meeting place, shielded by trees and stones.

"The game is up, Michael, get out while you can," Simon heard his voice anew. The sound of a horse reverberated in his head, and the shouts of Danny O'Dwyer, calling out to the Fenians, a voice that grew dim as Danny galloped away. "Over one hundred fusiliers are coming this way from Fermoy. You're dead men if you don't run."

"No, Simon, we've run off enough now. We'll stay and fight, fight like men," Mike said. "I'm leaving our sister in your hands. You're just the man to look after her."

Camped outside of Appomattox, they had spoken at length of the Irish Republican Brotherhood, had taken the oath together, and spent many hours talking about girls. Vows were made then, to look after the women should one of them fall in battle, fighting for a free Ireland. Michael had taught him a few words of Irish, to turn the head of a pretty colleen, to turn the head of Mary Claire O'Dwyer. The hazy dreams from one battlefield became real on another. "My God, Mike, there's not a girl I've met that I haven't ruined," Simon warned, but he knew even then that he had fallen in love with Michael's sister without ever having met her.

"Mary Claire's a beauty, Simon, and that's not a brother's bragging," Ed said, to reassure a wavering heart. "Marry her, go on, and she'll make you more happy than any other girl on God's earth. She's a child and she's been spoiled, I'll warn you now, but she's fond of the boys, Simon. She'll kiss a lad until his lips fall off, and that was fine with three brothers keeping watch, but we're not going to be able to protect her anymore. We're giving Mary Claire to you, and let it be your lips she tastes for the rest of her days."

"You're the right sort of man for her," Mike concluded. "Swear to me that you'll take care of her for us. We're brothers in arms, Simon; become our brother and take our sister for your wife."

"I'll ride her, if that's what you're ordering, sir," Plowman joked, a soldier's bravado shared with a compatriot before battle.

"If I get word that you're riding my sister," Ed said, responding in kind.

There was more that Edward had said, but Simon never could recall what happened in the last few moments before John O'Reilly clobbered him on the back of the head. With that hard blow, Plowman maintained his cover and the excuse of an ambush was made real, at the cost of a lump on his skull that throbbed for weeks. Recalling the headache, Simon was pulled back to his home in Rathkeale, where his grandson Peter was nudging his arm, demanding to know how his mother's uncles got to America.

"I told some of Uncle Michael's friends from his regiment in New York where to hold up the police van, and they came and set them free, to run away to a steamship and be brought to America. The authorities were quite upset to have lost a couple of Irish necks to stretch, so they went after your grandmother to make her pay."

"How did you get married?" Maura asked.

"I was given the honor of guarding the Fenian soldiers on the transport ship, and I made sure that your grandmother was transported with them. We almost did not get married, though, because I fell in love with a beautiful convict in Portland Gaol and forgot all about my promise to Michael and Edward."

"What happened to that girl?" Grace asked.

"That girl turned out to be the very girl I was looking for. So you see, your great-uncles were right all along, I was in love with your grandmother before I met her." He stopped a moment, looking out over the people who meant more to him than life itself. "I always believed that I hardened her on that voyage, made her a rock so that she could carry out our mission. I never did any such thing; she was already hard as stone. All I did was rub off the Irish moss and carve my initials, to claim her as my discovery."

The details of Mary Claire's military training were left for Eireann to share with her mother. With dawn approaching, Simon detected a need inside him, an urge to get everything else out before he ran out of time.

"In Fremantle, she earned the trust of the important people by pretending to spy on the Fenians, but only one of the Fenians knew who she really was. Messages passed from sailors to their lady friends," Simon couched his terms with delicacy for the children's ears. "And Mrs. Simon Plowman was collecting them in her missal. The name of the ship for John

O'Reilly's escape, the place where he could meet the merchantman. Right under their noses, and Mrs. Plowman was leading the entire operation."

"Did they execute her?" Michael broke in.

"They never knew, Michael; never did they see what she was up to behind her façade. She knew the entire plan, and part of it she had to invent herself. Of all the people who helped her, she was the only one who had all the parts, so that the plan would not come undone if one or two players were lost. She kept quiet, and that was the key to her success," Simon concluded with sound advice.

"So the O'Dwyers were true to their word," Anna said. Simon had not noticed her before, standing in the doorway. "They got their fellows out of prison."

"She died of childbed fever," Simon grew morose. "Injustice killed her. Injustice drove my parents apart and killed my wife."

Unaware of time passing, Eireann continued to read. Her mother's journal had been both wonderful and horrifying, as an essay on Rathkeale's happy times segued into an episode from the *Hellebore*. The daughter met a mother of uncommon valor and daring, unlike the indistinct image of a grand lady in a carriage. She also met a father who was not the man she had grown up with, because this man was a hardened instructor, drilling a raw recruit, compressing years of combat experience into a few short months.

The final words that Mary Claire wrote to her child were penned in the early hours of August 2, 1868. "I must close now, my darling," Mary Claire wrote hurriedly. "The *bean sì* has called my name and I know my time has come. When I was fourteen, my fortune was told, and it has all come to pass. You have before you the passage through hell in which I atoned for my sin of pride and vanity. While I was in torment, my brothers sent me their brother who was not my brother, and my brother's brother came to me to be my husband. As the tinker predicted, he opened the door to paradise for me and took me to heaven on earth, filling me with happiness until I was bursting with joy. You are our happiness, my sweet child, and while I cannot stay, I leave you behind with a father who loves deeply."

Tears flowed from Eireann's eyes, blurring her vision. She blew her nose and pulled herself together, to go on with the end of the saga. "One day he will reveal himself to you and you will understand how much we loved one another, and how much we love you. Love your father, be obedient and be kind. I have known since I was fourteen that I would die in a parched and colorless land, and I am in that land, prepared to face God and confident of His mercy. I love you, and I kiss you every morning from heaven. God Bless Ireland. Eireann go Bragh."

Her father had specifically pleaded that she not turn away at the end, and Eireann now understood his request. At the very instant that she finished the journal, she felt an upwelling of hatred and revulsion for her father, for using her mother so callously. Out of a sense of duty, she forced her hands to untie the string and open up the letters, the dates encompassing the span of her life.

Spreading the pile on the bed, she first picked out a telegram, the paper yellow with age. On the back, she saw a hastily scribbled note that her father had penciled. Swiftly turning the paper over, she read the cable, a brief note from her mother in Fremantle. "All haste. God speed," her mother had wired, and her father decoded the telegram, "O'Reilly sailing on *Speedwell* out of Bunbury."

She read the cable and the notations at least four times, befuddled, baffled, and then so shocked that she began to tear into the rest of her father's papers. Everything was there, in the letters inked in her father's neat hand and the coded telegrams that had been sent by Mary Claire. What her mother did in Fremantle was clarified in her father's explicit text, from the plot to free John O'Reilly to the actions that laid the groundwork for the escape of the six Fenians years later. There was much more, because Simon had written to Mary Claire long after she was dead, using letters to record his career, as if he wanted to assure his wife that he was continuing the fight for freedom while he appeared to be an average politician.

Eireann's father, the Conservative from Limerick, had made it his life's work to root out informers in the Irish Republican Brotherhood, and he had used his façade as Anglo-Irish M.P. to win the confidence of those connected with Whitehall. The dynamite plot of the '80's, the forged letters that implicated Parnell: Simon Plowman had been there, gathering intelligence for his colleagues, providing evidence that Lord Salisbury was the true ringleader, prepared to murder the Queen to put an end to Home Rule.

There were brief debates in the essays, where Simon argued the need for armed force while decrying the use of dynamite bombs and terrorism against innocent civilians. Eireann Plowman Lytton finally met her father, and she discovered that he had manipulated her into taking up a position of stiff resistance to British rule of Ireland. Aunt Anna had not been given free rein to raise her niece, she had been instructed all along, from the time that Simon returned to Dublin. In letters to Mary Claire, Simon had described their lovely daughter, not resembling her mother in her face, but in her mother's beautiful voice, a voice that Simon trained to speak Mary Claire's words, to sing of freedom as Mary Claire once had. He had used such subtle craft that Eireann never saw it happening.

"You promised to tell us why Uncle Ed sends you a coffee bean every year," Maura reminded Simon.

"Ed O'Dwyer threatened me, when I ran into him in Kilclooney," Simon spoke, an air of melodrama in his tone.

"But what does the coffee bean signify?" Grace pleaded.

"He threatened to do something to me if he learned that I was behaving dishonorably towards his sister," the grandfather warbled with menace. "And while I do not recall exactly what he said he would do to me, I believe that he did it."

"I always thought they threatened to kill you," Roger said. "But obviously that never happened."

"Mike had developed a fondness for coffee when he served in the Union Army," Simon explained. "He tried to convert me, because the Americans had shunned tea as a protest to British rule and he felt all Irishmen should do likewise. When I arrived back in Dublin after I left your grandmother in Fremantle, I received a gift that was delivered by an Augustinian priest who had been visiting America, raising money for a seminary."

"That coffee service was your wedding gift," Anna said, and she burst out laughing.

"The bean is sent every year to commemorate my wedding day," Simon concluded with his heart aching. "Mike used to send me one, before he passed on."

The sound of feet racing down the hallway disrupted the long saga. Eireann appeared in the doorway, slightly out of breath with running. She pointed a finger at her father, eyes blazing with hurt and anger. "That priest who comes to see you once a month," she accused. "He comes to say Mass, doesn't he? You're a Roman Catholic, aren't you? A Roman Catholic Fenian."

Roger looked at his father-in-law, mouth opening and closing like a trout. "You lied to my father, Sir Simon. All those years he was led to believe you were someone else."

Simon looked at Eireann, smiling like an indulgent father, looking immensely pleased with his little tricks and deceptions. "I never lied to him, Roger, any more than I ever lied to you. Neither did I disabuse either of you of your flawed impressions."

"I'd like to slap that smile off your face," Eireann hissed. "I could throttle you. Why could you never trust me, your own daughter?"

"Your mother took the oath as well," he added. "I did that of my own accord. How could I deny her just because she was a woman? She earned the right, as much as I had, and she did far more than I could have done."

"To keep all this from me," she spluttered, furious and deeply wounded.

"I urged my contacts to hound you until you joined Cumann na mBan and when you signed on to the Citizen Army we knew that we had someone who could work undercover." Simon rested his elbows on his knees, his back aching. "Don't let the men run you around, making them tea. I taught you how to shoot a gun so you could fight, not boil water."

Peter had been listening with his head down, as if puzzled. "When I thought my eyes were deceiving me, it was you near Liberty Hall," he said. "How could I not have recognized my own grandfather?"

"Because you did not see your grandfather, the colleague of Carson. My silence, my smoke and mirrors, my illusionist's tricks, have all spoken louder than Parnell and Davitt and Connolly," Simon replied. "They maintained the secret that only they knew so that I could do my work in my own way. I was waiting for the call, back when we hoped

Russia and England would go to war. Now the time has come, but I am too old. It is up to you to answer the call on Monday."

Simon got up and walked to the window, pulling the drapes aside to watch the sun rise over Cullen's Meadow. Eireann was at his side, not yet finished with her father. "Why did you wait so long to tell me all this?" Eireann asked, grabbing his arm to command his attention. He took her hand, relieved to lay down his burden at last.

"No one could know, not while I was of use to the cause. I wanted you to know before I died, Eireann go Bragh." He turned his eyes to the distant hill and saw her standing there, the pink glow of dawn behind her, creating a rainbow on her green linen frock. Her arm was upraised and the handkerchief in her hand fluttered in the breeze. "We gave our lives for Ireland, for freedom, and I hid from you, Eireann, because I could never let anyone know who I was. Your mother gave up so much, lass; don't let her sacrifices have been in vain."

"You still miss her," Eireann squeezed her father's hand, a gesture of love and understanding. Somewhere in her grasp, he detected her admiration, something that he had sacrificed long ago for the sake of the revolution.

"Not a day has gone by that I have not missed her."

The wind scattered dry leaves across the back garden and she came closer, smiling, her lips moving, and he heard the breeze whisper, "Simon, *mo stor*." He felt the pain in his chest again and had to sit down but he did not want to leave her, not as he had the last time, when she stood on the pier in Fremantle until the ship was out of sight. His knees gave way and he buckled to the floor.

Twenty-Seven

Simon insisted that he was perfectly fine and he could not be talked out of returning to Dublin after Easter Mass, which was said in the dining room of the cottage so that he could take Communion with his family for one time in his life. Before they left, Anna packed three small suitcases for herself and the girls, all three of them prepared to make a run for Boston if things went wrong. As for Simon, he would remain behind on Merrion Square, where the Lyttons would find safe haven in the event of surrender.

Eireann expected the good-byes to be tearful, but she wanted to be strong for her daughters and so she smiled, hugged them, and focused her mind on the thought that they would survive, either in America or a free Ireland, but they would not experience the inequality that was about to come under fire.

Michael drove the car, with Peter next to him, and neither one had much to say, as if they knew what was coming and had yet to formulate words that might be their last. Roger held her left hand from Rathkeale to Dublin, while her father tucked her right into the crook of his elbow and kept his eyes down. It was odd, but she no longer was furious with him because it all fell into place in the blink of an eye during Mass. He was successful at what he did because he created images that people accepted as reality, and he had taught her the same skills. She craned her neck and planted a loving kiss on his wrinkled cheek.

"Thank you," she said. For being her father and training her to be a soldier, to carry on the family business when that business was rebellion. He looked at her with a happy sparkle in his eye and she lost every speck of doubt. How could her mother not have been madly in love with such a devilish rake as Simon Plowman?

Farewells were made to their home in Rathmines at dawn on Easter Monday. Roger drove them to Merrion Square, they said good-bye to Simon, and then the soldiers split up. It was difficult for Eireann to part from her husband and Peter, to be separated and not know how they were faring, but her parents had survived such an ordeal and she would do no less. With Michael at her side, she walked along familiar streets, passing St. Stephen's Green where her grandfather once took her riding, and where Constance Markievicz was waiting with her division.

Along Grafton Street, Dublin's citizens were strolling and window shopping, unaware that the woman they passed had an Enfield rifle hidden under her skirt. They had no idea that the leather satchel carried by the young gentleman at her side was filled, not with legal briefs, but Colt revolvers, cartridges and bullets. Michael's face gave nothing away, with an impassive mien that reminded Eireann very much of her father, who her son most resembled.

Her step grew more determined as they reached Sackville Street, with every bump from the rifle serving as a reminder of all that her ancestors had sacrificed for liberty. Simon had invested heavily, far more than the one hundred fifty pounds it had cost him on a prison ship bound for Australia. She was going to the General Post Office on Easter Monday to recoup more than his loss. Her mother's family had been driven off their land, her mother had been put in chains, her uncles had been sent into exile, and she was marching into battle, to lay claim to debts that had come due. All that the British understood was bloodshed; her father had taught her that in his secretive way, and the lesson had been passed on to her children. They had learned well, all of them.

Michael pulled open the door and stepped aside to let his mother pass. Eireann paused, to take one last look at an image of Dublin that would be forever changed before the day was over. From his post next to a pillar James Connolly nodded to her, his face reflecting the grim nature of their business. The war had begun when James Larkin called out the men and the industrialists had responded with a lock-out; on Easter Monday in 1916 the fighting would escalate and blood would flow.

"In the name of God," Padraig Pearse spoke outside the entrance of the building, "and of the dead generations from which she receives her old tradition of nationhood, Ireland through us summons her children to her flag and strikes for her freedom."

And so it began.

THE END

Proof

Made in the USA
Charleston, SC
30 March 2011